I0543670

The
Isolation
Of Men

Jonathan Supran

The Isolation of Men

Paperback Edition First Publishing in Great Britain
in 2014 by aSys Publishing

eBook Edition First Publishing in Great Britain
in 2014 by aSys Publishing

Cover Artwork

'The Wanderer Above the Sea of Fog' by Caspar David Friedrich is reproduced by
permission of © bpk, Kunsthalle Hamburg, photo: Elke Walford.

ISBN: 978-0-9929796-9-0

aSys Publishing
http://www.asys-publishing.co.uk

Disclaimer

This is a work of fiction. Names, characters, businesses, places, events and incidents
are either the products of the author's imagination or used in a fictitious manner. Any
resemblance to actual persons, living or dead, or actual events is purely coincidental.

For:

My wife Liora, Talia, Debbie and Amelie

About the Author

Jonathan Supran worked in the finance and investment sectors in the UK and overseas, before becoming a fraud investigator at the financial services regulator and the Bank of England.

He followed this with several years teaching English to foreign students at a language school in west London.

He currently serves on the board of three charities.

He's married, and lives in Hertfordshire. 'The Isolation of Men' is his first book, and he is currently working on a second, an historical novel called 'The Hill of Riches'.

Contents

Emperor

'Power corrupts and absolute power corrupts absolutely."

He was dressed entirely in black, all his guards were dressed in black, and there were black flags on the parapets, blowing in the breeze. Jet black—the colour of the deep, cold water that was his most propitious element, the one that had relentlessly overcome the weaker ones, the wind, earth and fire, of his many opponents.

He was sitting alone on the terrace of one of his many palaces, thinking of such matters as he often did now he had the time, watching the town below, the people scurrying to and fro like an army of ants, only the occasional sounds drifting up to disturb the silence.

Alone? He was never really alone. There were guards stationed all around the terrace. More were inside watching every entrance and exit, except, known to very few, the hidden doors and the maze of tunnels under the palace that had been built in conditions of great secrecy. Although he could not help wondering if, despite all his precautions—he had of course ordered the killing of the workmen and architects who'd worked on them—they still remained a secret.

He'd doubled the guards recently in response to reports he'd received about new plots against him, but careful as he was—the massed bodyguards, the tunnels, the food-tasters and the spies—his enemies might one day succeed. Besides, he thought, even if they didn't, eventually he'd be taken by the fate that awaited every human being from the highest to the lowest. It was, unfortunately, inevitable.

Naturally he had the use of the best doctors in the kingdom, but he doubted if despite all their skills, they could extend the span of his life more than an additional fifteen years, twenty, if he was lucky.

A sound coming from below disturbed his reverie. He started, noticing out the corner of his eye the guards readying themselves to bow their heads should he get to his feet. Good lads, the best, each one specially chosen, their background checked to see if there was any matter—a relative executed or sent into exile, an estate confiscated—or some other issue that could cause the slightest degree of resentment against him.

He was confident the bureaucrats had been most thorough with their investigations, knowing it was their heads that would fall should any oversights occur. You could never be completely sure, though. He knew from past experience that mistakes were made. Men were foolish. Weak. Easily distracted. Covering up their anxieties and blunders when they spoke to him. He could smell it, see it in their eyes, despite all their protestations. Only their fear of him kept them in line.

No. When it came down to it, when it really came down to it, he could only trust himself. All the myriads of courtiers, soldiers and peasants counted for nothing. It was his will, and his will alone that moved them.

* * *

A figure appeared, prostrating itself before him.

A minister, requesting an audience later in the day, some topic or other to do with the treasury. He waved his hand in acknowledgment, angry his concentration had been disturbed from recalling, how a few months ago he'd come up with the most exceptional idea to protect both his life and his privacy.

Summoning his top engineers he instructed them to devise a special floor that would make a loud noise if stepped on, even lightly. So if, for example, he was sleeping or reading he would be forewarned of anyone approaching, and could take whatever steps were necessary to prevent them getting any closer.

He gave the engineers one month to present him with their proposals, but when the time came he could tell immediately from their worried expressions and nervous voices, constantly interrupting each other, stumbling over their explanations, that the news was bad. As he'd anticipated, they informed him, hands shaking as they opened page after page of plans and drawings, everything laid out so meticulously, characters and numbers perfect in their symmetry, that they'd failed in their task.

Despite many experiments it had proved impossible to construct a surface of the type he required. They opened their bags to show him all the different types of wood and metal pins that . . . He was already getting bored.

He considered making an example of them, but decided to order them back to their workshops to continue working on the problem. They left, bowing and scraping, no doubt relieved to have escaped so lightly.

He smiled to himself at the thought of them labouring away at all hours, trying desperately to find an answer, constantly terrified of a call from the palace. And who knew? Maybe, spurred on by their fear, they would one day come up with a solution. For the meantime, though, he would have to rely on the guards and the tunnels.

* * *

His eye was caught by the sun glinting on the head of one of the gigantic bronze figures he'd placed around the walls of the palace, facing in the four primary directions.

Years ago, after he'd first united the country, he'd ordered all unauthorised weapons throughout the Empire to be gathered together and bought to a large field outside his new capital.

He was informed after two months that the area set aside for this was completely full. Permission was sought to use another space nearby and, a few weeks later, a third. Puzzled, he rode out with his guards to see what was happening.

He could barely see a blade of grass in the first and second fields so clogged up were they with pile upon pile of weapons. As for the third, it was already half full, a long line of carts lining up to be unloaded, their drivers striving to keep the horses under control, the overseers striding to and fro yelling instructions, cracking their whips as the half-naked peasants levied for the task hurried to empty the carts while others gathered the weapons together and stacked them up in straight lines.

He rode slowly round the area, amazed at the enormous quantity of weaponry laid out before him. Swords. Spears. Bows and arrows. Clubs. Knives. Only then did he truly realise that although he'd prevailed over his enemies, his lot in life was destined to be one of constant, unremitting vigilance.

He immediately ordered the wooden handles and shafts of the weapons to be burnt and the metal melted down, but it was not until sometime later that he decided what to do with the great, untidy piles of ore that had been left lying beside the furnaces.

After consulting with his astrologers he'd decided that twelve guardian figures, each almost four times the height of the tallest of his warriors with girth to match, would be constructed from the ore and placed outside the walls of his palace, designed to strike awe and fear into the hearts of everyone who saw them.

* * *

He was constantly amazed at the skill and ingenuity of the craftsmen who made things for him, from his giant bronze figures to the tiniest objects, more beautiful than nature herself could ever imagine. The ability to produce a fine glazed vase; jade carvings so thin you could see through them; a statue of a prancing horse that seemed about to leap from its stand into the air; gold and silver pieces of the most exquisite intricacy. The list was endless. His palaces were full of them.

This skill. Where did it come from?

Some of it was no doubt mechanical and had merely to be learned and refined by repetition, like the tasks performed by the thousands who produced goods for everyday use and the workers who were being taught to manufacture by rote the arms, bodies and legs of the great army that would in due course be made ready to guard his tomb.

This he could understand. It was the others. The special ones, the master craftsmen, who bothered him. He knew from talking to some of them that they were ordinary men, not born to high bred families. Not having the benefit of an advanced education.

So . . . Where did this come from? The skill to catch the smile on a woman's face, or the motion of a bird's wing.

Where on earth did it come from?

There was only one answer. It was *him*. It was his will alone that moved these men to greatness.

* * *

He was content to leave the day to day running of the Empire in the hands of Li Su. Capable, efficient, yes, he couldn't deny it, but at heart nothing more than a cold spiritless bureaucrat, a man, however, so useful and competent it was said that if he didn't work for the Emperor he would surely have had to be killed for fear he'd offer his services to his master's enemies.

A rationalist, Li proudly called himself. A philosophy, that, the Emperor had to admit was admirably suited to the efficient running of the state. Yet did the so clever, so rational Master Li ever pause to consider the forces that had brought him, an obscure clerk from one of the recently conquered states, to his Emperor's attention?

What did his philosophy make of that?

And had Li realised that a slight, barely noticeable look of disdain passing across his face had been observed on more than one occasion when the astrologers and soothsayers were advising the Emperor on important matters of state?

Yes. Rational Master Li had better watch himself and do well to remember that, for all his cleverness, he could be brought down just as easily as he'd been raised up.

In truth though, despite these concerns, the Emperor needed an official like Li Su to deal with the boring, time-consuming, day to day matters that were an integral part of governing the Empire. After all, didn't the sages believe that a monarch should, as it were, float above mundane, worldly affairs, yet still be the controlling mechanism, working in all kinds of subtle and secret ways to impose his will upon the nation. Unseen. Mysterious. Like a god. Appearing when and where he was least expected so all his subjects from the highest to the lowest remained in a state of the utmost agitation as to his whereabouts and motives.

That was why he'd had the secret passages as well as covered roads built so no-one could tell where he was. Often departing his palaces in disguise, sometimes using doubles, leaving them on the throne in his place, but not for too long in case they presumed to get ideas above their station.

And when he left a palace whether for a day or a longer period, only a handful knew his destination. A precaution required after several attempts on his life and the unearthing of a number of plots against him.

Like the young aristocrat who held a grudge for the downgrading and disinheriting of his family, who'd realised that getting close enough to the Emperor was well-nigh impossible, and meant certain death for the assassin whether he succeeded or not. So what had he done?

Well, the cunning devil had recruited an exceptionally strong man who'd proceeded to throw an enormous pointed metal weight, specially made for the purpose, onto the Emperor's convoy from a ridge overlooking the road, crushing the first carriage, and killing the occupants.

It wasn't the Emperor who'd died though. He'd been travelling further down the line, not in the leading carriage, a magnificent, gilded affair, but in a smaller, plain one like his servants used.

Ignoring his courtier's exaggerated protestations of shock coupled with their pleasure at his astonishing escape, he'd quickly given orders and the plotters had been caught by his cavalry within the hour trying to escape on the horses they'd left on the other side of the ridge.

He smiled, recalling how he'd stage managed the conclusion of the drama. The plotters bought in chains to where the carriage lay overturned by the side of the road, smashed into pieces, the weight still lying on top of it. His entourage and guards crying and screaming in grief. The triumphant look on the face of the aristocrat and his accomplice . . . until . . . until . . . he stepped out from behind one of the carriages, completely unharmed, not a mark on him.

He thought the two of them would die from shock as the false tears of his men turned to laughter, mimicking his own, and the plotters were thrown to the ground in front of him, their heads pushed into the dust, realising he still lived.

The night after the failed attempt on his life there were terrible storms for three nights in a row—thunder, lightning, torrential rain.

The astrologers informed him the heavens were celebrating his miraculous deliverance. What he didn't tell them or anyone else about were the dreams he had for weeks after of being trapped beneath a massive weight pressing down on his chest, unable to move, limbs broken, lungs gasping in vain for air.

* * *

This was not the only attempt on his life. One of the worst, that was almost the end of him, was by a soldier he'd foolishly permitted to come into his presence to show him the head of one of his enemies, who'd hidden a knife in the rolled up map he'd bought to explain to the Emperor exactly where the dead man had been seized.

The assassin had him at his mercy as alone and completely off guard, he was bending over the map, peering to see the location of the place more closely. And then providence, that oh so beneficial providence which hovered over him at all times, protecting him from harm, cast her spell.

For some reason—he would never know why as the idiot guards killed the assassin too soon—the killer hesitated after pulling out the knife, giving him time to evade the blows until he'd managed to raise the alarm and the guards rushed in and cut his attacker down.

The guards who'd failed to find the weapon were all executed, as well as the ones who'd hacked the man to death without waiting for his command. He'd wanted to prolong the assassin's death, and, most importantly, find out why he hadn't struck when he had the chance, vital information which could be used to save his life should another such occasion arise.

A further deliverance from Heaven, the astrologers told him, blaming their failure to warn him in advance on unexpected movements in the planets and the exceptionally complex nature of his aura.

They'd examined the knife afterwards. Razor sharp, with poison on its blade. He'd watched them test it on some prisoners. The first one, just a nick. The second, a scratch. The next, a shallow wound. The last, a deep cut. They'd all died except the first who'd eventually recovered after a severe fever and attack of vomiting.

Strangely, the one with the deepest cut took the longest to succumb. Maybe the poison had lost most of its strength by then.

* * *

Would they never give up?

It was the people he trusted, those he'd allowed too close, that troubled him the most. The last one who'd tried, a musician of all people, who he'd had blinded for his part in a previous plot, then stupidly pardoned after a year or two and allowed back into the palace to play for him, as the man, damn him, was a most excellent flutist. Exceptional. Why else would he have pardoned him, allowing him access into his inner quarters, his bed chamber no less, an honour granted to so few?

The musician had played for him for almost a year. Was well rewarded for his efforts, past transgressions quite forgotten, before the guards, incompetent as usual, had failed to notice that one day the bag he carried his instruments in was particularly heavy.

The reason? One of the flutes, the large one used for solemn music, the kind which moved the Emperor the most, had been filled with lead.

He'd felt the weight of it afterwards, more than heavy enough to stave in his head.

He still recoiled at the memory of what happened. Listening as he lay in his bed chamber, savouring the beauty of the composition. The blind man finishing one piece, announcing he would next perform one of the Emperor's favourites, one that always brought tears to his eyes.

Carefully laying down the flute he was playing, he picked up the instrument he'd filled with lead, and got to his feet. Though surely he would know not to stand without permission while his Emperor was lying down? But there were no guards in the room, and the Emperor—the foolish, trusting Emperor—eyes closed in anticipation of what was to come, blind as his assailant—couldn't see a thing as the musician started to lift the flute, a weapon now, with both hands over his head.

What was it that caused him to open his eyes? The sensation of a slight, barely perceptible movement? A change in the composition of the air?

Whatever disturbed him, wide awake now, he rolled across the bed to avoide the blow, before running round his own chambers, his robe flapping open—how degrading to have to flee from a blind man—before he managed to draw his sword and disable his attacker.

The man, needless to say, had been given a particularly lingering and grue-some death, the recalcitrant guards executed.

His courtiers gave thanks for such a miraculous delivery. Yet another sign, they said, of the Grace of Heaven descending on him.

The Grace of Heaven was all very well, but in the meantime he would have to take steps to protect himself here on earth.

In future all musicians, and dancers would be checked most thoroughly before being allowed into his presence. Even the seemingly harmless dwarfs and jesters who he permitted to amuse him would be subject to this imposition.

And yet . . . The assassins were cunning, and men, including his guards, were weak and foolish. It would be so easy. All it would take was one of the dancing girls, a particularly pretty one, who he'd called into his presence, to flash her eyes and avoid the guards' attentions. How could he be sure she hadn't hidden a blade under her clothes or in her thick, lustrous hair, and when he was sleeping.

* * *

Plots. Always plots.

Was there no-one he could trust?

He made a mental note to order a complete change of the officers of the palace guard. It was long overdue.

It was well known that men such as these officers were the most dangerous to a ruler. Halfway men, he called them. A little education. A position, though not one so high they were afraid to fall from. Often from old, but impoverished families. Men with little to lose. It did not do for them to become too familiar with his habits and the layout of his quarters. They'd have to be replaced. And while he was about it he'd also order the shifts of the rest of the guards to be changed.

He rang the bell that stood on the table next to his right hand. An official scurried forward. Pen and paper were brought. He quickly penned and sealed a note to the general in charge of security setting out his requirements to be implemented by the evening watch.

* * *

Later that night, when the concubines had left, he found himself thinking about something he'd discovered by chance the day before when browsing in his library. Something so vital for his welfare he should have addressed it immediately, but unfortunately urgent matters of state had intervened.

He rang the bell beside his bed once for attention from his servants—twice would bring the guards running.

After they'd dressed him, two of the servants followed him carrying torches as he hurried along the corridors, the guards at every point bowing low when he passed.

Although initially pleased to find the new men alert and well turned out, he could not help noticing that their numbers needed increasing at a number of key points—in two of the ante rooms, and at the top of one of the staircases.

That, however, could wait till the morning. What he was looking for was far more important.

* * *

The library was a long, narrow room, its shelves crammed with books and scrolls from throughout the Empire.

After placing several guards outside, he closed the door behind him so he wouldn't be disturbed.

He'd considered ordering the official in charge of the collection to attend, but thought better of it. This was a task best done in complete privacy. If you wanted something done, or at least something as important as this, you had to do it yourself.

He commenced his search, quickly finding the book he was looking for, its battered binding making it stand out from the ornate ones around it. Clearly it was old, exactly how old he didn't know, and wondered how it had escaped the mass burning of books on history and religion he'd ordered when he came to power. Maybe it was fate that had saved this particular one for him, leading him, to the precise page, the *exact* place that held the key to eternal life.

He thumbed impatiently through the pages, looking for the paragraph that had caught his attention, stopping at one point to read.

"The wise man must be sure to make adequate provision for his funeral, and in particular for his tomb, according to his situation."

"According to his situation."

But no-one had been in his situation before. Emperor of the whole of China.

He continued reading details on the type of tomb appropriate for various types of individual, auspicious dates, and so on. Page after page of instructions. Boring. Why should he be interested in the rules and customs for mere lords and kings? Certainly not the previous rulers whose tombs lay near the city of Xian, in the centre of the country. He'd campaigned in the area several times, remembering the artificial mounds scattered at random on the empty plain, and marvelling at the effort that had enabled such massive works to be thrown up.

Well, he would overpower them in death as he had in life. He would have something constructed for himself so great it would put them all to shame. Surveyors were already on their way to the plains of Xian as well as other locations to report on possible burial sites.

* * *

He carried on flicking through the pages of the book until he found what he was looking for.

Yes. There it was. Just a few lines, exactly as he'd remembered.

"It is said that the ancients, who dwell on three islands in the eastern emerald sea, possess an elixir that can greatly extend their life span and, in certain cases, can even make them immortal."

There followed a detailed consideration of whether the gaining of immortality would render a man, a god. Such speculation he found uninteresting. What did thrill and excite him though—mere words are not enough to express the intensity of the feelings that were coursing through his veins at that moment—was the thought that these pages, known only to him, showed how it would be possible for him to achieve immortality.

He could feel his heart beating faster as he read about the location of the islands.

He was still relatively young, and, the doctors told him, healthy. But as he knew full well, death could come at any time. Sudden. Unannounced.

There was no time to lose.

He made his plans.

Firstly, based on the information contained in the book, he drew up as detailed a map as he could showing the location of the islands. Maybe not as expert a job as he could have got a professional scribe or mapmaker to do, but there was no way he would allow a mere underling, no matter how skilled they were, to undertake a task of such supreme importance.

He replaced the book, hiding it behind some scrolls, locked the library door, took the key, and instructed the captain on duty to place guards there day and night to ensure that no-one could enter on pain of death.

* * *

Back in his chambers and too excited to sleep, he ordered one of his most experienced sea captains to his presence, no guards or officials present.

After showing him the map he'd drawn up, the Emperor told him he wanted him to take two of the fastest ships available and, as quickly as possible, locate the islands where the elixir was to be found.

The captain was to handpick the crews using men who could be relied upon to hold their tongues. Money was no object. It was absolutely necessary to get the right people—he was to pay them however much it took to secure their services.

Once they'd reached their objective they were to give the guardians of the elixir whatever they required for a quantity of the substance sufficient for the Emperor's purposes.

There was no doubt, he told the captain, that a very high price would be demanded to secure the elixir, and gave him written authority to draw gold, jewellery, precious stones and silver from the treasury to be handed over to the guardians at the captain's discretion.

"I expect to see you back within six months." The Emperor told him, making sure to repeat the lucky number six, before adding. "This is most precious to me.

If you're successful your crew, and in particular yourself, will be rewarded most generously. But . . . "

He commanded the captain to raise his eyes so he could look into them directly.

"Remember this is highly secret, and I will punish with the utmost severity any leak of information about the voyage, its purpose, and where you're bound for."

Adding, for good measure, that he would hold the captain personally responsible for any such leaks.

As for failure, this wouldn't be tolerated, the Emperor repeating that the punishment handed out for this would be extremely harsh, so the captain would have no doubts as to the seriousness of the matter.

The captain was readying himself to get to his feet and make his exit, but there was more.

"There is something else you should know about." The Emperor said, lowering his voice, although no-one else was present in the vast room.

Why was nothing in this world straightforward? He'd discovered something in the section of the book following the description of the elixir and its location that could jeopardise the entire expedition.

A giant fish had been given the task of patrolling the seas off the eastern coast to protect the elixir islands from any interlopers. An extremely worrying development that would need to be speedily dealt with.

"The oceans off our coasts are patrolled by a giant fish." The Emperor said, leaning forward. "It's been placed there to stop anyone reaching the islands. You won't be able to kill the fish, only I can do that, but if your ships are fast enough you may be able to outrun him. If however, he's too quick, you must be prepared to sacrifice one of your vessels—I leave you to decide which one when the time comes—so the other can escape. I hope to have disposed of this monster by the time you return, but I don't have the time before you leave. You must therefore take the utmost care once you've left port. Do you understand?"

The captain, who was trying his best to hide his growing disbelief at what he was hearing, mumbled that he did.

"Good. And one more thing. You mustn't in any circumstances tell the crew or the captain of the second ship about the real reason for the voyage or the dangers from the fish until you are at least three days out from land."

The captain mumbled his acquiescence once more.

"Good. Get to work and come and see me by the end of the week to report on progress." The Emperor said, clapping his hands to indicate the audience was at an end, before waving the man out.

* * *

The following day the Emperor ordered his most senior armourer to construct a crossbow similar to those issued to his troops, but with certain important variations. It needed to be much larger than normal; made from the lightest available materials; its mechanism allowing for smooth and quick reloading; the bolts the largest and heaviest the weapon could take.

It should also be easy to sight the target and, most imperative, its accurate range must be as far as possible.

If the armourer was puzzled at this request he knew better than to show it, or even worse, ask the reason for such an unusual weapon. The will of the Emperor was not to be questioned—even in the slightest way.

The purpose of the weapon? To put an end once and for all to the giant fish.

The Emperor, unusually, did not hurry the work. This was not because he was minded to relax the pressure on the armourer. Merely that he wanted the crossbow to function perfectly, and besides, he was not planning to visit the coastal areas until the summer heat had abated, well before the return of the ships.

In the meantime they'd set sail according to plan, laden to overflowing with treasures that would surely be more than enough to persuade the guardians to part with a quantity of the elixir.

The captain was instructed to obtain as much of the substance as he could but in the final analysis, if only permitted to take a small amount, even just a vial, he would have to accept the offer.

On his return the doctors and scientists would analyse the contents of the elixir so sufficient quantities could be produced for the Emperor's use.

* * *

The crossbow was ready within the designated period, and a demonstration arranged in one of the pleasure parks close to the palace.

It was a fine morning, the sun warm as the Emperor arrived with a small entourage, the majority of guards and retainers having been left at the entrance to the park.

The armourer and his assistants were waiting outside a tent specially erected for the occasion, while some distance away, several of the deer that roamed the park had been herded into a roped off area and were trotting round and round, their hooves kicking up the long grass.

Two small tables sat in the middle of the tent. One, with a selection of refreshments should they be required, the other with the crossbow and several dozen bolts on it. The Emperor was pleasantly surprised at the size of the weapon, almost twice as big as an ordinary one, the bolts much longer and wider than usual.

"If you'll permit, my lord." The armourer said, picking up the crossbow, and, with both hands outstretched, handed it to the Emperor—who hesitated a second before taking it, fearing to show any sign of weakness when he took up the weight. Then covering up his relief at the lightness of the weapon, barely heavier than the ones his soldiers used.

His soldiers . . . Wait . . . There was something wrong. Of course. The fools. The crossbow was constructed of plain wood and iron, just like the ones his soldiers had. No inlaid metals or precious stones. No decoration.

He looked at it again. No. He wasn't mistaken. Nothing, not even the imperial crest. What was he? A person of no importance, nothing more than a common militiaman?

He'd been so pleased with the weapon he was intending to give the armourer a substantial bonus on top of the sum he'd been promised.

And now. . . .

He felt his temper rising at the insult. His doctors had warned him that every disturbance to his equilibrium could shorten his life span by hours, maybe days. And now this. He would have the armourer punished, whipped, or worse, for his impertinent behaviour.

Out of the corner of his eye he could see the wretched man, his head still bowed, move away and kneel again.

He checked the crossbow a third time just to make absolutely sure.

Nothing.

He was on the verge of shouting to his guards to seize the fellow, when the armourer, still kneeling, made a gesture with his right hand for his assistant to come forward and lay two more objects on the table.

The Emperor motioned one of his entourage to lift them up so he could see them better.

The first was a bag made of a thick canvas material, a dragon emblazoned on the front, an eagle on the back. When opened up four rows of leather clasps could be seen, each holding one of the bolts. Maybe sixty of them in all.

The second, made of leather, was a quiver for the crossbow, lavishly decorated with deer, birds and entwined flowers and vegetation. A true leather-master's work. After, the Emperor thought, he must remember to get one of his officials to establish who'd made it.

"We left the weapon unadorned." The armourer's voice broke into his thoughts, his voice shaking, whether from fear or pride it was impossible to say. "So as to make it as light and efficient as possible."

The Emperor gave a slight nod in acknowledgement.

An embarrassed silence followed, until the armourer asked for permission to demonstrate the weapon on the deer.

Getting to his feet he took one of the bolts from the table and carefully loaded the bow, before following the Emperor out of the tent.

* * *

The deer were still moving nervously around the enclosure. The armourer lifted the bow, and squinting, sighted it carefully before releasing the mechanism.

The bolt flew out, faster than the eye could see. No sound, just a slight disturbance of the air. A second, maybe two, passed before the watchers made out one of the deer stagger with the impact before collapsing, its feet kicking out as it thrashed about in its death agony, the other animals running around in circles frantically trying to avoid the fallen creature.

There was silence outside the tent, only briefly broken by an involuntary gasp from one of the younger officials, soon choked off. The Emperor stood looking into the distance for a moment, before ordering his entourage, the armourer's assistants, and anyone else in the area to wait at the entrance of the park with the rest of the guards, leaving him alone with the armourer. It would not, of course, do for anybody to see any weakness or errors he might make in firing the weapon.

He watched them hurrying away, telling them to move faster in his eagerness to try the crossbow for himself, all thoughts of security forgotten.

"Give it to me." He said, grabbing hold of the bow immediately they were out of sight.

He loaded the weapon and quickly loosed off a shot which flew over the heads of the deer, which by this time had quietened down, causing them to start moving again.

His second effort went wide, smashing into the branch of a tree with a loud crunch.

"My lord." The armourer said nervously. "If . . . If you'll permit me . . . Maybe you should go a little closer. Until you master the weapon. And . . . If you lower the sight a little, and aim to the . . ."

"Yes. Yes. Come on then. Show me." The Emperor said, already walking up the slight incline towards the enclosure.

It took four more shots before he struck home, hitting one of the creatures on the haunch, injuring, but not killing it, moving in closer to finish it off, then further away for his next attempt.

The Emperor learned fast, no doubt because of his long military experience, and by the time the bolts were almost exhausted was hitting the target accurately on the majority of his attempts, his final few shots being taken at the limit of the weapon's accuracy.

The armourer having taken some more bolts from the tent, they walked up the slope to inspect the enclosure.

Most of the deer had been downed, dead or injured, the bolts exploding into their bodies throwing out gouts of flesh, blood, and bone. Three of the animals had somehow avoided being hit, still on their feet, cowering in one corner, eyes wide, flanks shaking with fear. These and the injured ones the Emperor shot from close range, kneeling and turning on his heel to make the shots more difficult.

Thinking of what was to come he realised he hadn't felt as exhilarated as this for a long time. In fact not since his last campaign—and how many years ago was that?

This time the thrill of the pursuit and the kill would not be against the animals in his parks, herded in, easy to kill.

Even the great striped cats they brought from the jungles were no real threat to him, a line of guards waiting with spears to drive the snarling beasts away should they get too close.

This time he'd be meeting a foe worthy of his attention, and with this weapon in his hands—he could not resist looking at it, touching, almost caressing it—the fish, however large and ferocious it turned out to be, would surely be destined to meet its end.

Before sending the armourer to fetch his entourage, he told him to produce a second weapon, identical to the first, also to enclose more deer for the following morning, when he wished to master the art of shooting the crossbow from horseback.

* * *

An exhausted messenger arrived from the coast, where the fishermen had been given substantial amounts of money to keep an eye out for the fish, with more to come if they succeeded in finding it. They were ordered though, not in any circumstances to harm the creature. That honour was reserved for the Emperor himself.

The news the messenger blurted out, kneeling before him, trying to catch his breath, was that a great fish, far larger than any could remember encountering before, had been sighted two days earlier a few li out to sea.

Throwing caution to the winds, the Emperor had the fastest horses saddled up immediately, not caring who saw the preparations, riding through the night and most of the next day with his picked guards until they reached the small fishing village near where the fish had been seen.

* * *

Tired though he was he found it impossible to sleep, tossing and turning, up before dawn hurrying the fishermen and soldiers to ready themselves. Questioning the men who'd seen the fish. Mustering the fishing boats together with several warships stationed on the coast for this very eventuality. Checking the ropes and tackle, the weapons, and, most important of all, his two crossbows.

The gods had favoured the enterprise. It was a fine, clear day, the sun glistening on a calm ocean, small waves breaking on the sandy shore as he was rowed out to the largest of the war ships.

Four of the fishing boats led the way to the place where the creature had been spotted. The sun was well up by the time they told him they'd arrived at the place, though how on earth they knew in all this immensity of sky and sea he could not fathom.

He ordered the warships to anchor some distance away from each other with the fishing boats in the middle and at each end, his captains having given out flags—black of course, to guarantee a successful outcome—to be displayed immediately the fish was sighted.

It was nearing midday by this time, the sun high overhead. He took some lunch and a little wine, and lulled by the gentle movement of the ocean, exhausted from the hard ride and two sleepless nights, fell into a deep sleep.

He dreamed he was walking into a deep cave or tunnel towards a great round chamber lit by candles, rank upon rank of soldiers standing to attention along the walls. As he neared the centre the soldiers drew their swords and . . .

"My lord! My lord!"

He woke, blinking in the bright sunlight, to find one of his captains bending over him.

"My lord!" The man said again, dropping to his knees as the Emperor stared at him, the sleep not yet completely gone from his eyes, angry at his dream being interrupted.

"My lord. They've spotted it."

The tiredness disappeared at once as he ran to the side of the ship where his captain was pointing.

* * *

It was not until they'd managed to drag the creature onto the sand, using the men and horses, and he'd walked around the carcass, that he realised how big it was, a veritable mountain of flesh.

Brown, mottled with white blobs, an enormous mouth that could easily swallow a man, its large eyes stared lifelessly at him, the bolts he'd loosed off in a frenzy of activity sticking out of its head and back.

He wondered why it hadn't fought more ferociously, attributing this to its acknowledgement that it had met a superior force, and had no alternative but to succumb to its fate.

He gave orders for the body to be burned, leaving the beach when the nauseous, fishy smell became too strong to bear.

What the fishermen hadn't dared to tell him was that the fish, whilst rare in these waters, and larger than the ones they were accustomed to seeing, was definitely not unique, a peaceful creature, content to go about its business, no danger to anyone.

* * *

The prudent man always makes provision for the unexpected.

The Emperor, usually so suspicious and untrusting, had accepted everything he'd read without question in the case of the elixir. He did not however completely dispense with his reputation for caution in the eventuality that the expedition to the guardians may prove to be unsuccessful.

So, if for any reason the mission turned out to have failed, he was continuing the steps to plan his final resting place, and retain his position in the world of the spirits.

A number of sites having been surveyed, he eventually chose to build his tomb on the plains near Xian, which had been his preference from the beginning.

There were two reasons for this.

Firstly, future generations would be able to come and marvel at how greatly his efforts surpassed the funeral mounds of earlier, lesser kings.

Secondly, the mountainous area of Wutai was nearby, a place of which he was very fond and where he kept a private retreat. Terraces, pools, and pagodas had been built on the slopes for his relaxation, while below paths wound past streams and waterfalls, through wooded ravines, and sweet smelling pine forests, filled with the cries of birds, and a profusion of spring and summer flowers.

A serene, restful place. One where, after death, his soul, undisturbed, could spend many a restful hour.

The tomb itself would be hidden underground in the centre of the site, a hill would be raised over it for additional security, and an army of terracotta soldiers would guard him in the after-life.

The preparations having been completed, he gave orders for the work to commence in earnest.

No delays or obstacles, whatever their nature, would be accepted.

* * *

The time he'd given the captain to return with the elixir was rapidly approaching. Now he'd disposed of the fish there was nothing to do but wait.

He nervously counted and recounted the days on the calendar, and when he reckoned it was time, travelled to the coast to await the arrival of the ships.

A week passed in vain. Then two. Messengers arrived, requesting his presence at the capital. He refused to see them.

Three weeks, and still no sign.

The weather, reflecting the foulness of his mood, had changed. Heavy winds and torrential rain lashed the camp unremittingly, day after day, making the area muddy and waterlogged. Great, booming waves broke heavily on the shore throwing up spray so thick it was impossible to see through it.

It was not until the fourth week when the storm had abated somewhat and some of his men had started to go down with fever that he grudgingly considered upping tents and returning to the capital.

And still he could not force himself to leave, sitting for hours at a time, staring out to sea.

More men fell sick. Some died. New messengers arrived. This time he read the messages.

Reluctantly he ordered the return to the capital the following morning, leaving a small party behind in case the ships arrived.

He turned in his saddle for one final look at the grey, choppy sea before whipping his horse and riding away.

* * *

The bad weather persisted, and when they eventually reached the Yangtse, they found it swollen from the rains, logs and branches hurtling down the frothing, brownish, yellow water, tossed this way and that as if they were twigs. Any attempt to get to the other side was out of the question.

They had to wait for three days, the Emperor's temper growing worse by the hour, until the flood subsided. Even so two of the barges they were using to cross, laden with men and equipment, were swept away and sunk farther downstream.

In his anger, his first thought was to order his men to whip the recalcitrant river like common criminal. But this would be over in an hour or so and immediately forgotten. No, what was required was something more permanent so everyone passing this way would understand the culpability of the river, and the consequences of going against the Emperor's will.

A monument? A column of some sort recording what had happened?

Not dramatic enough. The solution came to him as he was standing on the river bank after he'd safely made the other side, watching the water raging past like an angry beast, its rage though not as deep and strong as his, which sometimes he felt could consume the whole world.

Pacing up and down the shore, waiting impatiently for the final barges to disembark, his guards and entourage knowing the signs, keeping well away from him, he noticed a hill overlooking the place where the crossing had been made.

He had the answer in an instant. The hill would mark the spot for eternity as a symbol of the river's sin.

* * *

A frustrating day passed while messengers fetched the governor of the province. The man kneeled before him, pale, trembling, anxious perhaps about some wrong he may have done—the Emperor made a mental note to have officials check the governor's records once the work he wanted was complete.

"Do you see that hill over there?" He asked, pointing across the river.

The governor nodded, his expression changing from fear to puzzlement.

"Do you see it?" The Emperor repeated.

"Yes . . . Yes, my lord. I see it." The man's voice was shaking as he replied, still uncertain whether his head was safe on his shoulders.

"Good. How many men do you have in prison at the moment?"

The governor hesitated.

"Come on. How many?"

"Three, maybe four thousand."

There was silence as the Emperor stared up at the hill.

"I want you to bring them here." He said eventually. "All of them except the ones who are traitors or are facing execution. Set them to strip that hill of everything that's growing on the side facing us. Every tree, every bush, every blade of grass."

Although by this time the governor was completely mystified at the Emperor's unusual, some would say demented, demand he knew it was more than his life was worth to express any concerns, let alone question the instructions in any way. All he could do was wait for what else was to come, and hope to get away in one piece

The Emperor looked up at the hill again.

"With the men at your disposal that should take three weeks. And, once the hill is cleared the same men must paint it red from top to bottom. Do you understand?"

"Yes. Yes my lord." The governor said, bowing low, his head touching the ground.

"Exactly the same colour red as criminals are made to wear."

The head bowed low once more.

"Do you know why?"

"I'm sorry, my lord. I. . . . "

"Of course you don't. You can't see further than your nose. The reason is obvious. The reason is so that everyone who passes here understands that this river committed a crime, an act of treason, against the Mandate of Heaven."

"Yes, I . . .

"Wait."

The governor's expression turned to fear again.

"When the job is finished you will get an artist to do a painting of the hill. This big." The Emperor indicated with his hands. "And send it to me."

Another bow.

"Good. Then off you go. And remember, get it all done in three weeks."

The governor got to his feet and backed away, his eyes on the ground.

"Wait."

The man stopped.

"Check the hill twice a year for new growth and whether any repainting is necessary."

The strange look the governor gave as he left the tent went unnoticed by the Emperor. He was already giving the orders for departure.

* * *

Back in the capital.

Still no news of the ships.

Fearing the worst, he found himself unable to sleep at night, prey to all kinds of fears about his death.

The fools he'd sent in search of the elixir having failed him, he ordered more men to be put to work on the tomb and the army that would guard it, paying a visit to the site to establish if all was going according to plan.

In the meantime he had his astrologers and scientists working day and night on developing an elixir. If the ancients had found the solution, then surely he, blessed with all the resources at his disposal, couldn't fail to do the same.

Will, patience and pressure. That's what it would take to get the job done.

* * *

One night, almost nine months after the boats had left, he was woken from a deep sleep by one of his officials.

For a moment he didn't know where he was. A second or two of panic, until he heard a voice saying.

"He's here, my lord."

A feeling of anger at not grasping what was being said to him, hearing himself, as if in a dream, shouting.

"Who? Who's here?"

Then recognising the name, and remembering his instruction to be disturbed day or night, wherever he was, when the captain returned.

* * *

Quickly pulling on a robe he hurried to the audience room where the captain was waiting having come straight from the port, two day's ride away.

The Emperor could barely recognise the figure prostrating itself before him, exhausted, eyes heavy, clothes covered in dust.

Although he was eager—no, not just eager—on fire to see the elixir, he forced himself to keep his voice calm and ask the captain about the voyage, holding back his impatience so the man would not think him too beholden to him.

The captain proceeded to explain in great detail the dangers, the storms and strange monsters he and his men had encountered—the great fish the Emperor had killed surprisingly not among them—until he and his men eventually made landfall on the islands where the elixir was kept.

How one of the boats and all its crew had been lost in a storm that swept them off course, so when they eventually. . . .

The Emperor could contain himself no longer.

"The elixir. What about the elixir?" He asked, his voice growing shrill with agitation.

The captain lowered his head so it was touching the floor.

"My lord." Came the muffled response.

The Emperor had learned to judge men over the years, and this one's actions and tone of voice did not bode well.

"Yes. Yes." He shouted, no longer bothering to conceal his impatience. "Continue."

"My lord . . . I . . . I don't have it."

"Not a drop? Not even one drop?" The Emperor was screaming now, his voice echoing round the walls.

"My lord." Came the voice, fainter than ever. "My lord. They said. . . . "

"You gave them the treasure and they gave you nothing. I'll have you. . . . "

"Excuse me, my lord. They said they will give me the elixir, if. . . . "

"They will? When?" The Emperor jumped to his feet in his excitement.

"The guardians took the treasure as proof of our good faith, but they know the value of what they hold is priceless. It took me much argument, but in the end I persuaded them to give me a small amount. . . . "

"So where is it then?"

The captain briefly looked up at him before dropping his head with an expression which, if the Emperor did not know better, could have been taken for distaste, or maybe even contempt. No. Such a thing was surely not possible. Still, when this was all over he must remember to have an eye kept on the fellow.

"They promised to give me several vials." The captain continued. "If I returned within a year with double the amount of treasure."

"Good. Good."

The Emperor sat down again, thinking.

"Right." He said eventually. "You'll have what you want. But you must go back in two weeks."

"My lord. It'll take me at least. . . ."

"Two weeks. No longer."

"And . . . I'll need more men and a second boat."

"Yes. Yes. Get them. But be ready in two weeks. No later."

It was only after the captain had left, that the Emperor realized, that in his excitement, he'd completely forgotten to tell him about the fish.

* * *

The prudent man plans for the future.

Having had to accept the delay in acquiring the elixir, there was, his scientists informed him, an alternative. The same as was to be used in his tomb to replicate the rivers and lakes of his kingdom.

A substance, very rare, that amongst its other qualities was reputed to greatly prolong life.

They would obtain quantities of the purest kind, refine them for his use, and turn them into pills for ease of consumption.

It would have to do until the ships returned with the real stuff.

* * *

He took a bite of one of the quicksilver pills. A nasty, bitter taste, though the very fact of its unpleasantness pleased him, for, as was well known, the foulest medicines were the most potent.

He forced himself to swallow the rest.

* * *

Meanwhile, hundreds of li away.

In the coastal town they'd chosen as their base because of its fine climate, picturesque location, and, most importantly, its situation far to the south, remote from the Emperor's authority, the captain and his men were celebrating the marriage of one of their number, now a rich man like they all were, to a local girl, the eldest daughter of a customs official.

As they sat in an inn overlooking the bay where their ships rode at anchor, satisfied after a heavy meal, the captain, somewhat the worse for drink, rose a little unsteadily to his feet.

"To the Emperor." He said, raising his glass. "Without whose generosity none of this would be possible. Long life to the Emperor!"

And the rafters rang with the sincerity of their cheers.

Heretic

Pierre was one of a group of armed Believers who'd been sent to kill a party of monks heading for their town.

They'd been told that the monks were inquisitors, sent to spy out the land and report back to their masters on the extent of the Believers' activities and support. Following this, their informant told them, the forces of law and order would descend on the area to eradicate once and for all the Believers and the intolerable and sacrilegious heresies they adhered to.

The intelligence proved to be correct. Pierre and his companions discovered the   monks late in the afternoon hurrying along a road in a forested area to the north of the town, no doubt keen to reach the safety of the city walls by nightfall.

The monks, six in number, had no escort to speak of. Just two men at arms, one at the front, a little ahead of the group, the other guarding the rear. How arrogant of the devils to think themselves safe, Martin, the leader of Pierre's group, whispered. Did they really think we'd be content to sit like lambs awaiting slaughter, shaking in fear, suffering the humiliation of wearing the yellow cross of the heretic until the sword came down on us?

They followed the monks for several minutes, keeping hidden in the thickly wooded slopes, until their quarry reached a bend in the road where the way narrowed to not much more than a track and the trees grew dense and overhanging.

Now Pierre could see the men they were going to attack up close, he felt something was wrong. The look of them, the way they carried themselves.

He was about to warn the others when. . . .

"Let's do it." Martin yelled. "Kill the guards first." And Pierre, despite his misgivings, got to his feet and followed.

The men at arms were hacked down in seconds. Time to finish them off later, if they still lived, once the main job was done.

Meanwhile, the monks, dressed in the black robes of their order, hoods covering their faces, retreated to the middle of the road in a tight group, awaiting their fate.

Afterwards, Pierre remembered thinking how calm they seemed, not terrified as most men who were about to die would be, but supposed at the time it was their faith, however twisted and corrupt, that caused them to behave so unnaturally.

"Say your prayers." Martin said as he advanced, raising his axe to strike. Then staggered back, the hilt of a knife imbedded in his chest as the monks threw off their habits to show the glint of chain mail beneath, the long swords in their hands.

"It's a trap. Run!" Martin managed to cry, before he was hacked down.

But it was too late. Their attackers were already upon them.

Pierre saw young Jean and one of the others fall under a hail of blows, as he closed with the man nearest him, slashing and thrusting, seeing his opponent clutching at his arm, blood dripping through his fingers, his sword falling to the ground. As he lifted his weapon to strike again, he felt a tremendous blow to his back. He staggered, then recovered and swung round to face his attacker.

Too late. Another blow caught him on the side of the shoulder.

He crashed to the ground, dropping his weapon.

"A tough one, eh. Keep him alive." He heard a voice say faintly, as if coming from a great distance.

* * *

Pierre wasn't really an adherent—more a hanger-on. What the Believers called a waverer. Someone who attended their gatherings, but did not fully have faith. It was his wife who forced him to go to the meetings and sermons even though he was uninterested in anything to do with religion. Never one for preachifying and talking, he tried to get out of it, he'd far rather have been in the tavern or at one of the fairs that visited the town from time to time, but she always insisted on him putting in an appearance.

"You must be patient." One of the elders told his wife. "The truth will come to him eventually. It is like you teach a child. Slowly. Until he comes to properly understand. And I promise you in time he will understand. God will not permit one of his flock to remain in ignorance forever."

For the moment, though, most of it went over Pierre's head. So far as he was concerned life went on as before. He continued working at the mill plus some other jobs on the side—a bit of poaching; some thieving and strong arm work. No matter, as long as there was money in it. To hell with what the Believers taught about right and wrong. You had to take what you could get, and besides, he had a wife and a child to feed.

* * *

It had started with a knock on his door the night before.

A friend outside in the cold. Not really a friend, just an acquaintance he'd had a few beers with from time to time.

"Listen Pierre." The man told him. "There's a job coming up tomorrow. Some travellers to be robbed on the road. We need another man. Rich pickings, if you're up for it."

It hadn't taken much to persuade him to go along. He needed the money.

It was only when they were well on their way that Martin, their leader, had informed him the people they were waylaying were their enemies, and none were to be left alive.

"No. I don't want anything to do with it." Pierre said, and feeling his anger rising, started to walk away.

"Wait Pierre." His friend said, taking him to one side to calm him down. "Listen. You know what I was? A thief, a fraudster, my right hand for hire. Well. I changed a few months ago. I'm one of them now. The Believers. It's like the army. I do what they tell me."

"I don't want anything to do with it."

"These men are coming to do us harm, Pierre. Anyone who's a Believer. You. Your family. All of us. They have to be stopped. One of our men got ill last night. You're one of us, and you're handy with a blade. I immediately thought of you."

"I don't want to. I . . ."

"They'll be carrying gold." His friend said, interrupting him. "Plenty of it. To pay informers. Bribe witnesses. You can have my share. I don't need anything like that anymore."

Gold? Gold was always good, thought Pierre, and like a fool he'd agreed.

* * *

Water. Cold and icy. Dripping down his face, and a voice, little more than a whisper, coming from behind.

"Well, Pierre. Do you have anything to tell us?"

How in God's name did they know his name? How did . . . ?

A brand was pressed hard into the flesh of his upper arm.

Fool, he thought, what a fool I was agreeing to go with them.

He heard himself cry out, a high piercing scream, as they jabbed him a second, a third time.

He passed out.

* * *

The torturer came into view, his face blurred, like looking into a pond, holding a pair of glowing pincers.

"Come on Pierre. Tell us" A voice, a different one, nearer this time, next to his ear.

The pincers moved closer. He could feel their heat on his face.

"Well, Pierre. I'm waiting."

Martin and the others tricked me he thought. To hell with it. And told them everything he knew.

* * *

As he looked down at his arm, just a light red discoloration, no worse than you got from accidentally touching a hot saucepan, his first feeling was one of shame that somebody as tough as him had succumbed so easily.

One of the things he did remember from all those hours of sitting with the Believers, was them saying how better it was to die like the martyrs who'd gone before them than betray their comrades or deny their faith, and if you did die how good it was for your soul to leave this stinking world of filth and corruption where the devil held sway, for an eternity in God's heaven.

"Don't think about the pain." The instructors had said. "It's only momentary. Think of our Lord's passion, and the joys awaiting you in paradise."

He'd heard of places far away, towns and villages where Believers, young and old, had literally been torn apart rather than cry for mercy, or if they survived, burnt at the stake or strangled, and yet here was he, tall, strong, in the peak of health, crying like a woman at the torturer's first caress, telling them exactly what they wanted to hear

If they were surprised at the quickness of his submission they didn't show it, although he noticed two monks, the ones, he assumed, who'd questioned him, standing to one side of the room, whispering to each other before slipping out, leaving him alone with the torturer and his assistant.

* * *

Time passed. The room was stuffy and hot. Pierre felt himself growing faint as he sat on a stool trying to hide his nervousness, his tormentors' flickering shadows looking like demons from the pit.

The only thing he could do was carry on staring at the floor, avoiding the eyes of the two hellish creatures, averting his gaze from the various instruments of their trade hanging on the walls, shrinking into himself, trying his best to become so small they wouldn't notice him.

Impossible. There was nowhere to hide. Soon they'd be getting bored, frustrated. Angry, he was sure, at the swift curtailment of their pleasure, tempted to hurt him some more, even though he'd heard the taller of the monks tell them that if he found another mark on their captive's body when he returned, it would go ill with them both.

"*If* I find a mark." Were actually the words the monk had used.

He was sure they knew ways of hurting him without leaving any marks.

Surely it was just a matter of time before they decided to. . . .

He heard the sound of footsteps outside, the door opened, and the two monks swept in, a welcome breath of cool air following them. He felt relieved to see them for a moment, before cursing himself for his stupidity. They were no friends of his. They were probably the messengers of his death. They hated and despised him and all the Believers. And now he'd confessed there was only one way forward. All that was in doubt was the means.

One of the monks told the torturers to leave immediately, which they did, slamming the door loudly behind them.

"Water?" One of the monks asked after they'd gone, handing Pierre a dripping ladle taken from the bucket that stood near the brazier.

He took it, drinking greedily, not caring what the bucket had been used for, what filth or blood it contained, the water splashing the dull grey robe he'd been given to wear,

"Come with us." The same monk said when Pierre had finished the last drop.

Pierre got to his feet, legs shaking, and followed them out the door.

* * *

The two soldiers who were standing outside fell in behind them as they made their way along a low, dark passage lit by spluttering torches at intervals on the wall.

The corridor, which felt cold after the heat of the torture chamber, seemed endless, with turns to the right and left, Pierre's bare feet slipping occasionally on the slimy floor—they'd taken his shoes away—feeling pain each time he took a step, his back and shoulder hurting badly where he'd been struck.

The monks kept up a brisk pace, passing dozens of cells, occupied or not Pierre couldn't tell, although from time to time he heard a dull groan or a cough, and once was startled by a loud scream as if coming from a soul in torment.

After several minutes, they reached a flight of stairs. One of the monks unlocked the door at the top, and ushered him through.

The night air hit him, causing him to gasp. They were in a large, open courtyard, open to the sky. The night was clear—he could see the canopy of stars twinkling above. It was cold. Very cold. Snow was falling, and the fountain in the centre of the courtyard was frozen solid.

Where in God's name were they taking him? Execution, it had to be execution. They would want to get it over with quickly. Throw his body outside the walls in a pauper's grave. His heart beat faster. He felt a moment of panic and stumbled, almost falling, only saved by the hand of one of the soldiers holding him up.

The monks hurried him across the courtyard, and down another corridor for a few more steps before one of them opened a door, telling him to follow them in, after ordering the soldiers to wait outside.

* * *

A plainly furnished room lit by candles. Warmth. Light. A bookcase against one wall.

An older monk who he'd not seen before was sitting at a small table in the middle of the room.

"Sit." Pierre was told, the two younger monks standing on either side of him.

"Drink this." The old monk said, pouring a glass of wine from a bottle on the table.

Pierre took a sip. Less sweet than what he was used to, but not unpleasant.

He drunk some more, immediately feeling it going to his head.

Why were they doing this? Why? He felt his head spinning. It was impossible for him to think straight. All he wanted was to lay down, put his head on the floor, no matter how hard it was, and rest.

"Well, Pierre." Said the older monk, leaning forward in his chair. "What on earth are we going to do with you?"

Then continued without waiting for an answer.

"You're condemned out of your own mouth. You've confessed not only to heresy, but also to various other sins against the laws of both God and man."

"But I'm not one of the Believers. I'm not. I swear."

"Be quiet, you damned infection" One of the other monks shouted, spittle spewing from his mouth. "Do you think we're fools? You've admitted everything. You're going to burn, and after—you'll rot in hell forever."

So there it was. They were going to kill him after all. In his heart he always knew they would. His only hope was to tell them again how he'd been tricked into attacking the monks.

But it was too late. The other monk, the older one, was speaking again.

"My brother is right of course." He said. "You *are* a confessed heretic and as such you should die at the stake. But don't look so frightened Pierre, there may be an alternative."

"No! No alternative." The first monk spat out.

"No alternative." Repeated the second one, who had not said a word so far.

"With respect, brother, I think there could be." The old monk said, looking up at him.

Pierre could feel his heart beating so hard he thought it would burst from his chest as his eyes moved from one monk to the other. They're playing a game with me, he thought. Like we bait bears in a pit. If I was a man I'd tell them what a rotten, filthy lot they are, and to go to hell with all their posturing. Tell them to do their worst.

He was just about to open his mouth when the old monk continued.

"In exceptional circumstances, I repeat, *in exceptional circumstances*, if a man or woman confesses without defying us unduly or hesitating, and also recants in the same spirit of contrition, the sentence of death can be suspended indefinitely, giving the person concerned the opportunity to redeem themselves. Of course." And here he looked at Pierre intently. "If there is the slightest attempt at fraud or backsliding the penalty will take immediate effect."

"I've never heard of such a thing. A heretic is a heretic, and that's the end of it." Said the other monk.

Whereupon, the old man got to his feet and, bending over the monk, whispered something, that Pierre, try as he may, couldn't hear.

"We'll have to take instructions." The old monk finally said, and ignoring Pierre the three of them left the room, locking the door behind them.

* * *

It was a long time before they returned, the two younger monks with expressions on their faces like children who've been reprimanded for some wrongdoing.

"So, Pierre." Said the old one, speaking slowly so Pierre could understand. "Firstly we need to know that you truly appreciate the seriousness of your situation, that you are an assassin and a heretic, and as such should bear the full consequences of such grievous sins."

Still not having an understanding of what was happening, Pierre, as he usually did in such circumstances, thought it best to say nothing, and just nodded at the monk.

"No. You have to say it." The monk said impatiently. "Repeat after me."

And taking a large Bible from the book case, put it on the table, and placed Pierre's hand on it.

"Right. Repeat. I am an assassin and a sworn follower of the sect of heretics known as the Believers. As such I should be punished for these sins with the utmost severity."

31

Words. More words. As Pierre slowly repeated them he wondered why they just didn't get it over with, rather than making him mouth words so long and complicated it was impossible to understand them.

"Good." Said the monk when Pierre was finished. "I hope you understand why you should be punished. I also hope you appreciate what a fortunate man you are. By the grace of God you're being given the opportunity to save yourself from damnation, but on one condition. That in future you do what you're told without fail. Can you promise to do that?"

Pierre nodded again, still not knowing where all this claptrap was leading.

"Keep your hand on the Bible, and say that you promise to do whatever is asked of you. Repeat after me. I swear on this Holy Book that I will follow whatever instructions I may be given in recompense for my transgressions. If I fail to do so I understand the full authority of the law will be invoked on me and I will die a heretic and a sinner. Come on. Repeat—I swear on this Holy Book . . . "

Pierre had no choice. He did what was asked, without having the slightest idea what any of it meant, although wasn't there something the monk had said earlier, before they left the room? Pierre tried to think. What was it? Something about circumstances? Except . . . Exceptional circumstances. That was it. But before he could gather his thoughts together the old monk was speaking again

"Don't look so alarmed Pierre." He said, his voice soft and cloying. "Nothing will happen to you. You have my word on it. Not if you do exactly what you're told."

The voice hardened, and grew louder.

"You will recant, sign a confession, and a solemn undertaking not to sin again. Then you'll be escorted to another city in secret so no-one here knows where you've gone. Immediately you arrive there you'll be taken to a man who will be known to you as the Handler. The Handler. Do you understand?"

Pierre mumbled that he did.

"The Handler will be the person who you take your instructions from and report to. You'll obey him without question, whatever he asks of you."

One of the other monks coughed loudly, the speaker glancing at him briefly before continuing.

"I see you're still puzzled at what I'm saying, so I'll explain it again." He said, speaking slowly.

"I want you to think carefully about your situation, Pierre. You've sinned most grievously, and should be made to suffer for it. However, in our mercy we are giving you the chance to redeem yourself. Very few are granted such an opportunity. So, you will well understand our great anger if you betray our trust. If you're thinking of escaping or telling a soul about anything that's happened here today or happens in the city you're being taken to, you'd do well to remember it is not only you, but also your family who'll be punished with the utmost severity. I repeat, with the *utmost* severity."

The younger monk coughed again.

"Come." The speaker continued. "Brother Marc is growing impatient. I need your answer now, Pierre. Will you do as we say?"

"But what . . . what will I have do when I get there?" Pierre managed to ask before the monk could continue.

"That is for the Handler to say. I can tell you this though. Your first task will be to deliver some letters to certain people in the town."

Well, that shouldn't be too difficult, Pierre thought, his self-confidence growing by the second.

""But what about my family? Can they . . . " He started to ask.

"No more questions, Pierre. I can't tell you anything else. I want your answer now."

Pierre nodded his agreement.

"Say it."

"I agree."

"Good."

There was silence in the room.

Pierre took another sip of wine.

"I want you to see something before you leave here." The old monk said to him, and rang a bell rope by the side of the fireplace.

"Take him to the castle." He told the sergeant at arms who appeared with two other soldiers. "You know what for."

* * *

The snow had eased off, but it was still deathly cold. The soldiers escorted Pierre through the deserted streets, until the bulk of the keep loomed out of the darkness ahead.

It seemed they were expected. They were immediately taken along a dark corridor stopping by a small grill situated at eye level on one of the walls.

"Look." Said the sergeant, pointing.

Pierre had a dreadful premonition of what he was about to see.

Below him was a room, lit by several torches. On the floor were two sleeping pallets. His wife, young son, and his mother were sitting on one of them, and a man in his late twenties—his brother—was leaning against a wall. They seemed to be talking, but it was impossible for Pierre to hear what they were saying.

His escort was ready for his reaction. As he turned to smash and attack, a knife was put against his throat and two sets of arms held him tight.

"Tie him." Said the sergeant.

Pierre's arms were fastened behind him, as, cursing and struggling, he was taken from the keep and led back to the old monk, roughly pushed down onto a chair in front of him.

"You've seen them." The monk said. "They're safe as long as you behave yourself and don't do anything foolish. I promise you Pierre, when this is over you'll be reunited with your family and they'll be a tidy sum for you to do whatever you want . . ."

But Pierre wasn't listening any more. He felt tired and hungry. His head was spinning, and his back and shoulder were aching again.

" . . . You understand?" Came the cold, hateful voice again, this time showing a hint of impatience. "Do you understand?"

"Yes." He spat out, wanting to choke the smooth, educated words from that soft throat.

"Good." The monk said to the sergeant. "Untie him. And one of you go and get Claude and the documents."

The soldier returned after a while accompanied by the two monks who Pierre had seen before, and a third man, a clerk by the look of him, carrying ink and pen which he carefully set down on the table.

"Can you read and write?" The clerk asked, laying three sheets of paper in front of Pierre.

Pierre admitted he couldn't.

"Right." Said the clerk, and after a whispered consultation with the monks, proceeded to read out the words on the first sheet, religious and legal stuff Pierre could barely follow.

"Put your mark here." The clerk said when he'd finished reading. "And tell me your full name and your father's"

These were added beside his mark at the bottom of the paper, together with the signatures of the two monks as witnesses.

The next two sheets followed. More of the same.

Once everything was finished the soldiers escorted him back through the icy courtyard to the dungeons. Just as he thought he would collapse, he was pushed into a small cell, a pot in one corner, a filthy blanket on the floor, and a plain wooden crucifix on the wall. He could hear the voices of the other prisoners, but they were too far away for him to make out what they were saying.

A flap at the bottom of the door opened, and a bowl of thin, lukewarm soup, some stale bread and a flask of water was pushed through. After he'd finished them, he lay down on the cold floor, covered himself with the blanket, and slept.

* * *

He woke, not knowing if it was night or day. One of the monks was standing in the doorway, flanked by the sergeant who'd taken Pierre to the keep, and two soldiers holding torches.

A cloak and Pierre's shoes were thrown into the cell.

"You're leaving." The monk told him. "Put on the cloak. Pull the hood over your head, and don't say a word."

"My family? What. . . . "

"Not a word. Now move."

* * *

It was dark outside, the only source of light a sliver of the moon. One or two in the morning, Pierre guessed.

They passed outside the city walls through a gate guarded by several soldiers. The monk turned back towards the gate without another word, leaving Pierre to be led some distance away where four horses stood waiting, held by another soldier.

"Come on then. Let's get moving." Said the sergeant, indicating a grey and black horse.

"I can't ride." Pierre said.

"I might have guessed. Right. Get up behind me and hold on tight. And no tricks. I can tell you it would give me and my mates great pleasure to cut you into little pieces, you damned heretic. Now get up, damn you. We've got to be there by dawn."

* * *

They rode through the night, the snow that had fallen earlier muffling the sound of the horses' hooves. The party had two brief stops to water the animals, and have a drink of water accompanied by bread and cheese, a little of which was grudgingly pushed in Pierre's direction.

It was still dark with just the merest hint of light in the east when the turrets of a city came into view. The horses were whipped to a gallop for the last time, only slowing when they climbed the steep incline leading to the main gate, the dark walls rising high above them.

They had to wait a while for the gate to be opened, before clattering down deserted streets to a large walled mansion standing in its own grounds.

They dismounted after the guards had let them through the outer gate, the sergeant knocking on the massive front door which was opened almost immediately by a middle aged man, who judging by his attire and the manner in which he addressed them, was the master of the house.

"Come in. Come in." He said in a low voice, looking around before closing the door as if checking that no-one had seen them.

Gleaming, polished floors. Rugs and tapestries. Paintings on the walls. Heavy, carved furniture.

It was the first time Pierre had been in a rich man's house. The people he'd done the odd bit of dirty work for in the past may well have been as wealthy as this, but they'd never dealt with him directly, always using intermediaries, so if he was caught he couldn't betray them, even if he wanted to.

The man led them into large sitting room lit by a log fire. Pierre could immediately feel his frozen face and hands getting warm from the heat.

"You have some papers for me?" The man asked the sergeant, who opened the leather bag he was carrying, taking out a bundle of letters tied up with string.

"Yes, monsieur." The sergeant said, handing them over together with a sealed letter. "And a letter from Monsieur. . . . "

"No. Don't say his name." The man interrupted, breaking open the seal, and quickly skimming through it.

"Good." He said to the sergeant, after putting the letter away in a drawer and locking it. "We'll look after you and your men until you leave. But not a word to anyone as to why you're here. If anyone asks just say private business. Nothing else."

He picked up a bell on the table beside him, and rang it twice.

"Take them down to the kitchens and give them a good meal." He told the servant who appeared. "And tell Monsieur Bergere to give them enough money for food and lodging for one night. No. Not you." He said to Pierre who'd got up to leave with the others. "You stay with me."

"Sit down." He told Pierre after they'd left.

"Do you know who I am?" He asked, staring closely at Pierre.

"The Handler?"

"Yes. The Handler. And do you know why you're here?"

"No monsieur. Not really."

The Handler told him.

* * *

Pierre was to take the bundle of letters to the leaders of the Believers in the city, and say he'd been sent to them as it was unsafe for him to remain in his own town. He'd be given a forged letter of introduction to corroborate his story.

The Believers would, as was usual in such cases, find him work as well as accommodation with one of their families. All Pierre had to do was come to the Handler's house once a week, making sure he wasn't followed, and report on whatever was going on in the Believers' community.

He was to inform the Handler if any plans were being made for assassinations of those the Believers considered their enemies, or, more seriously, for a general uprising, and also if he heard that any important men of the Believers were coming to the city to preach.

He was particularly to keep his eyes and ears open for two men whose names the Handler didn't know, but were known to the Believers as the Counsellor and the Confessor.

"These are very dangerous men, Pierre. Very dangerous." The Handler said. "You must let me know immediately, *immediately* you hear anything about them or their whereabouts. Day or night. The guards will be told to let you in. Do you have any questions?"

Pierre's brain was in such a turmoil he found it impossible to think of any.

"Remember." The Handler said leaning so close that Pierre caught a whiff of the man's perfume. "You're here on sufferance. You know what will happen if you don't do exactly what you're told. The sentence will be reinstated. And not just on you, on your wife and son as well as your mother and brother."

The Handler drew back, smiled a thin un-warm smile, and rang the bell.

"On the other hand if you do as you're told with no tricks you'll find me most appreciative. Think, Pierre." He continued. "A shop or smallholding for you and your family. I'm sure that's what you've always wanted."

The smile vanished as a servant appeared at the door.

"Go with him to the kitchen and give him some food." The Handler said before turning to Pierre. "Someone will come and take you to your lodgings, and show you where to go tomorrow."

* * *

Two months had passed and winter had turned to spring.

This isn't so bad after all, thought Pierre. Although missing his family terribly he had food in his belly and coin in his pocket. A family had taken him in, and he'd been given a job in a mill owned by a Believer on the outskirts of town.

The only problem was he was obliged to attend every one of the Believers' prayer meetings and gatherings, secretly held in the houses or outbuildings of supporters, and had to take care not to be seen going into taverns or attending cockfights and the like—entertainments considered immoral by the Believers.

He passed odds and ends of information to the Handler, who seemed surprisingly patient given the paucity of Pierre's reports, even handing him an extra coin or two on several occasions.

But of the two men Pierre had been told to look out for, not a whisper.

Then, two weeks before Easter, the festival the Believers considered the holiest of the year, there was a special announcement at the end of prayers.

"Brothers and sisters." The preacher proclaimed. "I don't need to remind you that a time of great joy is approaching. And this year we will be doubly blessed. One of our most holy men, the one we call the Counsellor, will be joining us at Easter. More details of the arrangements will be given to all our congregations at next week's Sunday service. All of you, I'm sure, will be proud that the Counsellor is honouring us with his presence, but I must urge you to exercise particular vigilance at this time so as to ensure his safety and that the rightful, uncorrupted word of God will continue to be preached to the faithful in this city.

Our enemies will be seeking to do us and the Counsellor harm, but we will prevail over the forces of darkness as did our Lord's true begotten Son, and with his help we will be kept safe from all the evils that beset us. So go about your business normally, and take care not to mention a word of what I've said to anyone unless you know them for certain to be fellow Believers."

* * *

As instructed Pierre immediately told the Handler the news that the Counsellor was due to arrive in the town for Easter.

"When exactly?"

"I don't know yet, but they'll be a lot of big services on the Good Friday."

"And where's he going to be preaching?"

"I don't know. They're telling us next week."

The Handler thought for a moment.

"With someone as important as the Counsellor the Believers will want all their followers to see him." He said. "But they won't want the gatherings to be too big. They'll be frightened of being discovered, and anything more than a small number of people will draw attention. They'll need to hold a number of smaller services. I need to know exactly when and where these will be held. You must let me know as soon as you hear."

Pierre, thinking the Handler was finished with him, took up his cloak to leave.

"Wait a minute." The Handler said, bringing a bottle of wine with two glasses from a cabinet, and a small bag which he emptied onto the table in front of Pierre.

Money. Coin. Much more than he'd been given before.

"You've done well, Pierre." The Handler said, pouring out the dark red liquid, and handing one of the glasses to Pierre.

He divided the coins into two piles.

"Take this." He said pointing at one of the piles. "It's yours. The rest will follow when you tell me the whereabouts of the Counsellor."

* * *

Excitement. Word of the Counsellor's visit had spread to all the Believers. It was the only thing Pierre's employer and the family he was living with were talking about.

It was not, however, until the following Sunday, the last before Easter, that the congregations were given details of where they would be meeting during Holy Week.

The barn that Pierre's group of Believers used for their gatherings was almost full as the preacher explained that because of the need for security during the Counsellor's stay separate services would be held over Good Friday and Easter Sunday for groups of between fifty to sixty people or "souls" as the Believers referred to them.

The members of each group, identified by a particular letter of the alphabet, would gather at different times at predetermined meeting places, in the town or in villages nearby. Only then would the group leaders tell them exactly where they were bound.

As for the Counsellor, he would be escorted from place to place by a special group of guards, leaving immediately after each service was concluded.

* * *

Pierre hurried to the Handler's house the moment Sunday's evening prayers were finished.

The mansion was a blaze of lights. Guests arriving on horses and in carriages, servants with torches ushering them inside.

Pierre waited until it got quieter before approaching the guards on the gates who by this time knew him quite well.

"You're out of luck mate." One of the men said when Pierre asked to see their master. "There's a big feast on tonight, so they can stuff themselves before Lent's finished."

"He'll see me." Pierre said. "It's important."

"More important than his big shot friends? I don't think so."

Pierre was wondering what to do next when the sergeant came up, and whispered something to one of the guards.

"Well, there's a turn up." The guard said. "You're being allowed to go in. Off you go then. And try to grab a chicken or two for us on the way out."

* * *

Pierre was shown into a room he hadn't seen before. Small, just a desk with some books and papers piled up, and a couple of chairs. The door had barely been shut when the Handler swept in, face flushed, dressed in dark blue velvet with a heavy chain around his neck, and bulky rings on his fingers. Gold like the chain, Pierre thought. Must be worth a fortune.

"Sit down, Pierre. Sit down." The Handler said good humouredly.

"I'm sorry to interrupt you . . . but . . . but I've got some important news." Pierre said.

"No. No. You did right to come here. Have some wine." The Handler said, taking a bottle from the desk and pouring Pierre a glass.

"So, what have you got to tell me?" He asked rubbing his hands together.

Pierre told the Handler the arrangements as best he could remember. He was expecting this news which made it so difficult for anyone to track down the Counsellor to have angered the Handler, but it seemed that his cheerful mood was barely affected. Almost . . . Almost as if this was what he expected to hear.

"Excellent. You've done well." The Handler said, looking across the desk at Pierre. "But there's one more thing I need you to do. If you do it correctly, I'll give you not only the rest of the money you saw before, but a decent amount on top. And you'll be free to go back to your family."

Although he'd only taken a couple of sips, the wine was making Pierre sleepy, the Handler's face moving this way and that like a puppet's as his eyes bored into Pierre all the time.

The Handler paused before continuing.

"This Counsellor is an evil man, Pierre." He said. "He does the devil's bidding. He turns men against their Church and King. If we allow his wickedness to continue there'll be chaos and disorder everywhere. He has to be stopped. Look at me Pierre. Look at me." He said, his voice harsh and demanding. "It is God's work to kill this man, but the Believers are cunning. Even if we managed to find where the Counsellor is they'll have watchers to warn them of any attack and he'll escape. Only someone who's near to him can do the job."

Pierre felt trapped in his chair, his eyes darting round and round vainly seeking a way to escape, as through the mist and confusion it suddenly dawned on him what the Handler required.

"The Counsellor will officiate at the laying of the hands ceremony." The Handler continued apparently not noticing Pierre's discomfiture. "Where he puts his palm on the head of each member of the congregation and blesses them. You'll be close to him then. That's when you have to do it. Use a knife. Easy to hide."

Pierre felt himself getting warm and took another sip of wine. His head was spinning. He couldn't think. He couldn't. . . .

"But how will I get away? They'll kill me. They'll kill me." He blurted out.

"No they won't. You may be able to get away in the confusion, but even if you can't they won't kill you. They'll want to find out who sent you and what else you know before they harm you. Besides, the moment it's done we'll hear about it, and send our men in to get you out. Pierre. Are you listening? Do you understand what I'm saying?"

"Yes. I understand."

"And you'll do as I ask?"

"I can't. What will happen to my family?"

"They're safe. I told you that before. They're safe for now, though I have to warn you that if you refuse I've got no control over what harm could happen to them."

Pierre couldn't breathe. He felt like he'd fallen into a deep well, and was drowning, the air being sucked out of his lungs.

"Do I have a choice?" He eventually asked

The Handler smiled.

"Oh yes, of course you have a choice, Pierre." He said. "Do as I ask, and you and your family will be free with enough money to do whatever you want, but if you refuse you can forget about any more money or seeing your family again, and I'll make sure word gets to the Believers that there's a traitor in their midst."

Pierre didn't reply.

"Come Pierre. No more playing around." The Handler's voice burst in, interrupting his thoughts. "I want an answer. Now. Will you do it?"

"I don't know what . . ."

"This man is evil. And Pierre. Remember your family."

"Alright. Alright. I'll do it."

"Good. If you manage to get away, come straight here immediately it's done. Otherwise we'll get you out."

The Handler got to his feet.

"I have to get back to my guests. Someone will come to escort you out." He pointed at the table. "Don't worry Pierre, and have some more wine while you're waiting."

* * *

The larger groups went to services in barns and villages outside the city walls, while Pierre's congregation, amounting to less than forty follows, was taken to a house in the merchant's quarter of the town in two's and three's to avoid suspicion.

Their leader knocked twice at a door in an alley behind the house, hidden away from the main street. A couple of young Believers ushered them nervously inside.

The service was held in the largest room in the house, barely enough space for all the congregation even with the furniture cleared out and piled up in the hall outside.

As he waited near the back, Pierre noticed that the key was left in the door after it had been locked. He'd learned from experience that most people froze when confronted with violence, and as for the two young lads on the door . . . Maybe getting out of here wouldn't be so difficult after all.

* * *

There was a buzz of expectation eventually hushed by their leader as they heard sounds coming from the hall. The door opened, and the Counsellor was led inside.

Seeing the Counsellor, Pierre wondered what all the fuss was about. Tall, distinguished looking, dressed in a white habit similar to a monk's, but just a man like any other.

It was only when he started to speak, the deep, sonorous voice echoing around the room, that the overwhelming power of his presence struck home

The service passed Pierre by in a blur, and as for the sermon—something about the noise and bustle all around them, and how the Believers should value peace and silence—it was completely over his head. All he could do was think about his family and the mess these damned Believers had got him into.

The sermon dragged on and on, but eventually it was over and as the Handler had said, the Counsellor asked the congregation to line up for his blessing and the laying on of hands.

Pierre placed himself near the front of the queue as he reckoned he could get out more easily with people away from the door. As it was, the line moved along at a snail's pace, the Counsellor exchanging a few words with each person. How long will this take, Pierre thought. In God's name what are they talking about? But slowly they moved.

Now there were only three in front of him. Two. One.

He was about to reach for the knife when he felt hands grabbing hold of him.

He was only able to lash out once before he was pushed roughly to his knees, the knife yanked from beneath his robes.

There was uproar and shouting all around him, rushing through his head like the blowing of the mistral wind, and faintly, as though coming from far away.

He felt the weight of a hand being placed on his head, and flinched, waiting for the blow. But the blow never came. The hand was soft and caressing.

"Get up." He heard a deep, calm voice saying, as hands raised him to his feet.

"What is your name, my son?" The voice asked.

"Pierre."

"Look at me, Pierre. Look at me."

Pierre lifted his head and looked into the eyes of the Counsellor. Dark like pools of deep water. Boring into his very soul.

"You were misled into betraying the Believers and trying to kill me." The Counsellor said. "You're not the first, Pierre, and you certainly won't be the last."

The voice gained in strength as the eyes left him to look around the room.

"Men are weak." The Counsellor said, raising his voice. "The devil finds his way into their souls. Just the slightest gap or frailty, no wider than the breadth of a hair, is enough for him to enter and do his sinful work. This poor, misguided sinner has been led astray, and it is only because of the rightness of our faith that I have been saved from his evil intentions, and those of the enemies who guided his hand. But unlike them, we are merciful. If he confesses his errors with a true heart we will take him back into our fold."

The Counsellor took a step towards Pierre and placed both hands on his head.

"This is the most holy time of the year." He said. "The time Our Lord chose to show mercy to mankind and give us the hope of redemption if we follow the right path. Likewise." He said raising Pierre to his feet. "My poor deluded brother who has sinned, we will show you mercy, and welcome you back into our congregation." The Counsellor paused for a moment. "There's one more thing I have to say to you brothers and sisters before I bless you all. I need your solemn promise that what happened here today will not go any further than this room. No-one else must know, not even other members of the Believers."

Then, softly, into Pierre's ear.

"You'll be brought to me later."

* * *

Pierre's heart was thumping with fear as, after all the amens and hymns, he was escorted by several Believers to a large room at the back of the house, plain, whitewashed walls, no decorations, pictures or crucifixes.

The Counsellor was sitting at a table in the middle of the room with two men, military by the look of them.

"Sit down Pierre." He said, indicating the chair opposite him, after telling the escort to leave. "Don't be frightened. You're among friends. All I ask is that you speak frankly and answer all our questions."

"My family. They're holding my family." Pierre shouted without thinking what he was saying.

The Counsellor leaned forward and put his hand on Pierre's.

"I know Pierre. I know that's how they forced you to betray me."

They know? But how? Pierre thought. They know about everything. The ambush. The attempt he was to make on the Counsellor's life. It was no accident they'd grabbed him before he could strike. They were waiting for him.

"The Handler will find out I failed. I have to go back to my wife. I must get. . . . " Pierre said, stopping as he realised he was raising his voice again.

"Pierre, my son." The Counsellor said, squeezing Pierre's hand "Listen to me. It's impossible."

"Your town has recently been sealed off, placed under siege by the forces of darkness." Said one of the military men. "At the moment there's no way in or out, but when the siege is broken as it will be with God's help, you'll be the first in there, and I promise you you'll be reunited with your family."

"Pierre." The Counsellor said quickly, apparently wanting no more discussion on the matter of Pierre's family. "I told you we forgave you. And we do, I swear it with all my heart. But when someone sins as seriously as you have done there is a price, a penance for their wrongdoing. And this price has to be paid. "

He waited a second or two for his words to sink in before continuing.

"Who told you to murder me?"

"He calls himself the Handler, but I heard the guards talking. His name is Luc. Luc . . . Bon . . . Bon. . . . "

"Luc Bonnard." Said one of the military men.

"Yes. That's it. Luc Bonnard." Pierre said.

"Of course. I might have guessed." The military man continued.

"And this Bonnard." Asked the Counsellor, looking at the two military men. This man, this devil who told Pierre to kill me. Where does he live?"

Pierre noticed the two military men nodding and exchanging glances.

"We can't risk an all-out attack on his house." One of them said before Pierre could reply. "But someone he knows could get in there."

In a blinding light Pierre realised what they required of him.

No. Please. Not again.

He could feel himself starting to sweat, his stomach contracting as it always did in times of stress.

There was the sound of a chair being pushed back as the Counsellor got to his feet, his voice, loud and resonant, filling Pierre's head.

"We're peaceful people, but we have to defend ourselves when we're attacked. This man, this Handler as you call him, has sinned against the laws of God and man. He must be punished and sent to hell, where he belongs. And God has sent you to us, Pierre, as the instrument of his wrath."

"I can't." Pierre blurted out. "I can't. I'm frightened. I'm a coward. I. . . . "

He tailed off, unable to continue.

The Counsellor smiled. A smile similar to the old monk who'd sent him to this damned town in the first place.

"And yet you were brave enough to try to kill me. Surely you'd rather do God's bidding than that of the devil? Besides, you're no coward. A couple of our men are nursing the bruises you gave them and we've heard how well you fought at the ambush outside your town."

They know. They've always known Pierre thought, but before he could think of anything to say, the Counsellor was talking again.

"You failed to kill me because your faith was weak, Pierre." The Counsellor continued. "But now you're with us your faith will make you stronger than ever."

Will he never shut up, Pierre wondered, his head bursting from all the words buzzing around inside it like angry bees.

"And my family, what about them?" Was all he could think of to say.

The Counsellor continued as if he hadn't heard the question.

"What we ask of you won't be easy, but you have erred greatly, and remember, Pierre, there is nothing so precious to our Lord as the soul of a redeemed sinner."

"Isn't there nothing else I could do?"

The Counsellor's voice hardened again.

"No. Nothing else. Not if you want to see your family again. An eye for an eye. Only this particular penance will suffice. Now, will you do as we ask?"

It was all too much. This lot were as bad as the others. So many things, so many questions, buzzing around in his head that Pierre found it impossible to answer.

"I can't think." He eventually managed to say. "I can't think."

The Counsellor sighed with impatience.

"Come over here, Pierre." He said, going over to the window. "Look outside. Can you see any soldiers on the street? No, and our watchers haven't reported any. The Handler would have left you to your fate. He doesn't care if you live or die."

He put his hand on Pierre's arm.

"And what do you think he'll do to you and your family when you tell him you've failed? And it's not only you that's in danger. We've got supporters in the garrison here. They've told us that the numbers of troops have been increased over the past two weeks. The moment the Handler hears I'm not dead he'll give the order to round up our people. We have to start dispersing immediately. Leave this town for safer places. Do as I ask and you'll give us more time. Every hour more of us will be able to escape. I repeat. Killing the Handler is the one chance you have to redeem your sin. If you don't do as we wish, we have no more use for you. You can go back and take your chances with the Handler. Now Pierre, what's it to be?"

"Alright. Alright. I'll do it."

"Good. When were you going to see him next?"

"After I'd killed. . . . "

"After you'd killed me." The Counsellor said with a smile, and continued, looking across at the military men. "As if this Handler thought we would have let an assassin walk out free as a bird once he'd done the deed."

"He must go immediately." Interrupted one of the military men, glancing over to his colleague, who nodded. "Before Bonnard gets suspicious."

"You're right." The Counsellor said after thinking for a moment. "Go with these two Pierre. They'll tell you what to do, and show you where to go when it's over. I'll be waiting for you there. And remember, Pierre, God will guide your hand, your faith will make you strong."

* * *

Early evening. Pierre made his way to the Handler's mansion, a long bladed knife, the same that was destined to kill the Counsellor, hidden in the pocket of his cloak.

The guards on the gates opened up for him as soon as he knocked, and he was shown to the library, where the Handler was sitting behind a desk, a bottle of wine and a glass in front of him.

"You're late. Everything's too quiet. What's happened?" He asked angrily.

Pierre didn't reply.

"So, did you get him? Did you get the Counsellor?"

"No."

"What do you mean, no? You told me the ceremony was today. You said it would be this afternoon."

"They cancelled it."

"Cancelled it? Why? Did they say they suspected something?"

"No. They just postponed it. They didn't say why."

"So when are you seeing him?"

"Tomorrow. Tomorrow morning. "

"Tomorrow? You're sure?"

Pierre nodded.

"Well my friend." The Handler continued. "You'd better listen carefully. If I don't hear he's dead tomorrow, you know what will happen to your wife and the rest of your family."

Pierre didn't reply.

The Handler pointed at him, wagging his finger, as if talking to a child.

"Do you understand, you oaf?"

"Yes. I understand." Pierre said, taking out a sheet of paper with the list of false names that one of the Counsellor's men had given him. "I've got something for you."

"What's that?"

"Some names."

"Show it to me."

The Handler took the paper and looked at it.

"And what's this supposed to be?" He asked.

"It's a list of people in the city. Believers and their main supporters."

The Handler studied the list again, his brow furrowed. Thinking.

"I don't recognize any of these. Wait." He said, looking up at Pierre with a puzzled expression. "You can't read or write. So how d'you know what's on it?"

The Handler jumped to his feet, knocking over the bottle, the wine spilling across the desk, but it was too late, the blows from Pierre's knife were already raining down on him.

"You don't. . . . " He said, looking up at Pierre as he slumped to the floor his blood spreading over the rug, mixing with the dark wine.

Once a thief always a thief. Pierre couldn't resist opening the cabinet from where he'd seen the handler taking the bag of coin he'd given him, to see if there was anything inside. Nothing, not even a sou, damn it, empty as a poor man's larder.

One more thing. He bent down to look at the dead man's fingers. No, none of those rings he'd seen on that night he'd come to the house.

It was time to go. Pierre left the knife on the floor, put his cloak on, and walked out, closing the door behind him.

* * *

"You were quick." Said one of the guards as he unlocked the gate.

"Yes. Nothing much to talk about." Pierre replied, hoping they wouldn't hear the trembling in his voice.

"Nothing much, eh. Well, have a good night."

The door slammed shut behind him.

* * *

It had been easier than he thought. Now all he had to do was get to safety before the news of the Handler's death filtered out.

He made his way to the house in the poor quarter of the city where he'd been told the Counsellor would be waiting for news of his mission.

The house was in darkness. He knocked on the door. No answer. He checked. Yes, this was the one, just down from a tavern, its doors and windows painted a dull yellow exactly as they'd said.

He knocked again, louder this time.

The window opposite opened, and a woman leaned out.

"You won't have any luck there." She yelled. "They left, horses and all, about an hour ago. Now be quiet and let me get a decent night's rest."

* * *

He managed to avoid being apprehended by the soldiers who'd appeared on the streets, and made his way to the mill where he worked, spending an uncomfortable night in one of the outhouses, leaving early in the morning before the other workers arrived.

Where could he go? There was only one place, and that was to the east of here. Home.

At least he had the money the Handler had given him, well hidden in his jerkin, promising himself not to spend even a sou until he was reunited with his family.

Joining one of the groups of men heading out before dawn for the fields and workshops outside the city, he slipped away once they were well out of sight of the city walls and watchtowers, and started in the direction of home, hiding in woods and ditches to avoid the military convoys that passed from time to time marching briskly along the road in the direction he'd come from.

* * *

It took a week of stealing whatever food he could find, supplementing this with berries and roots, avoiding people and villages, sleeping in the woods, curled up against the cold like an animal, before Pierre made it back to his home town.

It was the middle of the afternoon on a warm, clear day. He'd heard an occasional boom like distant thunder, and when he crested the final hill his heart fell. The ground shook, the noise grew overwhelmingly loud, and he realised it was the sound of guns ringing out as they pounded the city walls.

He'd seen guns before, but never as many as this. From his vantage point he could see the lines of ditches and soldiers circling the perimeter of the city, the plumes of black smoke rising from inside the walls, and hear the sound of small arms' fire in response to the constant bombardment. It was obvious there was no way in or out. It would be suicide to try.

He hid in the trees on the hillside, watching the soldiers marching to and fro, the cavalry charging up and down, and the guns being dragged ever closer to the walls.

Several hours passed without him moving. It was only when night came and the gunfire died down that he turned away, the tears flowing down his cheeks.

* * *

He spent the next two days under cover, but within sight of the road that led to the town, not daring to venture forth, drinking from a nearby stream, the few scraps of food he had left barely sufficient for his needs.

On the second evening the sound of the explosions and gunfire reached a crescendo, and as it grew dark the sky was lit up with flashes and the glow of fires. A little later he heard what seemed to be great shouts or cheers coming from the direction of the town. He couldn't bring himself to go and look, crept back into the hollow he'd found, covered himself with his cloak, and eventually fell into a fitful sleep.

* * *

When he woke it was morning, and, he realised, quiet.

He lay watching the road, until, later in the day, long columns of horse and foot soldiers and wagon after wagon laden with booty left the town, followed after a while by a crowd of bedraggled refugees.

He crept down the slope as close as he dared to try to see if he recognised any friends, his brother, wife, anyone he knew, among them.

Not a soul. All the faces seemed the same. Exhausted. Drawn.

Their clothes in rags. Huddled together, holding onto each other to protect themselves, as they were herded on by soldiers with swords and staves.

* * *

He hid for another day in case the soldiers returned, only breaking cover when he saw some raggedly groups of people making their way back towards the walls.

After cleaning himself up as best he could, he followed them into the town. Or what was left of it. The main gate destroyed. Great, gaping holes in the walls. Fires burning everywhere.

As for his family, nobody could say what had happened to them. Whether they were taken and killed, condemned by his confession, or were slaughtered with hundreds of others when the king's armies overran the cities of the Believers, Pierre would never know.

As life in the town slowly returned to its old routine, he clung to the hope, as men do in such circumstances even though they know in their hearts their optimism is probably misplaced, that by some miracle they'd managed to survive and would one day be reunited with him.

In the meantime all he could do was wait.

Interpreter

It started with a simple mistake. A minor one, which he noticed immediately he'd translated the word, but was too preoccupied with listening to the rest of the conversation to try to remedy it, and too frightened to admit his error to his Spanish masters.

Besides, who was concerned about the odd incorrect word or two—when, as was often the case, the Spanish and Quecha languages were not precisely compatible? What *was* crucial, the Spanish had told him, was that Pizarro and the other commanders were given the correct sense of what was being said to them by the Indians, and likewise that the various natives they dealt with were made to understand the general import of their words.

This, they'd drummed into him time and time again, was of major importance to the success of their endeavours, and if he served them well in this regard he would benefit greatly.

So, when he made the occasional error he didn't revise his translation, for fear they would think him incompetent, and the glowing future he saw unfolding for himself and his family would disappear like a puff of smoke.

* * *

His name was Paullu. His mother and father had always said he was bright, but parents always say that about their children. In his case, though, it was true. He learned quickly, and in particular had a gift for picking up languages. Not just the language of his own people but also of the two neighbouring tribes, and, more importantly, Quecha, the language of the Incas, their masters for almost three generations.

Wealth and status awaited those who rose high in the service of the Incas. Maybe, his parents told him, your knowledge of languages could be useful to them. When you reach the right age, you should put your name forward to be trained as an administrator, helping them to govern the northern quarter of their Empire, where our people live.

He nodded at this suggestion without committing himself. Maybe, in the future. Maybe.

* * *

And then, when he was ten years old, the Incas took his sister, only fourteen, but already the most beautiful girl in the village, to serve the royal household in Cusco, their capital.

"Don't be sad." His father told him and his brother. "It's a great honour for us. Your sister will be taught to weave the wool of the vicuna. It's so fine and soft it's reserved only for the Inca and his family. She'll also make garments for them from the feathers of the brightest birds, and if she acquits herself well, she could even become one of the special ones the Chosen Women who are selected to undertake the rituals in the Temple of the Sun."

But after dark, when his parents thought the children were both asleep, Paullu pressed his ear against the thin dividing wall and heard them whispering softly, his mother referring to the Chosen Women as "the Inca's whores", and listened to her crying every night for the child she was about to lose forever.

"We'll never see her again." She sobbed. "I've heard that when the Inca dies they kill all his servants and women and bury them with him."

"No, I can't believe that." His father said.

"I tell you it's true. You must stop them before it's too late. Give them back their blood money. Tell them she can't go."

"Can't go? They'll take her by force. And if we try to interfere. . . . "

Paullu didn't hear any more. His brother stirred, and he ran back to his bed, covering his ears with the thick blanket, swearing under his breath never to help the Incas as long as he lived.

* * *

Day followed day. Season followed season. Nothing changing, except for the yearly increase in the portion of the crop the village was required to set aside for the Inca's use.

Paullu grew to be a tall, handsome youth, working alongside his brother and father in the fields. The taking of his sister and his hatred of the Incas almost forgotten, until his older brother, with a number of other men from their village, was forced to fight in the war of the two brothers for control of the Inca Empire.

After almost a year the family was told by one of the men who eventually made it home that although they'd fought on the side of the eventual victor, Ata-hualpa, who now declared himself the Inca king, Paullu's brother had been killed in a skirmish in the mountains, his body buried in a mass grave.

After the period of mourning the work continued alongside his father in the fields. Harder than ever. Four hands instead of six. Ploughing. Harvesting. Ploughing. Harvesting. Day after day. Season after season. Nothing changing until the day the Spanish came.

One afternoon late in November after the harvest, when the granaries were full, and the seas were rich with migrating fish, some fisherman, on their way out in the early morning, ran back into Paullu's village shouting for everyone to come and see.

Three ships, larger than any of them had ever seen before, were anchored close to the shore. Great floating castles, white sails billowing in the wind like the wings of three enormous birds.

* * *

Paullu had been frightened of the Spanish at first. Big, strong men, darkly bearded, clad in hard shining steel. Wielding swords and lances that could slice deep into flesh without effort. Metal tubes which could kill at a hundred paces with a loud boom like the thunder that from time to time rolled across the slopes of the mountains. Their barking, slavering dogs, trained to hunt and pull down the quarry on their handlers' order, and, worst of all, the great snorting beasts that made the ground shake as they ran, so fast no man could outpace them.

But that was at the beginning. He quickly learned the Spanish were the same as other men. Some easy to deal with. Some difficult. Some kind, and some cruel.

He even conquered his fear of their horses, plucking up the courage to touch them when they were tethered for the night, finding them surprisingly docile, running his fingers through their thick manes, feeling their hot breath on his face.

He hadn't chosen to work for the Spanish. They'd chosen him.

After landing, they camped near the coast at Tangarara for several months waiting for the rainy season to end and reinforcements to arrive from their colonies in Central America.

A number of people from his village, including Paullu, were forced to work for them as cooks, servants, and kitchen helpers, serving them in the evenings when they relaxed, laughing, shouting, and drinking the foul red drink—he'd once foolishly tasted a mouthful left in a glass, and spat it out immediately—that they referred to as vino rosso.

Paullu wasn't assigned to their leader, Pizarro, but one of his most experienced captains, Sebastian de Benalcazar by name, a short, barrel of a man he'd seen beating one helper who'd spilt food on the table, and another who was too slow in serving the soup.

He soon picked up the Spanish for different kinds of food and drink, as well as objects in the kitchens and the camp. First, individual words, then more complicated ones and simple phrases, running them through his head at night, speaking out loud to judge if the pronunciation sounded correct to his ear, translating first into his own tongue, then Quecha, because, as he quickly realised, it was the Incas that interested the Spanish.

The other tribespeople working in the camp thought him crazy.

"It's just something to while away the time." He told them by way of explanation.

And it was true. It *was* a way to fill the endless, boring hours. You couldn't even leave the camp, the Spanish making it clear it would go hard for anyone who tried to escape. Besides, as neither side knew the other's language—signs, gestures, and the occasional simple word, were all that were used—it was virtually impossible to make any more complicated requests or explain any problems.

The thought came to him one night as he practiced his Spanish in a whisper, trying his best not to wake his sleeping neighbours.

He would act as a bridge between the Spanish and the people from his village who worked for them. Yes, he said to himself, that's what he'd become—a bridge.

* * *

The thing he had the most trouble with was increasing his vocabulary.

Words like plate, knife, fork, that he heard every day, were easy. It was the ones he'd only come across once or twice, often heard in a cacophony of sound at the dinner table or in the kitchens, mixed up with other voices that proved difficult.

Still, he persevered, remembering what he could, relying on his wits and memory, trying his best to learn as much as possible. For instance, he knew Brutus was the name of de Benalcazar's horse, so when the name was spoken at table he picked up the word for horse and whip so when he heard them in a statement about Brutus he could at least get the general idea of what the conversation was about.

He tried harder. Concentrating so intently on what was said by the diners that on several occasions he was within a hair's breadth of a beating for being too slow at his work.

In three months he could create simple phrases. In six, more complicated ones, taking pleasure at the look of surprise on the face of the Spaniard in charge of the kitchens when he asked for things in the man's own language, and thanked him in Spanish when the man gave him leftover food and drink.

After this incident his confidence grew by leaps and bounds. This, though, was almost his undoing.

* * *

It was during dinner one evening. Paullu was serving at the table. Outside it was raining heavily as it had done for several days, the large drops pattering on the roof of the tent.

De Benalcazar asked, of no-one in particular.

"When in the name of heaven is this damned rain going to stop?"

Without thinking, Paullu said in Spanish.

"One week. Two weeks. Then it will get hot."

"Who said that?"

De Benalcazar asked.

There was silence round the table. All Paullu could hear was the drumming of the raindrops, louder than ever.

"I asked, who said that?" De Benalcazar repeated angrily, looking in Paullu's direction.

"Me, senor." Paullu replied, cursing himself as a fool for replying in Spanish.

"Come here boy."

Paullu came apprehensively around the table until he was face to face with De Benalcazar.

"What's your name?"

He told him.

"You live in the village nearby?"

"Yes."

"How long have you worked here?"

"A long time."

The others seated round the table remained silent as more questions followed which Paullu answered as best he could, his voice, he was sure, shaking from fear, until his inquisitor eventually leaned back in his chair.

"Well." De Benalcazar said, staring at him through narrow eyes, the colour of a winter sky. "It seems we have a spy amongst us. A crafty spy who didn't tell us he could speak our language."

"Senor, I work, I am no spy." Paullu blurted out.

"You only speak when you're spoken to, boy. D'you understand?"

Paullu nodded, his mouth too dry to answer.

"So." The commander said, looking around the table. "What shall we do with this spy in our midst?"

No-one responded to this question as it was clear it would be de Benalcazar who would be supplying the answer.

Paullu was wondering if he should try to make a run for it when he noticed the thin, plainly dressed man, a priest in the Spaniards' religion, who was sitting on de Benalcazar's right, leaning over to say something in the commander's ear.

"You're in luck." De Benalcazar said when the whispered conversation was finished. "If it was up to me I'd have thrown you to the dogs, but de Valverde has other ideas. Come here tomorrow morning after breakfast, and ask for Father Morales."

Then laughed as he continued "That is if your Spanish is good enough to understand what I'm saying."

* * *

His "instruction", as Father Morales called it, once it had been established that Paullu could speak Quecha as well as several other languages, began the following day.

After an appropriate time, Morales told him, speaking slowly so Paullu could follow, once his knowledge of Spanish was sufficient he'd be taught the main elements of the true faith. He'd then be given a proper Christian name, be baptised and required to swear an oath of allegiance to the Spanish crown, before working for them as an interpreter.

Despite the priest's attempts to explain everything simply, Paullu barely understood a word, but thought it best to indicate his agreement by nodding once the priest had finished.

"Good." Said Father Morales, rubbing his hands, a gesture which in the priest's case, Paullu learned, indicated pleasure.

* * *

The Spanish, on the whole, treated Paullu well, apart from the occasional slap or chastisement when he experienced difficulties in learning the subtleties of their tongue, or persisted in making the same mistake over and over again.

"Persevere, Paullu. You must persevere." Father Morales told him after a particularly gruelling session.

He persevered, and after two months of hard work, morning till evening, every day of the week except Sunday when he had to undergo religious instruction, Father Morales expressed himself satisfied with his progress, and ready for baptism.

Despite his tutoring the ceremony passed Paullu by in a barely understandable blur, but at the end of it he'd sworn allegiance to the crown and had been christened Francisco, the name, the Spanish told him, of their leader, and also one of their most holy saints.

"A good name." Father Morales told him with a smile, explaining how the holy man could converse with the animals. "He also learned to speak in a tongue far removed from his own. In some ways like you."

Finally Paullu, or Francisco as he was now called, was obliged to place his right hand on a large leather bound Bible and swear an oath, a "most solemn oath" the Spanish called it, representing something they referred to as "fealty".

Insofar as he understood, it seemed to him that this thing called fealty had the effect of tying him body and soul to the king of the Spaniards.

He repeated, nevertheless, what was required of him, but did not dare tell any of the villagers or even his family about what had happened for fear he'd be called a traitor, although in his own mind all he'd done was replace one distant overlord with another.

* * *

Having more or less mastered the language, he was bombarded hour after hour with interminable questions about the Incas, particularly from Pizarro himself.

The Incas, always the Incas. Their armies. Their cities. Their allies. Their religion. The sources of their wealth. On and on, without respite, till his head spun with it.

How could he, not even of the Inca tribe, who lived so far from Cusco, be expected to know all of this?

Too proud to show his ignorance, Paullu replied as best he could, occasionally embellishing the facts, or, if he felt particularly bold, making them up, happy to see Pizarro nodding and talking animatedly to his captains when the information pleased him.

Like the time when Paullu told him about the struggle for the crown between the Inca king, Atahualpa, and his half-brother, resulting in the bloody civil war which had split the country in two until Atahuapla had emerged the victor.

When Paullu had finished Pizarro leaned forward and asked him to repeat what he'd said about the war. When he'd done so a strange half smile flitted across the commander's face, and he clasped Paullu on the shoulder, hard, but not in an unfriendly manner, before turning to one of his brothers who was sitting beside him.

"You see, Gonzalo." He said, "You see. God or fate, whatever you choose to call it, is surely on our side."

Later that day Paullu was given two silver pieces, and a black jacket with shiny buttons, a little big on him, but nonetheless very smart, the first of many such gifts.

Over time he accumulated a goodly pile of silver coins and other valuables which he hid safely away until the day when he'd find a good use for them.

In addition his belly was always full, first rebelling against the Spaniards' way of cooking, but soon becoming accustomed to it, eventually enjoying the taste as the soldiers began to take up with native women, and the dishes started to acquire many of the familiar spices and sauces that he was used to.

* * *

During his instruction Father Morales had told Paullu that an interpreter should be both truthful and honest, never allowing his personal. . . . What was the word in Spanish? His personal pre . . . prejudices. That was it. Never allowing his personal prejudices to effect his behaviour.

He wasn't sure if he'd understood this correctly. After all, how could someone set aside their feelings particularly where their family was involved? How could he not forget what had happened to his brother and sister, and the hatred he'd felt towards the Incas?

Still—"When in doubt, keep quiet". So it seemed best if he didn't mention their fate to any of the Spanish, not even Father Morales, let alone Pizarro.

* * *

There was another month of instruction before Paullu was allowed his first real taste of interpreting. Simple affairs, mainly to do with obtaining supplies from the local villages in preparation for the imminent march to Cusco, the reinforcements having arrived.

To Paullu's mind the Spanish army—that is if you could grace the small group of Spanish soldiers with such a grand name—still only amounted to a mere handful of men given the enormous numbers the Inca could call upon. The Spanish were well aware of this, he was told by Father Morales. They weren't foolish, of course, they had no thought of instigating any battles against the Incas; that would be ridiculous, suicidal, given the smallness of their force compared to the mighty power that confronted them.

They would defend themselves if attacked, that was the right of every man, but if they were left in peace there wouldn't be any fighting.

No fighting. No battles. All the Spanish wanted, Morales said, was to see the wonders of the land, explain their religion to Atahualpa, trade some goods, and transmit the desire of the King of Spain to maintain a mutually cordial and beneficial relationship with the Inca, his royal equal.

* * *

Paullu had only once seen Pizarro really angry.

That was when, despite the arrival of the reinforcements, one of his officers advised him not to risk marching into the interior, but wait the year or so it would take for a more substantial army to come out from Spain.

"You fool." Pizarro burst out, leaping to his feet, eyes blazing, so that Francisco thought he would strike the officer. "You damned fool. Why? D'you think it'll be easier to hide yourself from danger if there were more men on the march?"

Before continuing he glanced across at his brothers who were ready to retaliate should things turn nasty.

"I won't dignify you by giving my reasons for leaving now." Pizarro said, staring hard at the fellow. "Except to say if you, or anyone else, feels the same way, you can stay here with our sick and wounded, and if you can summon up the courage, help guard the camp. Better that than me hearing your whining and complaining on the road. Now get out and tell me by tomorrow what you prefer."

* * *

Paullu was allowed a few days back in the village with his family shortly before the army was due to leave.

On the last night, his father took him to one side after they'd eaten, and Paullu had handed over some of the gold coin he'd accumulated to help tide his family over during his absence.

"We live in terrible times." His father said. "First the war between the brothers. Then the long beards coming. They're strong, but there are few of them. If it comes to fighting no-one knows whether they or the Incas will prevail. As for you, you must keep yourself safe whatever happens. Do whatever you have to to survive. But Paullu. . . . "

His father grasped Paullu's hand so hard that he winced with pain.

"You must always remember where you came from. And promise me you'll never forget who was to blame for what happened to your brother and sister."

"I promise." Said Paullu. "I promise."

"Never forget." His father said once more, as he let go of Paullu's hand, and turned away, wiping the tears from his eyes.

* * *

The small Spanish force made its way into the mountains, guided by Indians opposed to the Incas who'd also agreed to act as bearers.

The way was hard, becoming narrower and more difficult as they climbed higher and higher. The men were exhausted, particularly at night, when the cold light of the moon replaced the warm, life-giving heat of the sun.

It took two weeks of struggle, several men and animals sick or dead, which they could ill afford, before they descended from the mountains to more equable parts.

What Paullu couldn't understand was why the Incas hadn't ambushed the Spanish on the heights when they were at their most vulnerable, the soldiers tired and cold, their horses' effectiveness greatly reduced by the narrowness and unevenness of the terrain.

It was only when he understood the Inca king, Atahualpa, better, that he decided this error could only be put this down to the Inca's overwhelming pride and arrogance. Secure with his army, victorious over the other claimant to the throne, what possible threat could this small, insignificant force pose against him, safe in the heart of his kingdom?

Later, in Cusco, when he'd been interpreting for the Spanish for some time, and had overcome his initial awe of the Inca, realising he was a man, just like himself, Paullu had plucked up the courage to ask him why he'd allowed the Spanish to continue into his kingdom unharmed.

Atahualpa looked at the interpreter as if he were a fool, and when, even more audaciously, Paullu asked again, Atahualpa stared at him with an expression that somehow managed to convey a combination of hatred as well as incomprehension that anyone, particularly someone as low as a mere interpreter, would have the impertinence to put such a question to him,

"Because I was curious." He replied after some time, before turning away and caressing the long, black hair of one of his women.

Paullu, though, caught the fleeting look of remorse that darted across Atahualpa's face, and realised then, with a feeling of triumph, that the raising of this subject was like digging a knife deep into the Inca's guts.

* * *

It was around the time of their lunch halt on the day after they'd completed their descent from the mountains—having recommenced their advance almost immediately because, tired as they were, Pizarro refused to countenance any delay—when two of the scouts arrived in a cloud of dust and galloped to the head of the column, gesticulating, and talking excitedly to Pizarro and the other commanders.

The march continued, the men left wondering what the fuss had been about, some speculating whether an attack was imminent, but nothing untoward occurred, and after an hour or so Pizarro called a halt for the day, somewhat earlier than usual.

Word came for everyone to gather in front of Pizarro's tent immediately they'd finished partaking of their refreshment.

A buzz of nervous conversation circulated around the camp until Pizarro came out and announced he'd received intelligence that the Inca and his army were camped a day's march away.

He said nothing else except they should rise early, and every soldier was to clean his armour, and make sure his weapons were ready for battle before they moved off the following morning.

They set off the next day in formation, bearers and foot soldiers in the middle, the precious cavalry split between the vanguard and the rear, no-one knowing what the day would bring.

In the event the morning passed without incident, and by afternoon they'd reached the edge of a steep escarpment overlooking a valley green with crops and trees.

In the distance a river, glistening in the sunshine, wended its way towards a small town built in the Inca style, the main buildings grouped around a large central square.

The men though weren't interested in the town, which was roughly an hour's march away, or the beauty of the landscape. Shading their eyes they were pointing at a long line of tents stretching along the top of a ridge a little way beyond the town.

Paullu did likewise, squinting against the glare of the sun, noticing the men around him chattering among themselves apparently unconcerned at such a vast array, although in his case the sight sent a shiver of fear down his spine.

* * *

The scouts rounded up some Indians they'd found nearby and dragged them, wide eyed and terrified of the iron clad warriors and their horses, before Pizarro who'd insisted the men remain in formation and the cavalry mounted.

When Paullu interrogated them, the Indians told him the town was called Cajamarca, and confirmed the camp was that of Atahualpa and one of his armies.

The Inca king was relaxing, taking the waters prior to his return to Cusco to formally receive the crown, having a long last finally defeated and killed his half-brother.

"So." Asked Pizarro. "He's now the sole ruler?"

"Yes. All the Empire follows him."

* * *

If Pizarro was concerned at the size of the forces ranged against him, he didn't show it. On the contrary he was all smiles and cheerfulness as he turned in the saddle to his brothers who were on their horses beside him.

"Only *one* of his armies, eh." Paullu heard him say. "So we deserve only one. How disappointing."

The order was given to march on Cajamarca. The natives they found in the town were driven out, after which Paullu, accompanied by twenty or so horsemen in full armour, was instructed by Pizarro to proceed to the Inca camp in order to request Atahualpa's presence in Cajamarca the following day.

"There's no time to waste." Said Pizarro, who insisted on giving the orders personally so Paullu should be in no doubt as to their importance.

"Tell him I'd be honoured to receive him here in Cajamarca. But it must be here, not his camp, and it must be tomorrow."

And pulling off one of his rings said. "Give him this to him as a token of my affection, and tell him if he has any dangerous enemies we would be happy to help him deal with them."

Then repeated. "Don't be put off by any excuses Paullu. You must persuade him to come here tomorrow."

* * *

Paullu had never been on a horse before. Two of the soldiers helped him up to everyone's amusement at his discomfiture, though how the Spanish could laugh and jest at such a time was quite beyond him.

"We'll be going full out." The rider he was sitting behind told him. "Don't be frightened. Just put your arms tightly around my waist."

Paullu had been obliged to ride a mule on a number of occasions as the army made its way through the mountains, but this was the first time he'd been on a horse, and the thought of travelling on one of the gigantic beasts at a gallop represented, at that moment, a far greater terror than his fear of being attacked by the Inca's troops.

"Relax lad. You'll be alright." The soldier yelled as they gathered pace, the wind whistling through Paullu's hair, the sound of the animal's hooves drubbing on the thin grass of the plain, hanging on for dear life as they rode towards the camp.

Mercifully, the journey was short, and the line of tents stretching across the ridge at the side of the valley, soon came into view. It was only now that they could make out an open area in the heart of the encampment where there were a number of small, unusually shaped stone buildings with steam rising from their roofs. It was here the Inca was taking the baths, Paullu was told by one of the perimeter guards who'd scattered in terror at the approach of the horses and their riders.

Three of their horsemen were left at the edge of the ridge should there be a need to warn the main force, while the rest thundered towards the camp.

"Full gallop, and don't slow down for anyone till we get there." The captain shouted as they moved off. "Give the bastards the fright of their lives."

The tents passed by in a blur, the Indians hurrying to make a way for the fearsome beasts and the men clad in bright, shining steel that rode them, some even averting their eyes from the horror that had come into their midst.

Paullu was helped down in front of the stone buildings, gasping for breath, his legs weak, trying hard to regain his composure.

"Be quick." The captain said to him, looking at the hundreds of Indians surrounding them. "And remember what the commander told you. He must come tomorrow."

* * *

The Inca king didn't deign to come out to meet the Spaniards in person, sending instead a number of his nobles, recognisable by their rich clothing and large gold earplugs.

Paullu noticed they were most careful not to come near the horsemen supposing, he was later told, that the horses and their riders were one fearsome being.

Once he'd passed over Pizarro's ring to a nervous, older noble, he did as Pizarro had told him, requesting that Atahualpa come to the town the following day so the Spanish could pay their respects to him, and pass on messages of friendship from their king.

The resultant negotiations took place through the Inca noblemen, who disappeared from time to time into Atahualpa's quarters before emerging with yet more questions and demands for information, Paullu constantly having to move between the two parties.

The Spanish in the meantime remained in their saddles, guns and swords at the ready, the horses circling around snorting and stamping their hooves as their riders struggled to control them.

After a number of lengthy delays, and myriads of questions from Atuhualpa about the Spanish, the size of their forces, their intentions and so on, it was eventually agreed that he would come to the town the following day, in the afternoon, when the sun had passed its peak.

Paullu breathed a sigh of relief as they left the camp, the Indians moving hurriedly out of the way to allow them to pass

The journey back was far easier. Just a slow, gentle canter, into the setting sun, the tension lifting as men relaxed, laughing and joking among themselves.

* * *

"Good." Said Pizarro, clapping Paullu on the back when he'd been told the result of the negotiations. "Well done." Before striding off, his officers gathered around, hurrying to keep up with him.

That night one of the captains handed Paullu a bag of gold and silver coins, far more than he'd ever been given before which he hid away with the rest of his cache.

Shortly after the men had settled down in the houses and other buildings, with a heavy guard on the outskirts of the town, Paullu was passing one of the Pizarro brothers' quarters when he heard the following words wafting out of an open window: "There's no choice. If you want to kill a snake, you've got to cut off its head." Followed by laughter, and later a snatch of conversation where he heard a soldier referring to "a throw of the dice which could finish us off for good."

He paid no attention to either of these as the Spanish often joked or spoke in riddles. It wasn't until the happenings of the following day that he understood what they were referring to.

* * *

After he'd finished his evening meal he stood on his own for a while outside the small house he was sharing with several others.

Night had fallen, the town silent, peaceful in the darkness, with only the occasional stirring of the horses, and the faint clink of armour as the guards were doing their rounds.

Looking at the flickering fires of the Inca camp in the distance, it was, he thought, as though the naval of the world—the name by which the Incas referred to Cusco their capital—had somehow been miraculously moved to Cajamarca, and all the people of these lands were watching this one spot, holding their breath in anticipation of what was going to happen in the next few hours.

Surprised he hadn't yet been informed about his role in the meeting with the Inca, and nervous of whether he would be adequate for what would be demanded of him, he found it difficult to sleep, and later, when all was quiet, slipped out once more, and was surprised to see the lights still burning in the building Pizarro had commandeered for himself. They're probably discussing the final details, he thought. They'll tell me what they want in the morning.

As he walked back to his quarters he thought how the months of learning, the hardships of the march, the loneliness he felt away from his family, had led inexorably to this one moment, when he would stand together with Pizarro and Atahualpa and act as a bridge between them.

* * *

He woke shortly before sunrise to find the Spanish already astir, horses being brushed, the breath from their nostrils hanging in the cold air; weapons being sharpened; armour cleaned till it shone, the men obviously wanting to look their best when they greeted the Inca.

Quickly donning his smartest outfit, he hurried to find Father Morales.

Morales, Paullu was told, was at prayer with Pizarro and the other churchmen and commanders, and the guards outside the building that was being using for the service insisted they were not to be disturbed under any circumstances.

He was forced to spend over an hour—much longer than morning prayers usually took—waiting on tenterhooks for them to emerge, rushing up to speak to Father Morales when he saw him coming out, but before he could utter a thing the priest took him to one side, and said softly.

"Come with me, and not a word till we get to my house."

Once inside the house Morales was using, Paullu's frustration at the wait quickly forgotten, he asked what his responsibilities would be, what attire would be appropriate for the occasion, and so on.

So many questions pouring out of him, his words stumbling over each other in his enthusiasm.

"Sit down." Morales said, after Paullu had finished, his voice seeming sharper than usual.

In his eagerness to hear about his role Paullu had barely given Morales a glance. Now, startled by the tone of his voice, he looked at him intently.

The priest seemed old and tired, slumped in his chair, his body shrunken, his face pale and drawn under the tan.

"Is anything wrong?" Paullu asked, shocked by Morales' appearance.

"No. Nothing." Came the brusque reply. And, after a pause. "Your services won't be required this afternoon."

"Not required? Why? Is someone else translating?"

"No, there's no-one else." Morales stared at the floor as if unwilling to continue.

"No-one else. So why aren't I . . . ?"

"All I can say is that you're not required."

"But the Inca. When he meets Pizarro. Who will interpret their. . . . "

Morales looked up at him, his eyes blazing.

"Don't you understand, you fool. There'll be no interpreting. It won't be men, but guns and swords that will do the talking. They're going to. . . . "

The priest stopped mid-sentence, as if unsure of what to say next.

"I've said too much already." He muttered, getting to his feet

"Wait here. I'll be back shortly." He said, before hurrying out.

There must have been a mistake, Paullu thought as he waited. He's gone to rectify it.

Morales returned after several minutes accompanied by a soldier.

"Go with him." He said. And then, as Francisco followed the man out the tent, whispered softly.

"You'll get your chance to interpret, but not today."

* * *

As they walked through the narrow streets, the soldier not talking, occasionally looking back to see if he was keeping up, Paullu found it difficult to take in what Morales had told him. What was that about guns and swords, and why come all this way to meet someone only to be unable to converse with them? It just didn't make sense. Could it be that he'd misunderstood? Or maybe the Inca had his own interpreters.

Impossible. This was the first time except for some brief encounters on their journey that any of his people had seen the Spanish let alone having the opportunity to learn their language.

Or was it that he'd done something wrong? No. Pizarro had seemed pleased with him. Look at all the money he'd been given. Hardly a sign of disfavour.

Thinking about it there was only one answer. It had all been a terrible mistake, and he was being taken to Pizarro to rectify it.

Any hopes Paullu retained were quickly dashed as he was taken, not to Pizarro's or one of the other commander's houses, but to a large building on the edge of the town, behind the square, guards on the door.

The soldier who'd escorted him unbarred the door and indicated him to go inside.

* * *

He was greeted by the sound of muted voices which stopped immediately he was brought in, only starting again when the door was shut and barred behind him.

He looked around. He was in a long, barn-like room. Cool, with a little light filtering in through small windows placed high in the walls. Stalks and the odd ear of maize on the ground. He guessed it was a granary, empty now until the next harvest.

As his eyes got used to the semi-darkness, he realised that most of the other native servants and bearers were also there, talking nervously among themselves in small groups, some standing, some sitting, the chatter only dying down when two more bands of men and boys were led in.

* * *

He slumped down in a corner, head spinning, trying like everyone else to comprehend what was happening, listening, but not bothering to join in the conversation and wild speculation around him,

After some time the door opened again and some soldiers appeared carrying maize cakes and water which they placed on the ground seemingly oblivious of the questions which rained down on them from the Indians. Fools, he thought, they don't understand what you're saying, and was thinking about asking in Spanish when he heard his name being called.

"Ah." He thought as he jumped to his feet. "Morales was wrong. They need me after all."

But it was Paullu who was wrong. All they wanted was for him to tell the people inside the granary to remain quiet until they were let out later in the day. They wouldn't be harmed, but should know there would be guards outside, and if there was any noise or other disturbance, the culprits, whoever they were, would be executed immediately.

"But why are we being kept. . . . " He started to ask.

"No questions. Just repeat what I said, so they all understand."

* * *

Three hours, maybe more, passed. He couldn't tell for sure. Some of the men lay with their backs against the walls of the granary. Others slept on the hard, earth floor, seemingly oblivious of the discomfort they were in.

Although the talking and the sounds from outside had stopped, he found it impossible to sleep, and sat aimlessly playing with the maize stalks he found lying around, until, after a while he heard the clank of armour and movement outside, and from a distance, voices in Spanish, loud, but not so loud that he could make out the words, then what seemed to be cheering, before all went quiet once more.

He'd eaten one of the maize cakes and was just having a drink of water when he heard a sound, from, he guessed, the north of the town, the direction of the Inca's camp.

At first he couldn't make out what it was. He shouted at the others to keep quiet, so he could listen. The sound grew louder, and as it did he realised it was the slow, deliberate stamping of hundreds, no, not hundreds, thousands of feet, on the ground.

Louder. Louder. And now he could also hear chanting. High-pitched. Rhythmic. And drums, pipes, and the deep, booming, repetitious blowing of conch shells.

The Inca was coming.

* * *

The noise grew in strength, getting closer and closer. He felt the fear seeping through his body just listening to it, and wondered what the Spanish were thinking as they saw the great host coming towards them?

Closer. Closer. Louder and louder the noise came, overwhelming the small town with its intensity. Until suddenly it stopped. He craned to hear. No stamping now, just a low buzz, like a swarm of bees, before he perceived it was not bees but the sound of men breathing.

He tried to imagine them standing row upon row, motionless in the hot sun under the Inca's gaze, frightened to move a muscle until he gave the order; the bright colours; the plumes and feathers; the sunlight gleaming on gold and silver; and finally the Inca himself, proud and imperious, carried on his golden throne. Nothing for four or five minutes. Then voices. Shouting. Gunshots. The buzz Paullu had heard before interspersed with screams. The occupants of the granary on their feet now, some crying out in fear, others pounding on the door.

Horses neighing. More shouting and screaming. Feet running here and there in disorder.

A great crash in the distance. After, Paullu was told it was a wall collapsing as the Inca's men tried in vain to escape being hunted down and killed by the Spanish.

More gunshots and screaming, the sound of horses' hooves, galloping.

Then silence.

* * *

The door to the storage room was flung open, the last of the day's sunlight flooding in to reveal several soldiers, dirty, covered in dust and blood, swords at the ready, their shadows long and threatening on the ground.

The natives shrunk back, some crying in fear of their fate, but one of the soldiers shouted out that it was over and they should come out now and perform whatever tasks were demanded of them. Paullu translated—adding his own words that they should all remain calm whatever they saw or heard or their own lives would be forfeit.

One of soldiers who was waiting outside called out Paullu's name.

"Pizarro wants you. Now." He said roughly, and taking Paullu by the arm hurried him along in the direction of the commander's quarters.

Paullu couldn't help noticing the dried blood on the soldier's hands and spots of it, like the red dye they used in his village to colour their clothes, spattered over his breast plate.

Despite the lateness of the day it was warm and bright with a slight breeze which as yet had failed to disperse the stench of death hanging over the town.

The smell grew stronger, and as they passed the square Paullu could see the cobblestones still running with blood, the walls splashed with great streaks of it to the height of a man, and the piles of bodies choking the open space and filling the gap where the wall had been pushed down.

Some of the Incas had managed to make it to the streets beyond the square, and Paullu and his escort had to make their way around, or climb over corpses, the gaping wounds still seeping blood.

One they passed, a lad a year or two younger than Paullu, was still moving, groaning in agony. The soldier escorting him bent low, took out his knife, and with a swift movement slit the boy's throat. A soft sound came from somewhere deep within the soldier's chest. Paullu couldn't tell if it was a laugh or a cry.

More bodies. Bloody, scattered. Broken instruments. Feathers trampled in the dust. Cast off sandals. Soldiers in their shirt sleeves or naked to the waist slowly picking their way amongst the corpses, finishing off the injured, tearing off necklaces and bracelets.

Paullu felt sick to his very heart. His legs almost gave way, but he forced himself to continue until they reached their goal.

"Keep calm." He said to himself. "Keep calm. Your life depends on it."

They arrived at Pizarro's quarters, a large group of soldiers standing guard outside.

Paullu barely had time to pause to catch his breath and gather his thoughts together, before he was pushed through the door.

* * *

The main room of the house was crowded. More soldiers, Pizarro, his brothers, and several captains, all of them still in their blood-splashed armour, as well as Father Morales and de Valverde.

At their centre was an Inca about forty years old. Seated on a low stool. Expressionless. In a garment of the purest white, edged in silver, but torn, and stained with drops of blood. Heavy gold bangles on his arms and wrists. A necklace of dark red stones around his neck. A gold diadem on his head with a thin silver veil that covered the top part of his face.

Atahualpla.

Paullu felt himself sinking, as he dropped to the floor, prostrating himself, only to be pulled to his feet by one of the captains, and hearing the friar, de Valverde,—the same who'd saved Paullu from de Banalcazar's attentions—say angrily.

"You're a Christian. You don't bow your head to a heathen."

Then the friar asking Pizarro.

"Will he be up to it?"

And Pizarro, despite his triumph, looking older and more tired than Paullu had ever seen him before, answering.

"He's the best we've got." And then. "Talk to him, Morales, and let's get on with it."

Father Morales took Paullu to one side and, giving him a sip of the sweet drink the Spaniards called sherry, told him not to be overawed by the occasion, and to keep calm as a great obligation had been placed on his shoulders, as it was now his opportunity to interpret between the two greatest men in the land.

Finally, adding, as he clasped Paullu by the hand that he, Morales, had faith that Paullu would undertake this task to the best of his ability, and treat it like he had the other missions he'd performed with distinction.

Then held out the glass of sherry, saying.

"Have another sip. Quickly. Pizarro is waiting."

Surprisingly, Pizarro didn't seem concerned at the delay. Later, when Paullu understood the situation better, he realised even a little thing like keeping Atahualpa waiting—a man who up to that afternoon had been used to having every one of his desires instantly attended to, whose slightest word or gesture could mean life or death—keeping such a man waiting for someone as lowly in the order of things as an interpreter suited the commander's purposes very well.

The room was hot. Paullu's head felt giddy from the drink. All he wanted was for the proceedings to be over with as soon as possible so he could go back to his quarters and lay down and sleep.

"Tell the Inca." Said Pizarro in a soft, calm voice. "That he is welcome here, and should have no fear as he is under my personal protection."

Before he'd had a chance to utter a word Atahualpa, staring at Paullu with flashing eyes, showered him with insults—"scum", "filthy traitor", and worse, and when he started to translate he could hear more mutterings and curses under the Inca king's breath. Not against the Spanish who not much more than an hour or two ago had slaughtered his followers in their thousands, but against Paullu, calling him a snake, a traitorous devil, son of a whore, as if he, a mere interpreter, was personally to blame for the disaster that had befallen him.

"What did he say?" Asked Pizarro when Paullu had finished.

"He said . . . He said he appreciated your attention, my lord."

A lie, but one he felt that Pizarro wanted to hear.

"You're sure? He seemed angry."

Paullu wanted to say—"Would you not be? Master of the world one minute, a captive the next."

Instead he replied.

"Yes, my lord. He is angry." Paullu paused, readying himself for another lie, a really big one this time.

"He also said he wished his men had been armed so they could have killed you all, and it would have been your bodies not theirs lying in the dust for the wild beasts to devour."

Pizarro smiled.

"And who could blame him for feeling so? Tell him I'm truly sorry for the loss of life."

"My master says he rejoices all your men are dead and pose him no threat." He told Atahualpa.

Everything was happening too fast. Paullu felt like fleeing from the room, running, running, until he reached his home village, but his feet couldn't move an inch. It was like he was in a bad dream—his brain not functioning, his mouth saying things his ears weren't hearing.

Rather than becoming the bridge he'd dreamed about for so long, in a few short minutes he'd begun the construction of a barrier between the two leaders.

* * *

It seemed all the fight had gone out of Atahualpa. No more insults followed, and he made no reply to the questions Paullu put on behalf of Pizarro, staring straight ahead, not moving, and refusing to touch the food and drink Pizarro had brought in for him.

Eventually Pizarro said to no-one in particular.

"I don't think his majesty's in the mood to talk any more. For now we'll keep him in the style he's accustomed to, and none of you dare lay a finger on him."

He turned to Paullu and patted him on the shoulder.

"Well done, my boy." He said. Then looked into Paullu's eyes for what seemed to be an eternity. "You're sure all that stuff about wanting to kill us—that's exactly what he said?"

"Yes, my lord. I'm sure."

* * *

Later that evening Father Morales told Paullu what had happened in the afternoon.

The Inca and his retinue, five, maybe six thousand strong, nobody knew how many for sure, had come into the city square unarmed. There was some cursory talk between Pizarro, accompanied by his spiritual adviser, the friar de Valverde and Atahualpa, which neither side understood as no interpreters were present, after which the friar handed Atahualpa a bible, the spidery black words incomprehensible to the Inca who threw it to the ground in a rage, whereupon de Valverde yelled out that this insult could not go unavenged.

A signal was given, and the Spanish, who'd been hiding in the buildings around the square rushed out to attack the defenceless natives.

The sound of their guns and war cries, and the vision of their war horses bearing down upon them terrified their opponents who were slaughtered almost to a man.

But not quite all. Atahualpa had been captured unharmed, by the hand of Pizarro himself.

"I knew, Paullu. May God forgive me, I knew what was going to happen. It was all planned in advance. The throwing down of the bible was just an excuse. All I can say is you can thank yourself lucky you didn't have to witness what I did." Father Morales said with tears in his eyes.

Seeing Morales like this Paullu wanted to get down on his knees and confess to the various falsehoods he'd invented, but the moment passed, and he went back through the darkness to his quarters, making his way past the bodies still lying in the streets, and spent the rest of the night tossing and turning, unable to sleep, trying unsuccessfully to find a reason for his misrepresentations.

He could blame his lies on the drink, his shock and confusion at the day's events, the looks and words of contempt the Inca had addressed to him, or the voices of his lost brother and sister crying out for revenge. But in truth there was no proper explanation as to why he'd done what he had.

It was as if some sort of evil spirit or devil had taken hold of him. Whatever the reason though, once he'd started on this game, because that was what it was at first, a game, he'd found it impossible to stop.

* * *

The Spanish gave Atahualpa one of the largest houses in the town, allowing a number of his jesters, courtiers, and servants who'd been brought from the Inca camp to stay with him, as well as some of his women, the Chosen Ones, or the "Inca's whores" as Paullu's parents had called them.

Paullu didn't care what they were called. He'd never seen anything so beautiful, and for a fleeting moment hoped he might recognise his sister among them. But, of course he didn't. So many years had passed since she was taken he doubted he would recognise her even if she was standing in front of him.

A guard was kept on the Inca's house at all times. In fact the whole Spanish army was on a high state of alert in case any attempt was made to rescue Atahualpa.

The Inca was not a prisoner, Pizarro assured him, he was an honoured guest and the soldiers guarding his house were necessary for his protection. Protection from who? The Spanish? Paullu wondered as Pizarro was talking.

"Tell him we've heard those still loyal to the memory of his half-brother wish him ill." Pizarro said, showing as ever his uncanny ability to judge what his listener may be thinking. "And also that we want to make sure his women aren't interfered with."

Paullu however chose not to repeat these explanations nor Pizarro's statement that he and his commanders regarded the Inca as their guest, merely mouthing some platitudes he made up on the spot and telling Atahuapla that he wouldn't be allowed to leave until the Spanish said so, and he should forget any ideas he had of rescue or trying to escape.

* * *

The Inca refused to eat until his special plates and drinking vessels were bought to him, and Paullu was forced to make yet another of those terrifying horseback journeys to the natives' camp in order to obtain the objects in question.

"Make sure they understand exactly what's wanted." He'd been told by Pizarro's brother, Gonzalo.

As Paullu left he heard Gonzalo mutter under his breath to the captain who was going to accompany him.

"Don't come back without all the stuff. We can't have the bastard dying on us."

* * *

In the event there was no need for Paullu to repeat Atahualpa's request. The slightest demand of the Inca, even though he was not among them, had to be immediately obeyed. Several servants appeared within a short time carrying the items requested.

Happily, the return journey was somewhat slower so the Inca's servants could keep up, jogging behind the horses, leaving after depositing their burdens at the Inca's residence.

Back in the relative safety of Cajamara Paullu couldn't help wondering why the Indians, who, despite their losses, still greatly outnumbered the Spanish, had not attacked them while they were in the camp, and had then gone on to assault the town.

He'd noticed that the horsemen stayed in their saddles until the servants were well on the way back no doubt because the Spanish wanted to perpetuate the fiction that horses and riders were one terrifying creature.

This, he thought, and the Incas' fear of the Spaniards' weapons and ruthlessness, were the main reasons why they hadn't been set upon. He recalled the words he'd heard the night before the slaughter—"If you want to kill a snake, cut off its head." Well the snake's head hadn't been cut off, but it was well and truly caught in a trap and if any of their number were harmed the Spanish could well take revenge on him. Paullu guessed the Indians would rather do nothing for the moment in the hope that their king would eventually be released. Time enough for revenge once he was free. Paullu would do exactly the same in their place.

* * *

The items, all fashioned from the most exquisite gold and silver, having been delivered, Paullu was told to wait outside the Inca's room in case any further demands were forthcoming. There were none, but as there was no-one else about Paullu took the opportunity to observe Atahaupla at his meal—something afforded to nobody outside the Inca's most intimate circle—creeping upstairs to an empty storeroom, and watching through a crack in the floor boards.

The first thing Paullu noticed was how something as simple as the partaking of food had been turned into a ritual so elaborate as to appear almost ridiculous, at least to someone seeing it for the first time.

For a start Atahualpa made no effort to deal with his food himself. Only the Chosen Women were permitted to be present at the meal, taking it in turns to display dish after dish to him, the contents already cut into small pieces, so he could pick the ones that he fancied.

The Inca having chosen a particular food, the woman in question would hold up a small piece before giving it to him, so all could see her, and swallowing it. Only then, presumably convinced the food wasn't poisoned, would the Inca partake, the Women passing it to him a bit at a time, like they were feeding a child.

Likewise with whatever the Inca drank. First the Women would pour a little into a wooden beaker—the gold and silver ones apparently being reserved solely for the Inca—and drink from it, followed by Atahualpa—sip by sip—as though frightened to take down too much in one gulp.

The end of the meal was indicated by the Inca washing his hands in a large silver bowl, whereupon one of the Women clapped her hands, and the servants streamed in to gather up the plates, cups, and bowls, as well as the uneaten food and any other implements that had been used.

Paullu quickly got to his feet and hurried downstairs just in time to intercept the servants carrying the various items, and direct them to the kitchens outside so everything could be washed.

"Do you expect our king to use the same dishes more than once?" One of them said, looking at him as if he were mad. "They must be thrown away. All of them. New ones will be brought tomorrow."

And so it was. Everything, including the uneaten food, even the clothes the Inca had worn, was buried by the servants on some wasteland on the outskirts of town, and early the next morning, before the Inca had risen, a new supply of utensils was bought by runners to his quarters.

"Where did they bury them? Where?" The captain demanded when Paullu told him.

He showed them the spot outside the walls.

During the night a party of soldiers dug up the ground. The cups and dishes were cleaned of earth and food, and, gleaming like new, were taken to Pizarro's quarters, as were the clothes if any gold or silver was found to be attached to them.

* * *

Any Indians, men and women, going in or out of the Inca's quarters were checked for weapons.

The first time this happened Paullu was ordered to hurry to the Inca's quarters, as the women objected to being felt all over by the soldiers.

He found Atahualpa reclining on cushions and blankets surrounded by a number of his Chosen Women and retainers, the Inca wearing a long cloak made of a darkish brown, shiny material that Paullu had never seen before.

One of the servants later told Paullu it was fashioned from the wings of a bat found in isolated caves near the eastern borders of the Inca Empire. Only the Inca himself was permitted the use of these creatures whose location was a closely guarded secret. When Paullu repeated this to the Spanish, they laughed, saying the Inca was welcome to wear the skin of such an ugly animal, however rare it was. For their part, they said, they were more than happy with clothes made from the wool of the humble sheep.

Paullu tore his eyes away from the vision of loveliness that were the Chosen Women to where two Spanish captains were waiting for him to find out exactly what was happening.

"Find out what the trouble is. And be quick about it" One of them told him impatiently.

He asked one of the retainers what was wrong.

"The Inca says he cannot have his Chosen Women searched by common soldiers." The man said nervously, his eyes darting one way, then another.

"Tell him." The captain said to Paullu when he passed on the complaint. "That we're concerned agents still loyal to his half-brother may try to assassinate him. That's why everyone must be searched for weapons. We have a solemn obligation to protect him. He's much too important to be harmed in any way"

This is nonsense, Paullu thought, as he was translating, purposely failing to mention Atahualpa's half-brother. There was no outside threat to Atahualpa, or at least none that he knew of. Surely everyone realised by now that all the Spanish were interested in was keeping the Inca as a hostage, and the searches were to stop weapons being smuggled in that may be used in an attempt to free him. In any case, feeling those beautiful creatures was hardly the most onerous task for a man.

He saw Atahualpa lean back and relax when Paullu told him the captain had said he was much too important to risk being harmed.

He may have been an almighty ruler, to be obeyed without question, but, Paullu could not help thinking, what a foolish fellow he was, allowing an appeal to his vanity to so easily sway his position.

A compromise was eventually arrived at. Only the men servants would come and go, and be searched. As for the Chosen Women, they'd remain in the house with Atahualpa.

If any of the women felt disgruntled on learning they were to be kept cooped up like chickens in a pen they didn't show it. Their king had spoken and his word was law. No dissent.

It wasn't like that with Pizarro, Paullu thought. Oh yes, his word was law alright, but until he'd actually pronounced his final decision, his captains and even the lower ranks were free to debate and argue with him.

Round the dinner table, on the road, in camp, lively, spirited discussions which Pizarro, if not always following to the letter, certainly took note of. Atahualpa, he was sure, would never permit such a thing. That, and his overweening arrogance, was why he'd been tricked so easily.

I could have made the whole incident much more troublesome, Paullu reflected afterwards. I should have told Atahualpa that the Spanish didn't give a damn about his women's feelings, and would do whatever they wanted with them.

A mistake.

By now the whole thing had become far more serious. It was no longer a game. Paullu's misrepresentations had become the instruments of his revenge.

In future he would make sure to choose his words far more carefully.

* * *

His lies and falsifications continued. Like dripping poison drop by drop into a cup of water.

It was inevitable, though, that his luck would run out.

It happened during a session between Atahualpa and Gonzalo, one of Pizarro's brothers, a fiery character who nonetheless managed to keep his temper under control when addressing the Inca—no doubt under Pizarro's firm instructions.

Paullu had exaggerated some of Atuahalpa's complaints, and translated Gonzalo's responses as being somewhat less accommodating than they actually were.

It was a short session, but as Paullu stepped outside he was confronted by one of the newer Indian interpreters, an older man whose work was mainly concerned with the gathering of supplies and food for the Spanish.

"I heard." The man said, his eyes blazing.

"What did you hear?" Asked Paullu.

"What you were saying in there. It didn't make any sense. I don't know what you're up to, but I'm telling my captain about it straight away."

Paullu could feel his heart pounding so hard he thought it would jump from his chest.

"Listen. I'll explain." He said, trying frantically to think of what excuses he could possibly make.

He led the man away from the building.

"It's . . . It's Pizarro." He eventually said in a whisper. "He told me what to say."

"How could he? He wasn't there."

"I can't say now . . . I have to go and report to Pizarro . . . I'll tell you what. I'll meet you this evening after the meal, by the river, and I'll tell you all about it."

The man nodded.

"You'd better." He said. "Or. . . . "

"But not a word to anyone." Paullu interrupted, making a cutting sign across his throat. "You know what Pissarro's like if he's annoyed.

* * *

Paullu skipped his meal, and rushed to the meeting site as dusk was falling.

He looked around until he found a suitable rock by the river bank, hid it under his garments, and waited.

It was almost dark by the time the interpreter arrived.

"Right." He said, when he saw Paullu. "What's this all about?"

Paullu came close to him.

"As I told you." He said. "Pizarro. . . . "

"There's no need to whisper. Why would Piza. . . . "

Paullu pulled out the stone and smashed him on the head with all his strength, and again, and once more, until the man slumped to the ground, his blood pooling around him.

He felt no remorse, just that it was a job that needed to be done. Nothing was to interfere with his quest for revenge.

* * *

He dragged the body to a shallow depression in the ground and piled rocks and branches over it.

Once he was missed it would be assumed that the interpreter had run off. His disappearance or death, if the body was found, would be regarded as nothing more than a minor inconvenience. Nobody, least of all the Spanish, would pay much attention. Life, particularly Indian life was cheap.

* * *

The next few weeks passed by in a state of considerable tension, an attack feared at any time, but once it appeared that none was forthcoming for the moment, the soldiers, as men often do when an imminent threat is lifted, started paying greater attention to matters closer to their hearts.

They hadn't come halfway across the world, the men complained, to be stuck in this shit hole. No entertainment, no women, nothing but hot, boring, days and freezing nights. Gold. It was gold they wanted, and soon—that, and to be away from this godforsaken place as soon as possible.

Pizarro, always one to pick up on any potential problems, convened a meeting with his commanders to decide how best to get the thing they all desired. The result being that Paullu was sent to inform Atahualpa that the Spanish wouldn't release him until he'd supplied them with a ransom of silver and gold appropriate to his stature.

Shortly after the Inca was brought, surprisingly without any complaints, to a block of empty storerooms where Pizarro ordered one of his tallest soldiers to raise his hand as high as he could against the wall of the largest room in the building. Next, someone stood on a chair and marked the spot at the end of the man's outstretched fingers. This, Paullu was told to translate, was where the ransom had to be piled up to.

A second, slightly smaller room, was marked out in a similar fashion.

The larger room was for the gold, the other for the silver.

Impossible, Paullu wondered, surely there can't be so much gold and silver in the whole world. But then he saw Atahualpa give a smile, a small, secret smile that seemed to say.

"This task is nothing for me. Just child's play."

Paullu didn't know if anyone else had noticed, but thought to himself.

"You stupid, arrogant fool. Even now, after everything that's happened, you still don't understand these Spaniards. They won't be satisfied. All you'll be doing is whetting their appetite for more. Don't you realise that once they've got these rooms filled they'll have no more use for you?"

Paullu smiled his own small, secret smile.

* * *

Atahualpa had told the Spanish that messengers had been sent across the Empire to gather the treasure, but almost a month passed with very little of it having arrived, just some small, insignificant pieces from a couple of towns nearby.

The Spanish started to grow uneasy, and Paullu, who'd fuelled their concerns by dropping the odd word about the possibility of the Inca's messengers being sent to muster armies rather than treasure, heard the soldiers complaining on several occasions about the delays. Even Pizarro, usually so patient, showed some impatience at the slow progress.

"Ask him what's happening." He said, twisting his ring, a sign, Paullu had grown to recognize, of nervousness.

Atahualpa looked at the interpreter as if he was the worst sort of fool for presuming to ask such a question.

"It will come." Was all he would say, with that self-satisfied smile again.

When Paullu came back to Pizarro he told him the Inca had promised the treasure would start flowing in large quantities in three or four days, hoping it wouldn't arrive, and Pizarro and the rest of the Spanish would become even more angry at the continuing delay.

In the event though, on the morning of the fourth day when Paullu was looking forward to more mumblings of discontent that the ransom had still not materialised, the sentries saw a large cloud of dust approaching the escarpment that overlooked the valley. The soldiers were put on full alert, guns loaded, horses saddled and ready to mount, the killer dogs armed with their heavy spiked collars.

All unnecessary. As the cloud came nearer they could see it was raised not by an attacking army but by hundreds of llamas and native bearers accompanied by a small troop of guards and Inca officials.

Paullu was sent forward with a contingent of cavalry to escort them back to Cajamarca.

A buzz of excitement went around as the caravan entered the town, and made its way to the building earmarked for the gold and silver, with comments of surprise that such a great treasure had travelled safely through open country virtually unaccompanied.

It had come in the main, one of the Inca officials told Paullu

from the temples and palaces in and around Cusco, although great numbers of ordinary people had also donated their private possessions so as to speed the release of their beloved king, and then, whetting the Spaniards' appetite even further, informed them that two further shipments were being gathered together from places further afield, and should be with them shortly.

* * *

Pizarro and his commanders stood in the street outside the storeroom, the troops craning to see as the bearers' sacks and the llamas were unloaded and their contents placed on the ground to gasps of astonishment from the onlookers, Pizarro permitting himself a look of triumph as the first items were displayed each seemingly more impressive than the one before it.

The process took most of the day. Paullu had seen gold and silver before, but nothing like the quality and fineness of what was piling up before him. Dishes. Plates. Cups. Great beaten sheets of gold taken from the walls of the Temple of the Sun, the Incas' most important shrine. Figures of animals and men some so heavy it took three, sometimes four, of the strongest soldiers to carry them into the storeroom.

The sun grew hotter. Chairs were called for, and a canopy erected over the commanders.

Throughout all this Pizarro did not take his eyes off what was happening, occasionally getting to his feet to examine some of the choicest pieces, telling the clerks who were noting the items, to put a mark or comment next to the ones of particular merit or unusualness, but when, as night fell, the last of it was taken inside it still only filled the storerooms to just over the height of a man's shoulder.

"Not enough." Paullu heard Pizarro murmur as the rooms were sealed and guards put on the doors.

He needn't have been concerned. Almost every day columns of bearers and llamas bought more to Cajamarca, although, despite all the riches that had fallen into their grasp, not all the Spanish were content.

Rumours, in which Paullu had a hand, started to circulate that the Inca had given orders for the most precious items to be moved to secret locations in the jungles and mountains so as to keep them out of the hands of the interlopers.

* * *

The treasure kept on flowing, but once the marks on the walls of the storerooms had been reached, the flood of precious items stopped, as though a stream had been dammed, not even the slightest drop of water allowed to trickle through.

But if Atahualpa thought that the filling of the two rooms would buy his freedom, he was sadly mistaken. Playing on the Spaniards' fears, Paullu started spreading more falsehoods casually to those he knew from past experience would repeat it to everyone in the town.

A word here, a word there, that he'd heard that Inca armies were gathering in the mountains, ready to strike the moment the ransom was delivered; that Atahualpa had sworn to wreak revenge on those who'd tricked him the moment he was released, and would be sure not to make the same mistake of underestimating the Spanish again.

This time there would be no mercy.

Each day the Spaniards sent patrols out only to see them return hours later with no sightings of the enemy. Despite this the rumours about the Inca's deceitfulness, once they'd taken root didn't die out, if anything they grew in intensity.

Paullu continued stoking the fire.

The skill of misrepresentation like any skill, improves with practice, so when Paullu was eventually made to question Atahualpa about Pizarro's and the mens' concerns, he was far more subtle in his approach, generating a feeling of unease in the minds of the Spanish by translating the Inca's protestations of innocence into something far less positive, giving an impression of an evasive, cunning adversary who couldn't be trusted under any circumstances.

Drip. Drip. Drip

* * *

A few weeks after the final load of treasure was delivered, Atahualpa was taken to trial.

The charge. Treason. Planning to attack the Spanish immediately he was free.

Paullu accompanied the party of soldiers sent to bring the Inca to Pizarro, telling him that the commander wished to see him in his quarters to advise him of something to his advantage. Atahualpa only realising too late that he'd been lied to, when they placed the shackles on his hands and feet and locked him away under heavy guard.

Tricked yet again.

Clearly, Paullu thought, a man so conceited, so stupidly sure of his invulnerability, that he was incapable of learning from his previous mistakes, deserved the fate that awaited him.

* * *

Paullu's services were not required at the trial which was held early the following day. Another interpreter, of which several had been trained recently, was to be used. He didn't complain. In fact, he was relieved not to be involved, neither needing nor wanting to face Atahualpa's wounding looks and words of hatred, or to hear his protestations of innocence, and inevitable cries for mercy.

All this, when combined with the lies and falsehoods of the Spanish, concocted to ensure a conviction, would have been too much for him to bear. It was enough to know that he, a mere interpreter, a man the Inca thought not fit to wipe the dirt from his shoes, had had a hand, however small, in his downfall.

The words of his father kept echoing in his brain.

"Promise me." He'd said before Paullu left with the Spanish. "That you'll never forget who was to blame for what happened to your brother and your sister. Never forget."

It was enough for Paullu to know that he hadn't.

* * *

Paullu barely closed his eyes the night before the trial, only falling into a fitful sleep shortly before morning, which no doubt accounted for the particularly vivid dream he had.

He was walking in a valley, not unlike the one they were in now when suddenly he heard a tremendous noise, and turned to see a herd of llamas thundering towards him at breakneck speed. He hesitated, realising there was something not quite right about them, but it was only when they were almost upon him that he saw they had the heads and tails not of llamas, but horses.

Rooted to the spot with shock, he dived behind a rock with just seconds to spare, crouching down until the creatures had passed by leaving a cloud of dust behind and two crumpled bodies on the grass.

He was about to go to see who they were when he started awake, screaming and covered in sweat, not knowing for few seconds where he was, until he heard the voice of one of the men who worked in the kitchens saying.

" . . . decided. He's guilty."

Paullu felt nothing. Neither happy nor sad. Just empty. Like a broken pot no longer required.

* * *

News of the verdict spread through the town like wildfire. All were put on full alert lest the natives undertake a last minute effort to save their king.

The execution, Paullu was later told by one of the soldiers, was done that very night in front of Pizarro, his brothers, a handful of guards, and Father Morales.

The Inca was strangled, having adopted the Christian faith, Paullu's informant told him, to avoid the indignity of being burnt at the stake, and was promised a burial according to his traditions.

Another lie. Atahualpa's body was burned, it was rumoured, rather than buried, for fear the site might become a place of pilgrimage and remembrance for those natives still loyal to the previous regime. So, up to the very end, the Inca was misled by his captors.

* * *

Once the Inca had been taken care of it was time to deal with the treasure.

For some days following Atahualpa's execution Indian labourers had been busy constructing stone kilns under the direction of the Spanish on the outskirts of the city, out of sight of the Inca camp. Immediately the work was finished the fires burned day and night as the Spanish melted down the ransom they'd collected and then poured the molten liquid into wooden troughs.

As he watched the contents of the storerooms being hauled out, then dragged along and manhandled into the kilns, Paullu wondered what the hurry was now the Inca was no more. Was it fear of being attacked? The desire to move on to Cusco where, people were saying, even more valuable treasures were either being hidden or moved away to other locations? Or, knowing the greed of the Spanish, were their leaders concerned that the men may attempt to take more of their allotted share by force?

Already, two soldiers had been hanged for trying to smuggle out objects, an example to anyone else who was contemplating a similar act.

But not everything was consigned to the flames. A number of the choicest items were left untouched to be sent to Spain, as part of the crown's fifth share of the proceeds so the king could see for himself what marvels had been unearthed in his latest possession.

"What sort of man is he?" Paullu asked one of the soldiers as they watched the remaining treasures together with the roughly melted down bars of gold and silver being loaded onto the backs of llamas for the long journey to the coast.

"Who?"

"Your king. What's he like?"

The soldier smiled.

"How would I know? They say he's pious. Well mannered. True to his wife. A good man."

A rich man now, Paullu thought, as he watched the heavily guarded convoy making its way slowly out the valley.

* * *

Would the Spanish never be content? Immediately the treasure had been melted down and distributed to the army, they started getting him to question the imprisoned Inca nobles who'd survived the massacre.

So many questions, and as he would have expected, mostly about gold and silver.

Was there more treasure? Where was it hidden? Where was the gold and silver mined? Did they know of any other rich kingdoms? Did the Incas trade with them? How far away were they?

The responses the nobles gave were vague at best, even when the Spaniards told Paullu to threaten them with torture.

"Do you know what will happen when you no longer have the Spanish to protect you? You filthy traitor." One of the younger Inca nobles shouted at Paullu, as he warned them what would happen if the Spanish remained dissatisfied with their answers.

All Paullu could do was walk away, face burning, pushing past the guards, hearing his tormentor's words as he left.

"That's it. Run. Run. You cursed, filthy coward."

He attended the first of the torture sessions in case anyone yelled out some information in their agony, but could detect nothing of any value in the mumblings and screaming he was obliged to witness.

Two Inca notables died and several others were badly burnt or injured without divulging anything useful.

He could tell from the looks on their faces that the Spanish didn't believe him when he told them the prisoners either didn't know, or wouldn't tell their tormentors whatever secrets they may have been party to.

They think everyone is like them, Paullu thought, cruel, greedy, interested only in their personal wellbeing.

In fact he doubted if he would have bothered to tell them even if he'd heard something useful.

* * *

Shortly after he was replaced by one of the new interpreters. As if a different face, another voice, would persuade the nobles, who wouldn't move a step without their ruler's authority, to divulge anything, if indeed there was any information to reveal.

For his part Paullu was left wondering if his services were merely being dispensed with, or as had happened to a number of others, he was about to be accused of treachery with the inevitable consequences.

* * *

More reinforcements from Spain arrived from the coast, doubling the size of the army, and Pizarro gave the orders to prepare for the march on Cusco, the Inca capital.

Somewhat surprisingly Paullu was to be one of the interpreters accompanying the expedition.

* * *

Since the news of Atahualpa's execution most of the Inca's army had melted away, the Indians that were left seemingly stunned, unable to move with any purpose, like an animal that had been badly wounded, or was waiting the slaughterer's axe.

Not Paullu, though. He'd had his bellyful of both the Spanish and the Incas.

He left early one morning before the camp was astir, slipping away a couple of days before they were due to leave for Cusco.

He took with him some supplies and the stash of coins and other valuables he'd accumulated, leaving behind his uniform and the Spanish Bible he'd been given, and looking like any other of the hundreds of Indians milling around the camp.

Walking briskly, his lungs taking in the cool, clean air, the camp and the town of Cajamara soon disappeared in the distance as he climbed out of the valley towards the mountains, their peaks catching the rays of the rising sun, and his home.

Renaissance

It was shortly before the hour of two as I made my way to the inn where we'd arranged to meet, trying to avoid the afternoon sun by keeping to the shady parts of the streets, anxious, and cursing myself for being late, today of all days.

We'd agreed in advance that, were our assassination attempt to fail, Giovanni, Stephano and Paulo would wait at the inn, while myself and Mateo would go to the dealer and collect the horses that we needed to make our escape. In the event only four of us had got away. We'd left Mateo dying on the steps of the duke's palazzo, the rest of us splitting up, Paulo, Stephano and Giovanni going to the inn, while I would make my way to the horse dealer as quickly as possible.

I'd arrived at the stables on the edge of the city at the time arranged. The horses were waiting, the price previously agreed, but as they were being led into the yard it was clear that one was pulling his back leg badly. Whether it was lame or had some malady or other, I did not know nor care, just angry that the dealer thought he could palm me off with an inferior beast, particularly as I'd insisted I wanted the best available.

In normal circumstances I would have refused point blank to pay the cheating rogue, forcing him to reduce the price or walking away from the deal because of his damned trickery, which, in the event of a pursuit, could have caused our deaths. But not today. There was no time to go anywhere else, I felt tired and dispirited, and the gash to my shoulder, whilst no longer bleeding so heavily, was still painful.

Most importantly, I'd told the others that I'd be at the inn at half an hour past one so we could get away before there was time for the authorities to start searching in earnest for the perpetrators of a crime as heinous as the one we'd committed. Or to be precise, had tried to commit.

So, biting my tongue, I agreed a higher price for a replacement, handed over what was demanded, and led the animals to the secluded copse outside the city walls where I'd previously secreted supplies and changes of clothing in the event it proved to be necessary to make our escape.

I washed and patched my wound, changed my bloody clothes for some of the ones I'd hidden, and, having secured the horses, hurried away in the direction of the town as quickly as I could.

Fate plays strange tricks on us. In fact I probably owe my life, such as it is, to the delay caused by the horse trader's deviousness.

* * *

I didn't see the soldiers until I turned the corner opposite the inn, some standing in front of the alley I'd exited from, more in the square, bright in the sunlight after the shady dimness of the streets I'd come down.

And across the square . . . Five or six others at the door of the inn.

How had the Duke's men found us so quickly? A chance remark about several men reserving a room for a just one night? Stephano, ever the hothead, arguing about the price, needlessly drawing attention to us?

Or maybe it was Mateo.

But he was dead for sure. I knew when someone was done for. I'd seen him with my own eyes, blood pouring from his wounds, clearly with only minutes to live unless . . . he'd somehow survived.

Had they managed to revive him and persuade him to divulge everything with his terrified, dying confession?

A vision flashed through my mind of one of the priests beholden to the Duke, crouched over Mateo like a dark bird of prey, whispering in a seductive, cloying voice.

"You've committed a most terrible crime, my son. One for which you will will suffer forever, burning in the deepest depths of hell. You have one chance left before you depart this life. Just one. If you confess and tell me the truth I can absolve you of your sin before it's too late."

* * *

My first instinct was to turn and run. Try to get away and take my chances in the narrow alleys I knew so well, but it would have been hopeless. I was tired, in pain, considerably older than the soldiers who'd be pursuing me, and unarmed except for the dagger I wore beneath my shirt, my sword having been left at the scene of the attack.

My sword! I felt a cold feeling in my guts, thinking for a moment I'd taken my favourite one with me with our family's crest on the pommel, before remembering it was a plain weapon, without identification.

The panic passed. I had to do something. But what? I needed to find out what had happened to my comrades, and before I knew what was happening, I found myself walking across the square, towards the inn, my feet carrying me as if I had no control over them.

As I got closer I could see the soldiers' faces and hear their voices, an older one giving orders as another shouted down at him from an upstairs window of the inn.

By now one of them was staring intently at me and yet I still continued.

There's no knowing how it would have ended if I hadn't heard the sound of a babble of conversation coming from my right, and, turning my head, saw a small crowd held back by several soldiers on the far, shady side of the square.

It was if a spell had been broken. I changed direction, forcing myself not to hurry, and made my way towards them, my limbs shaking as I realised how close I'd come to discovery, trying all the while to calm the turmoil of my thoughts.

The clothes I'd changed into, akin to those of a tradesman of the lower classes, now stood me in good stead being similar in look to the people crossing the square about their business, and the members of the crowd into whose midst I now walked.

I stood near the back of the crowd and, trying to disguise my voice to match my physical appearance, asked the unkempt looking man next to me what was going on, making my question sound as casual as possible, thinking all the time he could surely hear the pounding of my heart.

"I don't know for sure." He replied. "The Duke's men arrived a few minutes ago and surrounded the square. Some of them went inside the inn, and . . . Look." He said, pointing.

There was a shouting of orders. The men outside the inn stood to one side as the door opened, and a number of soldiers come out carrying a corpse, followed a few seconds after by more of them bearing a second dead body.

The crowd grew silent.

Giovanni. My brother. Please God don't let it be Giovanni.

I wanted to leave knowing it was over, our plans all come to nought, but could not do so without knowing what had happened to him.

I tried to crane forward to see the faces on the corpses. Impossible with all the people in front of me. I broke out into a sweat and a sinking feeling came over me. My eyes glazed over, and I was forced to lean against the wall behind me for fear of collapsing in the street.

I'd barely recovered when a third group of soldiers emerged from the inn, and headed towards the side of the square where I was standing.

They were leading two men, whose wrists secured with lengths of rope, the first, stocky with a slight limp, I recognised as the innkeeper. The second was Giovanni.

By now he was only a few yards from me. As he walked by like a man in a trance, I could see his shirt, bloody and torn, the wounds on his arm and chest, and the bruise on the pale skin of his cheek.

One of the soldiers struck him a blow in the back, causing him to stumble, almost falling.

I felt an anger rising deep within me and my hand went to the knife hidden underneath my shirt. Draw it, a voice said inside my head. Draw it. Throw yourself upon them and die like a man alongside your brother.

But to my shame I did nothing, shrinking back into the crowd, trying to avert my face lest his gaze light upon me and draw attention to my presence.

I needn't have concerned myself. Head erect, long, golden hair glinting in the sun, eyes firmly to the front, his back straight once more, wearing his wounds like a badge of honour as they led him to his fate, there was little chance he would notice me, while I, like a feeble woman, turned away from him in his hour of need.

I guessed they were bound for the fortress which sat on a hill overlooking the town. Knowing what fate awaited him in those cruel dungeons and torture chambers I would have preferred him dead like the others.

Then they were gone, leaving the onlookers and the rest of the soldiers in the square.

* * *

The crowd broke up, their entertainment for the afternoon finished, and I started walking away, choking back the tears, my mind in a turmoil, only to be disturbed by a voice in my ear.

"I wonder what that was all about." The man I'd previously spoken to asked, walking beside me.

I looked at him, trying to gather my thoughts together.

"What d'you reckon happened there?" He asked once more.

Through all the confusion and the roaring in my head I felt there was something not quite right about him. Something bothering me that I couldn't quite put my finger on.

"Well. What do you think?" He asked again, and then I had it. His dirty clothes and shoes and unkempt appearance completely belied the mode of his speech.

I knew the authorities were in the habit of sending spies into the streets to indulge in seemingly innocent conversations with passers-by, hoping in this way to unearth any criticism of the Duke and his family, maybe, if they were lucky, sedition or heresy. Given what had happened barely three hours ago these rats would be swarming all over in an attempt to find out whatever they could about the plot.

"I asked what you thought." The man's voice crashed into my head once again. "What?"

"You seem distracted my friend. What do you think that business at the inn was about?"

It took all my self-control to demur from telling him he was no friend of mine, and strike him with all my might, or even better stick him in the guts with my knife, and have done with it, and while I was about it take some of the Duke's soldiers with me before they cut me down.

No. Remain calm if you want to live.

"It's nothing." I replied, turning towards him and forcing myself to smile. "I'm a little tired that's all. They were probably smuggling or owing money. Something like that."

"With so many soldiers around? No. I reckon it's something else. Maybe a conspiracy of some sort against the Duke."

He leaned towards me, dropping his voice.

"Look at us. Scraping a living while he and his minions grow fat on our backs. A lot of us think there ought to be a plot. Get rid of the whole damned bunch of them. That's what I say."

He paused, waiting for my reply, no doubt hoping I'd say something incriminating so he could have me hauled in for interrogation.

Keep calm, I repeated to myself. If he had anything specific on you he'd have had you picked up already.

"I don't know what you're talking about." I said, forcing myself to stare at him as if it was he who was acting suspiciously.

He was not, though, put off so easily.

"We should talk more." He said. "D'you want to come for a drink?"

"No thank you. I must be going. I've got an appointment. And a word of advice my friend. Be careful. You could get into a lot of trouble, the way you're talking."

With that I walked away from him, doing my best not to hurry. Step by step, the sweat running down my face, all the time fearful of a hand on my shoulder or the prick of a blade in my back.

But nothing happened. By the time I glanced nervously back he was already in conversation with another passer-by.

* * *

Once away from the square, and certain that no-one was following me, I gathered pace, rubbing the tears and sweat away with my sleeve.

My legs felt heavy, and the wound in my shoulder was hurting again. More soldiers went hurrying by. I needed to think. I ducked into a tavern and ordered a glass of wine and a plate of stew—I hadn't eaten since morning—but had no appetite for it, leaving half the food untouched, sitting alone, the buzz of conversation and laughter all around me, my mind still in a tumult, trying to work out what best to do.

For the life of me I couldn't remember whether or not I'd told Mateo the name of the horse dealer. Surely not, or they'd have been waiting for me when I was there earlier. Or maybe they were there now, searching the area.

My hand drifted to the belt under my shirt to check if the money pouch I was carrying was still safe. It was. I breathed a sigh of relief. At least I still had a fair amount of money, including the sum to pay for our lodging and other expenses.

Our lodging and expenses. That was wrong. It wasn't *our* lodging and expenses. I was the only one left.

* * *

There was only one place I could go.

Several months earlier when the plot had first started being seriously considered, I sold some property and other assets, and under an assumed name, bought a rundown, isolated villa on the eastern shore of the Lake of Como, burying the money that was left over from the transaction together with some jewellery and other valuables in the grounds.

I hadn't told a soul about this, not even Giovanni. Maybe even then something deep in my soul was telling me our plan was destined to fail.

I decided to leave immediately for the lake, travelling on foot, keeping to the back roads, sleeping rough for a couple of nights, not purchasing a horse until I was well away from that damned, accursed town.

* * *

The villa, which I purchased from a wealthy family in Milan, hadn't been in use for several years because of its isolated position and distance from the roads. It had been allowed to deteriorate, and in truth was barely habitable. Holes in the roof. Broken windows. A few old pieces of furniture. A couple of creaky beds.

Let the wind and rain come in.

Maybe when some time has passed I'll undertake some repairs and improvements, but I haven't the heart or energy to do anything at the moment.

If I'm still alive by then. The Duke's men will be pursuing all avenues to find the final assassin who managed to evade their clutches.

* * *

The terrace of the house overlooks the lake. Each morning I watch the birds winging their way across the water, and the fishermen's boats, their catch for the day having been taken, gliding slowly back to the villages along the shore. An eagle occasionally soars overhead. Deer and foxes visit the garden.

I call it a garden, but in reality it is so unkempt and overgrown it is more like a wilderness. Once I discovered a family of wild boar on what is left of the lawn snuffling and digging among the roots. I let them be, a few more holes and disturbances would make little difference.

After weeks of idleness, made worse by my recollections of that awful day, and my constant reflecting on whether we might have succeeded in achieving our purpose of killing the Duke and his brother had we'd done things differently, I started exploring the area, walking the rough trails that criss-cross the forested hills that skirt the lake, armed at all times with sword and dagger, and loaded pistol at my belt, as protection against wild beasts or any of their human counterparts I might encounter.

* * *

It is said that wolves and bears live in these parts. As yet I have seen neither, although the other day when I was on my way home as dark was falling I heard a rustling sound coming from the bushes in front of me. I moved quickly away from the path, drawing my sword, and stood listening, my breath coming in short gasps until I saw a small rabbit hop out, and pause for a second before disappearing into the undergrowth.

I smiled ruefully at the pass I have come to—a man who dared attempt to slay a tyrant, frightened of a rabbit.

I only go into the nearest village for food and supplies when absolutely necessary, engaging if I have to in some idle chit chat, but no more, in case questions are asked or suspicions aroused, for the arm of the Duke is long and, knowing him as I do he will never give up the chase for me however many years and how much gold it takes.

Still, for the time being, I feel, if not completely safe—this I will never be—at least reasonably content. No. Not content. I will never be that after what happened. Just somewhat more at peace than when I first came here, and I have to admit that I've grown surprisingly fond of it here, or at least as much as one can be of a place of exile. Someone in my position can hardly ask for more.

* * *

I was fortunate it was summer when I came here and could enjoy the long, hot days when the waters of the lake shimmered in the sun, and all of nature enjoyed its bounty. And then the autumn, cooler, the air fresh, walks though the forests on a carpet of multi-coloured leaves.

Now that winter's arrived, the birds and animals have gone, and the lake is a choppy, dull grey, the clouds from the north blowing in over the mountains, and bringing rain almost every day.

I've had to spend some time patching up the roof in several places and nailing pieces of wood over the windows where the water comes in.

The days are cold and the nights draw in early forcing me to spend time indoors and leaving me weary with boredom. My only pastime, apart from keeping this journal, is reading and re-reading the books I found at the bottom of a cupboard in one of the upstairs rooms. Most of them are not to my taste, still I give thanks to whoever left them there for giving me something I can occupy my hours with.

In truth, though, I feel more isolated than ever, missing the company of men and women far more than I would have thought possible. So intensely did I experience this lack of company, that one day when the weather was brighter, a cold clear, winter's day, a touch of frost on the ground, I made my way to the tavern in the nearest village, and exchanged a few words with the locals.

They soon realised from my accent that I was not from these parts. The inevitable questions followed, which, I must admit, I answered somewhat brusquely, before excusing myself and leaving in a hurry, rather quicker than I had intended.

Fancy me, afraid of peasants and farmers.

It will be some time before I avail myself of their company again.

* * *

The weather's grown worse, flurries of snow forcing me to shorten my morning and afternoon excursions. That is why I started writing this journal. It fills the time and exercises my mind. Each night when I've finished I hide it behind a loose brick in the chimney. God alone knows why. No-one ever comes here. But this is what I've become, a nervous, cowardly man, frightened of his own shadow, still too fearful of discovery to visit the local villages more than once or twice a month, let alone venture into the town of Como—barely two days ride away.

Fearful. Frightened. Who was known before as a man who wouldn't hesitate to stand up to anyone who crossed his path, and not much more than half a year ago tried to kill the Duke and his accursed brother.

Still, time has a habit of changing things. Maybe when the weather improves I'll regain something of the spirit I used to have, and make the effort to go to Como. Buy some books and a few luxuries. Indulge myself with a woman.

Yes. Even stay there a night or two. Nothing lavish. An inn, a plain inn, just like the one where I saw Giovanni for the last time on that fateful day in July.

* * *

Last night, it must have been about two o'clock, I was woken by a noise coming from the back of the house. I crept to the window, and, standing to one side, looked out over the garden. The sky, dark. The garden empty. Nothing to be seen. Probably a wild animal, I thought, sniffing around for food.

Then the moon came out from behind a cloud, and in its cold light I clearly saw the figure of a man standing under one of the trees, gazing up at the window where I was standing.

I ducked back into the room, grabbed my pistol, and waited a minute or so before carefully glancing out again. There was nobody there.

I hurriedly put on some clothes, covered the bed, placing the pillow under the covers so in the dark it could be taken for a human form, and tiptoed into the hall and along the corridor to the plainly furnished room—just a table and a chair—where I keep the few books I found and where I write this journal.

Leaving the door open, I moved the chair to the side of the room, at an angle where I could see the staircase and hear anyone coming up, keeping my pistol cocked and ready to hand, my sword on the floor beside me.

I lost track of the length of time I sat in the chair, trying not to fall asleep, before the first dull light of the winter dawn filtered through the window.

I felt tired and stiff. I suspected I'd dozed off once or twice during the night, and once had to leave my post to go and relieve myself, the dribbling of my piss sounding to me as loud as a waterfall amid the dark silence.

Nevertheless, here I was, still alive, and not a mark on me.

* * *

It was not until after breakfast that I summoned up the courage to venture out. Armed with sword and pistol I walked round the house to see if there was any sign of an attempted entry—I keep the windows and doors barred at night—but could find none.

Next I went across to the tree where I'd seen the man to check if he'd left any footprints or other signs of his presence. Nothing.

I also examined the ground my boxes were buried in to see if any of them had been disturbed. Everything was exactly as I'd left it.

It was as though nobody had ever been there.

* * *

I've had difficulty in sleeping since I saw the man in the garden.

Before I retire for the night I set various plates and glasses beneath the windows, in doorways, and on the stairs so as to warn me if anyone comes into the house.

I lie in bed fully clothed, weapons close at hand, and get up several times during the night to check downstairs and peer out the windows.

* * *

He came for me almost a month after I'd first seen him, on a night when there was a most terrible storm. Thunder. Lightning. Rain lashing against the window panes. The wind howling, blowing the branches wildly this way and that.

I should have guessed it would be on a night such as this that he would decide to strike.

* * *

I fell into an exhausted sleep an hour or two before dawn, and woke with a start to see a strange looking crossbow, much smaller than is usual, aimed at my chest, the figure holding it a mere shadow in the darkness beyond.

My hand crept slowly towards my sword as I readied myself to jump up and run at him, not caring if I was killed in the attempt, rather than dying without a fight like a lamb led to slaughter.

The crossbow moved a fraction, following me. I steeled myself for the bolt to slam into my flesh.

"Relax. I'm not here to kill you. I'm here to talk." A voice, soft and calm, came from behind the crossbow. "Now, light a candle. Slowly now. No tricks."

I lit the candle with trembling hands, and as the flame flickered into life I saw before me a man in his late forties of average build, with a greying beard and a pale scar on one cheek, bending low and laying the crossbow on the floor.

He remaining crouching, clear blue eyes, seemingly unconcerned, looking up at me.

"I don't intend to harm you." He said, spreading his hands wide to show he was unarmed. "If it makes you feel better keep your weapon to hand. But hear me out."

I said nothing, but held my sword down by my side, so it was easy for me to swing or stab with it.

"Good." He said. "I'm going to get to my feet. And now I'll get rid of these."

Three, vicious looking, short bladed knives appeared one after another as if by magic, and were laid on the floor next to the crossbow, followed by a short curved sword of the type the Moors use.

"Are you convinced now?" The man asked, getting to his feet, holding his hands out to show they were empty. "I repeat, I don't intend to harm you. After all, why should I hurt the man who's had a hand in saving me?"

He took off his soaking wet cloak, and sat down on the bed.

"I'm cold, wet, and I'm hungry." He said, rubbing his hands together as though he was an old friend come to visit. "Aren't you going to offer me something to warm me up?"

"Yes. Yes. I'll get you some wine and food." I said distractedly, thinking there was something familiar about him. Had I seen him somewhere before? The Duke's court? The inn in the village? My mind was in too much of a turmoil to think about it.

"I'll explain everything when I've eaten." He said, somehow sensing my growing confusion. "Bring your sword with you if you want to".

He insisted on walking in front of me to the kitchen, looking around with an amused expression at the traps I'd taken so much trouble to set.

He stopped and turned around when the bottom two stairs creaked loudly as they always did.

I tightened my grip on the sword.

"Don't worry." He said with a smile. "Your hearing isn't at fault. I didn't come this way. It was over the roof at the back. That's how I got in without falling for any of your little tricks. I took off some loose tiles while you were out walking, and hid in your loft until I was sure you'd dozed off. I got soaking wet up there. You really need to repair those holes properly. That damned storm kept you awake for hours. I thought you'd never . . . but, here we are. Let's open a bottle, and I'll tell you all about it."

* * *

I took out a bottle of wine, two glasses, and some bread and cheese, thinking all the time that none of this makes sense, racking my brain to understand what was happening.

I lit some more candles, filled the two glasses, and sat down opposite him, still on my guard, watching him eat the bread and cheese, and taking the opportunity to observe him more closely. I hadn't been mistaken. He *was* familiar. Though not absolutely sure, it seemed to me he was the man I'd seen that night in the garden staring up at me.

He nodded when I asked him, telling me that it was indeed him I'd seen, and also, what I'd assumed was the case, that it was the Duke and his brother who'd ordered my assassination.

"In the most painful, drawn out way possible, they commanded." He said, adding. "They pay me well, and they trust me to do what I'm told."

"But how did . . . ?" I asked.

"Wait. All in good time."

The first thing he'd done was hide in the woods close to the house so as to ensure himself I was the person he was looking for. Once certain I was his man he'd come back to kill me on the same day in the early hours of the morning, but by the grace of that providence that I'm now convinced is protecting me he disturbed a fox on his return. It was this noise, he guessed, that had woken me.

Despite my efforts to conceal myself he'd seen me at the window, and realising his presence had been discovered, decided to return to his lodgings in Como and wait several days before returning, by which time, he reckoned, I would have lowered my guard.

He'd concluded, rightly, that I wouldn't run, but if I did, had taken the precaution of paying men to watch the road out of town.

"So how did you find me in the first place?" I asked.

"I was told where you were. It's not my business to ask how they tracked you down. You know you're a very lucky man." He continued. "You should have been dead by now, but you've been protected from my attentions not once, but three times. Maybe the fates have some great enterprise in store for you."

"Three times?" I asked, my surprise growing by the second.

He leaned back in his chair, took a sip of wine, and explained that the day before he was going to return to my villa, intending on this occasion to catch me when I left the house for supplies or a walk, a messenger arrived at the inn where he was staying ordering him back to the city with the news that the Duke and his brother had been executed for crimes against the people, and their families killed or exiled after an uprising led by one of the Duke's own condottieres, a man paid by them and trusted to protect their lives.

"And so through the Duke's death your life was saved again." The assassin concluded with a smile.

"Unless I'd killed you first."

He smiled and shrugged.

"Maybe. If you were lucky."

* * *

"And the third time?" I asked.

On his return to the city he was informed that I wasn't to be pardoned, on the contrary, the contract on my life was to be reinstated.

"How could we allow such a man to survive?" He was told by the new ruler. "A man who attempted to assassinate his lord? Think of the message that would send to anyone who was contemplating the same against me or my family. No-one should ever suppose he can lay his hand on those above him with impunity."

"Go back." The assassin was ordered. "And finish the job."

And was offered double the original sum when he bought proof of my death.

So, I thought as he was telling me this, this is the type of lying, vengeful hypo-crite who lords it over us now, no better than the bastards we'd tried to kill.

Tears came to my eyes as I thought of Giovanni, Mateo, and the others who'd died that day, only for me to see one tyrant replacing another.

It is I think, this perfidy that hurts me the most.

* * *

The assassin had returned to Como, this time deciding to revert to his original plan of coming upon me by night. As he put it. "Less chance of such a valuable prize slipping through my fingers."

"I checked my weapons the day I arrived." He continued "The tools of my trade, so to speak. My crossbow, just as accurate as a pistol, but quieter. A sword, of course, and my three knives. Specially made for stabbing or throwing. One in the front of my belt, another in the back, and the third in the top of my boot."

"I was well prepared, my friend." He said, draining his glass. "After all you're a very dangerous man. I had to make sure this time. Professional pride, you could call it."

"More?" I said, pouring the wine, and asked him why he'd gone against his new master's instructions in the knowledge that having failed to accomplish his task he could never return to the city. A very great loss financially, for surely a man of his skills would find himself in considerable demand during the troubled times we were living in.

"As I said before." He said. "You're very lucky. This time I decided to wait a few days in Como before I tried again. Relaxing, enjoying the town. There was no rush. I'd been given more than sufficient for my expenses, and I was convinced you wouldn't run. It was on the second day there that I met a woman purely by chance. Younger than me. A widow. Childless. I arranged to meet her the next day, and after that we were inseparable."

"It was completely chaste." He said, staring into my eyes as if daring me to contradict it. "All we did was walk by the lake, sit and talk, watch the world go by.

And then, one evening as we were strolling back to the town, I don't know what possessed me, but without thinking what I was doing I started telling her about my past. All of it. Like a confession in church. I held nothing back. I couldn't stop myself. She listened without saying a word to what I had to say about the killings, the assassinations, the whole tale of murder and betrayal.

When I'd finished I felt sick inside, convinced she'd refuse to have any further congress with me. Instead. . . . ' "

His voice shook with emotion.

"Instead she looked at me with a smile, placed her hand gently on mine, and said. You have sinned. So have many others. The question is, have you the strength to give up your sinning? If you have, then anything is possible. If not then you're damned, and no decent person will want to associate with you."

"She said no more, but I understood exactly what she meant."

* * *

"I saw her twice more after that. There was no further discussion about what I'd told her. Instead we spoke about simple, mundane things—the people about their business on the lake, the beauty of the countryside round about, her work, and suchlike. The things normal people talk about, and by the end of the week I'd decided I would turn my back on the life I was leading."

He gazed at me once again with that direct, challenging stare he had, but I said nothing.

"Look at me". He said, touching his head. "I'm turning grey, and to tell you the truth I've been fed up with this work for some time now. In a few years someone younger will stick a blade in my guts. I told you I had pride in my profession, but even that's going sour. I've got plenty of money stashed away, and now by a stroke of luck this woman has appeared out of nowhere. I've been given a chance. I could settle down with her, maybe have children. But for that to happen. . . . "

The intense stare appeared once again.

"You, my friend, will have to die."

I could feel my heart beating faster as I fumbled for my sword, hearing my voice sounding shrill. Distant.

"But you, you said you wouldn't. You weren't. . . . "

He laughed, leaned across the table, and placed his hand on my arm.

"No." He said "Don't be alarmed. You're not going to die. Not for a long time I hope. At least not if I bring them sufficient proof that I've done the job."

He lifted his hand, and smiled again, I supposed to reassure me.

"Don't worry. I'm not going to take your head. No. Not your head. Something else. But it must be something they'll take seriously."

It was only then what he was suggesting dawned on me.

He stared at me, his face creased in thought.

"Your finger with the signet ring showing your family crest." He said after a second or two. "That should do it. It's the only way I won't be suspected, and if that providence of yours continues to watch over you, you should be able to live in peace."

"Not my right hand, and not the ring. It's been in my family for years."

"It's just a ring. Think. Do you want to live? If you do, I'm afraid you've got no choice."

I thought for a few moments. He was right. It *was* only a ring. Nothing special. I had better ones buried in the boxes in the garden.

And yet I couldn't help remembering my father giving me the ring to me, and an identical one to Giovanni when we were young lads, the two of us so full of pride, showing them off to our friends. No. No. Forget all that. That's in the past. I was alive *now*, and by God, I wanted to carry on living.

"All right. I'll do it." I said, pulling the ring off. "But it must be my left hand."

The second finger of my other hand was the only one it would fit.

"We've got to do this straight away." The assassin said once I'd forced the ring onto my left hand. "A representative of the new Duke is waiting for me in the next town, and I don't want his suspicions aroused by too long a delay. We'll get a fire going. And I'll need an axe, a small one if you've got one."

He got to his feet.

"You know." He said, staring out the window. "I've seen many men die. Some easy. Some hard. I've no idea whether they went to heaven or to hell, and I certainly don't know what's going to happen to me. One thing's for sure, though, I can't undo the past. What's done is done. But what I do know is with her I can have a decent life here, on this earth."

He pointed. "Come. Look."

I joined him by the window.

The storm had stopped. The early morning mist had started to clear, the sun glinting on the water, the grass and leaves fresh and green after the rain.

"You see how beautiful it is." He said. "I want to enjoy this while I can. While there's life left in my bones."

Then he turned to face me.

"Come on. Let's get on with it."

* * *

I found him an axe, and started a fire to heat the cauldron I'd filled with water drawn from the well.

When I came back the assassin was sitting outside, sharpening the axe with a stone he'd found. I felt my stomach go cold at the sight of the sun's rays gleaming on the blade.

I tore a clean white shirt into strips, and, on his recommendation drank half of some brandy I had, feeling it burn my throat and going to my head almost immediately.

"We'll do it in quarter of an hour." He said. "When it's over I'll make you as comfortable as I can before I go."

* * *

I lay on the bed, my head spinning from the drink, feeling though, more alert than I would have liked to be.

The room was hot from the heat of the fire the assassin had made in the grate, within which was a piece of red, glowing metal to cauterize the wound.

"Are you ready?" He asked, bending over me, his eyes cold and expressionless.

I nodded, unable to speak for the piece of shirt he'd thrust in my mouth.

He said nothing, grasped my hand hard with his left, and raised the axe above his head.

He means to kill me after all was my last thought.

Then intense, blinding pain, followed by oblivion.

* * *

When I woke, it was growing dark, the weak rays of the sun barely penetrating the room. I had a splitting headache, and my whole arm was throbbing. I felt dizzy as I forced myself to sit up in bed and look down at my hand.

The stump of my finger was neatly bound with one of the strips from my shirt, stained reddy-brown. A bowl of bloody water was on the floor, and a small table had been set next to the bed, with a flask of water, a glass of wine, and some bread, cheese and meat on it.

The sight of the damage inflicted to my person made me feel sick to my very stomach, and I fell back against the pillow, lying there in a state of despondency for several minutes before I managed to gather myself together and gulp down most of the water—I was experiencing a most terrible thirst—and sip a little of the wine, but couldn't bring myself to touch the food.

The drink restored my spirits somewhat—after all, I thought, what's one finger when it could have been my life itself that was taken.

Eventually I fell into a troubled sleep from which I didn't wake until late the following morning. The headache had gone. My hand still hurt, but not as badly as before, and I felt extremely hungry.

It was not until I was up and halfway through the food the assassin had left me, that I realised he hadn't told me his name.

* * *

I've taken to sleeping in a small room at the back of the house in my clothes, weapons by my side, sword unsheathed, gun primed. I've left the various warning devices in place, and I secured the roof and nailed up the loft immediately I felt strong enough to undertake the work.

I only go out into the villages when I need necessities. Fully armed, hiding my weapons under my clothes, suspicious of everything and everybody, taking care at all times, constantly turning, checking, to see if I'm being followed or under surveillance.

I wonder what the villagers and fisherman I sometimes encounter make of me, the almost silent stranger who sometimes appears amongst them, then vanishes.

They probably think I'm a madman or some kind of hermit. At least their natural reticence and distrust of strangers stops them asking questions or delaying me in idle chit chat. I trust these same qualities will prevent them from mentioning anything about me to outsiders or the townsfolk who appear in the area from time to time to trade in furs, agriculture, and other business.

* * *

The weather has improved recently, the sky clear and the rain stopping, the first time for over a week. I ventured out early this morning, armed as always, heading towards the hills until the slippery, muddy, tracks drove me back home.

Later, sitting upstairs, writing my journal, I got up to stretch my legs and glanced out the window towards the lake, calm at that moment, without the dull, threatening grey clouds and choppy water so prevalent for the past few months.

As I watched, a flock of geese with orange markings flew in low from the north, their raucous cries piercing the silence as they elegantly skimmed the surface of the lake, and landed, barely disturbing the water. Where they'd come from or were bound to I could not hazard a guess, except it was most unusual to see them at this time of year.

I grabbed my cloak and hurried to the edge of the terrace which afforded me a closer look. I'd barely been there a couple of minutes when I heard the sound of footsteps crunching on the gravel at the front of the house. I felt at my side. No weapons. In my haste I'd forgotten them. It was far too dangerous to try to get back inside, all I could do was wait and listen and hope whoever it was wouldn't find me.

I concealed myself behind a clump of bushes, cursing my carelessness, as I heard the crunching on the gravel getting ever closer.

The footsteps grew louder. I shrunk further back into the undergrowth, and bent down to pick up a piece of wood to defend myself. How in God's name could I have allowed myself to be caught like this? All those months of remaining on the alert after the assassin had gone, thrown away in a moment of stupidity. If only. . . .

I was startled by the shrill calls of the geese as they took off, wheeled overhead, and flew towards the south. When I listened again the crunching sound had faded somewhat, and then it ceased altogether.

I forced myself to wait several minutes before creeping round to find out what had happened, and immediately saw the imprint of footprints in the gravel. Only one person. Small. A child's or a woman's by the look of it, leading up to the front of the house and then away. On the top step was a letter, jammed under the door. I took it inside and broke the seal.

* * *

The letter, neither signed nor dated, was written in a small, neat hand.

"My Dear Friend", it began, and continued, "If I may still call you that, given the harm I was obliged to inflict upon you.

I trust you are well, and recovered from my handiwork. I would have wished to write earlier, but circumstances rendered it impossible.

You will be pleased to hear that my story, accompanied by the evidence I took from you, was, I believe, accepted.

Over the years that I plied my line of work I learned that the so-called great often bore of the very thing that previously had seemed so important to them, leaving the little people whose lives they have affected to their fate -whether good or ill. By the time I arrived back the new Duke had far more important problems to contend with than the likes of you and me.

So, for the moment, I believe you are safe, but would urge you not to lower your guard for some time to come.

As for me, the tools of my trade lie somewhere deep in the lake, although I must say, as I dropped them over the side of the boat, watching them splash into the water, I felt a pang of remorse like leaving a place you have come to know well for the dangers and unknowns of another town or country. Still, it is done now, and by the time you receive this letter myself and the woman I told you about, soon to be my wife, will be well away from this part of the world.

I doubt if our paths will cross again. In the meantime I wish you well, and thank you for leading me, albeit inadvertently, to what I trust will be a better life.

Do you remember what I told you that morning when we were looking out over the lake? I said the world was beautiful and I wanted to taste of it. It *is* beautiful, and what this woman, God bless her, has taught me is it is only like this because of the good offices of both He who created it and His one begotten Son. The same Creator and Son who brought us two sinners together for delivery into their hands.

Think on this my friend, and save yourself.

Yours in Christ our Redeemer."

* * *

After I'd finished reading the letter I went out to the terrace again. Looking across to the opposite shore, I could feel the tears welling up in my eyes. As I wiped them away I thought I could smell a hint of spring in the air.

* * *

Almost a month has passed since I received the assassin's letter, and finally spring has arrived, the trees in blossom, the air heavy with the scent of grass and pollen. Even the lake water smells fresh and clean.

For the moment I am content to remain here. The ebb and flow, the daily noise and struggle of life in the city no longer hold the same appeal to me as they did before, although I have to admit, they still retain some of their attractions.

As soon as the weather improved I ventured into Como having bought a horse from one of the farmers who live nearby, staying for three nights at a cheap but clean inn on the outskirts of town.

Passing myself off as a visiting merchant I did everything I'd promised myself when I was sitting in the house during those long, cold winter days and nights—ate and drank well, bought several books and other items, and availed myself of the services of some of the women of the town.

* * *

The trip, short though it was, seemed to have the effect of energizing me, and on my return to the house I started to clear the garden of the undergrowth that was choking it. Once I've dealt with the weeds and brambles I'll start to plant some shrubs and maybe even some flowers.

It is a difficult, time consuming task not made any easier by my missing finger, the loss of which I still haven't got completely used to.

In truth, though, I only occasionally miss the finger, when tying a knot or doing some more intricate task, and sometimes, when the weather is damp or particularly cold I feel a dull itching in the place where it used to be, barely a pain, more a slight discomfort.

It is strange how quickly we can learn to do without something that previously we thought so important.

* * *

The other day, as I was finishing off clearing the section of the garden nearest the lake I discovered a statue lying on its side beneath the matted, tangled vegetation. I pulled it free and dragged it into the house so as to have a better look, and once I'd scraped off the moss and mud, and washed it clean, realised it was a finely carved figure of a young man, about two thirds life size, made of marble, the right arm outstretched, a finger pointing towards the heavens. When the garden is complete it will take pride of place in the centre of the lawn on the empty plinth where I guess it originally stood.

* * *

Two years. It is almost two years since I first came here.

Evening is approaching. The garden is thriving. The statue casts its shadow on the grass.

The house had been allowed to decay for the several years it lay empty before I arrived. Now the garden is satisfactorily completed I've decided to start refurbishing both inside and out, and to repair the terrace before it reaches a state where mere renovation is insufficient to save it from further deterioration. I've spoken to a number of people in the nearest village, and have found various craftsmen who are willing to help me with the work.

Who knows, once everything is finished and the house looks presentable I may even start entertaining a little.

There are a number of other villas scattered around the lake, most of them much larger and grander than mine. I have up to now avoided any contact with whoever lives in them, but recently have been thinking that perhaps the time has come to pay one or two a visit to see how the land lies, and decide which, if any, I wish to cultivate, introducing myself and concocting some story about the past that will satisfy their initial curiosity while leaving them wanting to know more. An air of mystery does no harm to a man's popularity, especially if there are ladies involved. My missing finger for example, could be explained away by a story of battles fought against the Moors or some other exotic foe.

I feel like an actor in a play, free to invent whatever background he wants for himself. Just a little rehearsal to ensure my story hangs together, and I will be ready to row across the lake in the small boat I've recently acquired, and make my first acquaintances.

I will first have to go into town to buy some new clothes, appropriate to the status of whoever I decide to become. Despite all my expenses there is still plenty of cash and valuables buried in my boxes, although I do not care to contemplate what will happen when, as is inevitable, they eventually run out. Maybe by the time that happens my excursions around the lake will have unearthed an heiress or a rich widow who will solve all my problems.

Still, for the moment, I am more than satisfied to sit here on my terrace, looking out on the lake and the mountains beyond, reading a little, keeping this journal, and making my plans.

I smile to myself, and go back happily to my idle contemplation.

* * *

Some news has filtered through from the city I fled from. I heard it when I was in Como buying clothes last week, the third occasion I've ventured there.

According to a merchant at the inn where I was staying, the new lord is now well established, having eliminated the previous Duke's family and seen off various challenges to his rule from supporters of the old regime, people who resented having their privileges taken from them in favour of the new man's friends and kinsmen.

As he put it—"Another flock of birds are wetting their beaks now."

These threats having been eliminated, the city, so he said, is now at peace and thriving under its new master, although, he added, nothing has changed for the ordinary folk who still fear the tap on the shoulder or a knock on their door in the middle of the night.

I couldn't bear to hear any more, slipping quietly away while the merchant was occupied with excited questions from other onlookers, eager to hear any gossip or information that could benefit them.

* * *

I've not heard anything further from the assassin—not knowing his name I am still obliged call him this. He has, I assume, moved on with the woman he told me about. Or maybe all his plans had come to naught, and he'd been killed or tortured for disobeying his instructions. If it was the latter he may have told them everything. . . .

I jolted from shock. No. No. After all, well over a year has passed since his letter. If anyone was coming for me, it would have been by now.

* * *

The first leaves have started to fall though the days are still warm and sunny. Early each Sunday the church bells ring out around the lake, but despite the counsel of the assassin I have so far ignored their entreaties.

So far as I do think of the Almighty I prefer to contemplate His works in the nature all around me, than sit bored in His house, waiting impatiently until I can escape at the end of the service. I've never been a great churchgoer. I have little time for all the paraphernalia of priests, cardinals and the like, and in truth wonder why any rational man should believe that his sins, however wicked, could be wiped out by the mere act of confession.

How in God's name could the Duke's weekly visits to the cathedral have eliminated his abominations, practiced each day, not even with the excuse of passion, but with a cold and merciless heart? If there is any justice in this world or the next he and all those who aided his endeavours will rot in hell.

And Giovanni. Dear Giovanni. How could his last confession, tortured out of him by the pain of the rack or the hot iron in those cold, dark, filthy dungeons, have ever. . . .

No. No. No.

Go outside and breathe the clean, fresh air.

Think of other things.

* * *

I've continued my explorations of the area, learning the skills of persistence and stealth so as to best observe the nature that abounds in the region.

When I was walking in the woods yesterday I came across a lynx, the first I've seen round here, standing by the side of the path, head to one side, large, pointed ears cocked and listening, yellow eyes looking straight at me for a brief second before it turned and walked unhurriedly into the thick undergrowth.

As it moved away I noticed one of its back legs was just a stump, maybe caught in a hunter's trap or injured in a fight. At least, I thought, although damaged, it has managed to survive—so far. A survivor just like me. Hunting, though, would be difficult for it. I decided I would try and help it live, and returned later in the day, by which time I hoped it would have regained its courage, and left some raw meat near to where I'd first encountered it.

By the time I came back to the spot the following morning not one piece remained. I stood concealed in the bushes for over half an hour, the sound of birdsong all around me, eyes peeled, barely moving a muscle without any sign of the cat.

Nothing. Not a murmur disturbed the peace of the forest.

I'll try again this evening, I thought, leave it some more to eat. Maybe it will eventually get used to my presence.

The soft wind caused some leaves to tumble slowly to the ground. I sighed. A relaxed, contented sigh. Yes, as the assassin had said, the world was beautiful, and I was a part of it

As I smiled and started to make my way back home I heard a movement on the path behind me. I turned to see what it was.

Apart

Tsar Ivan IV, better known as Ivan the Terrible, ascended the throne of Russia in 1547 at the age of seventeen.

Eighteen years later, after many instances of a growing brutality, he imposed a reign of terror on those of his subjects he considered disloyal or threatening to his power. Neither the nobility, the church, nor the ordinary people were immune from attack.

The instruments of this oppression were a military brotherhood personally beholden to Ivan, known as the Oprichniki, or "Men Apart".

* * *

Oprichniki oath.

"I swear to be loyal to the Tsar and his Empire, the Tsarevich and the Tsarina, and I swear to reveal anything I know or have heard or may hear about any evil enterprise directed against them by any person or persons.

I swear not to eat or drink with people outside of the Oprichniki, and never to have any relations with them. I also swear to deny my family, and to forget my father and mother.

In witness thereof I kiss the true cross in the knowledge that I will suffer fit retribution should I break any part of this sacred oath."

* * *

Vassily should have realised something funny was up when his uncle told him to come to the monastery dressed entirely in black.

His uncle had been very specific—not brown or dark grey. It must be black. Boots, jerkin, trousers, and, most important of all, this, his uncle said, handing him a long cloak with a hood.

"It's what we all wear." He told Vassily. "So whoever we're dealing with knows it's us, and we're about the Tsar's business."

Vassily's mother though, was not so respectful.

"Well, bless me." She said, laughing, as he was preparing to go to the monastery on the edge of the village where his uncle had arranged for him to meet the Oprichniki officers. "Do you know what you look like? A monk. Exactly like monk."

* * *

Vassily was his name, though they called him "Bull" on account of his strength.

A fighting man, a tolerable rider, skilful with the blade and, more particularly, the axe, flogged and dismissed from the local lord's army for insubordination, lucky to still be alive. Not beyond violence, either for the fun of it and, when the opportunity arose, the odd beating up, thievery and poaching for a few kopecks, qualities, his uncle told him, that would commend him to the people he was about to meet.

Despite this he couldn't help brooding over whether or not he should go with his uncle. These Oprich . . . or whatever they're called. They're soldiers aren't they, he thought. What'll happen if I don't tow the line? It could be a beating, the knout, or worse. Besides he was happy in the village doing whatever he wanted to. Why change that for something he knew nothing about?

Vassily's doubts and suspicions of authority must have shown in his eyes

"Come on, boy." Said his uncle, clapping him on the shoulder. "Drink up. There's nothing to worry about. They don't give a damn about your past. Only that you give a good account of yourself."

His uncle poured some more vodka.

"Look at me." He said, showing Vassily the rings on both hands and point- ing to the fur coat slung over the back of his chair. "I barely had two crusts of bread to feed myself with. Now I dine on meat and drink wine every day. And if you're smart you'll have the same. A lot better than being stuck in this stinking shit-hole."

He drunk deeply before leaning forward.

"They call us the Oprichniki. Men Apart. We owe allegiance to the Tsar. Only to *him*. Not to any merchant, boyar, priest or Jew. We do whatever he commands. He's promised us land, and we're allowed to take whatever spoils we want when we're about his business. But remember Vassily, if you do get in you can only do *his* business. If you try anything on the side. . . . "

His uncle drew his finger across his throat.

"I've seen men impaled, thrown to the bears, torn to pieces by dogs, you name it, for going out on their own. But if you behave, and do as you're told you'll be fine. Believe me, there's plenty for everybody. Gold. Furs. Whatever you want. So long as the big shots get their share."

He laughed. "We call what we pocket a fine. Sounds more legal that way. And the women, Vassily. There for the taking. You can do whatever you want with them. I've had young ones, old ones. Merchants' wives and daughters, even boyars' women sometimes—their skin so pale and soft it's like silk. And if they don't like it, we just cut the bitches' throats."

He took another swig and leaned back in his chair, a smile on his face.

"They'll only pick one or two, but you're a big, strong fellow, and I'll put in a word for you. And once you're in you'll do alright, I promise you. So what's it to be?"

Vassily finished his drink, thought for a bit, and agreed to go.

"Good." His uncle said, getting somewhat unsteadily to his feet and smiling encouragingly. "I'm sure you'll do well, but Vassily, whatever you see or hear up at the monastery, keep your trap shut."

"One more thing." Said his uncle, throwing his coat over his shoulders, the black fur shining in the firelight. "Don't forget to wear black clothes and the cloak I gave you, and bring an axe that's nice and sharp."

* * *

Vassily reported to the monastery early in the morning together with a number of other men from the neighbourhood.

After he'd answered a few questions about where he lived, his family, and military service—nothing too complicated—he was taken outside and one of the Oprichniki brought up a horse.

Vassily had to ride the animal several times round the open area in the centre of the monastery. As he did, he noticed some black clad Oprichniki inside the chapel. He was cantering fast and concentrating on keeping the frisky beast under control so he might have been mistaken, but it looked to him as though they were prising the icons off the wall above the altar.

"They won't like that." He thought, wondering where all the monks had got to.

Next they told him to show them his axe work on some logs. When he'd finished one of the Oprichniki went into an outhouse and emerged pulling a dog along by a rope tied around its neck, by the look of it one of the strays that hung around the village searching for food. A large brute, but thin, ribs showing through its skin.

"Kill it." Vassily was told.

Vassily hesitated, wondering if he'd heard right, before approaching the dog which growled and barred its teeth.

"Come on. Don't piss about. Kill it." The voice repeated. "Use your axe."

No problem. He'd dealt with dogs before.

One blow from the axe and it was over, the animal giving a low moan before collapsing in the dust, twitching twice, then lying still.

"Right." The voice said. "Now cut off its head."

He looked up, puzzled once again.

"You heard what I said. Cut off its damned head."

He stood over the animal, lifted the axe, measuring the distance before striking down sharply, cleanly separating the head from the body.

A sack sailed through the air, landing near his feet.

"Alright you're in. Put the head in the sack, stick it in some vinegar when you get home, and make sure to bring it back with you. Come here three days from now, Thursday, first thing in the morning. We'll show you the ropes, equip you out, and find a horse that can carry a big fellow like you. Come over here."

The man handed Vassily a few coins, telling him to use them to buy a broom and bring it with him when he reported for duty.

"A broom?" Vassily repeated, surprised.

"Yes. A broom. A new one."

* * *

His uncle laughed when Vassily asked him about the broom and the dog's head.

"We hang them on our saddles, so people know who we are. The broom's to sweep away all the shit that's been ruining this country."

"Why a dog's head?"

"Can't you guess? We're the Tsar's dogs, snapping at his enemies' heels. Faithfully doing whatever he wants."

* * *

They gave him a splendid horse, black, like all the horses the Oprichniki rode to complement the effect of their uniforms. He decided to call it Satan, on account of its colour.

"You know, we're not only soldiers, we're also like monks." The captain told him at the end of his first week's training, adding when Vassily creased his brow, not really understanding.

"We're a sort of brotherhood with our uniform all in black and our special oaths. Not tied to anyone except the Tsar. That's why we're called the Men Apart, and that's why the fuckers are so damned afraid of us."

* * *

Nothing was disallowed.

On the contrary, as he was informed. "The worse, the better. Makes them even more terrified."

By the end of the first year Vassily was sick to his guts of the constant round of killing, burning, raping, looting and torture. But what could he do? He'd sworn an oath on the Holy Book, and everyone knew what happened to people who broke sacred oaths. They went straight to Hell, and if that wasn't bad enough, there were all the awful things they'd do to you in this world if they caught you trying to desert.

On the other hand, as his uncle had promised, Vassily was eating and drinking well for the first time in his life. Meat every day. Decent beer, not that evil tasting swill they made in his village. Money in his pocket, and women pretty well whenever he wanted.

Besides, his mates, Dimitri and Vladimir, really smart fellows, and the rest of the company, put up with the bad stuff without any problems, so why should he be any different?

At least, he reckoned, you could take a bit of comfort from the knowledge that there were some in the brotherhood who were even worse than you.

It was whispered that three hundred Oprichniki, specially picked by Ivan himself, lived at Alexanderovskaya Sloboda, where the Tsar spent most of his time.

An isolated place, deep in the forest, a hundred or so versts from Moscow, surrounded by moats and a double line of walls, one of wood, the other of stone. No-one could enter or leave without permission, guards being stationed at all times on the narrow tracks that led to the place.

It was like a monastery, Vassily was told, austere and cold, gloomy rooms, simple furniture, except for the Tsar's quarters, full of gold, silver, and great chests overflowing with precious jewels, furs and other treasure.

Like a regular monastery, there were prayers and fasting, but here they were interspersed with feasting, orgies, and long intervals of torture.

Jesters and women were brought in for entertainment, and prisoners were thrown to the hunting dogs or the bears kept in pits outside the walls, and also . . . at this point the whispering became even lower, and whoever was telling the story glanced around nervously to make sure no-one else could overhear . . . there were hundreds of "special" captives, dear to Ivan's heart as deserving of exceptionally careful attention, kept in underground dungeons where only Ivan and his chosen Oprichniki were allowed to venture.

Constantly replenished by new victims, these "specials" were subjected to all sorts of ceremonies and tortures too terrible to mention, even by the hardened dogs of the run of the mill Oprichnicki. It was rumoured that Ivan was always present at these sessions, not only to encourage his minions, but also to join in the proceedings.

Was there any truth in this, or was it yet another trick of the Tsar's to instil even more fear in the hearts of his opponents?

Vassily wasn't clever enough to judge.

* * *

He only saw the Tsar twice.

The first time was about eighteen months after he'd joined up.

Vassily was a member of a party of Oprichniki sent to an estate in the country to teach a lesson to the boyar Kolychev, who'd upset the Tsar in some unspecified way.

"Do what you want with them, but none are to be left alive." Was the order. "Not him or his family. None of his servants and retainers. Not even the animals."

Nothing unusual. A typical operation—like many they'd done before.

What *was* unusual was that after twenty or so versts on the road they'd been met by Tsar Ivan, accompanied by a party of guards, and Malyuta Skuratov, the commander of the Oprichniki, who, it was said, was the most dangerous individual of all, after the Tsar.

"Don't look at him." One of the older men whispered as Skuratov rode by. "His eyes are yellow, like a cat's. Men have died for a wrong glance in his direction."

* * *

Followed by several wagons they thundered down the road into the hamlet where the boyar lived in a large timber house with balconies and intricately carved doors and window frames.

Vassily and his group were ordered to dismount and throw a cordon round the village so no-one could get in or out.

In the meantime, Ivan's men flushed the villagers out of their homes and crammed as many as they could into the boyar's mansion. Those for whom there was no room were cut down or shot, the bodies left on the ground, a similar fate awaiting the few that tried to break through the cordon.

From where he was stationed Vassily could see the doors and windows of the mansion being barred with pieces of wood nailed across them while the Tsar and Skuratov rode up and down shouting out instructions.

The rest of the black cloaked Oprichniki scurried around, carrying several large boxes from the back of the wagons, and placing them against the walls of the mansion and in the spaces underneath.

Once they were done the majority withdrew leaving some of their number laying long pieces of what seemed to be twine or rope along the ground to the boxes.

Vassily turned to his friend, Dimitri, who was standing beside him.

"What are they doing?" He asked.

"Wait. You'll see." Said Dimitri with a smile.

After a short while the remaining men ran back to the rest of the Oprichniki having lit the pieces of twine from tinder boxes they were carrying.

"Why are they . . . ? Vassily had just started to ask, when his ear drums were assailed by a tremendous explosion as the house was blown into a thousand pieces, timber, bits of household goods flying everywhere. He could have even sworn he saw parts of bodies and a couple of chickens sailing through the air.

There was a second or so of silence broken by the Tsar's men yelling and screaming with laughter, running around like mad people.

He felt a nudge to his arm.

"Look, Vassily. Look at Ivan, see how he loves it." Dimitri whispered.

The Tsar, struggling to control his horse, which had been startled by the blast, had come close to the cordon. His thin, gaunt face, Vassily saw, was creased with laughter, and a keening, coughing sound came from his throat as he yelled instructions to the Oprichniki to finish off anyone who'd somehow managed to survive the detonation.

* * *

That night, after the village had been burned to the ground and most of the animals slaughtered, a great banquet was held in the open to celebrate the destruction of the Kolychev clan.

Terrified young girls and women were brought in from the villages round about, the tables groaned with food and drink, and the entertainment was provided by the musicians and clowns who'd accompanied the Tsar.

The sight of Ivan, Skuratov, and the rest of the big shots grinning and drinking at the top table, their faces lit up by the flames of the fires lit to take the chill off the autumn air, reminded Vassily of the vision of hell painted on the wall of the church that had frightened him so much when he was a child.

* * *

Things got worse. Vassily had difficulty sleeping. Nightmares. Sweats. A constant pain at the back of his head.

"I want to leave." He blurted out to the captain one day, without thinking what he was saying.

"Why? Said the captain. "Our company not to your liking?"

"No. No. It's not that."

"So what is it?"

"It's . . . It's just that I should . . . I have to see my mother. She's old. She's . . . "

"Your mother, eh? Ah. Vassily. You're a good man. A true Russian heart. But what d'you think the little Father would say if he heard you wanted to leave his Oprichniki? I can tell you. He wouldn't be at all happy. He would ask, why is this Vassily so ungrateful? This man who swore a solemn oath to serve me, who I've protected, nurtured like he was my own son? And then he'd say to me, Andrei, in the name of everything that's holy, what have you done to make this man hate me so? This man who I've raised from the dust? And what would my answer be to that?"

"But I'm not . . . "

"I know Vassily. I know." The captain said with a smile. "But that isn't the way *he'll* see it. He can't stand men who betray him. God has given him the power to reward and punish as he wills and nobody, nobody, leaves the Oprichniki without his authority."

The captain leaned back in his chair regarding Vassily.

"I'll tell you what I'll do. I'll stick my neck out. Make some enquiries. See if we can't let you have some time off to visit your mother in a few months. Maybe next winter."

"Next winter?"

"That's the best I can do. Take it or leave it."

Needless to say, the captain had no intention whatsoever of sticking his neck out in any shape or form, particularly not for a simpleton like Vassily.

* * *

A new captain came. Even more brutal and uncaring than the one he replaced.

Not a chance of Vassily being allowed home, not even for just a short spell.

"We'd never see hide nor hair of you again." The new man told him, flanked by a couple of guards in case Vassily made any trouble.

"Besides. There's work for you. For all of us. There's a big operation coming up. You wouldn't want to miss that, would you?"

* * *

The operation the captain was referring to was the city of Novgorod.

Novgorod the beautiful. The great. Novgorod of the golden domes.

Treacherous Novgorod. Or so Ivan believed

Shortly after the Christmas holidays the Oprichniki were ordered to gather a few versts outside Moscow.

Vassily had never seen so many of them in one place—there must have been three or four thousand, maybe more. How many had been left in Moscow, Rostov, and the rest of the country was a closely guarded secret.

Some said just a few hundred were more than enough to keep the people in line, they were that terrified of them. Others reckoned many thousands, but only the Tsar and his closest advisers knew for sure.

Ivan. Skuratov. All the big shots were there.

"They're his specials from Alexanderovskaya." Dimitri, who seemed to know everything, said, pointing at a group of hooded Oprichniki who kept close to the Tsar at all times.

"And look at that lot. Yuradivye, they're called. Bloody mad, the lot of them."

Vassily looked to where a number of horseman, unkempt, their beards and hair long, cloaks, filthy and stained, were waiting at the side of the road, people manoeuvring to avoid coming too near them.

"Right bastards." Dimitri continued. "They say they're holy men, monks who've left their monasteries to serve the Tsar. More likely they were chucked out. There's not an ounce of decency in any of them, and they stink like pigs."

"Time to move off lads." The captain said, galloping up to their party.

* * *

They laid waste to the countryside like a swarm of black bats.

Tver. Pskov. Klin. Torzhok. Towns, villages, their names meaning nothing to Vassily and his comrades. All destroyed. Piles of bodies in the streets. Houses, churches, burning. Torments the Tsar's men inflicted on their victims the like of which Vassily had never seen before.

Giant pans for frying people, a special rough rope used to saw them in half, and worst of all, the water treatment—ice cold, then boiling hot until the victims died, screaming for mercy.

Vassily's headaches got worse, and a couple of times he was almost sick at the horrors he was obliged to witness.

And then it was Novgorod's turn.

* * *

The slaughter and destruction in Novgorod continued for six weeks, only coming to an end on Ivan's orders, as suddenly as they'd begun.

Vassily, though, was done before that, after four weeks, to be precise.

Fate, or whatever you choose to call it, had played a hand the day after his company had been told about the Jews.

* * *

"Right." The captain said having gathered his men in a square in the centre of the town, ruined, looted buildings, some still smouldering, all around them.

"You lucky boys have been given a job by none other than Skuratov himself, so we'd better get it right. We're going to a place called Chudovsy. It's a small town a day's ride east of here. We've got to do a special on the yids there. No-one else to be touched, and that means no-one. If any of you lays so much as a hand on a slice of bread or a girl's tit—you're for it. A couple of priests'll be coming with us. For protection against the Jews' magic, and to deal with any of them who agree to convert. We're going to give them a choice. If they convert to our faith, fine—we leave them alone. But if they don't—and by past experience most of them won't—they're for the chop. Any questions?"

There were none.

"Good". The captain continued. "The Jews all live in the same part of town. You'll recognize their houses. They keep a kind of small tube attached to their doorframes. Probably some kind of curse inside, but don't worry, the priests will deal with it. It'll be piece of cake. No trouble. They won't fight. And we'll take whatever they've got. They're rich bastards. Easy pickings."

The captain looked around.

"We'll be leaving in a day or two, but we've got something to do right now. They want us by the river. There's a big consignment needs dealing with down there. C'mon. Let's move it."

Vassily let the others go ahead of him saying he was going for a piss and would follow shortly.

"I don't want to do it any more. I don't want to." He kept repeating to himself recalling those other times, when people, most still alive and crying for mercy, were lashed together and dragged, like bundles of wood behind horses and sledges to the water's edge, and pushed into the icy, frozen river, the Oprichniki circling round in boats, spears and hooks ready to push anyone under who some-how found the strength to surface.

But go Vassilly did, moving slowly off in the direction of the river after hanging around for several minutes.

Whether it was purely disorientation, or maybe a desire to avoid getting to his destination, somewhere along the way he took a wrong turn and found himself in a part of Novgorod where he hadn't been before.

A warren of narrow, deserted streets. Small, rundown houses, little more than huts, most burnt, the others with their doors and windows smashed in. Metal or wooden tubes on every doorpost, or at least on those still standing. It must be the Jews, Vassily thought. Like the other place the captain had described. What was it called? Cudov? Chudov?

No, Chudovsy, that was it. He crossed himself and hurried on.

* * *

As he was trying to decide what direction to take he heard screams, high and desolate, like a child's, coming from a half destroyed house nearby.

He went to investigate the noise.

The body of an elderly man, his throat cut, lay sprawled across the doorway. The screams, louder and shriller now, came from inside.

Overcoming his fear of the tube attached to the doorframe Vassily stepped over the body and peered into the semi darkness, his axe at the ready.

He smelled the stink of them before he saw who they were. Yuradivye. Two of them, laughing, pushing an old woman back and forth, one to the other.

As Vassily's bulk blocked the doorway, the taller of the Yuradivye turned, drawing his sword as he did so.

"Ah." He said, on seeing Vassily's uniform. "Welcome brother. You're just in time. We found two of the bastards skulking in here. I don't know how we missed them the first time, they must have been hiding somewhere. We're going to have some fun with this one, the old bitch, before she joins her husband."

He sheathed his sword and shoved the old woman hard, with both hands, she staggered and fell against the wall. As she went down she gave a low cry, and tried unsuccessfully to grasp onto Vassily for support. Her hands, he noticed, were red and chapped from a lifetime of work. Just like his mother's.

The Yuradivye grinned and rubbed at his groin.

"After me and Gregor have finished, you're welcome to have a try with her. That is if you like your meat well done."

Grinning. It was the grinning that finally did it. The full, red lips and the mouth, the mouth, black like an animal's, with a few stumps of teeth.

Something snapped inside Vassily. Without a word he took a step towards the Yuradivye and swung his axe with an awful, dull clunk into the side of his head.

The monk looked at him with a look of surprise before crashing to the floor, his blood and brains spattering all around.

The old woman started screaming again.

Vassily was instantly onto the second one, but not quite quick enough. A knife flashed in the half light, cutting his arm, fortunately his left.

He moved back swinging with his axe, his opponent easily avoiding the blow and drawing his sword, smiling, knife in one hand, sword in the other, feigning from one to the other, to and fro, to and fro, as Vassily watched the blood drip from his arm, mingling with the dead man's on the floor.

The sword stabbed forward, missing him by a whisker, the Yuradivye darting away, light on his feet before Vassily could counter, the axe giving him a disadvantage in the confined space.

All the Yuradivye had to do was keep away until the cut weakened Vassily or some other Opichiniki came by to see what was happening when they stumbled across the body in the doorway.

Another thrust just missed his wounded arm, the blood now flowing freely, throwing him off balance. The Yuradivye smiled, preparing himself for a new attack when his expression changed and he collapsed as though he'd been pole-axed on the floor next to his dead comrade.

For a moment Vassily couldn't make out what had happened. Then he understood. Somehow or other the old girl had summoned up the strength to smash a stool down on the Yuradivye's head.

She stood there sobbing, the stool still in her hand, while Vassily bent down and finished the man off with his knife.

"It's alright, grandma." He said, taking the stool from her. "You're alright now. We can't stay here, though. It's not safe. You're coming with me."

* * *

He suddenly felt hot and giddy, and had to sit to recover himself while the woman, still sobbing, went to a room at the back of the house, returning with a jug of water and some pieces of bread, her hands shaking as she offered them to him.

"I'm sorry. It's all I have." She said, speaking in a heavy, almost indecipherable accent that he hadn't heard before

Vassily drank deeply and chewed on the stale food, closed his eyes and desperately tried to think.

He felt her hand lightly touch his arm.

"My husband? Dead?" The woman asked.

He nodded, his mouth full of bread.

There was a low, almost inaudible sigh, a faint sob, then silence as she went into the back room again and came out carrying a small bottle.

"Drink." She said, handing it to him. "It will do you good." He took a sip, then another, draining the last of it. It was like vodka, but sweeter.

He felt a little better after a while, and managed to get to his feet.

It was time to leave, and quick.

* * *

The streets were still deserted. First he moved the body of the old man behind the house so it couldn't be seen, and then found a nearby water pump. After filling the jug, he went back to the house where he gave the old woman a drink and cleaned her up—just scratches and a bit of bruising, nothing serious—as best he could before turning to himself.

He examined his wound. It was deep, not too bad though, he'd had worse, but it did need binding up to staunch the flow of blood.

He washed the cut thoroughly, tore a piece of material from the bottom of his shirt and wrapped it tightly round his arm

"Right, grandma." He said when he'd finished. "It's time to go."

"Where? Where shall we go?"

"To . . . Chudovsy." He didn't know why he said it, it just came out. "Chudovsy." He repeated, as if confirming he'd actually meant what he said. "But first we need to get you ready."

* * *

Her eyes, staring blankly, were on him all the time. He wondered if it was shock or if she couldn't understood what he was saying as he explained what he was going to do, taking the cloak and hood off the smaller Yuradivye and, using his knife, cutting the them shorter so as to fit her better.

He filled a bottle with water, found some more stale bread, and put the cloak over her, with the hood up.

In the chaos and terror that was Novgorod there was virtually no-one about except the occasional Oprichniki who gave the odd looking couple—one, a big strapping fellow, the other almost a dwarf—a wide berth.

It had grown colder and had started to snow again. He could feel the old woman's hands shaking as he led her along the streets and alleys, stopping several times so she could rest.

They headed towards to the north of the town, away from the river, everything looted and burning, no supplies to be had, to an area by the walls, where Satan was waiting tethered, unguarded, with the other horses of their company.

* * *

He found some bits of cloth in his saddle bag which he wrapped around the old woman's hands, and lifted her, light as a feather, on to Satan.

"If we want to get out of here in one piece let me do the talking." He told her as he mounted up. "And hold on to me as tight as you can."

The snow was falling heavily by this time, the only good thing about that, Vassily thought, was at least their tracks would be quickly covered.

* * *

Everything went alright until they reached the last line of sentries in the woods some distance from the walls. Whether they had orders to be extra vigilant or something else aroused their suspicions, Vassily didn't know, but instead of waving him through as all the others had done one of the two guards on the east road stepped out in front of Vassily and signalled him to stop.

"Where're you off to, brother?" He asked.

Don't tell him where, Vassily thought. Say somewhere else. Anywhere.

"Tver." He said after some hesitation.

Out of the corner of his eye he saw his interrogator motion the other guard to come closer.

"Tver, eh. But this is the east road. Tver's to the west. And in any case, why would you be going there? There's nothing left of it." The guard said, looking up at Vassily.

"Orders from Skuratov. I'm taking someone a message."

"Skuratov, eh." The guard said with a smile. "Important message, is it?"

"I don't . . . I don't know."

"You don't know. I might have guessed. And who's that up there with you?" The guard asked, putting his hand on Satan's bridle.

"He's been injured. Got to take him for attention."

"To Tver? For attention?"

The guard moved his hand off the bridle, the second one now standing beside him.

"Let's have a look at him then. Tell him to take his hood off. That is, if he isn't too badly hurt."

Vassily turned in the saddle and with his left hand lifted the hood off the old woman, while his right grasped hold of the axe handle.

"What the devil. . . . " The second guard exclaimed, going for his sword. But it was too late, the axe swung, once, twice, the work of a second or two to down the both of them.

The old woman screamed as Vassily leapt off Satan and slit their throats.

His first thought was to trample his dog's head and broom next to the two bodies on the blood reddened snow. Tear off his black robes as soon as he could, and replace them with some other colour. Grey. Brown. Anything, so long as it wasn't that damned, abominable shade, but then he thought better of it. The fear people had of these symbols could stand him in good stead. Let them think he was still who he appeared to be.

* * *

Vassily turned in the saddle for a last look at Novgorod from the top of a hill on the outskirts of the town. How peaceful it seemed from this distance. Quiet. A white blanket of snow covering everything.

He looked again. No sign of the hell inside except for the odd column of dark smoke, rising into the clear, blue, winter sky.

The woman, who'd said nothing since she'd asked him where they were going, gave a low sigh and started to weep.

A cold wind started to blow. It wouldn't be long till darkness fell.

They had to keep moving, and get to their destination by morning if they wanted to stay alive.

* * *

Vassily pulled his cloak around him, dug his spurs into Satan's flanks, and galloped down the slope in the direction of Chudovsky.

After several versts he gave up trying to hear if there were any sounds of pursuit. If they came, so be it. There was nothing he could do.

The snow had stopped. He kept Satan moving at a swift trot, the woman trying her best to hold on to him, her breath coming in heavy, laboured puffs, her hands grasping him so weakly he had to slow down to steady her from time to time.

Vassily stopped occasionally to rest the horse, and so they could have a drink of water, sip some of the vodka he had to warm them up, and chew some of the bread, the old woman barely swallowing a crumb and refusing to touch any of the pieces of dried meat that he'd found at the bottom of his saddle bag.

"Come on grandma." He said, breaking a little of the bread up and softening it in the water. "Got to keep your strength up."

It was shortly after their third stop that he felt one of her hands then the other slip from around his waist.

He immediately bought Satan to a halt beside the road

"Anything the matter, grandma?" He asked.

No answer, her arms dangling to each side of the saddle, as she slumped forward against Vassily's back.

He jumped off to see better in the faint moonlight. Her face seemed pinched and shrunken like a child's. It's the cold he thought. Just the cold. Give her some more vodka to drink, maybe light a fire. Warm her up a bit before we move on again.

"Come on grandma." He said steadying her so she wouldn't fall. "Not much further to go."

He looked closer. No breath hanging in the cold air.

He lifted her down, lying her gently on her cloak, the bottom ragged where he'd cut it, rubbing her up and down, trying to force some vodka down her throat, the tears blinding his eyes as he tried again and again to revive her.

No good, the thin, worn body was already growing cold. He took her cloak and wrapped it round him for extra protection.

* * *

He couldn't dig a grave; the ground was frozen solid. There was plenty of wood lying around, but he couldn't risk making a cross in case any Oprichniki were in pursuit and would notice it. All he could do was move the body into the trees and pile snow over it in the hope that the wolves and bears wouldn't get to it.

The tears refused to stop as he stood beside the small mound of snow trying unsuccessfully to remember a proper prayer, only turning back to Satan when the cold forced him to.

"Sleep well, grandma." He murmured as he rode away.

* * *

He rode through the night, arriving exhausted at the city shortly after dawn.

The guards looked down on him from the gate tower.

"You're early, friend." One of them yelled.

"Urgent business." He shouted back. "Open up."

"Where do the Jews live?" He asked once he was in.

"Why d'you want to know?"

He forced himself to smile.

"We've got business with them."

"Teach them a lesson, eh? All by yourself?"

"I'm taking them back to Novgorod."

"Yeah. We've heard what's happening there. Why did the Tsar. . . . "

"I'm in a hurry. Where are they?"

The guard pointed.

"That way. Straight down. You can't miss it, it's the worst part of town. So you've come to teach the bastards a lesson. Good. About time too. Hey, do you need any. . . . "

But Vassily was already riding away.

* * *

He knew he was in the right place by the wooden and metal cylinders attached to the door frames.

The houses were exactly like the ones where he'd found the old woman in Novgorod, for the most poor and small; the streets narrow and winding, some just dirt tracks, others cobbled, the stones uneven and broken.

Although it was early there were already a few people up and about staring open mouthed as Vassily galloped past, bringing Satan to a halt in a small square in front of a two storied wooden building considerably larger than those around it.

Funnily he didn't feel scared at all; just hungry and very, very tired. He was wondering what to do next when he heard a voice beside him.

"Excuse me, sir. Excuse me." The voice said. Vassily looked down and saw an old man with a robe a bit like a priest's, a long beard and a strange sort of hat, like the ones the boyars wore.

Several other men of different ages, all of them bearded and with similar clothes, and a couple of women stood nearby, looking intently at Vassily who dismounted, keeping hold of his axe, ready for trouble.

"If you permit me sir, could I ask what your business is with us?" The old man said nervously. "We were wondering what. . . . As you can see we're poor people. We work hard and we're loyal subjects of the Tsar, and. . . . "

"I've come to warn you. The Oprichniki. They're coming for you."

"But . . . I don't understand. You're Oprichniki yourself, aren't you? We know what these mean." The old man said, pointing at the broom and dog's head.

"I was, but I'm not any longer. I wear all this for . . . for. . . . "

Vassily searched for the right word.

" . . . For protection. So they don't interfere with me."

"But if you aren't Oprichniki what do you want with us? Why are you here?"

"I'm Oprichniki no more. I killed four of them. I escaped so I could warn you. They're coming to kill you."

"To kill us?"

"I've come from Novgorod. They've killed thousands. A few more here and there doesn't bother them."

"But why . . . What do they want with us?"

"I told you, they're going to. . . . "

But before Vassily could finish he felt the earth start to spin out of control beneath his feet, air rushing through his ears. There was shouting all around, but faint, distant, as he crashed down, down, onto the cobblestones.

* * *

He woke to the sound of voices, speaking softly.

He was lying on a couch, two pillows under his head. The room, was warm, a fire glowing in the corner. His cloak lay on the floor beside him, and his arm had been bound with a clean cloth.

"He's awake." He heard someone say, as the old man appeared before him.

Vassily managed to prop himself up against the pillows still feeling a groggy, his limbs stiff and his wounded arm aching.

"Where's Satan?" He asked

"Satan?"

"My horse."

"He's watered and fed. How do you feel?"

"Much better."

"Good. Eat this it will do you good."

Another man gave him a bowl of hot broth, bread and water, and after, a plate of meat with a few potatoes. More spicy than he was used to, but tasty all the same. He could feel the strength flowing back into his bones.

"How long have I been here?" He asked when he'd finished the last of the food.

"Just over an hour."

"You must get away from here. Quickly. All of you. If you're lucky they'll be resting today, and gathering up their spoils, but they'll definitely be here tomorrow. They like to come in early in the morning or just before nightfall."

"And who are *they*?" The old man who seemed to be their leader, asked.

"I told you. Oprichniki. There's an army of them in Novgorod. If you want to live you must leave. Now."

Vassily repeated as best as he could remember what the captain had told his men.

"Wait here."

The old man went out of the room. Vassily could hear voices talking, arguing, some raised in anger.

"Someone's gone to gather the people together." He said to Vassily when he came back. "But I'll tell you now, not everyone will believe you. I do personally—we've heard rumours about what's been happening, but nothing certain. Tell me, are there no survivors?"

"I don't know. They're still killing there. No-one gets in or out."

"So how did you?"

Vassily pointed to his cloak.

"This. And I told you. I killed four of them. Look here. You can see the bloodstains."

The old man looked at the cloak and then stood there pulling at his beard, thinking.

"You said they'll spare us if we become Christians?" He said eventually.

"That's what the captain said." Vassily replied, tired of all these questions. "But I know what happens when their blood is up, and they see your wives and daughters. . . . " Vassily shrugged.

The old man left the room again.

"Alright." He said when he came back. "I'll try my best to persuade them."

Vassily got to his feet, still feeling weak and unsteady, rested a moment, his hand on a chair, and put the cloak on.

"Please." He said to the old man. "Be quick."

* * *

As they went outside the house they were greeted by the sound of conversation interspersed with weeping and moaning from the small crowd that had gathered in the square.

More and more Jews were arriving, bearded men, women with their heads covered; boys, stringy locks of hair hanging down the sides of their pale faces. It would be difficult enough to control the ones already in the square, but now, as he watched, more of them, no doubt disturbed by the noise, were crowding in, clustering around in small groups, talking agitatedly, some screaming and crying.

The captain was right, thought Vassily. This lot'd be a walkover.

"Damn it." He thought. "How did I get myself into such a mess?"

Despite what he'd told him not five minutes ago about the need for haste the old boy insisted on making a speech to calm the people down and convince them of the need to leave.

Standing at the edge of the crowd, only making out snatches of what their leader was saying—recognising odd words like Tsar, slaves, forty years—the rest impossible to understand as large parts were delivered in a language incomprehensible to him, Vassily found himself losing his temper.

"Come on." He mumbled under his breath. "For fuck's sake, come on."

Whatever was said, though, it did the trick. The people quietened down, and disappeared into their houses only to come out weighed down with bundles and bags and all sorts of household implements.

No. This was no good. No good at all. Far too much stuff. They'd immediately arouse the city guards' suspicion if they carried such a lot, apart from it slowing down their progress.

Vassily hurried over to tell them it was impossible.

More discussions followed. More speeches. More time wasted. Voices raised. Fists clenched.

What was wrong with these people? For a moment Vassily thought of taking Satan and riding out, taking his chances on his own. Just for a moment, until he remembered the reason why he was there.

Eventually common sense prevailed and a compromise was reached.

Each person would be allowed one bundle of food and belongings.

Vassily could live with that, just about.

* * *

He directed them to walk in front of him three or four abreast so it looked as though he was escorting them out the town.

He'd never learned to count high numbers, but using his fingers he reckoned the Jews amounted to the number of fingers on both his hands, repeated ten times—that is round about one hundred souls. In fact it was nearer a hundred and twenty.

As they left the town some people came onto the streets to watch and jeer. Vegetables were thrown, and he heard one voice louder than the others yell.

"Look at them. Rotten Jew cowards. Just one decent Russian, and he can control the whole filthy lot of them."

More of the same followed as they slowly made their way along the muddy, icy road until, just before they reached the gate, half a dozen of the local lads started laying about the people near the front of the line with sticks and cudgels.

Vassily moved his horse forward.

"Back off." He shouted, showing them the axe. "Leave them. They're ours."

The boys slunk off like whipped dogs, cursing under their breath.

"You took your time." One of the guards on the gate said. "We were going to see if anything had happened to you. Give you a hand. I bet you had a bit of fun with the women there."

"Yes. Plenty of fun."

The gates were opened without any questions, and they were out on the open road.

Vassily hadn't, of course, told the townsfolk that when the Oprichniki arrived and found their quarry gone, vanished under the inhabitants' very eyes, there was no saying what they would do.

Still, that wasn't his problem, he had far more important things to worry about.

* * *

Once they were well away from the town he had them quicken the pace, twice getting off Satan, telling them to keep quiet so he could listen, putting his ear to the ground.

Nothing.

He climbed back into the saddle and urged them on.

The snow, which had stopped falling in the morning, had started again. Good, thought Vassily, at least they won't be able to spot our tracks.

They continued at a fair speed along the road, for just over a verst until one of the younger men came up beside him.

"This is the road to Novgorod." The young man said, his voice high and shrill, nervously fingering at the white tassel Vassily had noticed the men wore under their clothes. "You're taking us back there aren't you?"

"He's taking us to Novgorod." The young man repeated in the strange guttural Russian they spoke, raising his voice so everyone could hear.

"It's a trick. It's a trick." The young man was shouting now as he turned to face the people who'd gathered around him. "He's taking us to Novgorod. We're all going to be slaughtered."

For a moment Vassily was tempted to strike him down.

Stop, he said to himself. Stop. Be calm, then spoke out loud, slowly. Addressing them simply, as if talking to children.

"It's no trick. We're not going to Novgorod."

He pointed back in the direction they'd come from.

"When the Oprichniki come, the people in the town will tell them that we went towards Novgorod. But after another verst or two, when we're sure no-one can see us, we'll go in that direction." He pointed again, this time to the east. "Put them off the scent. It'll be safer that way, but we must move quickly."

There followed some whispered discussions after which an older man, a stout, middle aged fellow, approached him.

"We'll do as you say, but if you try to trick us we'll pull you off your horse and kill you." He said, pointing to a knife in his belt.

Vassily couldn't help smiling at their impertinence.

"Quickly." He repeated. "We must go quickly."

* * *

There was a moment of panic late afternoon on the third day when one of the young boys cocked his ear and called for silence.

"Horses. I can hear horses." He said.

The people, gathering something was afoot, started chattering nervously amongst themselves.

Vassily quickly hushed the noise so he could listen for himself.

The boy was right—horses, a lot of them, and coming their way.

"Right." Vassily yelled. "Everyone off the road. Now. And not a sound."

He herded them as quickly as he could into the trees that grew at the side of the road, knowing that if they were fully on their guard the Oprichniki would almost certainly see the footprints in the churned up snow. If that happened all he could do was kill as many of the bastards as possible before the inevitable occurred.

Vassily could hear a kind of dull murmuring from the people beside him, like they were praying, though what protection their god, whoever he was, could give them as they were hunted down and slaughtered he had no idea.

The sound of hooves came closer, and now Vassily could hear voices shouting and the clatter of the wheels of the wagons the Oprichniki took with them to carry supplies and whatever booty they could get hold of.

He crept forward and peered through the trees into the gathering gloom as the first of the horsemen came into view.

Wait, it wasn't the familiar black cloaks, hoods, and horses he feared, but flashes of red, green and white mounted on grey and brown horses followed by wagons, the drivers yelling as they used their whips; speeding past them without a glance, merchants, no doubt, going hell for leather to reach the nearest lodgings before night fell.

He breathed a sigh of relief. Maybe this god of the Jews was some use after all.

* * *

Vassily kept his black garments on, as well as the broom and dog's head secured to his saddle, reckoning the sight of them would ensure, even in the increasingly remote places they were passing through, that no awkward questions would be asked, and any supplies he requested readily given.

He recalled what his mate Dimitri had told him after the two of them had cleared a village of its inhabitants before setting fire to the houses and farm buildings.

"You know, Bull." Dimitri had said as they were riding away, the glow from the burning buildings reflecting orange on the snow. "That's what I like about this job. The sight of just the two of us is enough to put the fear of God in the stupid fuckers. They see the black horse and the cloak and they turn to jelly. You can do whatever you want with them. I sometimes wonder if we even need to carry weapons."

"Weapons?" Asked Vassily.

"Only a joke, my friend. Come on. Let's get out of this dump. We've got two more to torch before dark."

* * *

The old ones and the youngsters badly needed to rest, so after another day had passed without any signs of pursuit Vassily slowed the pace.

Despite the deathly cold, for the first time since they'd left Chudovsky he could sense a distinct feeling of relief in the air, people laughing and chatting, the children playing in the snow.

One day during their mid-morning halt for food and drink Vassily sat down by their leader, the old man who the people called "Rav" or "Ravvi", or at least that's what it sounded like to him, and asked.

"What did you say to them that day we left?"

"I told them." The Rav replied. "That what was happening to us was exactly like something that happened to our people a long time ago."

"When you were young?"

The Rav smiled.

"No. A long time before I was born. A very long time ago."

"What happened?"

"There was a king. Like the Tsar. He also wished evil on us. After he'd been punished for it, he gave us a few hours to leave his country. We had to pack up quickly taking very little with us and go."

"Where? In Russia?"

"No. Far away, in a country we call Mitzrayim. You call it Egypt."

Vassily frowned, both names meaningless to him, but said nothing.

"I told our people." The Rav continued. "That this trial was exactly like what occurred all those years ago. It was difficult then but we survived, and with God's help we'll survive this."

Vassily nodded, though not really understanding what the old boy was getting at.

* * *

The Rav stared into the distance before turning to Vassily once more.

"Now it's my turn. May I ask *you* a question?" He said.

"Why not."

"Why are you doing this for us?"

Vassily could feel himself going red with embarrassment.

"I have my reasons." He replied, trying to avoid the old man's gaze.

For the first time Vassily noticed he had blue eyes, light blue, like a Russian, very clear for someone of his age.

"I see." Said the Rav, staring into the distance again when it was clear that Vassily wasn't intending to say anything more.

"Well then." He said after a while. "Let me ask you another question. Where are you taking us?"

"To be honest I don't know." Vassily said without thinking, then pointed west, back in the direction they'd come from.

"But one thing I can tell you." He said. "As far away from there as possible."

The Rav put his hand lightly on Vassily's arm.

"Don't worry." He said. "We'll know when we get there."

* * *

East. Away from the lands set aside by Ivan where the Oprichniki held sway.

Across the Volga, swollen with winter floods, using the gold Vassily had to pay for the ferries.

Trudging slowly along the roads and tracks—Vassily reckoned it was safe to use them now—the old folk and children slowing their progress—day after day across the frozen, flat, never ending steppe, barely seeing another soul.

Always towards the east, where the sun rose like a red ball in a cold sky.

Desolate. Empty. Cold. Deadly cold.

Huddled together at night round fires which had to be constantly replenished for fear the people would freeze.

Food. Just about enough with what they'd brought with them, and what could be purchased from the villages and farms they passed, or were given free when those people who knew what they meant saw the black cloak and the dog's head.

Occasionally they came across a place where the fear of Vassily and the payment of a few kopeks enabled them to sleep under a roof and between four walls for a night or two, and they could replenish their supplies.

There were deaths of course. Couldn't be avoided. Mainly the very young and the very old. Buried in the woods as deep as they could dig in the frozen ground, then praying and more speechifying from the Rav.

Yeah, Vassily thought, you had to hand it to the Rav, the tough old bird really held them together with his speeches about the trials and tribulations they were obliged to bear before they would be allowed to get to safety and what he called the promised land.

* * *

Nothing was simple with these people. The Rav always insisted on special foods. No game birds. No pig. Though why a nice juicy piece of pork was a problem was quite beyond Vassily's comprehension.

And there were other things.

They refused to move on Saturdays—even at the beginning when he warned that the Oprichniki could be on their heels—or cook or light fires—the silly sods would have perished if he hadn't done it for them. And they prayed, not just Saturdays, but every day without fail, morning and evening, always facing east. The men wrapped in a sort of silk shawl, swaying to a rhythm best known to themselves, and mumbling in a language he couldn't make head or tail of.

And that wasn't the end of it. Before they washed or ate they mumbled something to themselves. It was a blessing, someone told him, to thank their God for everything he had given them.

He had a glance at one of their books once. He couldn't read or write in Russian, but at least some of the letters were familiar, here it was nothing but a jumble of signs all higgledy piggledy like animal tracks in the snow.

What in God's name was he doing with these madmen and women? Sometimes he wondered if he'd ended up in a lunatic asylum and that he should have taken his chances on his own, and leave them to their fate. Still, he thought, he'd come so far there was no alternative but to see it through to the end—whatever that may be. There was no going back.

He was after all, their leader, well, not really their leader, the Rav was that, but their . . . what did you call it . . . their guide through the wilderness, maybe the same wilderness the Rav kept rabbiting on about during the talks he gave them each Saturday—one of the men Vassily had become friendly with whispering to him what was being said as he sat beside him.

* * *

Muddy, churned up tracks through thick, dark, forbidding forests.

Lakes, some big like the sea, their surfaces frozen solid.

The occasional glimpse of deer and elk, and once, a bear with her cubs.

Wolves howling at night. Only kept away by the fires and their fear of the size of the party.

East. Always east. Until . . . One day. . . .

* * *

For the past week or so the number of travellers they'd encountered on the road could be counted on the fingers of one hand, the towns and hamlets getting smaller, and more isolated, a day's walk, sometimes more, from each other.

The latest place they came to, called itself a town, but in reality wasn't much more than a village.

Vassily usually led the Jews in and arranged for food and accommodation—a stable or barn, sometimes a cattle shed, but never, the Rav had told him, never a place where pigs were kept.

For Vassily a room at the inn, often for free, the innkeeper, shaking in his shoes, bowing and scraping, calling him "lord" or some other complimentary title, a decent, hot meal, a drink of vodka or kvass, and a woman for the night if one was available.

Everyone scared of him, until in this one-horse apology for a town some children pointed at his saddle where the dog's head and broom were still secured, laughed, and ran away.

And more was to come. The men at the stables asking him, seemingly quite unafraid, who he was, what was his business there, and, most embarrassing of all why was he dressed in such a peculiar manner.

"What are you? A monk?" Asked one.

Once he'd told them, one of them turned to his companions and said.

"Yes. Oprichniki. I've heard of them. They work for Ivan Grozny."

Nothing else, before he said to Vassily, not a hint of fear or apprehension on his face or in his voice, if anything sounding somewhat put out at this intruder who'd turned up unannounced in their midst with a crowd of what looked like little more than beggars or runaways.

"Well, I suppose you and that lot outside can squeeze in here and the barns across the way for a night or two, but it'll cost you."

As Vassily walked away, he knew they'd gone far enough,

* * *

They'd come far enough, Vassily told the Rav the next morning.

It was time to find a place.

They located a spot that suited them after several days of scouting around. Just over half a day's walk from the town.

A small valley, sheltered, well wooded, with a stream, and of course far from Moscow or for that matter any settlement of importance.

Pooling the money they had left they bought three cows, some chickens, and a mare to be sired by Vassily's horse, now called Blackie, the name Satan deemed unsuitable by the Rav. Also some seed, wood, and nails.

Barely a week had passed after they arrived, and it seemed the nights were no longer as cold. More water flowed down the stream, and in some places where the sun shone the odd blade of grass poked through the snow as if smelling the air. Birds started to appear, and one of the men caught a glimpse of a herd of caribou moving north.

"It's a sign." The people said. "A sign from God."

Nobody disabused them that it wasn't a sign from Heaven, merely that spring was on its way.

* * *

They start to build a village, similar to the one Vassily had been brought up in, except in this one the inhabitants are all Jews, with a sprinkling of runaway serfs and other miscreants. People who need to avoid the authorities and have no desire to talk about their past, both of which qualities suit the other inhabitants fine.

The Jews call Vassily "Shor", the Hebrew word for bull. He can convert to their religion if he wants to, the Rav tells him, but it's a long, difficult process, made almost impossible due to the fact that he can neither read nor write.

For the moment though, he seems happy enough, undertaking various tasks around the village where he has his own small hut—wood cutting; ploughing using Blackie; loading and unloading; clearing out the cattle pens; all hard, back-breaking work for which he's well suited.

He also helps with the building of the barns and dwelling houses, as well as undertaking those tasks that Jews are not permitted to do on their sabbath and holy days.

He's always busy because the community is growing rapidly—the numbers swollen by new births, and people who've heard about this place, drifting in from time to time, although the inhabitants are careful not to advertise its existence.

* * *

Every place must have a name.

"We're calling the village Tikvah." One of the men told Vassily. "It means "hope" in Russian.

Hope.

Not a bad name, thought Vassily.

Not bad at all.

* * *

Vassily had seen inside the Jews' church on several occasions. Sometimes when it was empty, other times when it was crowded, lit with candles, the people swaying in rhythm and singing in words he couldn't understand. Not bad tunes, though, a bit like the ones he remembered from home

It was a strange place, he thought. No icons. No gold or silver. No decorations on the walls. And, on top of all that, no celebrations of Easter, Christmas or any of the saints' days.

Very strange.

* * *

He befriended a stray dog that started hanging around the village looking for odds and ends of food. A thin scruffy, creature, not unlike the one he'd killed that day they'd accepted him into the Oprichniki. I should have refused to kill it, he thought. If I would, all this mess could have been avoided. Still, no use crying over spilt milk. He was here now and he could do nothing but make the best of it.

He fattened the dog up with whatever scraps he could find, though in truth there was not much available in those first few months, just about enough to keep body and soul together.

As it was, several of the community died during the winter. Buried in the hard frozen ground in the small cemetery they'd set aside on the edge of the village. No crosses, just a large stone with strange letters carved on it to mark where each grave was situated.

* * *

He had to hand it to them, these people worked hard. Not many shirkers or layabouts that he could see. All of them chipping in, even the Rav himself.

Slowly things started to improve. Bread and vegetables, brought from the town nearby, appeared more frequently, occasionally fish and more often, meat. Plenty for him and the dog, because there were several parts of the animals they slaughtered that the people refused to eat. Why, he had no idea, but, as his mother used to say, never look a gift horse in the mouth, so he took whatever was offered without any questions.

To tell the truth he'd given up trying to understand their strange ways. It was all far too weird for a normal person to comprehend. In any case he remembered his mother telling him you should let people get on with whatever they were doing so long as they didn't bother you.

His mother. Goodness knew what had happened to her. It was high time he was getting back home, but all he knew was that his village was a long way from the place they'd ended up in, and most worrying of all, they, the Oprichniki, could still be keeping an eye out for him should he ever be so foolish to return.

No. Not *could* be keeping an eye out. *Would be.*

"The Little Father never forgets a wrong done to him." He'd been told when he first joined the brotherhood. "The greater the wrong, the greater the punishment."

He had no desire to know what devilish punishment Ivan had devised for him, and certainly didn't intend to find out.

* * *

Another year passed. The snow came and went, and still Vassily didn't move.

He'd met a girl on one of his visits to buy supplies in the town. She seems to like me, he thought, maybe one day we'll settle down together. She can live here with me, and when we have children we'll take them home to see my mother.

As for the black cloak, jerkin and boots, the dog's head and the broom, Vassily had wanted to chuck the lot of them on the great fire they'd lit during one of their festivals, but the Rav had said, taking him by the arm.

"Don't, Shor. I know how much you want to. But don't. Keep them, just in case. I hope with all my soul it won't be necessary, but maybe one day in the future you'll need to use them again to save someone's life. And believe me there is no greater mitzvah a man can do than that."

And so Vassily wrapped the objects up carefully in a blanket, and put them on top of the cupboard that stood in the corner of his hut.

* * *

The Oprichniki were disbanded after seven years of terror.

Ivan, having murdered his older son in a fit of rage, died at the age of fifty four, broken both physically and mentally.

The dynasty perished with him, his younger son being killed before he could assume power.

After Ivan's death Russia went through a long period of chaos and upheaval, known as the Time of Troubles.

* * *

Vassily never got to see his mother again, but he married the girl from the town and they had two children.

By the grace of God there was no need for him to take out the black cloak and jerkin, which, together with the broom and dog's head, now just a skull with a few pieces of flesh attached to it, remained undisturbed and eventually forgotten on top of his cupboard.

Taiping

'*T*he world turns. Each day the sun rises, casting its warm, unchanging rays over town and country. All bathe in its welcome glow.

Rich and poor. Peasant. Merchant. Lord. Emperor.

But what if a man took it upon himself to state that the sun only rose because of his will?

Of course we would say that such a man is mad. Fit only to be locked up with the other maniacs far from prying eyes.

And what if thousands, millions, followed him in this delusion?

What then?

Water ripples on a pond. Waves. Then a deluge.

Bowls and vases are broken. The Mandate of Heaven trembles, the world shaken to its core.

Corpses lie unburied in the fields. Living skeletons roam the land.

But we run ahead of ourselves.

All is at peace.

Each day the sun rises.

The world turns.

The peasant toils in his fields. Scholars walk, debating in groves of trees.

The Emperor sits secure upon his throne."

* * *

The Chinese word "Taiping" means "Heavenly Kingdom".

The Taiping Rebellion, which lasted between 1850 and 1864, was an attempt to overthrow the corrupt and inefficient Manchu dynasty, and introduce a form of Christianity to China under the leadership of Hung Hsiu-chuan, a messianic figure who claimed to be one of God's sons and Jesus's younger brother.

The rebellion, which occurred at a time of economic upheaval and intense agitation and unrest, also promised social reform, land redistribution and more equal treatment of women.

It appealed not just to the poor and dispossessed, but also to members of the middle classes and intelligentsia, disillusioned by the stultification of the regime and what they saw as China's weakness in the face of Western encroachments.

* * *

Having pooled their resources, archivists in Beijing and Oxford are now in a position to publish an account of the rebellion in the form of a letter and a diary written by an Englishman, James Havelock, one of a small number of westerners who joined the Taiping and fought alongside them until the conclusion of the revolt.

There is no record of any other letters written or received by Havelock, and it will also be seen that there are a number of substantial gaps, sometimes of a year or more, in his narrative.

It is not known whether any entries were actually made during these periods, but an examination of the diary indicates that a large number of pages have been torn out—mostly probably by James Havelock himself.

* * *

The form of Chinese names prevalent during the rebellion has been used wherever possible, and certain of the Taipings' and their opponents' proclamations have been included at appropriate points in the manuscript to give an idea of the views and attitudes of the opposing sides.

* * *

April 29, 1852

To Sir George Lancing, Commander, British Garrison, Canton.

Dear Sir George,

Having waited until I am a good distance from Canton I am sending you this letter, as well as similar ones to my family and friends, both here and in England.

After much soul searching and many sleepless nights I have decided to throw in my lot with the Taiping rebels.

I have been considering such a course of action ever since I learned about this remarkable upwelling of Christian beliefs, eventually concluding that it is my sacred duty to help the insurgents with whatever skills I possess.

I accept you and the men under my command have every right to question why I am doing such a thing, and to harbour feelings of anger and resentment as to my having deceived you over the past weeks and months in not making you privy to my innermost thoughts.

I beg you to put these feelings aside to reflect on this country, and the opportunity I have to help bring the one, true faith to the millions of souls who dwell here, and then to consider that this task, surely the greatest and most worthy a man can be associated with, can, by the grace of God, be accomplished in two, maybe three years. What a prize to be gained!

In deciding to join the Taiping I have ignored the prejudiced and ignorant talk about the movement I have encountered from those who are wedded to the current Manchu system of government, or should I say, misgovernment.

I have to say, though clearly incompetent and unable to rule, the dynasty seems largely immune from any strictures or criticism within our British enclave. I however, firmly believe there is a higher order to our lives than the mere worship of Mammon, status, and the seeking of worldly honours, which is why I am decided upon this course of action whatever criticism people may choose to level against me.

When the news of my destination emerges I will, I'm sure, be called traitor and worse, but I would beg you Sir George, to remind yourself of the glory of what I am doing, and think of the Apostles, and how our Lord and Saviour plucked them up to do His holy work.

Knowing and understanding this, I trust you will find it in your heart to forgive, or if not forgive, then at least understand the reason for my actions.

Yours sincerely,

Your friend and colleague

James Havelock

* * *

June 2, 1852

After a most difficult journey, conducted mainly at night so as to avoid the Imperial troops, I have arrived in the areas controlled by the Taiping.

After making myself known to them as one who supported their cause and was placing himself at their disposal, I was escorted under guard to their main camp, where I was interrogated by one of their captains.

My Chinese being extremely basic, his questions and my replies were translated by a Dutchman, one of several other Europeans in the camp, merchants and the like—though none of them, I think, is in my situation.

* * *

The examination was far harder than I'd expected, understandable given the daily threats the Taiping face from their Manchu foes.

Over almost two days of interrogation I sought to overcome their concerns through a combination of my zeal for their cause, my knowledge and affection for the Scriptures, and my wide experience of engineering and gunnery, areas which, I believe, could prove most useful to their endeavours.

Once their enquiries were finished I was locked in a cell, but was not in any way ill-treated, contrary to what one may expect after the wild and fallacious statements given out which imply that the Taipings are little more than wild beasts, killing and looting indiscriminately.

I am pleased to say that my interrogators came back the following day to inform me they had agreed I could stay with them and help them to the best of my ability.

On hearing this news I immediately put pen to paper as I intend to keep a detailed record of the progress of the rebellion, the Taiping way of life, and my various experiences of this great adventure.

* * *

Proclamation issued by the Taipings.

"Within the boundaries of Heaven and Earth is man not the noblest of all?

And though the people of the world are many, they are all created by God, and born of God. Their souls come from Heaven, and under Heaven all are brothers and sisters.

We have therefore established a new Kingdom. A Kingdom in which the children of God are all members of one family.

The land of the world must be tilled in common by the people of the world. If there is insufficient food in one place the people must be moved to another where food is abundant, so that the plenty in one place may relieve the famine in another.

Men will not hold things in private, but will pass them to our Sovereign Lord. The Lord will use them, and all people everywhere will be equal. For the whole world must enjoy the happiness given by God, the Heavenly Father.

Land shall be farmed by all; rice, eaten by all; clothes, worn by all; money, spent by all; so that there is no inequality anywhere, and nobody lacks food or warmth. For the whole world is the family of God, the Heavenly Father.

This is the edict of salvation especially enjoined by God, the Heavenly Father on the true Lord of the Taiping."

* * *

June 5, 1852

I am brimming over with observations to make about life under the Taipings.

In fact there is so much to write about I could, if my time wasn't so limited, probably write three or four times as many pages as I intend to.

I will therefore restrict myself to setting out what I believe are the main matters of interest.

* * *

One of the first things I have come to realise is that the Taipings have a completely different notion of privacy to us.

For example I am obliged to share my tent with half a dozen other men.

We are only permitted to keep sufficient of our labour to feed and clothe ourselves and our families, if we have them.

Any surplus goods produced are not for personal gratification or show, but are placed in our common Treasury. In this way we will avoid the extremes of wealth and poverty that are a feature of Manchu society, where many die of hunger while others feast on the fat of the land, so the peoples' thoughts are no longer concentrated on the mundane business of day to day living, but solely on the goal of bringing Christianity to China.

* * *

They have taken my clothes away, insisting I wear Chinese ones indistinguishable from the myriads around me, and have also required me to grow my hair long and flowing as they do.

The Taipings (or God Worshippers as they sometimes call themselves) wear their hair in this way as they say it strikes fear into the hearts of their opponents, and shows their contempt for the ways of the Manchu who have for many years forced the native Chinese to wear their hair in the style of what we refer to as the pigtail.

Surprisingly, they have allowed me to keep my beard, possibly because our Lord Jesus is commonly shown having one and they also envisage the Almighty as an old, bearded man.

Although I would be the first to admit that some of the practices of the Taipings may seem strange, even heretical, I'm convinced that in time they will develop a more ordered form of Christianity, albeit one that incorporates elements of their own culture.

You only have to look around the world at those previously savage peoples who have taken to the Christian way of life. Can anyone doubt then that the Chinese with all their natural intelligence and inventiveness won't succeed in doing so?

* * *

August 5, 1852

The Taiping camp is far larger than I had expected—they claim to have at least half a million followers, a good portion of them under arms, many more than the Manchus can put into the field.

The army is organised into squads of twenty five, then brigades of one hundred, and regiments of one thousand, consisting of both men and women. Yes, surprisingly, many of our main fighters are from the so-called weaker sex.

In fact we call each other "brother" or "sister" because our European notions of master and servant are anathema to them as they say we are all equal in the eyes of the Creator.

The Taiping, I am pleased to record, have done away with the horrible custom of foot binding young girls. Henceforth, women will, thank God, walk tall and proud, with no more of that foolish, shuffling gait this dreadful practice condemned them to.

* * *

The tents are laid out in neat rows stretching a mile or so in each direction, with the larger ones of the leaders near the centre. There is a constant buzz of activity from early morning until well into the night.

These comings and goings reflect an intense, directed purpose, emanating from our leader Hung, who is referred to in Taiping terminology as God's Younger Son or sometimes Heavenly Younger Brother.

I shall say nothing about these titles here, except they apparently place Hung on a much higher level than his foe, the Manchu emperor, and this appears to be one of the elements that encourages people to flock to his standard.

* * *

August 9, 1852

Let me say something about Hung himself.

He is in his late thirties or thereabouts, and originally hails from a village in the southern part of the country—an impoverished area which suffered badly under the current regime.

Realising his potential from an early age, his family sacrificed much to encourage his studies, and by the time he was a young man he'd reached a sufficient level to go to the city of Canton and sit the examination which gives access to the Imperial civil service.

He failed the examination not once, but three times.

Some may scoff at what I am about to write, but I see God's hand in this.

Had Hung succeeded in passing the examination he would have been lost, subsumed in the organisation of government, no different to the millions of others who go about their mundane day to day business throughout this great country.

As it was, he was saved, Hung himself would most likely use the word *chosen*, for the far greater task of bringing Christianity to China. For while in Canton for the examinations he encountered a Christian missionary who handed Hung a number of booklets translated into Chinese which explained the tenets of the Christian faith .

Was this merely chance? For myself I believe it was yet another example of God's intervention in the affairs of this land.

* * *

Hung returned to his village taking with him the Christian tracts he'd been given. He married, had a child, and obtained employment as a school teacher.

In the event it was not until several years later that Hung looked at the tracts he'd bought back from Canton, and immediately realising the truth of what he was reading, concluded it was his mission in life to teach the tenets of Christianity to his friends and neighbours.

* * *

He and a relative returned to Canton where they took instruction in the faith from a Baptist preacher from America, who was fluent in Chinese, and returned to their area to commence God's work in earnest.

The vast majority of the Chinese live hand to mouth in conditions of the direst poverty, so when Hung offered them the hope of escape from this hell on earth, and his intention for all land and the produce thereof to be held in common so hunger and poverty could be eliminated, people were drawn to his cause in ever increasing numbers.

The movement grew, and as it did, the authorities, frightened of any new belief that could threaten the status quo, took steps to curtail it. When these failed, they proceeded to attack Hung and his followers who were obliged to defend themselves and fight back, with the results we see today.

An army, honed in battle, disciplined, organised, obeying the will of our leader. Fighting against an evil opponent. Impossible to defeat because right is on our side.

* * *

Comparing themselves to the Israelites fighting for the one, true God against the hosts of idolaters and non-believers, the people here are in no way dismayed by the forces confronting them. On the contrary they are as one, full of hope and faith for the future, seeing, as I do, our eventual success in this war—for make no mistake about it, it is war—as inevitable.

As for the Manchus, who the Taiping consider not proper Chinese but interlopers who conquered the country when it was in a state of disarray, they refer to them as "Tartar Dogs", and the Emperor and his followers as "Demons". In my professional opinion when compared to the Manchus who rely on conscripted soldiers of the lowest sort, our numbers and discipline make us undefeatable, but more than this the main advantage we have is our belief in the absolute rightness of our cause.

* * *

September 27, 1852

Our army commenced its advance several weeks ago, overrunning a number of towns and villages with barely any resistance.

Our main objective though was Quangzhou, the regional capital, which we succeeded in taking, but only after a most difficult struggle accompanied by great slaughter on both sides.

Our miners, working like men possessed, dug tunnels under the city walls, and set explosives, trying to undermine the foundations, whilst all the time the defenders listened out for the sounds of digging so they could flood or blow up the tunnels, and destroy everyone within.

In addition to helping organise the tunnelling work—using a combination of the Chinese I have managed to learn and some simple signs and diagrams, I also had to lend a hand in bringing the bodies out, crushed beyond recognition, or drowned in the water and filthy sewage the Manchus poured in.

Given the grievous losses we suffered would anyone be surprised if revenge for their dead comrades was not in the hearts of our men and women as they rushed in once we eventually breached the city walls?

And yet . . . When it was over and the bodies of our enemies thrown like so much rubbish into mass graves I have to admit that I found myself contemplating how quickly the God of love and compassion is pushed aside by the God of battle and vengeance.

* * *

Proclamation issued by the Manchu Government.

"Throughout history our sages have upheld the doctrine which sets the pattern of men's relationships. Of prince and subject; father and son; high and low; noble and humble; in an order that may no more be reversed than the position of cap and shoe.

But now these brigands have stolen the ideas of the foreign barbarians, and honour the religion of their so-called Lord of Heaven. All of them from pretended princes and ministers down to common soldiers call themselves brother, and say Heaven alone is their Father, and human parents are no more to them than brother or sister.

Farmers cannot till their own fields and pay tribute, for all land belongs to their so-called Lord of Heaven. Merchants cannot carry on business for their own profit, for all goods belong to this Lord of Heaven. Scholars cannot recite the classics of Confucius, for they have another work, their Bible, containing the teachings of their so-called Jesus. While our Chinese book of

148

odes, and the books of history that, for thousands of years, have been our guides in manners and morals, are used to sweep the floor.

This is a rebellion not merely against the Dynasty, but against the doctrine of the sages. How can men of education and breeding sit with their hands in their sleeves, and do nothing?

It is the sacred duty of all patriotic sons of the Middle Kingdom to strike the long haired bandits to their black hearts. To pluck out their lying tongues. To burn deep the sockets of their eyes. To rip open their vile bellies. To rub salt into many cuts. To trim close their ears, and draw forth their nails.

Security to the government, and extermination to the rebels!"

* * *

December 29, 1852

I have spent my first Christmas with the Taiping, and after the joyful, but somewhat unusual celebrations, I have managed to snatch time before we move on to write some brief comments about Quangzhou.

It is a large and wealthy city, one of the most important we have taken so far, which has supplied us with much needed gold and silver for our treasury, as well as boats, supplies and, most importantly, a host of new recruits.

A good number of these had to be persuaded to join our cause, but no matter, I am convinced that in time they will come to understand the benefits of the Taiping faith both to themselves and society at large and will become as firm in their beliefs as the rest of us.

* * *

Proclamation issued by the Taipings.

"Each year the Manchus transform tens of millions of China's gold and silver into opium, and extract several millions from the fat and marrow of the Chinese people and turn it into rouge and powder.

Each year these demons collect Chinese girls from all over the country to be their slaves and concubines. All the women of China are put to shame by them.

Whenever there is flood, or drought, or famine, the Manchus sit and watch us starve without compunction. They let loose greedy and corrupt officials across the country to exploit us so that countless men and women are left weeping by the roadside.

To speak of such things moves the heart and befouls the tongue. Can the Chinese still deem themselves men if they do not rise in anger at China's shame?

The Manchus are non-believers and demons. They have usurped the throne and enslaved us. They are no better than swine and dogs, and a great reward is promised to anyone who strikes off the head of the Manchu emperor, the Tartar Dog, Hsien-Feng.

A barbarian monster devours us and sucks our blood. Hurl him back to the hell where he came from. Destroy him, and grind him to pieces as the farmer grinds the grain".

* * *

January 31, 1853

I am travelling up river on one of the hundreds of boats we recently captured, our army marching on the bank alongside.

Our fleet is led by local boatmen who know the eddies and perils of these waters, indicating by flags in the day and lanterns at night on which side of the river we should move so as to avoid hazards such as shallows and sandbanks.

Our soldiers have learned surprisingly quickly how to co-ordinate land and water operations by using a system of signals with flags, drums and gongs. We also utilise these devices in battle, thereby ensuring our men react speedily to changing situations, and our forces are moved to the areas of the field where they will have the most impact.

We have also developed a number of other clever ruses.

For example, when we attack a city, we set off fireworks throughout the night and ride horses up and down, dragging boxes filled with stones behind them, to keep the defenders awake and confuse them as to the real size of our army.

Once, when one of our battalions was obliged to evacuate a town through the pressure of vastly superior forces, the last of our men gathered together a number of dogs, pigs and other animals and tied pots and pans to their tails – exactly like the Bible tells us Samson attached torches to the tails of foxes to deceive the Philistines.

The resulting turmoil persuaded the besieging forces that our men still remained in the city giving them the opportunity to get clean away under cover of darkness.

* * *

I was most surprised to see what happened the first time we were obliged to build a bridge for our men to cross a river that was running too high and fast to forge.

When everyone had crossed, rather than leave the construction or destroy it to stop it falling into the hands of our enemies, our soldiers collapsed the bridge into manageable pieces to be carried with us for use at the next obstacle, every-one enthusiastically working together on the task at hand.

The Manchus can do nothing against such an unstoppable force except threaten dire punishments on their beleaguered troops, and as for their generals, many, I have heard, prefer suicide to the torture and execution that inevitably await them when their failure is evident. Compare this to the high spirits and optimism that pervades our men, and it is easy to understand why I am so optimistic about the future.

* * *

February 12, 1853

We have learned the hard way that pride comes before a fall.

Our land forces having been obliged to march inland due to the topography of the area, the fleet I was travelling with encountered a most deadly ambush which proved to be almost fatal to our venture.

The Manchu had used sunken boats and other obstacles to block the river at a narrow bend, forcing our ships to stop and become all massed together, unable to move forward or back. Whereupon we were subjected to an intense bombardment of gunfire and burning arrows from both banks, forcing us to abandon our ships, and try to avoid certain death by getting to the shore.

You cannot imagine the turmoil; the roaring of the flames; the screams and shouts of the dying and the injured; the neighing of the terrified horses; and the churning of the blood reddened water, as we sought to escape our foes under the very mouths of their guns, scrambling hand over fist up the steep banks into the shelter of the woods.

In truth I feared that it was all over for me, but by the grace of God, managed to make it to relative safety with nothing more than a couple of minor flesh wounds. They have healed well. Just the slightest discoloration of the flesh remains—a badge of honour I wear with pride.

* * *

Once in the relative safety of the trees I could see our boats drifting aimlessly on the river, on fire or sinking, and hear the fusillade of small arms and occasional cry as the Manchus finished off those of our men who had failed to escape.

Hung, thank the Lord, was unharmed. Even so, a pall of depression descended on us when we realised the magnitude of the disaster and in particular that Feng Yun-Shan, Hung's cousin, a man much loved by Hung as well as the rank and file, had died from his wounds.

Looking around at the shivering, disorganised, frightened men crowded together, sheltering as best they could from the gunfire, trying in my barely adequate Chinese to comfort the wounded and the dying, I must admit in my despair I thought our cause was lost.

Then, as our souls were at their lowest ebb, something miraculous occurred. A voice, soft at first, then gaining in strength, started to sing a Taiping hymn

– "Thanks to the Mighty Lord". Another joined in, then another, until all of us were singing, thousands of voices proclaiming our faith and lifting our spirits.

Hung spoke to us, raising his voice above the sounds of gunfire and screams coming from below. I could not follow everything he said, but I understood that having lamented the death of his cousin—I caught the words "a great tree has fallen"—and all the others who'd perished, he declared this setback was nothing more than another example of God testing our resolve, exhorting us to remain strong and continue the struggle, for with His help we would surely triumph.

* * *

We escaped that scene of destruction by crossing the mountains under cover of darkness, led by those who knew the area well. Even so we would have undoubtedly been finished had our opponents thought to block the passes. By some miracle they did not, and so, after enduring three gruelling days and nights of marching up and down steep wooded slopes, carrying our injured, many of whom succumbed from their wounds, soaked from the incessant rain, unable to light fires lest they lead to our discovery, exhausted and hungry we came down into valleys friendly to our cause where we were able to meet up with our comrades from that area, recover from our wounds, and recoup our strength, safe for the moment and among friends.

* * *

March 19, 1853

I am writing this prior to bedding down for the night. Above me, the glittering stars, all around, the flickering of our fires.

We are advancing by land and water, our previous losses more than made up with new recruits.

Wherever possible our boats travel in the middle of the stream, at night their lanterns looking for all the world like a host of fireflies, the soft splashing of our oars striking the water, the occasional shout breaking the silence, while scouting parties reconnoitre several miles ahead so the disaster of the previous ambush won't be repeated.

When a city or town is taken we leave a garrison of local recruits behind, stiffened by a small number of our veterans to guard the place and run it according to Taiping usage while the bulk of our army continues its progress.

* * *

April 22, 1853

We have taken Nanking! And I was a part of it.

This event will reverberate around the world. Nanking is the second city of China, and is a former capital of the Ming dynasty, with very significant religious and historic significance to the people.

We now rule half of China, and so shaken will the Manchus be by this latest blow it is surely only a matter of time before their whole rotten structure comes tumbling down and all the country is ours.

China is like the sea when there is a storm raging in its depths, calm on the surface, but seething below. And now, because of what we have accomplished, the sea is boiling and bubbling with a vengeance.

* * *

I will not go into the details of our campaign. Suffice it to say that our leaders decided they would take advantage of our rapid return to our full strength and the enemy's lack of knowledge of our whereabouts to make a bold and unexpected strike against Nanking.

We moved quickly, achieving our goal in just thirty days, three separate armies marching all day, often at night, and travelling on the rivers and waterways that abound in this area.

Having reached Nanking we took full advantage of the element of surprise, hitting the city hard by both land and water, concentrating our forces and coordinating our attack so to strike simultaneously on all sides, in particular the two sections of the walls that were identified as being the weakest.

* * *

The Taiping gunners, though enthusiastic and quick to learn, are not as well versed as we are in the best practices of artillery. I was therefore, I am pleased to say, able to give considerable assistance in the setting up of our guns at advantageous positions overlooking the city, using my expertise to try to ensure our shot caused maximum damage to the most vulnerable areas.

The walls, as one would expect given the strategic and economic importance of the town, were well built and the defences strong. Even with our overwhelming numbers and the element of surprise it took almost two weeks of constant bombardment and the activities of our miners, before we could effect a breach of such a size that our men could force their way through.

This first happened in the northern part of the city, which we had identified as one of the more weakly defended parts. Standing beside our emplacement I could see the dust flying as our shots increasingly found their mark, and the dense masses of our men running this way and that, carrying ladders, and battering rams to enlarge the gap the bombardment had made.

Eventually, thank The Lord, the breach was secured and our gunners, bodies slick with sweat and powder, stopped firing and cheered as wave after wave of our comrades poured in though the gaping hole in the wall.

And then a moment I will never forget. The silence broken only by the faint cries and gunfire coming from the town, as standing on the windy heights, heads bowed, our commander led us in a prayer to Him who had granted us this great victory.

After, each alone with his thoughts. Mine being how truly blessed I am to see with my own eyes the miracles that are unfolding here.

* * *

Once our men were inside the walls resistance crumbled more quickly that any of us had dared hope, the major part of the city being in our hands within a few hours, although the final redoubt of the Manchus, a great fortress in the centre of the town, took several more days to be reduced.

* * *

Having made a useful contribution, I believe, by instructing our troops in the best use of their guns, and helping breach the walls, I then achieved the greatest reward I could have asked for. Not silver or gold. No. I have long thrown off the love of these useless things.

No. The reward I received was to join the massed ranks of our victorious warriors, long hair blowing in the breeze, solemnly standing outside what remained of the city walls, the sunlight glinting on our weapons, our red, yellow and black banners bravely fluttering, as Hung surrounded by his victorious generals led us in a triumphant prayer thanking God for our success, then announcing to great excitement and enthusiasm the naming of Nanking as his Heavenly Capital.

A new Jerusalem. God's refuge here on earth.

My cup overfloweth.

* * *

April 24, 1853

As there is no other soul to whom I can confide my innermost thoughts, I feel constrained to write them down in this journal, at night when nobody is watching me.

I feel safe in doing this as the papers are well hidden, and, having proved my usefulness to their cause, I cannot imagine the Taipings having any interest in searching my quarters.

* * *

The slaughter as we entered Nanking and when we took the fortress was most terrible to behold, even for someone like myself, not unused to the sights of war.

I was told that over fifty thousand of the enemy, or devils as the Taipings call them, were put to the sword—most after they had surrendered. (I took no part in this massacre, preoccupied as I was with the placing of our guns on those of the walls which remained standing, to defend the city in case of a counter attack.)

After it was over the stench of the bodies, women and children among them, was almost unbearable as they lay strewn around the streets, around the fortress, and piled up inside it, until carts were bought and they were taken away to be buried in mass graves some distance from the town.

As for the remaining population, they were unharmed if they swore under oath to join us and follow our religious practices, except for certain Manchu merchants, mandarins, bureaucrats, and the like, who had sucked the life out of the people over the years, and were summarily executed.

Even given the grave injustices the Manchus had inflicted on ordinary folk, I must confess that the death and suffering handed out by the Taiping was worse, far worse, than I had ever expected.

No mercy of even the slightest nature was shown or contemplated.

Still, as I keep telling myself, our cause is just.

And yet when I saw the bodies, soldiers and civilians alike, laid out like so much . . . so much offal. . . .

But war is war, and what's done is done.

Our cause is just, I keep telling myself. Our cause is just.

* * *

May 3, 1853

Nanking is a most attractive city, situated as it is on bend of the Yangtse river, mountains in the distance, wooded hills all around and containing a multitude of historical buildings.

After the initial slaughter, the strict discipline of our troops spared the townspeople the general orgy of rape and pillage that usually accompanies victories of the Imperial troops.

Unfortunately though, there did follow a major destruction of the shrines, temples and books of the old religion, some of great antiquity. In particular the Porcelain Pagoda, situated on a small hill overlooking the city, and famed for its beauty throughout China, which after suffering some damage in the fighting, was reduced to a pile of rubble by the Taiping.

* * *

I visited the site of the Pagoda one afternoon. Barely any of the structure remained standing. Piles of bricks littered the ground, and statues, their heads and arms missing—representations of the Buddha if I am not mistaken—were lying among fragments of the beautiful green and blue tiles that gave the building its name.

I have to admit this instance, as well as the devastation of many other beautiful objects throughout the city, at first caused me considerable distress. Now, having thought more deeply on the matter, I believe I understand the reasoning behind it.

The Taipings take the second commandment literally in that they believe all false gods, graven images and the like must be destroyed. At present they adhere to this decree with all the zeal of the newly converted, not heeding the consequences of their actions. I am convinced, however, that with the passing of time they will temper these excesses, and will gain the confidence to keep the best items in museums to demonstrate to future generations the artistic glories of their past, as is the case in our own country.

Our own country. I wonder if it is my country now. The greed and hypocrisy shown by our politicians and businessmen, sicken me.

For the life of me I cannot comprehend why the so-called Christian countries have refused to countenance any dealings with the Taipings, people who follow the same faith as they profess to do. I can only imagine it is because they prefer to deal with a regime, though rotten and corrupt to the core, allows them their obscene profits on opium and alcohol—both rightly banned by us—as well as other useless, flippant goods of no benefit whatsoever to the general population.

Despite this I am convinced that once the people in these countries hear about the wonderful things that are happening here any scruples their governments may have about engaging with the Taipings will instantly be set aside.

* * *

May 24, 1853

It is mid-morning. For the past few days I have been encamped with a work detail, repairing and improving the defences of one of the strong points that guard the approaches to our Heavenly Capital.

We have just finished our midday prayers, and I am lounging on the grass with my comrades, eating my meal of rice and beef and listening to their laughter and chattering.

The mist and cloud have cleared. Below me I can see the sun glinting on the river and a myriad of boats plying their way up and down, and from bank to bank, while high above a flock of birds heads in formation towards the mountains.

Nanking appears in the distance, like a mirage in the warm air, the hand of God protecting it from harm.

The sound of prayer, and the bustle of work, fair and honest, reverberate through its streets as those ensconced within the safety of its walls go about their daily business free from want and fear.

All is right with the world.

Coin no longer accumulates in the pockets of the rich, but in the hands of working men and women, or the coffers of our Treasury, to be used for the good of all.

Harmony, faith, and justice prevail, and the divisions that formerly kept men separated from each other have one by one come tumbling down.

I feel tears come to my eyes, not of sorrow, but of joy that I have been blessed to live in such momentous times.

* * *

June 9, 1853

There is much to be done here—the rebuilding of the walls, improvement of the defences, repairing of houses and other buildings destroyed or damaged in the fighting, and the construction of food stores and chapels in every district of the town.

If we are indeed the bloodthirsty beasts our enemies portray us to be, why then with all the other calls on our resources do we spend so much time and effort constructing orphanages for the children whose parents died in the fighting or have been separated from them through the chaos of war?

Everyone has been set to work at the skill or trade he or she is best suited to—in my case the work of reconstruction, and for the past few weeks I have been exceedingly busy—a state I like to be in. Having said that, the labour I am engaged upon is very tiring and made much worse by the intense heat.

Each day apart from the Sabbath—of which more later—I fall into bed exhausted, happy though, in the knowledge that I have achieved something worthwhile for our cause.

* * *

June 21, 1853

It is not just the physical that the Taipings are concerned with. The moulding of peoples' minds is, if anything, even more important to them.

Almost every day orders, instructions and guidance on all sorts of matters, civil and religious, emanating in the main from Hung, are posted up so all can read them.

To take one example, men and women, even the married ones, are segregated under pain of death, until the blessed time—let it be soon—that our Heavenly Kingdom is attained for the whole country.

It is quite beyond me why such a restriction should be insisted upon as the scriptures clearly permit conjugal relations within the sanctity of marriage, yet despite this everyone apparently follows the prohibition without complaint, and is a measure of the constancy of their faith and the extent of their discipline that everybody seems to accept without question this restraint on their passions.

* * *

July 14, 1853

The immense task of printing the Bible in Chinese is well under way, and alongside this work groups of scholars are busy revising the texts of both Testaments so as to best reflect the Taipings' and Hung's beliefs.

As is often the case, though, new converts tend to be somewhat overzealous in their fervour, and I have gathered from the tenor of some of the questions put to me that some of their interpretations, are, I have to say, bizarre in the extreme.

For example, they declare that now there are not two, but *three* Testaments; the Old, New, and a third consisting of Hung's writings and proclamations.

One could, of course, take issue with such, but my view is that these deviations are a small price to pay for the dissemination of the true faith to the Chinese people.

* * *

July 21, 1853

The Chinese have always been great record keepers, and in accordance with this tradition meticulous details are kept of every aspect of our lives.

The town has been divided into neighbourhood areas, and everyone is obliged to register themselves, and their family so they can receive what provisions and goods they are entitled to, and, just as importantly, give whatever is required of them, including military service.

So necessary is this considered for the correct running of Taiping society that the penalty for repeated refusal to register is the execution of the head of the household. The same penalty applies to those caught taking alcohol or opium, the severed heads of these and other criminals displayed on the city walls as a warning against the flouting of these laws.

While this may seem somewhat harsh to our sensibilities, it clearly operates for the good of all, and I have been told that mercy is often shown in cases where there are extenuating circumstances such as a young person being led astray by an older one.

One thing the Taiping have done which I do not approve of is to release every prisoner held by the Manchus, with no regard as to the seriousness of their crimes, on the grounds that now the Heavenly Kingdom has been established these peoples' previous incarceration has no legitimacy in the eyes of God and Man. This seems to me to set a most dangerous precedent. Clearly not all the Manchu laws are unjust, so surely it is better to keep the good and discard the bad, rather than, as it were, throwing out the baby with the bath water?

* * *

August 14, 1853

The Taipings have decreed that the Sabbath should be observed on Saturday, because they contend, as do the Hebrews, that it was on this day of the week that the Creator rested.

Prayers are also held every day in the morning, midday, and the evening.

All activity comes to a halt as everyone files into the chapels that have been built in every part of town.

Sitting with my brothers in the quiet of our simple, unadorned halls, I feel an atmosphere such as must have been present in the early days of the Christian religion when the first believers gathered together in the Holy Land, secure in the eventual triumph of their faith despite all the problems that surrounded them.

I have to stop now as I can hear the gongs calling us to prayer.

* * *

October 6, 1853

Hung has appointed four so-called Kings—calling them North, South, East and West—to command our armies as well as to oversee civil matters.

Surprisingly, these Kings and most of the other commanders are not aristocrats or scholars. They are in the main common, uneducated, men from the very lowest classes of society and yet, with no previous training, they have turned their hands to the arts of war, diplomacy, and organisation as if they were born to it.

One of them, for example, is a man called Yang—or to give him his official title the East King—who was originally leader of the charcoal burners, a very poor, depressed group in the mountains where the movement started. He joined the Taipings in the early days, moving quickly up the ladder because of the forcefulness of his personality and his military prowess, and is now second in importance to Hung himself.

I believe it is the fact that people like Yang have risen so high as well as the Taiping threat to the established order that has caused such an excess of hatred in the minds of our opponents. For if such men can take over the levers of power so easily what need is there for the whole paraphernalia of mandarins, lords, priests and Emperor?

The Taiping are a source of continuing amazement to me on this point and many others, and once we have achieved all our goals I have it in mind to write a book about my experiences and the various unusual phenomenae of their rule.

* * *

December 14, 1853

A couple more observations.

In keeping with the highly charged religious environment that prevails, trade is banned within the confines of the Heavenly City lest it pollute its holiness, but is allowed to flourish outside the walls and in the towns and villages round about.

Despite these restrictions I have noticed a number of Europeans around the town, merchants, I gather, here for business of various sorts, and welcomed by us for defying their governments' ban on dealings of any nature with the Taiping.

But there are also an increasing amount of the lower sort of person, adventurers, soldiers of fortune, mercenaries, whatever you choose to call them, solely interested in hiring out their services to the highest bidder.

Why on earth the Taipings have any truck with types such as these, I have no idea. If it was up to me I'd send the whole lot of them packing. As it is, all I can do is try to keep out of their way, acknowledging them with the briefest nod if I encounter any on the street, and if they insist on talking to me, allowing just a brief conversation from which I escape as quickly as possible.

* * *

January 10, 1854

I mentioned Yang, the East King, in one of my previous entries. What I did not have time to write is that he has been in the habit of falling into deep trances, claiming he is suffering from a kind of divine sickness caused by his taking all the sins of the people on himself.

I am told by the Dutchman who I first encountered when I arrived at the Taiping camp, and who seems privy to much information about what goes on in what he refers to as "the inner circle", that after being in such a state for hours, sometimes days, at a time, Yang commences to pronounce on all sorts of matters of doctrine and morals, hesitant at first as though the words are being dragged out of him, then in a deep resounding voice so everyone around can hear whatever wisdom he has to impart.

Hung has decreed these pronouncements to be the direct word of God, and has recently given Yang the additional title of Lord of Eight Thousand Years only a little below Hung's own title of Lord of Ten Thousand Years.

Yang is also now referred to as the "Redeemer" or "Teacher", titles which no doubt serve to boost his high opinion of himself.

The Taiping are very keen on these graduations in hierarchy and titles, and the ordinary followers study them avidly for clues as to the relative favour and importance of the various leaders.

I have to say I find all this very bizarre and not at all like the Christianity we are used to, but you must bear in mind that the Chinese have a habit of adapting other cultures to their use while at the same time incorporating their own traditions. There is, I keep telling myself, no reason why their adoption of our faith should be any different. The important thing though, is that they are following the right path.

We will prevail.

We *will* prevail.

* * *

February 12, 1854

Whatever foul stories have been circulated by the Manchus regarding the morals of the Taiping women—they are complete lies.

Whilst it is true that the Taipings do count men and women as equals and many women join them so as to become free of oppressions such as the evil practices of child marriages and feet binding, the sexes are strictly segregated, and sexual congress, even between husbands and wives strictly prohibited until our final victory is secured.

* * *

This segregation does not, however, apply to Hung and his so-called Kings who, it is said, enjoy the company of concubines and dancing girls in the privacy of the palaces they have built for themselves. Palaces, I regret to say, which are every bit as grand as those of the Manchus they have supplanted.

Needless to say, the largest of these, even bigger than Hung's, is that of Yang, the East King, who I have mentioned a number of times before.

The city is awash with rumours concerning him, the main one being that of late he has been falling into his trances more and more frequently.

The Dutchman, who is surprisingly frank and open with his comments, informs me that Yang, still claiming all his utterings come directly from God, has now started being critical of the conduct and faith of his fellow Kings, and even of Hung himself.

* * *

Hard on the heels of this disturbing intelligence a directive recently appeared stating that not only us common folk but also Hung and the other Kings must kneel in Yang's presence whether he's in his palace or travelling in the town with his entourage.

No matter if it is raining or snowing, cold or warm, all, young, old, hale or sick, are required to bow the knee under pain of a beating from Yang's guards.

If this were not bad enough, his latest demand is for the same impositions to be followed before his two sons, the eldest, who, I would guess, is not much more than ten years old.

* * *

February 24, 1852

The other day it was bitterly cold, snow having fallen in the night. Making my way home, I spotted a procession in the distance. Judging by its size and magnificence that it was Hung, who we see extremely rarely these days, I hurried to see it.

But it wasn't Hung. It was Yang, the East King. As I approached I observed men, women, even children, bowing their heads low and kneeling in the snow, while the procession passed.

I have to say I was not inclined to follow suit. For Hung, yes. But not for this . . . this charcoal burner. That is until his guards brutally attacked a man who for some reason had not emulated those around him. Beating him, forcing him to his knees, pushing his face down on the ground.

I had no choice but to comply unless I wanted a similar treatment.

As I knelt in the snow and ice, feeling the cold seeping into my bones, I sneaked a look at the gilded palanquin, carried on the shoulders of a dozen men, and caught a glimpse of Yang peering out from behind the curtain, before they passed by, and we all clambered to our feet.

The Lord only knows how people feel about this imposition, but no-one breathes a word because Yang's spies and informers are everywhere.

Time alone will tell where all this is leading. For my part I'll continue to keep my eyes to the ground, do as I am told, and ask no questions.

* * *

April 6, 1854

Rumours. Whispers.

The atmosphere of distrust and betrayal has grown so great that no-one feels himself safe. All I can do is hope that no suspicion will extend to a figure as minor in the scheme of things as myself, though as one of the increasingly few remaining Europeans I stick out like a square peg in a round hole.

Just writing these words, should they ever be found, would place me in the gravest danger, so I've taken the precaution of secreting this journal in a more inaccesible place, for were its contents discovered there is no knowing what would happen to me.

The Dutchman reckons things have come to such a pass that Hung is now obliged to come out on foot like a common servant to greet Yang when he visits Hung's palace, and if any officials or officers neglect to show Yang the respect he considers he deserves, they are punished most severely. Beaten, on occasion executed or burnt alive if a suitably grovelling apology is not forthcoming.

Once, the Dutchman says, Yang threatened Hung himself with forty lashes for some minor infraction, only relenting at the last moment, claiming that God had begged him to show mercy!

I can scarcely credit all of this, but if only half of what I am told is correct, Yang seems completely out of control.

The man's arrogance is becoming so insufferable that the North King accompanied by one of our most valiant generals, has left the city ostensibly on a campaign, but in reality, it is said, to avoid Yang's overbearing presence.

* * *

July 19, 1854

Yang's palace has been set ablaze. He, his family and many thousands of his followers slaughtered on Hung's orders.

The stench of death hangs like a pall over the city. A fearful dread is everywhere, the killings continuing even as I write.

Each morning fresh corpses can be seen lying in the gutters and on the roads and pavements

The whole of Nanking is in a state of terror. Gangs of soldiers roam the streets day and night looking for any of Yang's supporters who may still be alive, proclaiming loudly on every corner the fate of anyone found to be harbouring fugitives.

* * *

The first I knew of all this was when I was woken in the early hours of the morning, the night rent by the sound of explosions and lit up by flames and flashes of gunfire coming from the area where Hung and his "Kings" have their residences.

Dressing quickly and grabbing my gun I ran into the street thinking we were under attack by Imperial forces, only to find hundreds of people nervously milling about, running this way and that, not knowing what to do because the great bells and gongs that are supposed to warn us of any assault were completely silent.

Despite all the melee that ensued I eventually managed to find several men from our section of defenders. As we started to make our way towards the square where we were supposed to muster in such situations we encountered a number of others from our group coming towards us.

"Haven't you heard?" One of them shouted as they approached.

"Heard what?" Replied one of our party.

"Yang's compound is under attack."

I felt a shock pass through my body as he continued.

"The North King and General Quin have come back into the city under cover of darkness to bring Yang to heel. Hung's orders."

By this time large numbers of soldiers were streaming towards the palace quarter from all directions, screaming at us to get off the streets if we valued our lives.

There was chaos as everyone rushed back to their homes, but even indoors it was impossible to sleep. Every few minutes I could hear more gunfire and explosions, the tramp of feet, voices shouting orders, and the clatter of horses' hooves.

The sounds and disturbances faded away shortly after dawn, only to be replaced by an ominous silence which I found far more disturbing than the cacophony of sound that proceeded it.

I peeked out my window until the sun was well up when I noticed some brave souls venturing forth onto the street. I plucked up my courage and went to join them.

* * *

A pall of black smoke hung over the palace quarter, and I could see a line of soldiers blocking any access in that direction. A group of us wandered aimlessly off in a different course along the empty streets, no-one talking, the occasional person joining us, until we came across a small crowd staring up at the Western gate where the blood encrusted heads of Yang and his family, their eyes staring blindly down at us, were stuck up on pikes for all to see, like common criminals.

But it wasn't over yet. Later in the day the sound of gunfire and shells burst forth again, resounding over the city for almost two hours.

Panic as before. People screaming. The streets emptying.

Several thousand troops loyal to Yang had been lured into the outer halls of Hung's palace ostensibly to view the whipping and public humiliation of the North King and General Quin for their part in the murder of Yang and his family. Upon which troops who had been hidden in the rooms around the halls and on the roofs turned guns and cannon on them at point blank range.

I was told that the corpses were piled up to the height of two men.

* * *

July 29, 1854

We desperately need reassurance and guidance from our leaders, but Hung has so far not thought it necessary to show himself and calm our fears.

In terrible times such as these there is, of course, the reassurance of prayer, but we also need the support of those who are supposed to rally us in times of trouble. As of now this relief is denied, and I am forced to the reluctant conclusion that Hung and his minions have neither the interest nor the desire to make any contact with us ordinary folk.

* * *

September 2, 1855

It has taken over a year, but at long last the atmosphere has started to return to something approaching normal following those desperate, dark days after Yang's fall.

It seems to me, though, that the recent convulsions have exacted a heavy price from the populace. Everything appears peaceful on the surface; people are going about their daily business, but there is little or no direction to our affairs and we are acting in what I can only describe as a kind of paralysis, a sort of trance or suspended animation, like the inhabitants of a dream.

* * *

September 11, 1855

I have little to do now that the work of repairing the damage from our internal feuding is done, and, to be frank, am becoming increasingly frustrated at the state of enforced idleness which has persisted here for the last twelve months or so.

During this time I, and many others, had been expecting to be given the orders to march north to attack Peking. Despite our problems the Manchus were staggering under the weight of defeat after defeat, and in addition to holding

Nanking we controlled almost the whole south of the country with its immense wealth and manpower.

All the advantage and impetus were on our side, and I am convinced that had we made our move we would have had little difficulty in sweeping everything before us, and once the capital had fallen the regime would have followed suit, and the whole of the country would have been ours.

As it is, a year has been allowed to pass, and here we are running around like headless chickens rather than taking the fight to our enemy, thereby handing the Manchu the opportunity to recover from their previous dire situation.

To add insult to injury the Western powers have agreed to work together with the Manchu to blockade us by both land and sea in an attempt to stop the shipments of arms and supplies that are essential to the success of our endeavours. Slowly but surely they mean to squeeze the life out of us.

And if this were not enough, we now hear that apart from the foreign adventurers who are swarming into China, paid handsomely to fight alongside the Manchus, an Englishman, Major Charles Gordon—a good Christian, no doubt, if he still has the gall to call himself such—has been appointed by General Stavely, the British commander in Shanghai, to train and lead a section of the Imperial forces against us.

I ask you. Is this what the people of England, France and the rest of them want done in their name?

Despite our problems it will avail them nothing, and I tell you, if Gordon, or any other of these interfering foreigners were in front of me on the field of battle, British or not, I would shoot them or run them through without a second thought.

* * *

October 14, 1855

The atmosphere has improved considerably since my last entry.

We are like a man who has been struck a mighty blow. He staggers, almost falls, but then his head clears, his vision returns to normal, and he is himself once more.

Hung has not been seen for several months, in fact not since the slaughter of Yang, seemingly content to cloister himself with his women, occasionally issuing edicts on obscure matters of ritual or etiquette, through rhyming couplets written on long sheets of paper which are secured to the walls of his palace, always ending with the exclamation—"Respect these Words."

I have to admit that, on reading these proclamations—my knowledge of Chinese is now greatly improved—the phrase "the Emperor's new clothes" enters my head from time to time.

I find some of them so difficult to decipher, and their meaning so subtle and obscure, I would go so far as to say they are completely removed from what passes as normal reflection.

Whether they are the product of a confused mind, or are intentionally vague like the predictions of the oracles of the Greeks which could be interpreted in a number of different ways depending on the inclination of the listener, I have no idea, but like everyone else, I certainly do not wish to query what they mean as it is not done to question, even in the slightest way, the words, however crazy they may seem, of God's Younger Son, as Hung now calls himself.

In these circumstances all one can do is keep reminding oneself of the righteousness of the end result—the conversion of millions of people to Christianity—and try ones best to keep soldiering on.

* * *

December 3, 1855

Imagine my surprise when, without any warning, it was announced that the ban on men and women cohabiting together has been lifted.

I guess that such a prohibition on men's natural instincts even within the confines of lawful marriage caused so much resentment it could no longer be sustained.

* * *

January 9, 1857

More bloodshed.

The killer, killed.

The North King, who was instrumental in Yang's downfall has met the same fate as his victim—he, his family, and followers slaughtered, their heads displayed on poles on the walls of the Heavenly City.

Heavenly City? I wonder why we still call it that when it has descended into so much savagery. . . .

I can remember the beginning when it was so full of love and brotherhood and the hope of things to come—compared to what it is like now when. . . .

Enough. All one can do when faced with such violence and dissension is to give thanks to the Lord we still have such numbers of brave men and women to call upon in the hour of our need.

February 27, 1858

At last some good tidings.

We have recently heard that the British have attacked the Chinese quarter of Canton following some dispute with the Manchu authorities, forcing the town to surrender to them. If true, this rift within our enemies' ranks may well mark a turning point in our fortunes, as the British will surely be far more prepared to consider aligning themselves with us, and once one of Western powers changes direction the others will follow sure as night follows day.

This, I am convinced, is the breakthrough we've been looking for all these years, for without Western support the Manchu regime will undoubtedly collapse.

In the meantime though the war in the countryside ebbs to and fro, neither side gaining clear advantage.

* * *

March 25, 1858

We have received the most excellent news that Sir George Bonham, the Queen's special envoy, is planning to visit Nanking with a high ranking delegation, the first official foreign dignitary to do so.

The delegation will be arriving in a month or so and I am convinced that once they have seen the wonderful, inspiring work that is going on, and spoken to our leaders and administrators, normal relations will soon be instituted between us.

I have volunteered my services to interpret for our side and translate any correspondence from the delegation, but refused point blank to meet any of the delegation face to face, insisting on placing myself behind a screen as I feared for my safety, and also that my presence could inflame tensions between the two sides.

* * *

June 13, 1858

The British mission has arrived, but without the presence of Sir George Bonham or for that matter any other notable individuals. Instead of the high level delegation we'd been promised, we were presented with nothing more than a sprinkling of middle ranking military men and civil servants, plus a selection of so-called merchants. Not at all what we had expected.

The reasons for this change were unclear, and I thought it advisable to warn the Taipings, who are somewhat naïve on such matters, that as it could be that most of the mission were spies sent to assess our military situation under the guise of trade enquiries and the like, on no account should they be permitted to enter the city.

After much debate they somewhat reluctantly followed my advice, insisting that the British remained outside the city walls, but still not understanding why their fellow Christians should harbour any evil intent against them.

* * *

My concerns about the intentions of the British were proved correct at our very first meeting—which consisted of them mouthing foolish platitudes without making any attempt to engage us in any serious discussions.

Before they left a member of the delegation handed us a list of questions without a word of explanation as to their purpose.

On reading them, though, it was clear that, in addition to a number of queries about our beliefs and laws framed in a most offensive and patronising manner, the rest had the sole purpose of ascertaining our military strength and organisation.

We of course refused to reply, and countered by submitting a number of questions of our own a couple of days later. Having subsequently read a copy—not being given the opportunity to comment on their original contents, I guessed from the bizarre subject matter that Hung had been instrumental in their composition.

They consisted solely of queries on such absurd things such as the size and physical features of God; the area of Heaven and the like, all of which I am sure would have seemed completely ridiculous to the British delegation, thereby cementing their prejudices and low opinion about us.

* * *

Needless to say, once this nonsense was delivered no further meetings took place, and the British, clearly in a state of some dudgeon, left shortly after, but not before informing us that in no circumstances would they sign any trade agreements with the Taipings, and adding it was their intention to pursue a policy of strict neutrality in the conflict between us and the Manchus.

Neutrality. How in God's name can they claim to be neutral when their man Gordon is training and leading Imperial forces?

Damn it, any fool can see that their so-called *neutrality* in fact means supporting the Manchus with whom they are coddled up to in all sort of trading and other cosy arrangements.

I am not privy to the British government's way of thinking which confounds any notions of common sense, decency, and their professed Christian faith, but there it is. They have chosen the easy profit to the wellbeing of this country, preferring to align themselves with its unbelieving, backward rulers rather than those whose faith and ideals are the same as they profess to follow.

If there's any justice in this world those who determine the Western powers' policy towards China will rot in hell, but before the Almighty's retribution is visited upon them, I would round up every one of these rogues and parasites and send them as far away as possible so their stink no longer pollutes the atmosphere of honest, decent, citizens.

To hell with the lot of them.

We will do without their help.

* * *

October 3, 1859

Our prayers have been answered. The head of the snake is to be cut off for good

Orders have been given for an army to strike north at Peking or "the den of demons" as the Taipings refer to it.

I will be accompanying them in order to help with our guns which, like Joshua's trumpets sounding at Jericho, will bring the walls of the city crashing down.

I count the days till we reach our goal, and every night pray to the God of battles for our final victory.

* * *

January 20, 1860

I am back in Nanking.

The attack was doomed from the start.

There were not enough of us. Barely fifty thousand rather than the hundred, maybe two hundred thousand, needed to do the job properly.

In addition winter came hard upon us as we neared Peking. Bitter and cold, snow falling almost every night, which we had neither the equipment nor clothing to face.

Despite these drawbacks we fought like tigers to within a hundred miles of the capital until vastly more numerous Imperial troops, aided by that damned traitor to his faith, Gordon, forced us to retreat, three of their armies closing in on us in a well-planned manoeuvre.

Being in the rear-guard I was one of the ones lucky enough to get out before the trap was sprung.

Those of us who were left managed to regroup, but after struggling back through snow and ice for over a week had to face yet another ordeal when trying to cross the Yangtse.

As we lined up on the river bank, our scouts trying to locate the barges which had been moored for our return, gunboats, British as well as Chinese—I clearly saw the Union Jack flags—loomed out of the spray, firing at us at point blank range. The cries and moans after the first fusillade died away reminded me of that other time we were ambushed on a river, shortly after I'd joined the Taiping, but the difference now was we were retreating instead of advancing.

While the boats were turning for another pass against us, we broke and ran in all directions, every man for himself, trying to gain whatever cover could be found while death and destruction rained down all around.

By the grace of God a thick mist suddenly descended on the river or we would surely have all been slaughtered. As it was, we only managed to get away after losing perhaps a third of our number, eventually managing to cross by tying ropes over a narrow ford some distance upstream, more of our men, unable to hold their grip on the cold, slippery cord, being swept away to their deaths.

It seemed that nature, who had aided our escape, was now conspiring against us for no sooner had we crossed the river when the temperature dropped and the snow, which had ceased for several days, started once more, a few flakes at first, then heavy, drifting across our path.

* * *

The journey back was hellish. Trudging exhausted and half-starved through snow and ice day after day, fearing attack at any time, I believe I only owe my life to my northern constitution, more used to such a climate than my comrades, many of whom succumbed to the cold.

Even so, the first few weeks were very hard, struggling through the drifts, little shelter or food, only driven on by the fear that the Imperial troops were most likely hard on our heels, until, thank the Lord, we arrived in milder climates and encountered several parties of our men, some of whom had only managed to escape by disguising themselves as Imperial soldiers.

Words cannot describe how welcome it was to see them and feel the warmth of the sun's rays once more.

* * *

Barely ten thousand made it back to Nanking, the rest dying on the battle field, on the river, of cold, and, I am ashamed to say, deserting to the enemy, their faith forgotten as they chose to place bodily survival ahead of the fate of their souls.

They persist in this course of action in the belief it will save them, even though it is well known that on numerous occasions, our troops, despite the promise of safe conduct if they surrender, have been slain most treacherously once they have laid down their arms.

The Imperials shave our soldiers' heads as a sign of their submission, and place white head coverings on them—white being the sign of mourning here—before killing every one, except for a handful, spared so they can return to tell us the fate that awaits us.

The thought of these poor wretches, these poor, misguided men and women—yes, women are not shown any mercy either—being led to their deaths like cattle brings tears to my eyes.

Do our enemies not realise that this threat, rather than alarming us, causes a terrible anger and convinces us to fight on even harder?

* * *

February 19, 1860

As our position worsens and the threats to our very existence grow more intense, the faith of the people who remain in Nanking, soldiers and civilians alike, intensifies.

I, though, am no longer sure that this will end well for us. In moments of weakness I find myself concerned about the eventual outcome of the conflict, and whether we will ever prevail against the ever stronger forces ranged against us.

So I read my Bible, and the knowledge that Our Lord Jesus overcame so many trials and tribulations, even death itself, gives me renewed strength in the justness of our cause and our eventual triumph.

After all I have been through the valley of death and survived.

All is not lost.

This thing is not over yet.

* * *

April 1, 1860

Our prayers have been answered, my optimism and that of my comrades rewarded. A cousin of Hung's, by all accounts a most intelligent, energetic and amiable person, has managed to make his way here, after a most difficult journey through Manchu lines. His arrival seems to have energised the whole town, and he has already been given the title of "Shield King" and appointed to head our armies and administration.

Apparently he speaks good English having spent some time in Hong Kong, and is full of ideas for modernising every aspect of the country.

I believe with all my soul that his arrival will give us the impetus we so sorely need.

In addition to this, a young man of humble origin who has risen swiftly through the ranks on account of his constancy to our cause and his military accomplishments, has been given the title "Loyal King" and made second in command to the Shield King.

These two developments give me more reason to be optimistic about our eventual success than I have felt for some time.

It is as if a bolt of lightning has been released into our midst, or the force of the sun has driven the dark clouds and all the enveloping mists of suspicion and apathy clear away, the air clean and fresh once more.

* * *

July 13, 1860

The Loyal King has struck eastward with an army of some of our best fighters, taking the enemy by surprise. Several cities have been already retaken, and Suzhou, a town of crucial strategic importance that we lost a year ago, restored to our control.

* * *

August 5, 1860

The Taiping, drunk with glory over their recent successes, are planning to attack Shanghai.

I imagine that this misguided idea stems from a desire to try to impress the Western powers of our growing strength and confidence, coupled with the naive belief that, ensconced in their special quarter of the city where they undertake their commercial activities and are free to follow their own customs and religions, the Westerners will allow us to pursue our attack while they do nothing so as to avoid conflict with us, their fellow Christians.

To say I have serious qualms about the wisdom of such a course of action is putting it mildly. I am convinced the Western powers will view any move on Shanghai as a threat to their interests, and that an attack such as this will reinforce their decision to support the Manchu dynasty. To antagonise them by attacking a place so important to their trade and reputation is in my view, little short of madness.

* * *

Stressing my loyalty over the years I explained my concerns to whoever would take the time to listen, insisting that my hesitation should in no way be viewed as cowardice, but arose solely out of what I believed were the best interests of our cause.

Suspicions of people's motives being rife since the crushing of Yang and the North King, I had to be most careful how I phrased any criticism, in particular lest it was construed in some way as censuring Hung. Even though he has been seen only by his inner circle for the past few months and his pronouncements are becoming increasingly strange, his word is still sacrosanct.

* * *

Everything I said was to no avail—the planned course of action will not be deviated from, although the Taiping leadership eventually agreed to direct the Loyal King to inform the Western powers before our attack, that they will be unharmed if they do not take part in the hostilities.

Having said this, I doubt very much if such an assurance will have any effect on the outcome of this sad affair.

* * *

October 30, 1860

My worst fears have been realised.

Once our army was encamped outside Shanghai the Loyal King wrote to the Western delegations promising them that neither their persons nor property would be harmed when the city was taken.

In the event, though, as I predicted, the Western powers, when faced with the choice between the forces of light and those of darkness, chose the latter, and helped repulse our attack, their guns and ships driving us off with heavy losses.

The only lucky thing in all this mess is that the defenders did not possess enough troops to undertake a counter attack, giving us the opportunity of an organised withdrawal.

* * *

January 16, 1861

Some small relief from the boredom and depression of spirit that has recently assailed me.

A most interesting character has arrived as an "honoured guest" of the Taiping leadership. He is the Reverend Issachar Roberts, the American preacher who first instructed Hung in the tenets of Christianity.

He is a tall, well-built fellow, in his early sixties, with a good head of hair and a flowing beard. A booming confident sort, full of enthusiasm, and apparently held in high regard by Hung.

Having been introduced to him only briefly, I did not have the time to establish why precisely he had come here, but took the opportunity to ask him when we met on the street two or three week later.

Dressed in a splendid set of silk robes, looking for all the world like some exotic western-style mandarin, he at first seemed disinclined to converse about his experiences.

Eventually, though, after looking around to check no-one was listening, he told me that he'd been tricked into kneeling and bowing his head before Hung, something which distressed him greatly as such a thing is not permitted by his branch of the Christian faith which only allows one to lower one's head before the Creator.

He'd also hoped to acquaint Hung with his objections to some elements of Taiping practices and beliefs, and his puzzlement at certain of their changes to Biblical texts—which he described to me as being "little short of blasphemous".

Not being able to raise these matters at their initial meeting, a high ranking official assured him that Hung wished for a private interview with "his most esteemed guest" to be held as soon as possible.

In the following days and weeks Roberts had been summoned to the palace on numerous occasions, then obliged to wait in the audience hall for hours at a time with no sign of Hung, merely receiving vague, contradictory answers when he asked what was going on.

"All sorts of courtiers, soldiers, women came in and out of his quarters." He told me. "But no call for me and not a glimpse of the person I came all this distance and under so much difficulty to see and talk with."

He then informed me that it was originally his intention to open a number of chapels in the Heavenly City as well as other areas controlled by the Taiping, and asked for my opinion as a "God fearing, Christian gentleman" on whether I thought it desirable for him to pursue such a course of action "in the light of all the rebuffs I have suffered."

I, for my part, merely gave him some bland reply, not wanting to give any hint about my own misgivings on the subject.

I could not help but see the look of disappointment in his eyes at my unconstructive response before his good manners took over, and he thanked me for my help.

* * *

As he walked away I thought, so this is what I have become. A coward and a dissembler without the courage to speak his mind. A pariah, only concerned with saving his own skin, cut off from everything he previously held dear, keeping silent time and time again so as not cause offense, yet still not certain if he has the complete trust of those around him.

What, in the name of God, is happening to me?

* * *

July 18, 1861

A heavy blow has occurred.
One of our main bases, Anking, has fallen.
Over twenty thousand lost.

* * *

December 9, 1861

I've come across the American preacher, Issachar Roberts, a number of times since his arrival. We usually exchange a few words about the weather or some other such topic as he does not seem inclined to talk further about his experiences or whatever concerns he may feel.

On the last occasion, though, he seemed willing, I would go so far as to say, eager, to talk frankly to me.

"Have you read Hung's proclamations?" He asked in a rush without any of the usual preliminaries.

"What?"

"Don't act the booby with me, sir. His proclamations. The ones plastered over the walls of his palace."

I nodded, somewhat taken aback by his tone.

"Then you will realise how misleading if not downright heretical they are." He continued, ignoring my obvious displeasure at the way he'd addressed me. "These Taipings seem to imagine they can change the text of the Bible at will. I do not know how familiar you are with the Chinese tongue, sir, but I am very familiar with it, and I can tell you that their translation of the Bible contains numerous errors. No. Errors is not the right word. Changes. Omissions. They seem to imagine they can alter God's word to suit their own purposes. Well, sir they have been badly advised on this point. Very badly indeed. I need to talk to Hung . . . I have to see him as a matter of urgency to impress upon him the error of his ways and set him on the right path."

He put his hand on my arm before continuing.

"If you have the slightest degree of influence in this madhouse, I beg you, sir, use it to obtain me an interview with Hung. I do not ask for much, just an hour would suffice. I would be in your debt for ever."

And with that he shook my hand and was off without waiting for my reply.

I told no-one of this conversation, knowing full well that Hung has his own views on matters of doctrine and all the power in the world won't persuade him to deviate from them one iota, and because I feared for the preacher's safety were his views to become known.

* * *

June 12, 1862

I encountered Roberts yesterday—the first time I've seen hide or hair of him for several months, still dressed in his Chinese robes, but looking much thinner than I remembered, almost shrunken, his former confidence seemingly completely dissipated.

I've no idea why he has stayed in Nanking so long. It could, I suppose, be because he still retains some charitable feelings for Hung because of their past association, or he could be being kept here against his will. Whatever the case, the hopes he had of being able to reform the Taipings' "errors and misconceptions", as he once described them to me, had turned out to be vain ones.

Ill at ease, constantly looking over his shoulder and shuffling his feet, he told me, in a state of the greatest agitation, that "every one of my proposals having been rejected with the utmost contempt", the day before, one of the "Kings", who he described as a "devil" had stormed into his quarters without any warning, violently assaulting him and his servant, for what reason he did not know.

"I feared for my life, sir. I feared for my life." He exclaimed, his voice shaking with emotion.

"I must leave this infernal place." He continued "And you sir, I most strongly advise you to do the same."

A week or two after this I was told that Hung had grudgingly given him permission to return to Canton.

* * *

Apart from this incident things have been surprisingly quiet for the past few months with little movement on either side.

My guess is that the Manchus are probably as exhausted—both physically and morally—as we are after the struggles of the past years.

It seems to me it is now purely a question of which side can summon up sufficient strength to finish the job.

* * *

February 11, 1863

Increasing numbers of our fighters are deserting to the enemy, being promised, and, given, safe conduct once they surrender their arms and join the Manchus.

I am sure this change in policy is at the instigation of the Western powers. Previously the Imperial forces indiscriminately killed our soldiers once they were in their power, any promises of mercy made during sieges and battles entirely forgotten. The foreign powers, though, are much more subtle. They know that the fear of being slaughtered was one of the main elements in preventing those who were minded to leave us from actually doing so, but now word has got out that they can safely surrender, our fainter hearted men and women are starting to drift away.

Among these was the Dutchman who interviewed me when I first arrived at the Taiping camp—the one man here I could truly call a friend, and with whom I could converse intelligently in English.

He vanished one night without a word, leaving me a note advising me to do the same.

Who can blame him? Since he left I increasingly find myself thinking of England, her rolling hills, her towns and villages, and at moments of weakness, particularly in the long, dark nights, when I feel so utterly distraught and alone, I thought to follow him—it is not necessary to join the Manchu—if you have some money, particularly European money, it is still possible to bribe one's way out.

But even if I was to leave and managed to make it back to Canton or Shanghai, what then? What sort of life would await me? I've been away for over ten years now. The sound of my own language sounds strange to me. Even my appearance has changed. Sometimes it seems to me that I look more Chinese than English.

And if I did go, imagine my reception. Treated as a pariah, most probably tried as a traitor. Unable to find employment. Shunned by those I once counted as friends and acquaintances.

Impossible . . . Enough of such thoughts. I'll stick it out to the bitter end.

* * *

February 18, 1863

A few days before he left the Dutchman told me about the latest example of eccentric behaviour in the court.

Hung's officials have taken to coaching ordinary soldiers, workers and the like, giving them weird and wonderful names and titles, dressing them up in the most outlandish clothes, and introducing them to Hung with great pomp and cere-mony as emissaries from neighbouring states or far flung countries and empires that have no existence outside someone's fertile imagination.

The whole thing is a complete farce of course, and all the officials and commanders know it. Only Hung apparently swallows the whole preposterous deception hook, line and sinker—the strange names and titles; the descriptions of non-existent places; and the glorious costumes.

He indulges in long winded and earnest discussions about affairs of state and religion with these so-called ambassadors—in particular the young and pretty girls—who are instructed to nod their heads in agreement at appropriate moments and offer Hung and our cause their undying tribute and support.

I sometimes wonder if the world has gone completely mad.

* * *

March 22, 1863

I feel obliged, no, not obliged, that is too weak a word, *compelled* to set down an account of what I witnessed on an excursion into the countryside in a vain attempt to locate additional supplies.

After so many years of war I feared I would find some sort of deterioration in conditions in the countryside, but nothing, I repeat *nothing*, had prepared me for the reality of the situation.

* * *

What I saw was nothing less than a vision of hell.

Complete devastation. Dwellings and storehouses burnt or destroyed. Grain and food virtually non-existent. Rivers and canals choked with foul-smelling rubbish, the debris of war, and piles of dead bodies. Hungry packs of dogs wandering the villages and countryside. Skeletons of cows, pigs, horses and domestic animals lying everywhere, stripped down to the last piece of flesh.

The roads, such of them as remain intact, were clogged with beggars, starving people who are little more than skeletons, and gangs of children, filthy, half naked, roaming around, searching in vain for some for any form of sustenance.

They say things have come to such a pass that people are starting to eat each other.

Is this, I ask what Stavely, Gordon and their like are proud of having imposed upon this land?

* * *

April 14, 1863

The desertions have accelerated. Men can only take so much, and having suffered so many defeats and disappointments they find little or no comfort here other than the promise of more fighting without the assurance of success that previously raised their spirits. All our leaders can do is on the one hand threaten the direst consequences for anyone caught trying to leave, and on the other intensify their promises of our eventual victory over the forces of evil.

Hung still remains unseen in his palace, but after a silence lasting for several months his proclamations have started to appear again, declaring amongst other things that the title Taiping Heavenly Kingdom will be changed to God's Heavenly Kingdom—as if this makes a jot of difference to our situation—and announcing the dawning of what are referred to as the Days of Peace, and the promise of salvation and final victory if only we hold fast.

As for his more outrageous claims that a Heavenly host will come to our aid to kill every one of the snakes and dogs, the demons and unbelievers who assail us, or that our opponents' bullets will be rendered harmless, I am afraid I ignore these as the ravings of a madman.

It is shocking how this superstitious nonsense still seems to resonate with the majority of the people here, despite all their instruction in the Christian faith.

Is it for this, this twaddle and gobbledygook, that I have spent the best part of the last eleven years fighting?

* * *

May 9, 1863

Our efforts are now concentrated on trying as best we can to defend our own territories, all thoughts of taking Peking or Shanghai set aside.

A great effort has been made to break through the Imperial forces that are continuing to encircle us.

Under conditions of absolute secrecy—necessary because it is rumoured that traitors in our midst are selling details of our plans and situation for Manchu gold and silver—two armies of our best troops, each I would guess, numbering twenty, maybe thirty, thousand men exited the city at night, one heading north, the other east.

I only know this because I happened to see the two immense columns leaving, involved as I was on guard duty at the time, and saw them marching silently through the gates, banners bravely flying, still proud and unyielding despite all they have been through.

* * *

June 20, 1863

Our attempt to break out has failed. The defeated remnants of the eastern column started to drift back at the beginning of this month, followed by the northern one a week or so later.

Outnumbered and outmanoeuvred. Many thousands lost.

From the talk of the men who did return it seemed to me that the Manchu forces were considerably better equipped and more disciplined than previously was the case.

I put these improvements down to the involvement of the British and others.

We are no longer fighting men like ourselves. We are also struggling against Imperial gold and Western skills and organisation.

How much longer will the God who, despite all our troubles we continue to worship so intently, permit us to suffer?

* * *

October 8, 1863

A sense of lingering unease hangs over the town.

Even the Sabbath services which used to be so lively and colourful are despondent and subdued.

Food and supplies are running short, the storerooms and granaries almost empty.

Our attempts to store essentials in central warehouses have largely failed because people are hoarding for themselves and their families against the inevitable siege.

I had the misfortune to be seconded to one of the patrols charged with the task of seeking out these people, expropriating their goods, and punishing them.

The trials of any wrongdoers we catch—that is if you can dignify such cursory affairs with the name of trials—are conducted on the spot by whoever is deemed the most senior man present, and the penalty, when they are inevitably found guilty, carried out there and then. Death by shooting for the head of the household involved, be they man or woman or, God help us, young boys and girls, their parents having been killed in the fighting over the years.

All I can do to justify such harshness is repeat to myself over and over again as we line them up, ignoring their cries and entreaties for mercy, that the good of the many must supersede the needs of the few. Surely any reasonable man can see the truth of this.

Thinking about it, I wonder if I still know the difference between right and wrong. All I can say is that when I look in the mirror I see a man barely recognisable to me, a man with something of the beast about him. Gaunt. Unshaven. Sunken cheeks. Eyes staring out with no expression.

In a civilised society I would stand apart, but here in Nanking, I am normal. Everyone is showing signs of decay. The captains no longer ensure that their men turn up for daily parade, but lounge around chatting without apparent purpose.

The warriors' long hair looks matted and dirty, their clothes torn and unkempt, something of the rabble about them, who less than six months ago seemed so disciplined, so full of pride and dignity.

As for the women, in the main they are slovenly, except for a number of the younger ones who strut the streets with painted faces—willing to prostitute themselves for a bowl of rice.

As I look around and see the misery that is forcing so many to such desperate measures, I cannot stop myself from thinking that surely our cause is lost, with only death and destruction awaiting us.

No. I mustn't write any more in this vein. No. In the name of the God we worship, we have to continue the struggle. We *have* to.

* * *

The other day, sickened by what we're doing, not to our enemies, but to our own people, I could take no more of it.

After we'd shot two women, sisters, widowed in the fighting, whose only crime was to set aside some small amounts of rice and vegetables for themselves and their children, I pleaded illness, and was permitted to return to my quarters, only after promising I'd present myself for duty first thing the following day.

Sure enough, early the next morning I was woken by several men from the detail knocking loudly on my door and insisting on waiting outside until I was ready to accompany them.

* * *

December 6, 1863

Suzhou. Beautiful Suzhou. City of canals and gardens, one of our main satellite towns, has fallen. By betrayal, it is said, the gates opened to let the Manchus in.

I am too distraught to write any more.

* * *

March 3, 1864

We cannot surrender even if we wanted to.

Now that the Imperial forces can smell the scent of victory any thoughts of mercy on their part have gone clean out the window.

One of our commanders surrendered to overwhelming odds on the solemn promise that he and his men would be spared. Immediately they lay down their arms they were butchered in the most brutal and cowardly manner, except for two of our fighters who were given safe passage to return here so they could tell us what had transpired and what sort of fate lay in store for us.

Some were most distressed, wailing and weeping at this dreadful news. As for myself, I am determined more than ever to continue to the very end and not go meekly like a lamb to the slaughter.

* * *

April 7, 1864

Our forces, such as they are, are pulling back to defend the city and the string of outlying villages and fortresses that protect it.

It is rumoured that the enemy is in the process of bringing up many more thousands of troops and peasantry, though where they are getting them from the Lord alone knows.

The final assault must surely be imminent.

* * *

April 22, 1864

They have taken the last of the strongholds that protect the city.

From my vantage point I can see their men gathering in the heights overlooking us, while thousands more are busy building earthworks and ditches to hem us in on all sides.

All that our counter attacks can do is delay, but not stop, this inexorable process.

* * *

May 4, 1864

Nothing gets in or out.

Food is becoming scarcer. No meat. A small bowl of rice a day with some shrivelled vegetables.

The livestock and horses disappeared long ago. The cats and dogs have all been devoured.

Hung's latest proclamation promises we will be relieved, like the Hebrews in the desert, by manna from heaven. But of course not one crumb arrives.

We have run out of room to bury the dead. At night parties with carts creep out to dump them in mass graves outside the walls.

The word on the street is that the Loyal King has left the city. Some say to gather reinforcements, others that he will carry on the struggle in the countryside.

* * *

May 20, 1864

We are caught like rats in a trap, the city completely ringed by the enemy.

Each day they bring up more and more of their boats until they have almost blocked the entire river.

Through my glass I can see Manchu banners on practically every hill and highpoint where ours once flew so bravely, and their men scurrying around like a horde of ants excavating a great ditch to the north and west to keep us completely penned in.

A desperate attempt to break out led by some of our younger commanders, has failed.

The noose is too tight.

More heads of supposed traitors appear on spikes.

Suspicion. Fear. Death all around.

* * *

June 12, 1864

Night. Everything is hushed. You could be forgiven for imagining that finally the world is at peace.

A gentle breeze blows over the city.

Strengthens. Grows stronger.

Listen carefully. Listen. Can you hear the sound of wings flapping?

Great wings. Swooping. Diving.

The host of angels promised by Hung has come at last. They are all around us.

Listen . . . The sound fades. Dies away.

The wind stops.

All is quiet once more.

* * *

Through the stillness I can hear men moving. Guns being readied. Ladders stacked for the final assault.

God watches over us.

And is silent.

* * *

June 14, 1864

The powder depot has been destroyed. The streets are full of people running desperately in all directions.

I and some others have rallied a number of our men to try to hold the Manchus back when they breach the walls, but our numbers are too small to resist them for more than an hour or two.

The streets are rife with rumours that Hung has killed himself by swallowing gold, as the emperors of old used to do, but in the panic no-one knows if this is true or not.

They say that before he died Hung decreed that those of us who are left should take our lives so the Manchus will find nothing but a stinking charnel house when they enter the city. Others claim the enemy is being lured in so a Heavenly host can destroy them where they stand.

For my part I discount such foolish notions, preferring to die facing the devils like a man, and maybe putting paid to some of my so-called Christian country-men who are fighting alongside them.

* * *

June 15, 1864

There will be no miracles.

I can hear the sound of our men outside preparing for battle.

This is my last entry before I hide my journal, hopefully to be found in the future by some interested party, most likely to be cast aside and destroyed by our conquerors.

I pick up my gun and sword and begin my march to paradise.

* * *

Nanking fell on 15th of June 1864.

Hung committed suicide as the Imperial troops broke into the city.

Many of the surviving Taiping supporters chose to follow their leader's example rather than fall into the hands of the enemy. Nearly all the rest were slaughtered.

Resistance in the countryside continued for several months before being finally crushed.

The Manchu dynasty survived, though shaken to its very core.

The Western powers continued their commercial activities unabated.

Some estimates put the number of people who died during the rebellion as high as twenty million.

Apache

I felt like a proper man for the first time in years as I clambered onto my horse and was handed a rifle and a bandoleer of bullets.

One or two disparaging remarks were made about me until Jed Holmes shut them up with the comment.

"I'd lay a bet he can ride and shoot as well as you lot."

And then we were off in a cloud of dust, waving and shouting to the townsfolk who'd gathered to wish us well, the town quickly disappearing from view, our horses' hooves drumming on the grass, the four spare mounts running alongside.

I confess to feeling increasingly nervous as we rode away from the sights and sounds I was so familiar with, the tension only relieved by the laughter and joking of my companions. I suspected that not a few of the posse, or at least those who were as inexperienced in such matters as I was, were most likely encountering the same gnawing trepidation as me, but also taking comfort in the fact that we were a dozen strong plus our tracker, and all of us well armed.

* * *

Our group of townsfolk, merchants and ranchers, were for the most part unskilled in the arts of warfare, but able to feel assured that at least the two men who were leading the party knew what they were doing.

Firstly the sheriff—Jed Holmes—a tough, dependable character who'd brought order to our town. A solid, upright type, good with his fists and a gun who would stand no nonsense from drunks or troublemakers.

And then there was Abe Newson. An old Indian fighter who owned a small holding on the edge of town. A man getting on in years, who kept himself to himself, with whom I'd never previously exchanged more than a few words.

All sorts of rumours circulated about him. That his wife, dead before he came here, had been a Cheyenne squaw. That he'd killed more than twenty, some said as many as thirty, Sioux and Cheyenne before heading south to settle.

Whatever the truth or not of all this, it was generally agreed that although in his late fifties, grizzled, and with greying hair, he was still a man to be reckoned with. The sort you'd want by your side in a tight spot.

* * *

We picked up the Indians' tracks without much difficulty, the savages having left a trail of death and destruction that was easy to find.

Our tracker, a Navajo, reckoned there were only five of them—Apaches, he guessed, most likely renegades broken out of one of the reservations, or possibly ones living deep in the badlands who hadn't yet been subdued by the government, who'd taken to raiding for guns and horses and whatever else they could lay their hands on.

Like everyone else in the town I'd heard talk about the fighting skills of the Apache, and the tortures they meted out to any of their foes unlucky enough to fall into their hands alive. I promised myself there and then that if such a fate awaited me I'd shoot myself in the head, rather than allowing the savages their perverted pleasures.

* * *

The Hobson spread was the first that had been hit, Hobson's wife and two young sons killed, George Hobson, lucky for him, being away on business for a couple of days.

Next to be attacked was the Franklin ranch, a smallholding where a young fellow, Tom Franklin, and his wife—no children, thank the Lord—had raised cattle and sheep for four years.

Jed Holmes had gone out to investigate early that morning when two, almost identical, columns of thick, black smoke had been observed rising from the vicinity of both locations. According to one man who'd seen him, Jed had come back so pale and drawn it looked as if "he'd been drowned in the lake and pulled out three days later."

Whatever it was that Jed had encountered, he speedily gathered together sufficient volunteers for a posse, deputised two men to help his assistant in his absence, and got us to gather in front of the saloon at eight thirty sharp.

"This could be dangerous work." He told us. "When their blood's up, there's no knowing what these Apaches can do. As Abe here well knows."

The Indian fighter nodded.

"If there's any concerned about their family or whose heart isn't in it," Jed continued, looking around him, I was sure holding his eyes on me longer than anyone else. "Then they'd better let me know straight away and they can drop out now with no hard feelings."

"Good." He said, when no hands were raised. "Then let's get moving, and pick up their trail."

The sheriff hadn't thought it necessary to mention it, probably for fear of upsetting us, but I noticed the undertaker and his assistant following us in a wagon, soon left behind as we galloped full pelt for the Franklin spread, me already struggling to keep up with the others.

* * *

The first thing we saw was the smoke still rising from what remained of Tom Franklin's ranch house. Then there was the stench, hitting us as we came closer, coming from the cattle and sheep that lay scattered around, dead from gunshot and arrow wounds, some with great bloody cuts on their flanks where the Apache had taken meat, presumably for the journey. Swarms of flies buzzing around the carcasses, the vultures no doubt arriving soon to finish the job.

Only Jed, Abe Newson, and the tracker went inside, no doubt to spare the rest of us the sight of the bodies, leaving us milling about outside, not saying much, each one alone with his thoughts.

The three of them came out shortly after, grim faced and subdued, and spent some time talking softly amongst themselves, the tracker and Abe Newson crouching down from time to time to check the ground.

"We're in luck." The sheriff said after a while. "They came here after they hit the Hobsons. We reckon they stayed most of the night eating and drinking. Probably left before dawn, four, maybe five hours ago. They took Tom's three horses, one of which is slightly lame. Could slow them down a bit."

He stared around him as if smelling the air.

"Come on then. Let's get out of here, and after the bastards."

As we rode off I saw the undertaker's wagon approaching in the distance.

* * *

The lame horse hadn't held the Indians up for long. We came across it after barely fifteen minutes lying by the side of the road, throat cut, eyes staring, mouth gaping open showing its large yellow teeth.

"Why couldn't they have just let it go?" Asked the man riding beside me, addressing his question to the fellow on his left, ignoring me as if I wasn't there.

"That's their way. They're savages."

Well, I could have told them, if it was us and the horse's lameness couldn't be fixed we'd have shot it, so where's the difference?

But, as usual, I held my tongue for fear of making a fool of myself.

* * *

The day continued with the tracker dismounting from time to time to check we were on the right trail, nodding to himself as he bent low over the ground.

There was a short break for lunch, and a longer one in the afternoon when it grew too hot to ride, seeking out the shade under the few trees that grew in that arid area. Each time we stopped we exchanged four of our horses for the four spare unladen ones, in a kind of rota so we could travel faster without over-tiring them.

We settled down to sleep as darkness fell, cold in the night air following a tasteless supper, because Jed had forbidden any fire, lest the Apache should see the flames.

I slept badly, my thighs hurting and with a worse pain than usual in my back and shoulder.

* * *

We were about to start up shortly after dawn having finished our breakfast, when one of the young fellows pointed towards a range of low hills in the direction where we would be heading.

I craned to see with all the others in the half-light before the sun came up, until I could just about make out a flickering red dot halfway up one of the slopes.

Jed took out his telescope, squinting, and moving the piece from side to side.

"Yes. I've got it." He said eventually. "I can't see much else, but it's a fire for sure."

"But is it them?" Someone asked.

"Who else would it be on those hills? Only a few hours away lads. We should catch up with them tomorrow."

We immediately cleared away our stuff so as to be quickly on our way, every-one excited, talking eagerly as if the Indians we were hunting were already dead or hanging from the gallows.

And me, all I felt was a growing nervousness in my guts, and, despite the few hours sleep I'd snatched, my back hurt even more.

* * *

It was a little after ten on the third day that the accident occurred.

Bill Rafter, a big fellow who worked in the general store, fell from his horse as his beast missed its footing on some stone or indentation in the ground, and crashed to the ground, its back leg twisting up behind it. I heard the loud crack as the bone snapped.

Bill followed, landing heavily next to the animal with a loud thump, clasping his left leg and screaming out in agony.

Someone took out his gun, but Abe Newson stayed his hand before finishing the animal off with his knife, looking old and tired, as if he was in some distress or discomfort, as he scrambled to his feet after doing the job.

I thought nothing of it. It was only later that I realised this was a taste of what was to follow.

"We've got to get him back to town, and quick." Jed said after we'd put a rough splint on the injured man's leg, him still whimpering and crying from the hurt and shock of the fall. "Any volunteers?"

A hand went up immediately, rather shamefacedly, from Dave Clifton, an older man who probably should never have come along in the first place.

"What Dave. Bored with our company already?" Jed asked sarcastically.

"No. It's just that I thought . . . "

"Never mind. I want you to leave right now. We'll give you some supplies. Don't travel too fast. Trot, don't gallop. You'll make it by tomorrow night or the next morning."

He pointed.

"Try to follow our trail. If you lose it, head due east—where the sun rises."

"The Indians, what if they . . . " Dave started to ask.

"Don't worry, they're ahead of us. The rest of us'll get after them pretty quick once you've gone and finish the job." Jed said, bending down towards Bill Rafter, who was still moaning on the ground.

"I'm sending you back with Dave." He said to the injured man. "It'll be painful, but you'll be home in a couple of days."

A few of the men managed to haul Bill onto one of the spare horses, heavy as he was, securing him by some rope so he wouldn't fall.

"Good riddance." Someone whispered as they rode off, the injured man's moans slowly fading away. "None of them would have been any good in a fight."

Jed stared at him, but said nothing as we saddled up.

In truth I'd wanted to put my hand up when Jed asked, for I was finding the riding most uncomfortable, and if I'd thought my presence on the posse would gain me some respect I was wrong. My so called comrades continued to treat me with the kind of half friendly condescension I was well used to, all of them, thinking, no doubt, I would be of little use when we met up with the Apache.

Something though, lord only knows what it was, stopped me from volunteering to go back. Thinking about it, I guess I was just too embarrassed to admit I wasn't as good as everyone else.

It's true, I reckoned, after Dave and Bill had disappeared into the distance, neither of them will be missed. In any case, there's still ten of us. More than enough.

Unfortunately, though, that wasn't the end of it.

* * *

Things started really going wrong that evening.

We'd made camp just short of a range of hills and were cooking dinner, a fire being permitted as we were in a hollow, well shielded from sight, when Abe Newson got to his feet, his face pale in the light of the flickering flames, and with a strange, puzzled look, cocked his head as if he were listening for something, and walked off without a word in the direction of a small gully that lay nearby.

I don't know if anyone besides me saw him leave, but I'm used to noticing things that others don't. It comes with practice, all those years sitting around watching the other kids' games, or seeing my mother bustling about the house or the yard, while I was sat shelling peas or doing some other chore she considered me suited for.

Maybe he thinks something's wrong, and he's checking it out, was my first thought. But if that were the case surely he would have spoken to Jed? No. He's probably gone to relieve himself or to have a moment on his own before supper. No. Everything's fine.

But I kept my ears cocked and my gun close to hand, just in case, trying my best to hear any unusual sounds over the men's low talking.

Nothing at all. Just my foolish nerves showing through.

* * *

Plates were handed out with beans, meat and bread, and steaming coffee to wash it down. Our first hot meal for two days. I hadn't realised I was so hungry, and was already half finished, busy concentrating on my food, before I noticed Abe wasn't back yet, his plate lying unattended by the rock where he'd been sitting.

Putting down my food, I went over to Jed.

"It's Abe." I said, speaking softly. "He's disappeared. He went over there." I pointed towards the gully. "About ten minutes ago."

Jed dropped his plate with a clatter, the contents spilling on the ground as he sprang to his feet, drawing his revolver.

"Put out the fire. Now." He hissed to the others. "Get your guns. And for God's sake be quiet."

Once it'd been done, he pointed at the tracker, myself and two others, speaking in little more than a whisper.

"Right. You four come with me. The rest stay with the horses. Don't leave them unless you hear gunfire or some other disturbance. And even then two of you must stay with them."

He turned to me.

"Now where did you say he went?"

* * *

It was growing dark as we entered the gully, Jed leading, me at the back with the tracker, trying my best not to make any noise or slip on the rocks that littered the area.

Twice Jed held up his hands for us to stop and listen.

We crept forward calling Abe's name.

Not a sound. The place seemed deserted.

And deserted it was—that is, of living creatures.

* * *

We found Abe some distance from the entrance of the gully, lying on his back, a peaceful expression on his face, his revolver still in its holster, knife in his belt.

"They must have caught him unawares." Jed whispered. "We probably scared them off. My God ... What a ... "

Before he could say any more we heard a sudden clatter of stones from the semi darkness behind us. The others turned, drawing their guns and blazing away, me stumbling, cursing myself for being too slow to react.

I thought I heard a scream as I followed suit, my hand shaking as I tried to aim towards the sound. There it was again, a scream, but this time followed by a voice high from fear crying out from no more than twenty yards away.

"Stop! The voice cried out. "For Christ' sake! It's us."

"Stop shooting. Stop, damn you." Jed yelled at the top of his voice.

There was silence for several seconds, followed by a yelling and a wailing that put the very fear of God into me.

We went towards the sound and saw it was Harry Turner, one of the men we'd left with the horses, blubbering away like a baby, pointing to what we realised as we came closer was a body of a man lying on the ground, his chest torn open by our bullets, dark stains on his shirt.

Jed grabbed hold of Harry, his fist clenched, eyes flashing blue murder.

"You fool. I told you. Only come if you hear gunfire."

"We thought we heard something."

"Well, you didn't hear any gunfire that's for sure." Jed shouted before breaking off and pointing to the body.

"Who's that?"

"Jethro. My sister's husband. He ... He ... "

Harry's words choked in his throat as he started weeping again.

"Quiet." Jed hissed. "For God's sake shut your wailing, damn you."

The rest of us kept quiet, too shocked to speak as Harry's tears faded into a muffled sobbing.

"Right." Said Jed, nervously looking around him. "We've got to get the bodies back to camp. Jethro first. Then Abe. And quick. If those damned Apaches didn't know we were coming for them, they sure as hell do by now."

* * *

Four of the men carried Jethro's body to the camp, followed by Abe's, all of them breathing heavily from the exertion of it.

Even by the pale moonlight the bullet wounds that put paid to Jethro were clear for all to see.

Abe was a different matter. His clothes were completely undisturbed, a close examination revealing not one tear or hole where blade or bullet might have entered. No sign of any bleeding. No bruising or marks on his head, face or neck. And, some recalled, there'd been no indication of any struggle or of any footprints or horse tracks in the soft, sandy soil, in or outside the gulley.

"You know." Said Jed, getting to his feet, having finished checking the body. "I think he might have died from some sort of seizure. He complained of feeling unwell yesterday, but put it down to the effects of a day in the saddle. I don't think there's been an Apache within miles of this place, but here we are with two dead men. Well then, don't let's hang about. Let's get on with it."

We buried the two of them side by side in shallow graves, each marked with a cross fashioned from the pieces of wood that we found lying around.

I wondered if the others were doing the same calculations in their heads as I was.

* * *

Later that night as I tried to get to sleep, I heard the two men who Jed had set on the first watch whispering to each other.

"I don't believe Jed." Said one. "He just didn't want to scare us. They crept in and killed Abe in some cunning way so the mark wouldn't show, or most likely used some of their magic on him. I've heard they have potions they just blow in a man's face and he drops down dead. You mark my words. That's what happened to him."

As I listened to them I cursed my stupidity for ever volunteering in the first place. The men thought I was useless, and though no-one had said a word I could tell by the looks I was getting that some placed the blame on me for causing the mess in the gully. When we got back to town they'd tell everyone, and . . .

No. Not *when* we got back. *If.*

A tear ran down my cheek, followed by another.

Luckily the two men's whispers covered my snuffles.

I couldn't bear to hear any more. I covered my ears, eventually falling into a fitful, dream-filled sleep.

* * *

The tracker left towards the middle of the night, shortly after the second watch had started.

No-one, including the two men on guard, heard a thing until there was the neigh of a horse and a yell. We all jumped to our feet, weapons at the ready, expecting an attack, but all was quiet. It was not until sometime later that some-one realised the tracker was nowhere to be seen, his pack and horse gone.

Some yelled out, swearing to hang the damned traitor for his cowardice in leaving us, with Harry Turner screaming and shouting that we'd all die in this God forsaken place, until Jed quietened him down.

"I'll deal with him. I swear." Jed said "When our paths cross, which they will do one day, I'll hang him myself. No trial. On the spot. Fuck him. There's still seven of us. We can still do the job and find our way back without his damned help."

He spoke in what seemed to be a calm, confident voice, but I, for one, could detect the strain in it, and the notion that the tracker preferred to take his chances on his own rather than with us terrified me more than the loss of Abe and the rest of them put together.

"Right then." Jed concluded. "Let's keep calm, settle down, and try to get a good night's rest."

But try as I may I couldn't sleep. I lay on my back, watching the stars, my ears straining to hear any sounds coming out of the darkness that surrounded us like a shroud.

Visions of Apaches crawling, their bellies close to the ground, like cats hunting, invaded my brain.

Although it was cold I could feel the sweat running down my face and body. Twice I almost leapt up, spooked at some noise or other, but it was only one of the men tossing and turning.

Eventually I slept, to be woken by the others moving around the camp.

All of us still alive.

* * *

It happened the following morning as we were riding out of a ravine, Jed having made us spread out for fear of an ambush. A shot, coming from the hillside ahead. Fred Holness, the man next to me, starting as if surprised then slumping forward in his saddle, blood pouring from his head.

We scattered, riding back for the shelter of the ravine as more shots from our unseen enemy rang out around us, somehow arriving safely and exchanging fire with our attackers from the cover of some rocks. That is until someone pointed out Harry Turner spurring his horse away at full gallop, not slowing down even when Jed yelled out for him to stop.

Jed gave a strange little smile, as if to say "Well, I did warn him", calmly took up his rifle, aimed, and fired once, twice, the shots echoing in the quietness of the ravine.

Harry tumbled to the ground, moved for a few seconds, then lay still.

"Leave him." Said Jed in a voice that brooked no dissent. "The Indians would have got him if I didn't. Let the coyotes take him if the vultures don't."

* * *

"Now listen to me." He said once the shots ahead of us had died away as suddenly as they'd begun. "And listen good. I'm not running back home like a frightened rabbit. There's a job to be done and I'm going to do it. And if any of you have any ideas about taking off, remember what happened to Harry just now. If you want to take the chance between me and the Apache or getting lost in those damned hills, you're welcome to try."

* * *

We waited a while after Jed's little speech, no-one speaking until we eventually ventured out from our cover in ones and twos, fully expecting to be attacked again. Everything though was silent and undisturbed. Only the two bodies lying on the ground with Harry's horse moping around near where he lay giving any sign of what had happened barely an hour before.

We buried Harry and Fred as best as we could before scurrying back to cover like the frightened rabbits Jed thought we were.

* * *

It was the death of Pete Evans, a cheerful, friendly youngster, to my mind the best of the whole miserable bunch of them that finally put an end to it.

We'd moved off after a while, guns cocked and ready, Jed kidding himself he knew where we were going, the rest of us following nervously, spread out for fear of another ambush.

I'd be lying if I didn't say I was scared, shit scared. Still, all was quiet and peaceful, until someone, I can't remember who, yelled out that Pete was nowhere to be seen.

Jed turned in the saddle, looked around, a puzzled expression on his face, before pointing us to go back in the direction we'd come from.

My first thought was that Pete had panicked and gone off to try and find his own way back. Whether or not that was the case we'd never know because after a few minutes we found him lying underneath one of the cactus trees that scattered the area, eyes open to the cloudless sky, and a great bloody arrow wound in his chest.

That did it. All of them gathered round Jed, ignoring me of course.

I came closer to listen, voice after voice saying enough was enough and it was high time to head home. And there I was, thinking I was the only one who wanted to get out of there as quick as my horse could carry me, while all the while, they, my dear brave comrades, were to a man thinking the same.

As for Jed he cussed at us for being the filthy yellow-bellied cowards we were, threatening us with God alone knows what unless we continued, 'til somebody shut him up by saying.

"And what you going to do if we don't stay Jed? Shoot the lot of us?"

Someone laughed, a short mirthless laugh, but had the sense to keep his mouth shut.

By the look in Jed's eyes I thought for one moment he would actually do it, but sometimes you're forced to see reason.

"Alright." He said, grudgingly. "Alright. But I'm coming back here to finish the job, and next time I'll make sure I have some real men with me."

And so, after some more swearing and blinding, we were on our way back, in the direction we should've been going several days earlier.

They've won, the Apaches have won, I thought, they've killed some of us and driven the rest away. And you know what, I couldn't give a hoot. I'm alive, fuck it. Free to go back, even though it's to a place I hate. But alive, damn it. Alive.

* * *

No-one spoke as we started in the direction of home on full alert, me, and I'm sure the rest, still fearful, expecting we didn't know what, only that it was certain to be bad.

In the event though nothing untoward occurred and, having made good progress, we made camp with a feeling of relief in a sheltered spot shortly before nightfall.

The tension lessened somewhat, men starting to talk and joke as they ate, Jed sitting to one side, an expression fit to kill on his face. Still, he was the boss, and, tired as we were, no-one objected when he put a double guard on duty, rotating every two hours while the others tried to snatch as much sleep as they could before making an early start the next day.

* * *

My shift done, I settled down under my blanket and closed my eyes.

It must have been only a couple of minutes before I fell into a deep sleep, the first I'd experienced for several days.

I dreamed I was in a valley, lush and green. A cool, welcome breeze. Water flowing along a shallow stream. I bent down low with none of the discomfort I usually feel, and drunk deeply. Sweet and cold—better than a beer on a hot day. I was about to have some more when I heard a faint sound from behind me and turned around.

It was a girl, resembling one of the ones I knew from our town, but this one's hair was not yellowy blonde. It was long and black, jet black, sleek and shining in the sunlight.

She had on a skimpy white dress, short, low cut, the kind of thing a whore would wear, certainly not something a respectable young lady would be seen in.

She came towards me smiling. Welcoming. Holding her arms open. Her eyes deep and dark as water in a pool.

I responded by going towards her, but when I got closer she shrunk away from me, opened her mouth wide, and screamed and screamed, and . . .

* * *

I woke to the sound of screaming as in the murky half-light just before dawn figures like ghosts or phantoms dashed towards us out of the gloom.

I leapt to my feet to catch sight of Charlie Morton and one of the others going down, struck by bullets and spears, the ghosts coming closer and closer while I pulled my revolver out of its holster.

I put the gun to my temple as they rushed in, and squeezed the trigger, my last sight being of Jed being hit on the head and dragged yelling to the ground by two of the savages.

I heard the click of the bullet in the magazine and the hammer descending, and winced in anticipation of the explosion to come.

Nothing.

I squeezed the trigger again, harder this time. Still nothing.

And once more, my hand shaking so much I could barely hold the damned gun straight.

A grinning, painted face appeared before me. The gun was pulled from my hand. I felt myself falling. I heard voices. Laughter.

Then oblivion.

* * *

It must have been the motion that woke me.

I was tied to the back of a horse led by an Indian brave riding in front of me. My throat felt dry. My head was throbbing, my limbs and back wracked with pain.

My first thought was that the tracker, damn him, must have been in league with the Apache, because, rather than the five or six he'd said there were, there must have been at least a dozen or more of the devils around me.

In fact, as I found out afterward, the tracker had been correct. There *had* only been five of them. They'd spotted us early, on the day when we, thinking ourselves so smart, had seen their campfire on the hills. The Apache had immediately sent one of their number for reinforcements. From that moment we were as good as done for.

* * *

I was sure Charlie and Jed were dead as well as the rest of the posse. Certainly, if any were still alive there was no sign of them, at least not as far as I could make out by moving my head slightly to see.

After, I learned that another war party of a similar size to mine had gone ahead with the three other surviving members of the posse, one dying of his wounds on the way, the body chucked into the nearest gully.

The horse jogged along. My stomach went cold knowing the fate that awaited me.

I shut my eyes and hoped to die.

* * *

We were almost two days and a night on the road. I say road, but there was in fact no road to speak of, sometimes a sort of rough track, but most of the time us going across open country, through hills, over a couple of swift flowing steams. Without our tracker there wouldn't have been a cat in hell's chance of finding the Indians if they didn't want to be found.

Food was some dried meat and a sort of hard bread thrust into my hands which were untied for the purpose, and also when I indicated I wished to piss or shit.

The weather had cooled down somewhat thank the lord, because I was only given water to drink twice a day, morning and evening.

They clearly wanted to reach their destination quickly—maybe for fear of pursuit. We only stopped after darkness had fallen to snatch a little sleep, and were up well before dawn.

It rained during the night. My hands and feet were tied—where on earth did they imagine I could run off to? Cold and wet, trying my best to shelter under some rocks, I couldn't stop the tears from coming unabated, until a couple of kicks in my back put to paid to that particular emotion.

* * *

We arrived at their village at the end of the second day, the final stretch through a narrow defile, guards perched on the rocks above, which opened up into a valley—exactly like the one in my dream.

Word had obviously gone before us because our way through the camp was crowded with people, faces distorted, screaming and yelling at me what I guessed were insults, or even worse, threats about the excruciating things they were planning to inflict on me.

I felt several blows to my legs and arms, and thanked goodness I was up on my horse or there's no telling what they'd done.

We eventually got through the crowd. I was dragged off my horse, and, having cut my bonds, they tore off my clothes and threw me naked into a hut nearby.

* * *

I lay on the earth floor of the hut for what I reckoned was three days, my clothes nowhere to be seen, just an evil smelling blanket for cover against the cold nights, the door barred against my exit.

They must've given me some kind of draft or drug with my food or drink because I drifted in and out of consciousness, alternating between a deep, dreamless slumber and periods of being wide awake before falling asleep again without warning, only the slithers of light coming through the small gaps in the walls and roof telling me if it was day or night.

I assumed they unbarred the door when I was sleeping, because twice a day there was food and drink waiting for me when I woke, and the large container that I evacuated myself in had been emptied of waste and filled with clean water that I washed in.

There was nothing I could harm myself with. Apart from the containers for food and water, the hut was completely empty.

* * *

It was on what I judged was the second day—and by the strength of the light coming in guessed it to be late afternoon—that I was woken by the sound of drums and chanting, so loud it seemed to be coming just a few yards from my hut. Louder and louder, without pause. The damned noise filling my ears and racketing through my skull. And then, when it seemed like my senses was fit to burst, silence. Peaceful, blessed silence, only to be to be followed by a yelling and a shrieking such as I'd never heard the like of, that sent a shiver down my spine.

I forced myself to listen.

What in the name of God was it? A man? No *men*. More than one. Two? Three? I couldn't tell, the voices inhuman somehow, more like the cries and howls of wounded beasts than those of human beings.

And even worse than the screams . . . The smell of burning. Faint at first, then stronger, seeping under the door and through the gaps in the walls until I thought it would choke me. Sickly sweet. The smell of burning flesh.

Pretty obvious what was happening, isn't it? And yet at first I was completely unable to put the evidence of my senses together. I don't know if it was the drugs they'd given me or it was just that I didn't want to know. And then it clicked, and all I could do was cover my head with the blanket, the sweat streaming off me, and scream at the top of my voice to try to block out the awful, ear-splitting sounds.

I was sure it was the savages' way of adding to the terror I felt until it was my turn to suffer the same dastardly fate.

The only thing I could hope for was that my body, weak as it was, would give out sooner rather than later.

If I'd been a religious man I would have prayed for the souls of my poor, tormented comrades, and also that my end, when it came, would be as quick as possible. But I'm not religious, never have been, never had much time for it. I could offer no succour to the men who were dying so horribly, nor for myself, no doubt soon to follow them.

* * *

The screaming continued without pause, if anything gaining in intensity, until suddenly, as the light between the slats of the hut faded from day to night, there was one awful, piercing sound and the shrieking stopped dead, just like you'd choked off the water coming out a pipe.

Silence at last. Blessed silence. But only for a minute or two, before that damned, infernal drumming and chanting started up again, louder than ever, eventually fading away.

All that was left were some voices talking softly. A faint cry from a woman or child. Then quiet. Dark outside.

Not a solitary sound, except the occasional bark of a dog.

* * *

I lay on the blanket, wide awake, unable to sleep, hate and fear seething in equal portions through my brain.

After some time I heard the wooden bar of the hut being carefully slid back, and the door opening. I pretended to be asleep, narrowing my eyes to slits, just wide enough to see what was happening.

Three shadowy figures entered, two moving silently towards me, the third standing by the door which he closed quietly so as not to disturb me.

I stayed motionless, trying my best not to move as one of the men bent down to pick up the old containers while the other placed the new ones on the ground, both fully occupied with their tasks.

For a moment I thought of making a break for freedom. But what was I to do? Jump up and disarm the two of them, as well as the one on the door? Hopeless. All they would do was laugh at my puny, feeble efforts as they pushed me to the ground, trying not to use too much violence, not wanting to harm me ahead of whatever entertainment was planned for me.

I continued laying still, too afraid to stir, trying my best to control my breathing, until, I hoped, they'd leave me in peace for the rest of what was most likely my last night on this earth.

But they didn't leave. After they'd finished they stood staring down at me, nudging each other, pointing, then motioning the one by the door to join them. No doubt, I thought, looking me over like a butcher inspects a piece of meat deciding how best to cut it. But in this case it was me who was the meat and what they were considering was where their blades and burning brands could be placed for maximum effect when my time arrived.

I could take no more. I screwed my eyes tight to block out the sight of them.

And then, so soft I was barely aware of it, I felt a touch on my hump, followed by another, and another. Stroking, running over it, light like an insect or the caress of a twig or a blade of grass.

I forced myself to remain still, as more touches followed.

The stroking stopped. A minute or two passed. I heard a whisper, then the bar being quietly closed.

I was alone once more. I took a sip of water, shut my eyes and tried to rest.

* * *

I awoke with a start, seeing painted faces in front of me, feeling hands hauling me to my feet.

Men with feathers in their hair, their costumes not the dull browns I'd seen before, but brightly coloured. Shades of red, green, and blues. Decorated with beads and shells. Their best finery to enjoy the show.

I was given a rough sort of jerkin, and told to put it on.

After I'd done so my captors led me from my prison into the open air, blinking as I emerged into the light, feeling the cool breeze on my face.

It was early morning. The sun not up yet. Only a few people and some scrawny looking dogs hanging around.

* * *

I wasn't roughly handled like when we first arrived, on the contrary I was guided gently with signs and the occasional soft touch on my arm until we reached a hut on the edge of the encampment.

If I hadn't known better I could have sworn the leading warrior bowed his head a little as if inviting me to enter, and the same again when I went inside, the door shut firmly behind me, leaving me alone once more.

The hut was considerably larger than the others in the village, and far better equipped than the one I'd been kept in. Open spaces in the roof and high on the walls, allowing the sunlight to stream in. A sort of tapestry showing hunting scenes with deer-like creatures, water, trees, and a ceremony of some sort taking place—small figures dancing round a fire.

The earth floor was covered with mats, and intricately decorated pots were scattered around. A large wooden tub stood in one corner. Several stools, a small table and a high backed chair, decorated with carvings of plants and animals, in the middle.

I hoped, having been left on my own, that I'd be able to find some material or a sharp object to strangle or cut myself with, but this was not to be. There was nothing that could be used for such a purpose.

I picked up one of the stools, feeling the weight of it, thinking to try knocking my brains out, but could not summon up the courage to do it.

Exhausted, I slumped down on the stool, and waited.

* * *

The door swung open. I could see several of the men dressed in their beads and feathers, waiting outside and staring at me.

Two of them came in, one patting the large chair in the middle of the floor, indicating me to sit on it.

No, I hadn't been mistaken the first time. There it was again, the head bowed, even lower than before, from both of the braves.

It's strange, is it not, how in times of trouble we cling to the slightest prospect of relief. So considerate were they of my wellbeing that for a moment I thought they were about to embrace me, take me to their bosom, all the bad blood between us forgiven and forgotten.

The moment passed and reality intruded once again. Who was I kidding? Of course there was no grounds for optimism. All they were doing was in their savage way granting me the respect you give to a condemned man. Relaxing me, so I wouldn't struggle too much and give up the fight for life too quickly.

They retreated backwards, bowing again, before standing to attention on either side of the door, heads lowered, eyes fixed on the floor but, I was sure, aware of my each and every movement.

It was then I decided that if an opportunity arose either before or after they took me from the hut, I would try to grab one of the knives I'd seen hanging at the guards' belts and try my best to hurt or kill as many of them as possible before taking my own life.

I was trying to think how best to accomplish this when there was a commotion outside, and the door opened again.

In my panic I almost leapt out of the chair, only sitting down when I realised it was two elderly women carrying dishes of hot, steaming food, and a couple of small earthenware pots, one large, one small.

All was carefully set down on the table in front of me, after which, eyes averted, accompanied by the now familiar inclination of the head, they retreated as the guards had done, backwards, towards the door.

* * *

The food smelled excellent, not like the cold, tasteless gruel they'd been dishing out to me the past few days. Two kinds of meat, the taste, unfamiliar to me, maize and several other sorts of vegetables.

Although very hungry, I had to force the first mouthfuls down, so knotted with fear was my stomach. Then the juices kicked in and I started to wolf it up, smacking my lips, the juices running down my chin and onto my chest, not giving a damn what the guards thought, the both of them standing, like statues, not moving, heads still bowed to the floor.

To hell with it, I thought, exaggerating the noise of my eating even more, smiling to myself despite my despair, as the phrase—"the condemned man ate a hearty meal"—flashed through my mind.

I took a sip from the larger pot to wash the food down—it was water—before trying the smaller one.

I guessed it could be alcohol, and I was right. Strong. Somewhat bitter to the taste, but not unpleasant.

I drank the lot, thinking no doubt that was exactly what the devils wanted. To dull my pain, at least at the beginning of the process, so I didn't succumb too easily.

Outside I could hear the sounds of the village coming to life. Dogs barking. Chatter. Laughter. The cries of children.

All the people, no doubt enjoying themselves, looking forward to the day's festivities.

Damn them, I thought. Damn the whole fucking lot of them to hell. Whatever they did to me I would try my best to comport myself like a man, giving them as little pleasure as possible at my discomfiture.

Then I remembered the screams from the day before and my heart sank.

After all I hardly cut an impressive figure. Short. Twisted. A slight limp.

And, worst of all, the horrible, great, ugly lump I carried on my back.

No. There would be no heroics. They would enjoy their fun, and I would die screaming for mercy just like all the others.

* * *

The door opened again, and some women entered, their long dark hair decorated with feathers and bright coloured cloth, coming swiftly towards me, eyes cold and determined.

I remembered what one of the posse had said. That the Apache women were even crueller than the men.

I flinched away from them. Too late. They already had their hands on me. Strong, solid hands holding me down, the back of the chair pressing into my back, one grasping the back of my neck so tightly that I was unable to move my head more than a fraction from side to side.

I screamed, all thoughts of comporting myself like a man forgotten, as the glint of a blade appeared before me moving closer and closer towards my face.

As I closed my eyes to block out whatever horror it was they had in store for me I felt a gentle pull to my hair. Nothing else. Then a second one, followed by another. No pain, not even discomfort.

Plucking up my courage I opened my eyes a fraction to see something dark drifting down in front of them. A piece of hair, a second, and a third, falling slowly onto the wooden floor.

I could hear the women talking amongst themselves. Happy, laughing, as my head was pulled this way and that, and a veritable cascade of hair fell past my half open eyes.

Although I couldn't see or even touch myself, my hands still being pinned to my sides, I reckoned by now all my long, thick locks had been shorn off. My hair, the only part of me I was truly proud of, all gone.

I was pathetic. I had lived pathetic, and I would die pathetic.

I felt a deep despair well up within me. So deep it took all my willpower to hold back the tears.

No. No tears. At least I could refuse them the satisfaction of seeing that.

Beard and moustache followed, the blade sharp as a razor. A caress across my face causing my flesh to creep when I thought of what was to follow. The cutting and slicing, the burning.

After it was done one of the old crones came in to sweep the floor clean.

But if I thought they were finished with me, I was mistaken.

More women arrived carrying pots of boiling water, which they proceeded to pour into the tub until it was full almost to the brim, the steam rising to the roof of the hut, then pulled off my jerkin, seemingly in no way concerned at my nakedness, and manhandled me into the tub.

I winced as the hot water touched my skin, but the women ignored me as they went about their business. Serious now, silent, just the sound of their breathing as they set about washing me, water spilling over the sides of the tub. Rubbing me with bunches of leaves and twigs, my private parts, hump and all, up and down, up and down, until I glowed red and warm.

Helped me out. Dried me. Slipped a long sleeveless garment over my head. Not like the one I had before. This one shorter, wheat coloured, almost white, with beading round the edges.

It was finished. They sat me down in the high chair before withdrawing, eyes averted, leaving me alone with the guards.

* * *

A short time passed before the door opened, and the guards helped me to my feet, and led me from the hut, the men who were crowding round the doorway making way as we came through.

It was warm outside, the sun shining brightly now, dazzling my eyes for a moment. I didn't know if it was because of the hot relaxing bath they'd given me, or the effects of the alcohol I'd drunk, but I felt strangely calm as I looked around me.

I could hear birds singing, and somewhere in the distance water babbling over stones, the sounds sharp and clear. Everything was clean and unsullied, the hills near the camp covered with thickly growing vegetation; a few small clouds moving serenely across an otherwise clear sky; the grass at the edge of the village, a rich, green carpet, moving slightly in the breeze.

The world, this filthy, rotten world I'd endured for so long, and that I was shortly to leave for good, had never seemed so beautiful.

* * *

Two of the men took me by the arms and led me as docile as a child through the village which was completely deserted, silent.

No-one spoke. All I could hear was the breathing of the men beside me and the occasional footsteps of the other warriors who were following some distance behind.

The silence, though, didn't last for long. It was broken by the sound of drums and chanting as we made our way towards the edge of the village.

Ahead of us I could make out drummers and people whirling and singing, kicking up great clouds of dust as they danced. Stopping as they saw me approach. Turning in my direction. Stopping. Turning.

I made a grab for the knife at the belt of the guard nearest me.

Hands clutched at me. Too late. I'd already grasped the handle of the weapon. I lashed out blindly, hearing with pleasure a cry of pain, and another.

Just one more. Let me get one more of the bastards, then they can do whatever they want with me.

I lashed out again, felt a blow to my back, staggered, was pushed forward, and forced down on the ground.

* * *

There was shouting all around as I was dragged to my feet. I saw one of the guards holding his arm, blood dripping through his fingers, and another with a slash to his cheek, before they pulled me along, still struggling, to where the crowd was thickest. People stepped aside to let me pass, heads bowed, the occasional hand brushing across my hump.

* * *

Four men, chiefs or elders of the tribe, I guessed by the quality of their robes and ornaments, were awaiting me, seated in the middle of an open space, a kind of grove surrounded by trees. A fire, the coals glowing red, was in a circle of stones beside them.

Half a dozen younger men each shaking a sort of rattle, and chanting in high, keening voices were standing to one side of the grove, wearing masks in the guise of a buffalo, bear, hawk, and some kind of cat or puma, dark, empty spaces where the eyes and mouth should have been.

This garb, which at another time and circumstance would have struck me as being almost clownish, struck the very fear of God into me. My knees gave way, and I almost fell. Somehow I managed to force myself to remain standing, the men on either side holding my arms to steady me, as the terrifying creatures approached, stamping their feet and shaking their rattles, circling round me while the drumming and chanting started again, faster, louder, more urgent than ever.

Round and round. Round and round, till I was dizzy from it, when suddenly the drumming and stamping stopped, the quiet even more menacing than the cacophony of sound that proceeded it, as two braves, the ones I'd attacked, still bleeding from the injuries I'd inflicted on them, appeared in front of me.

"So", I thought. "They're to be given the honour of giving me the first cut or blow. Well then, get on with it, damn you. Start your filthy business."

And sure enough, a knife appeared in the hand of the warrior I'd wounded on the cheek. While two of the masked creatures held my arms so I was unable to move, he passed his blade across my right palm, in an almost tender fashion, the shallow cut drawing a thin line of blood. Not much of a wound I couldn't help thinking as I looked down, no doubt the gentle start to the long, devilish, process.

Superficial as the wound was I winced with pain when one of the masked creatures forced my hand up and pressed it hard against the slash on the brave's cheek, holding it there until our blood mingled together.

* * *

More dancing and chanting ensued, followed by the cut on my hand being held against the arm of the other guard I'd hurt.

When it was done my hand was bound up tight, the flow of blood staunched, and I was led to the elders, priests, or whatever the devil they were, who proceeded to present me a bowl full to the brim with a clear, yellowy liquid.

"What the hell." I thought, and took a sip. Alcohol. Sweeter than what I'd drunk in the hut. I drained it in a couple of gulps.

I heard cheers and clapping; felt hands touching me; the crowd opening up once more, bowing low and nodding as I was led to a tall carved chair, similar to the one in the hut. Two of the chiefs taking it in turns to speak to the people, before turning to me, smiling.

Smiling? Surely I must've been mistaken, the alcohol playing tricks on my mind.

All of a sudden I felt drowsy, barely able to keep my eyes open, as though some force was pressing the lids together.

This was all wrong. Surely they should be keeping me alert, so I could feel the pain of each and every cut and burn, that is . . . unless it was a method of having my senses numbed, so as to prolong my agony.

Of course, that's what it was. I cursed my foolish stupidity in taking what my tormentors had offered.

The sun felt hot on my face, sweat was pouring down my body. The faces crowding about me were blurred and unnatural, the sound of their voices and the beating of the drums muted and faint.

I closed my eyes, and tried to think of something other than the horror that was awaiting me.

* * *

The air is clear and fresh here. No ramshackle buildings clutter the landscape. Birds and animals come and go as they please.

I'm already learning to speak the Indians' language. Not well yet, but sufficient to let my needs be known and express simple opinions.

My brothers in the tribe respect me. They've given me a wife, a sweet young girl, loyal and affectionate, who administers to all my needs. I've come to prefer her dark skin and black hair to those pale, blond girls in our town I used to so yearn for, who would flounce by ignoring me, noses in the air, or even worse, stare at me unashamedly, not bothering to hide the pity in their eyes.

And on those rare occasions when one of them deigned to smile or even, joy of joys, exchange a few words with me, thinking about it afterwards, lying hour after hour in my room—that horrible room looking out over the main street; noisy when they threw the men out of the bars at night; rutted from the hooves of horses and the wheels of carts and wagons; choking, dusty in the summer; muddy in the winter—daydreaming, hoping, she might one day show me some favour.

Nonsense of course. Pure nonsense. Not one of them ever did.

* * *

My name, as near as I can translate it, means "broken big back", appropriate, for in the end, it was the very thing, my damned hump, that had cursed me from the day of my birth, that was the saving of me.

The moment the Apache saw it a debate raged as to whether I should live or die, those arguing for keeping me alive eventually prevailing. For what is a deformity to us is considered holy by them on account of a legend they have about a humpbacked god who lives in the mountains above the snow and has control over the mist, and most importantly the rain.

It is not for me to scoff at this belief as it saved my life, and, as I've written here before, I've never had much time for religion, so I guess theirs is as good for me as any other.

* * *

Although still somewhat awkward, my skills on horseback—they ride bare-back—and with the rifle—have greatly improved under the patient tuition of two of the braves who've been given the job of instructing me in the ways of the tribe.

I've even started to use the throwing clubs and tomahawk. Their bows though, I find too difficult to draw on account of my deformity.

I'm not obliged to, but if the mood takes me I sometimes ride out with the men of the tribe early in the morning, hunting for deer or buffalo, joking and laughing as we gallop our ponies, carrying our supplies with us—dried meat, and roasted corn cobs. Free. Unconstrained. No longer embarrassed to show myself to my fellows.

And now my wife is pregnant, I am considered a true man by my brothers and sisters.

None of this, not one part of it, possible if I'd stayed in that awful god-for-saken town, where everyone knew what I was, a good for nothing cripple, all, or nearly all of them, I was convinced, laughing and gossiping behind my mis-shapen back.

* * *

My knowledge can, I think, be as useful to the tribe as theirs is to me.

I know about the ways of the world, and can advise them in their dealings with the various businessmen, among them no doubt a fair sprinkling of rogues and rascals, who, when things eventually settle down and they manage to over-come their fears of the Apache, will wish to trade with us. And the sweet-tongued land agents and government officials who I'm sure, will one day appear promis-ing much, but delivering little, for in their very deepest hearts I truly believe none of them wish any good for the red man.

For the time being, though, any thoughts of trade or negotiations are far from our mind. We are at war, and although they don't force me to take up arms against my fellow whites, I often do, proud to use whatever skills I possess to help my people, proud to wear the war paint, my pony decked out with bright coloured streamers, riding out to ambushes or other attacks.

Under pressure from the army, a much more difficult proposition than the rag-taggle posse I was a part of, we've been forced to leave our village and retreat to more remote areas in the hope of avoiding our tormentors.

* * *

Winter is approaching. Cold. Little food. And now, as they are coming against us in greater numbers, we have to move on again.

Travelling to secret places through the forests, hills and rocks, across rivers and lakes, quiet and swift as the animals that we worship—lynx and bear; wolf, hawk and eagle.

* * *

I've discovered I have a gift for weaving and basket making, and am surprisingly nimble in the sewing and decorating of our garments, no doubt due to the days I spent at home as a sickly child, helping my mother with her daily chores, the peeling and stripping, the scraping and polishing.

My most important roles though are assisting the priests, who they call medicine men, in ceremonies such as the great feast of the corn dance, and in dealing with the captives who are bought to the camp from time to time. A task my nimble fingers seem well suited for.

Castrating. Pegging out on anthills. Skinning alive. Impaling, and all the rest of the pain we have learned to inflict on those of our enemies unlucky enough to fall into our hands

Oh, my brothers, how they yell and scream when they see my bent, twisted figure coming towards them, carrying the knives and sharpened sticks that are the tools of my trade, and, struggling ineffectually against their bonds, watch me prepare the fire and the hot stones, never supposing that the fearsome painted beast, who so carefully and painfully administers to them, is one of their own.

Cop

All of them were *his* boys, though he always thought of some as more special than the others.

And why did he think some were more special than the rest? It was certainly not affection. If truth be known he couldn't stand the rotten so and so's. Scumbags and thieves the lot of them.

No, it was just that his special ones, usually the older, more experienced boys who'd been with him longer, gave him better and more regular information. Even, on occasions, real nuggets, leading to arrests and convictions.

And as for him calling them his boys. Boys? They were hardly boys. A few were already into their thirties. A couple even older. Involved in petty crime. Shoplifting. Fencing goods. The odd mugging or break-in. Nothing too serious. Low level stuff he didn't give a damn about. Only that the information they gave him was useful, in exchange for his turning a blind eye to their activities.

In fact what they told him was, for the most part, pretty pathetic, but occasionally, very occasionally, they came up with a nugget of gold glistening amongst the rubbish. A tip off of a more serious crime going down. A drug deal or a heist. Sometimes a person on the up who needed keeping an eye on.

He paid them small amounts in exchange for information. For his special boys regular sums with bonuses for the good stuff, but as far as he was concerned they were all cunning, devious, little bastards who you had to watch like a hawk, each of them needing extremely careful handling throughout their relationship.

Relationship? You couldn't dignify it as such. He was under no illusions. The only thing they were interested in was his money and his ability to keep them out of trouble. They weren't doing this because they liked him. On the contrary. He guessed most of them hated his guts. Whatever help they chose to give him was purely for his pay offs and protection, and more often than not their real reason was to settle a score or improve their position in the particular pile of shit where they conducted their activities.

* * *

He'd laid down a few rules. His rules. No-one else's. No violence, well, at least no serious violence, particularly to women and kids. No drugs. Fat chance—but nothing he wanted to hear about. And crucially, not a word to another living soul about their arrangements. That included everyone—brothers, mates, girlfriends, and certainly not other villains.

He wondered if they took a blind bit of notice, but any infractions he did hear about he came down heavy, and all their moaning and threats about exposing him for allowing them to break the law, counting for nothing.

"Say what you want." He'd tell them. "I'll deny it. And who in their right mind would believe the word of a scumbag like you against mine?"

Adding for good measure that if they gave him any trouble he'd spread the word that they were snouts for the police.

More important was that they clearly understood that playing him around wouldn't be tolerated. If the information dried up or they failed to tell him something they should have done, his money and his protection would stop and he'd come down on them like a ton of bricks. And on the occasions when that happened he made sure every one of the little toe rags knew about it.

* * *

In the end it was the money that was the problem. It was always the money. It was money that caused the trouble with his wife, or more precisely, finished it off with her. Trouble that had been brewing for years.

It happened when he was forty nine, a year before he was due to retire from the force—you had to go at fifty if you'd joined the force on leaving school whether you wanted to or not.

Only one more year to go, thank goodness. The bureaucracy was worse than ever. There were more and more lawyers, more and more rules and regulations. Be careful of this, watch out for that. More and more paperwork. You couldn't draw breath without written permission. And then—if, despite all the obstacles, you were lucky enough to get a conviction—some old fart of a judge handing out a derisory sentence, and, of course, a good ticking off. As if that scared a hardened criminal one iota, or would sufficiently compensate him for all the months of hard work, the late nights and weekends he'd put in to nail the bastard.

* * *

When he'd started on this game he'd ruled the streets. Now he was the one who had to watch his every step. And recently, on top of everything else, funding was tight. He'd been made to cut back on the money he was paying to informers, and besides, as one pipsqueak of a lawyer told him with a superior smile, the input of such people was often useless or tainted, and these days, computers and other advanced sources of information were far more valuable than relying on petty villains

Yeah, he wanted to say. Advanced sources. Like the ones that forgot to deport several hundred foreign criminals, and warned us about September eleventh or the London bombings. But he'd held his tongue. No point in making a fuss. It was a bloody waste of time. Like hitting your head against a brick wall.

* * *

His two kids had left home years ago. Settled down. His wife was bored, and though she never said it to his face, was, he guessed, worried about the state of their finances when he retired, and dreading the thought of him hanging around the house all day. She'd already started bothering him with talk about what he could do to supplement his pension. Maybe, she suggested, he could get work at a private detective agency, or one of the government regulators—she'd heard they were always on the lookout for experienced men.

He nodded, promising he'd do something about it nearer the time, though, to be honest, the thought of going into a new job didn't appeal one bit. New systems to learn, new masters to report to and people to deal with, mostly younger than him. Lawyers. Administrators. Accountants. He'd been fighting the bastards since he joined the force at seventeen.

Didn't he deserve some time off, for Christ's sake? Put his feet up for a few months when he retired. Maybe learn to play golf, do a bit of fishing, or get some other hobby before he started looking around for something else. Hobby? Who was he kidding?

* * *

Without telling anyone in his department he'd started supplementing the payments to his informers with amounts from his own pocket after the budget had been cut. He thought of them as "top ups". Absolutely against regulations of course, though after all, he thought, his superiors shouldn't complain—privatisation is all the rage isn't it?

Only small sums at first, but these things have a habit of growing. His bank account became more and more frequently overdrawn. No, not "*his* bank account", "*their* bank account" that he stupidly shared with his wife.

She confronted him waving the latest bank statement, demanding to know who was the tart he was paying money to. He didn't disillusion her, and swore he'd stop immediately, which he did, only to transfer money from a joint savings account to a new account set up in his name alone, which acted as the source of the top up payments to his boys.

Inevitably this new arrangement was discovered after a few months. His wife challenged him head on, accusing him of stealing from her, for good measure throwing in his face his two "indiscretions", as she called them, from the past, and finally, having so to speak, gained the moral high ground, telling him with a glint of triumph in her eyes, that she was leaving him.

She'd met a widower at one of her church committees.

"A nice, honest man who'll look after me." She said. "Not a miserable specimen who first ought to clean himself up before trying to save the world. Not a thief and a liar who's rarely at home, and never took me out or on holiday for fear that missing a couple of weeks at work would stop him finding the Holy Grail."

There was nothing he could say. He moved out to a rented flat the next weekend.

* * *

The divorce followed quickly. His share of their savings accounts and the proceeds from the sale of their home was just about enough to purchase a flat in an inexpensive part of town without the need for a mortgage.

He was now only a few months from retirement, and a letter from his wife's lawyer informed him that she expected half his pension, both the lump sum and the monthly income, to be paid over to her. He felt like telling the lawyer it wasn't his wife who'd had to work all hours of the day and night, and risk a knife in the ribs or a beating, but he didn't have the strength for a fight.

He signed the agreement to the split.

One night, a couple of months after he'd moved into his new flat, in a moment of weakness he phoned the two women who his wife referred to as his "indiscretions". One had moved away some years earlier. No forwarding address. The other had remarried, telling him in no uncertain terms to leave her alone, or, and he had to smile at this, she'd have the police set on him.

* * *

He was on his own now. About to retire.

He'd always thought of the boys as his legacy, nurturing and developing them, probably spending more time on them than his own kids, hoping to entrust them to his successor when he went, yet here he was, about to hand them over to some young whippersnapper so wet behind the ears he wouldn't be able to fight for the resources or have the nous to know how to use them.

The network he'd so painstakingly built up over the years would be lost in a matter of months maybe just a few weeks, either because some lawyer reckoned the informers were a waste of time or some slimy, faceless bureaucrat had been told to cut the budget.

It killed him to think of all that hard work being thrown away. Well. He wouldn't settle for the scraps from their table. If they were determined to louse up his operations, they left him no alternative but to fill the gap himself.

To hell with it. They were still his boys. *His* boys. After all, he thought, once he'd left the force he'd have more than enough time to pursue whatever lines of enquiry he thought fit without the distractions of mundane tasks, paperwork, and those damned political and organisational winds that blew with increasing regularity throughout the force.

He'd carry on paying them.

Yes, that was the answer. He'd keep his boys going on the quiet. That's what he would do. And to hell with the consequences.

* * *

So once he'd retired there was no break, no month in the sun or days on the golf course.

He continued the relationship with his boys as if nothing had happened, letting them think he was still on the force, paying their monthly retainer out of his own pocket. But only the special ones. There was no way he could afford the rest. In any case he'd had to hand over some names to his superiors to avoid suspicion.

He did the figures. His needs were small. Food. Expenses for the flat. The running of the second hand car he'd purchased out of his share of the pension lump sum. If he was careful his police pension, what was left after his wife had taken her cut, should be sufficient to carry on paying the remaining boys.

All of this completely against the rules now he was no longer with the police, and if he was ever found out, well, someone with his background impersonating an officer was a jailable offence.

So why take such a risk?

If you'd asked him he probably would have said he hadn't asked to retire at fifty. There was still plenty of work to be done. He was still fit, and, most important of all, there were villains roaming the streets who needed to be stopped. He would have bridled at the word "vigilantism", insisting all he was doing was undertaking a little investigation and information gathering in his spare time and at his own expense with the intention of handing the results over to the authorities when he learned something that could be of interest to them.

Things, though, rarely work out as we expect.

* * *

It soon became clear that, with the limited funds at his disposal, his bank account couldn't stand the strain of the regular payments he was obliged to make to keep the boys sweet. What a fool, to think he could continue with this on such inadequate resources.

He lay awake at night mulling over the alternatives.

Take out a mortgage on the flat? He'd still have to find the monthly interest and repayments. Equity release? Possibly. He'd seen an article in the paper about how you could release funds against the value of your property, and went so far as having a meeting with one of the larger operators of such schemes—he preferred dealing with companies he knew.

Despite his mistrust of such arrangements he was seriously thinking about going for it, actually preparing to sign, when he had an unexpected stroke of luck. A family tragedy. A childless aunt and uncle in their late sixties who he barely knew died in a car crash, intestate, enabling him to share their estate with two distant cousins who he saw for the first and last time at the funeral.

It turned out the old couple had built up quite a little empire. A couple of houses rented out in their town on the coast; shares they'd held for a number of years, now worth a tidy sum; cash in various banks and building societies. Expecting twenty, maybe thirty thousand pounds from their small old-fashioned bungalow he in fact received what turned out to be a pretty substantial amount even after the legal expenses and tax on the estate had been paid. Once the shares and properties were sold and everything settled his share came to over a hundred and ninety thousand.

Why on earth they hadn't spent more of their carefully hoarded cash he had no idea, but he drank a toast to their frugality, which meant he didn't need to look for work, re-mortgage his flat, or put into effect any other of the hair-brained schemes he'd been mulling over. He could devote all his time and resources to his hobby, as he called it.

* * *

His hobby. Barely the right word for something that consumed most of his waking hours, seven days a week, day in, day out, rain or shine. How could you call it a hobby, when the first thing he did when he got the cheque from the lawyers was buy an untraceable gun with a silencer and a box of bullets from one of his contacts (for protection, he told himself), making sure the fellow well understood that he wouldn't hesitate to tell the police about the business he was up to if he dared breathe a word to anyone about what had transpired.

Next he found a cheap room with its own shower and kitchen facilities in a converted house a few miles from where he lived, where he could keep the gun, his files and press cuttings and other bits and pieces so nothing incriminating would be found if for any reason his flat was ever searched.

He took the room using the forged passport and driving licence he'd obtained – top quality, no questions asked—under an assumed name for several thousand from one of his old contacts, making sure he paid the agent cash each month on the dot. The landlord was absent, living abroad, so as long as he paid up on time and behaved himself it was unlikely he'd be be disturbed.

Oh yes he knew all the tricks. It was now a question of using them to his advantage.

* * *

Months passed. Some results. Anonymous calls to the police or customs making sure he always used phone boxes or pay-as-you go mobiles purchased for cash. Speaking into one of those contraptions that disguised your voice.

Tipping them off about drugs deals going down, several houses where trafficked girls were being held, the whereabouts of lorries used to transport stolen goods, a warehouse where smuggled cigarettes and booze were stored. Good, solid, useful stuff, but nothing to get excited about though. Nothing to make his head spin or his spirits soar.

Inevitably there'd been one or two problems.

Like the time he stupidly forgot to leave his gun in the car when he went into his bank, setting off the alarm. Only avoiding serious trouble because he knew the manager and lied his way out of it, though the look on the man's face made him wonder if on further reflection the flimsiness of his explanation would become obvious.

Sleepless nights followed wondering if he'd be called down to the station to explain why on earth an ex-policeman was carrying a gun on the street, but in the event nothing happened.

There was a break-in when he was out of his flat. A few things taken. Nothing important. He didn't report it of course, and thanked providence he had all his important stuff in the rented room, though, as an added precaution, he waited till the other tenants were out, installed an extra lock, and rigged up an alarm system inside.

* * *

He carried on paying his boys, making sure that none of them knew about the others he was using. At this rate, he calculated, with the money he'd inherited this could last ten, fifteen years, maybe more. And by that time he probably wouldn't care anymore.

He carried on registering successes. Phone calls that disrupted the villains' activities for a while, some of them, he hoped, getting worried by now at the leaks that were interfering with their plans. Tip-offs that helped put people away. Only the small fry though. The foot soldiers, not the big shots. They were too far away from the action to be caught by the likes of him.

He knew who they were, though. And one day, he promised himself, he would settle scores with them.

* * *

At the end of the first year he treated himself to slap-up meal and a good bottle of burgundy, raising his glass and silently toasting his efforts as he sat alone in the restaurant, the laughter and conversation of the other diners passing him by.

He ordered another bottle.

What was that quote he'd heard in a film once?

"Down these streets a man must go. . . . "

He couldn't remember the rest of it. Something about a man on his own, lonely, doing his job, confronting the evil all around him. Honest. Incorruptible. Just like he saw himself, swimming against the tide of filth and lawlessness that was engulfing society. The trash swirling around under the surface like one of those submerged villages that had disappeared under water when the building of a dam flooded a valley. There, but invisible. A hint of something below, just a brief glimpse of it when the tide changed or the rains failed and you could see the roof of a house, or the steeple of a church emerge for a few hours, maybe even for several days before disappearing from sight once more.

You only had to look around you, for God's sake. The run-down estates. The graffiti. The parks laid waste by vandals. The tide of drugs and people trafficked in.

And the ones he really hated. The white collar criminals and money launderers. The bent accountants and bankers.

They made him sick. Criminals the lot of them. Able to employ the best lawyers. Every detail of the prosecution's case scrutinised for the slightest weakness or irregularity. After all, the law was the law, and if even the slightest breach was found, all you had to do was step through the gap into the sunshine—a free man.

And if you were unlucky or stupid enough to get caught in the first place, and even unluckier to be sentenced, with good behaviour you could be out in half the time set, and in the meantime run your enterprise from your cell and drool on the money that would be waiting for you when you walked out the prison gate.

And what about the times when he could have been at home, warm and comfortable? Instead he was sat in his car, freezing, chewing on a cold hamburger or a tasteless supermarket sandwich, watching them drawing up to their houses and restaurants in their big cars, escorting their sleek, attractive, well dressed women into the warmth, part of him wishing he could be inside with them.

And even more depressing on those few occasions when he permitted himself to think about it—what exactly was it that he was protecting?

Ignorance. Greed. Human frailty. People with their faces deep in the trough.

He sometimes wondered if it was worth the effort.

Think positive. Think positive, damn you.

* * *

His luck started to run out.

Two of his boys, arrested in quick succession, came to him for help that he could no longer offer.

"Put in a word for me." One of them said.

"C'mon, man. Help me out. I can't go inside again." Said the other.

And he mumbled that he would.

Who was he kidding?

Face facts.

No illusions.

And then, disaster. He was caught red-handed paying off one of his informants, and for added good measure recorded on camera. Not a leg to stand on.

He had no idea who'd tipped the police off. He guessed it was one of the bastards he'd promised to protect, and hadn't.

"A man of your experience ought to have known better." The magistrate told him. "Impersonating a police officer is a serious crime, particularly where the person concerned has previously been a member of the force."

* * *

He was committed for trial in the new year. Granted bail after his solicitor had stressed his years of loyal service and lack of previous convictions.

The only good thing was that the search of his flat yielded nothing. The rented room with his papers, files, newspaper cuttings, as well as the gun, was safe. This he did not mention even to his solicitor.

He went into a state of lethargy. Sleeping late. Not shaving. Only going out occasionally when he had to buy food and drink. Sitting for hours watching the telly.

* * *

He received the court order just before Christmas, the trial set for early April. He would, he was sure, be found guilty. Even without the contents of his room, the evidence against him was far too strong. A custodial sentence would be inevitable. Judges came down hard on policemen who went off the rails. He'd get two, three years minimum, maybe more. There was nothing the public liked better than seeing authority figures, or in his case, ex-authority figures, brought down and disgraced.

He'd be banged up with all the scum, living in constant fear of a knife in his back or a beating from those only too pleased to take out their frustrations on an ex-cop, alone and unprotected, conveniently placed in their midst. And if he did manage to get out in one piece, his information would be completely stale, his boys either gone or wanting nothing to do with him.

I know what I'll do, was his first reaction, as he lay in bed, the court letter lying crumpled on the floor where he'd thrown it. I'll defend myself. Tell them exactly what I think of them.

What was the point? I'll be a laughing stock, he thought. An old fool who couldn't give up playing cops and robbers.

It didn't bear thinking about.

But think is what he did. With a whiskey in his hand.

Within half an hour he'd made up his mind.

To hell with it, he thought, after picking up the letter and reading it a second time. I won't give them the pleasure, and think of all the money I'll be saving the country. They should put a plaque up in my honour he said to himself with a smile.

* * *

He cleaned and tidied his flat. The first time for a month.

Outside it was a cold, crisp December morning. Sunny and bright.

After a haircut and shave he walked to the rented room by a circuitous route, checking he wasn't followed.

The following day he bought some new clothes. Had his car cleaned inside and out. Started going to expensive restaurants. Met his son, daughter, their spouses, and their kids in town after the Christmas holidays, and treated them to a show followed by a meal.

They couldn't understand what had happened to him. Having moved away to different areas they had no idea of his appearance in front of the magistrates, which had warranted only the briefest of mentions in his local paper.

"Have you got a girlfriend, dad?" His daughter asked, as if that explained everything.

"Maybe." He replied.

"Let's do it again in a few weeks." He said, as they were going their separate ways. "I'll phone you in a couple of days, and we'll decide where you and the kids would like to go."

"Don't be shy dad. Bring her along." His son said with a smile, before disappearing into the underground.

He booked tickets for another show in March, a couple of weeks before the trial. The trial which would not take place.

* * *

He didn't have long. He would do what he'd decided before his trial, just before they put the clocks forward.

Luckily he still had the gun and ammunition. He wasn't a religious man, but he couldn't help wondering if some kind of providence or fate, whatever you chose to call it, had guided him towards acquiring them for this very purpose. In fact, if you were that way inclined, you could say it was God's work he was embarked upon. An eye for an eye. Punishing the evildoers. The wicked. Wasn't that what it was all about? None of this turning the other cheek. At least not to the trash he was dealing with.

* * *

He met up with his dwindling band of informants, explaining his lack of contact by telling them he'd had to go abroad on police work, paying them a fair bit more than usual, telling them he was under pressure to get results, praying none of them had seen the article in the newspaper.

* * *

Before his arrest three names had started to appear with increasing regularity in his boys' reports.

The first, and most dangerous, a major drug dealer and people trafficker.

Next, a loan shark, fence and racketeer.

Finally, a businessman who he'd known about from his days in the force. Low profile. Very clever. Fingers in a lot of pies—some legitimate, most not. Suspected to be involved in major money-laundering scams on behalf of both local and overseas criminals. Smurfing, false invoicing, overcharging. Every trick in the book you could think of.

He reckoned he'd need three, maybe four days, to deal with each one. In between he'd go to ground in the rented room for a few days until the fuss had died down a bit. The whole job done in a month, five weeks maximum.

And after, well, after he no longer gave a damn what happened to him. What was important was that he did the lot of them. Under no circumstances could he get caught before he'd properly finished the job. He couldn't allow that to happen. Precautions would be necessary. He wouldn't use his own vehicle for the hits—it was surprising how many criminals used easily traceable vehicles. He'd hire a car for cash using a forged licence—easy enough to acquire for a few hundred pounds. Always park some distance from the mark. Gloves would be worn and different clothes for each job, and he'd change his appearance each time through a simple disguise.

Once the killings were over he'd send a letter to a couple of national newspapers, before finishing himself off with the remaining bullets.

Nothing much else.

All he wanted was enough time to conclude what he'd set out to do, and then . . . Oblivion.

*   *   *

He'd never bothered to make a will, never seen much use for one. Things were different now. He made an appointment with a firm of solicitors. A name he'd found in yellow pages.

The woman he saw advised him that if he died intestate his children would inherit equally, although, she added, his estate would be much easier to administer if a will existed. After sitting down with her and doing a rough valuation of his assets—his flat, the cash he'd inherited, and various other bits and pieces, there was still a good amount left even after what he'd given his boys.

He signed a will there and then, nothing complicated, half to his son; half to his daughter.

*   *   *

Before he could do a thing the marks had to be tracked down.

He redoubled his efforts. Paid the boys more money. Stuck his head a little above the parapet.

A month passed. January went, cold and grey. Snow threatening but never falling heavily, just a couple of brief flurries.

February came. Nothing. He handed out more cash. Large amounts.

"What's the matter, guv?" One of the boys asked. "Won the lottery?"

Still nothing. Then, within the space of a week he had details on all three of them.

*   *   *

The drug dealer spent his weekdays in a luxury, portered, apartment near the centre of town, weekends at a place he owned in the country. Was driven around in a top of the range Mercedes, dark grey, its personalised number plate making identification easy. The driver, a big fellow, almost certainly a bodyguard, would need to be watched.

The businessman. His main factory and office, a front for several bent operations, located in a large warehouse on an industrial estate in the outer suburbs.

The loan shark would probably be the most difficult to corner. All that was known about him was he usually worked out of a building next to a second-hand car showroom he had an interest in, but spent a lot of time moving around to the various restaurants, pubs and clubs who owed him money.

* * *

"You're sure about all this?" He asked the boys who'd supplied him with the information. "Good. I'll pass this on to my team. We'll soon know if you've been lying. And then. . . . "

Rubbish of course, he wasn't planning to see any of them again, except for the one who had to try to find out where the loan shark would be on any given day.

* * *

He decided to deal with the drug dealer first.

He spent some time walking and driving round the area, inconspicuous in the crowds of shoppers and the heavy traffic. Found a health club across the road from the dealer's apartment block, and after checking it out, took an out of town membership for a month, paying cash, showing his forged driving license, his smart new suit giving weight to his story of being a visiting businessman.

There was a coffee shop on the first floor of the club which gave a good view of the entrance to the block. With all the comings and goings no-one took any notice of the middle-aged man having a snack and reading the paper. He ignored peoples' attempts to strike up a conversation with him, nobody's suspicions aroused by his impolite behaviour. That was the good thing about cities, as long as you didn't disturb them, nobody cared what your business was.

He had to watch the block on and off for three days before he was sure of the dealer's pattern of morning and evening movements.

His surveillance revealed the car arriving at six thirty on the first evening and leaving shortly after, but no sign of it on the subsequent two evenings when he watched up to eight o'clock before giving up.

The mornings were a different matter. The driver brought the car to the block at nine, give or take a few minutes. Regular as clockwork. Drove into the car park under the block and out again three or four minutes later with the dealer in the back.

He assumed the car wasn't left at the apartment because it was more convenient for the chauffeur to park it at his home overnight. He didn't care what the reason was, just as long as they stuck to the same routine every day.

* * *

The entrance to the car park was by way of a metal grill operated by a code which residents of the flats and their visitors punched in—much too far away for him to see what the numbers were. The good news though was you could slip inside in the time it took for the grill to descend after the car had moved through. It would have to be a quick in and out, in the hope that no-one would notice.

The bad news was the CCTV camera by the entrance. Impossible to dismantle without being spotted. However, if the people in the control room were actually watching—and he knew from past cases he'd worked on that often they weren't—they would have ten, maybe fifteen, screens in front of them. The chances of them seeing him in the few seconds it would take to sneak inside were extremely slim.

Getting out would be easier. There was a door by the side of the grill where you could exit into the street after parking your car. He was sure it would be opened by a simple catch from the inside.

* * *

Dress well, and the chances of anyone bothering you are reduced to almost zero.

His put on his best grey suit, a light blue shirt, and a suitably conservative tie. A blue cashmere overcoat that had cost him a fortune, and new shoes, well-polished.

For disguise, a wig. Longish hair, slightly greying, and glasses with plain lenses.

And finally, a brand new leather briefcase.

He looked at himself in the mirror.

A smart, middle aged businessman stared back at him.

Very distinguished.

* * *

He travelled by tube, getting off one station before the block of flats.

He strolled along the street, arriving at just after a quarter to nine. Stood on the corner, looked at his watch, and put the briefcase down on the pavement. Just a run of the mill businessman waiting for a colleague.

He looked at his watch again. Eight fifty five. No sign of the car.

Nine. Five past. Then, as his spirits started to sink, he caught a glimpse of the dark, slate grey vehicle slowly making its way through the traffic.

He looked around, picked up his briefcase, and walked a little behind the car, stopping briefly as it swung down the slight slope that led to the car park.

He waited at the corner as the driver's hand emerged to punch in the code, and the grill opened to let the vehicle in.

Once they were out of sight he sprinted down, slipping inside as the grill started to descend. In the unlikely event of anyone seeing him they'd probably assume he'd left something in his car.

He saw the brake lights glowing red ahead of him in the dim light of the garage as the car was manoeuvred into its parking spot.

The garage seemed deserted. He took the gun out of his coat pocket, and, crouching low, moved towards the car as the driver got out and opened the back door. The dealer, who must have been waiting in the garage for several minutes, muttered something to the driver as he stepped out of the shadows and slipped into the back seat.

It was time. He stood up and quickly came round the front of the car showing the gun to the driver before he got back inside saying "give me the keys", so they would think it was carjacking, not a hit.

No response.

"Give me the keys." He repeated.

The driver put his hand in his pocket. A glint of metal. A sudden burning on his left forearm where the bastard had cut him, the foolish prick.

He shot the driver twice. The silencer reducing the noise to a dull thud.

Hearing over the sound of the second shot the click of the car doors being locked from the inside, he bent down, took the keys from the driver's hand and opened one of the back doors.

The dealer, a small man cowering on the seat, eyes wide, his lips trying to talk, mumbling about giving him girls, money, whatever he wanted.

He barely listened as he aimed the gun.

"Filth." He whispered and shot the dealer once in the chest and twice in the head. Then, resisting the urge to spit on the body, put the gun back in his pocket, pressed the exit button to the garage and strolled unhurriedly into the crowds, hearing the police sirens in the distance a little later.

* * *

He jumped on the first bus that passed heading in the opposite direction to his room, and sat upstairs at the back, hoping no-one could see the dull red stain spreading on the arm of his overcoat.

Got off after a few stops. Went into a pub toilet. The cut was just a glancing blow, not as deep as it felt. Washed and cleaned it, and bound it up with his handkerchief. Took off his disguise and caught the underground home.

His hands didn't start to shake until he was back in his room, pouring antiseptic on his arm.

* * *

The killings made the news on TV that night. Shots of the flats and garage, and an appeal for witnesses—a sign, he hoped, that they didn't have any.

"A gangland murder." They called it. "The police were investigating."

Probably not too hard, he thought. Not when scum like the dealer were taken off the street. Not unless innocent bystanders were hurt or they feared this was the beginning of a turf war.

More about the driver than the dealer. A short interview with his young wife.

"Just an ordinary man doing his job." She said tearfully. "Gunned down like a dog."

He experienced a brief moment of shock when she said how their two children would miss him.

Then thought.

"Oh yes. An ordinary man. Then why was he carrying a blade and working for such trash?"

No-one was innocent.

* * *

He had a nightmare on the night of the killing.

He was in a rundown industrial estate. Ruined buildings. Broken glass. Debris everywhere. Quiet. Deathly quiet. The weather dull, overcast.

The sound of an engine. A car, with psychedelic designs all over it like the Rolls that belonged to one of the Beatles, moved slowly down one of the rubbish strewn streets, then stopped nearby, not more than ten yards away its engine ticking over.

There was just enough light for him to make out something sitting upright on the back seat. Large. Inhuman.

He knew he shouldn't approach the vehicle, but was drawn towards it.

He opened the car door. There was a deafening roar as the creature in the back rushed at him with irresistible force, knocking him to the ground.

A head appeared in front of him. Striped. Expressionless yellow eyes boring into him, mouth open, teeth bared, bending towards his. . . .

He woke up to the sound of screaming. It took him several seconds to realise it was his own voice.

* * *

Lying in bed half asleep, half awake, covered in sweat, feeling the beating of his heart slowly return to normal, he remembered a TV programme he'd seen a week or so before.

A forest, thick and green. Grasslands. Lakes and rivers. Hills.

Ruined palaces and lodges. Terraces and vestibules.

Chattering monkeys in the trees. Crocodiles sunning themselves on the river banks. Birds swooping low over the water. Deer, nervous, feet stamping, easily startled.

And ruling over them all, the tiger. Rarely seen. Greatly at risk from poachers and human encroachment.

Gliding, black and yellow, though the grass.

He'd wondered how such a magnificent creature could exist on this rotten earth.

* * *

Why not?

After gulping down a coffee and a piece of toast he went out and got some brochures from a travel agent and a couple of guide books from the local library.

After studying them for an hour or two back at his flat, he eventually chose a company, one of the more expensive ones—the cost of their holidays shocked him—that specialised in wildlife tours to India and the Far East.

He hurried back to the agent where he was told there was still availability on one of the company's tours, the one to Northern India that specialised in visiting a selection of game parks where tigers could be found. *Could* be found, the girl at the desk said, stressing there was no guarantee he'd actually see one, and he'd have to pay a single person's supplement which. . . .

"Yes. Yes." He said impatiently. "No problem. I'll take it"

"Have you got your passport with you Mr. . . . ?"

"Mr Norris."

Not his real name. Considered to be a flight risk he'd had to surrender his passport to the court. Thank Christ he'd got hold of a decent phony one when he started all this business.

He handed the passport over, and paying in cash, booked a two week holiday, flying out at the end of March, a few days after he should have finished his business, that is if everything went according to plan.

* * *

He phoned the solicitors the following morning.

In answer to his question the woman he'd seen before explained that any charitable bequests in his will would be free of inheritance tax.

"Right." He said, and arranged to come to see her later that afternoon.

His new will left a quarter of his estate to a charity dedicated to the conservation of tigers and other endangered species and the protection of their environment, stipulating the donation should be anonymous.

The balance, as before, to be split between his son and daughter.

* * *

He'd deal with the businessman next. Easier than the dealer. Or so he thought.

He waited outside the mark's factory in his hired car, quickly realising it would be impossible to do the job there, morning or evening. Far too many people coming and going, far too busy and exposed. All he would do was draw attention to himself by hanging around. No. The hit would have to be at or near the target's house.

* * *

The next day he followed the businessman to his home, a twenty minute drive away. A large detached house set well back from the road. Automatic gates. Alarm box on the wall and movement activated lights, but plenty of trees and shrubs for cover, and the garage separate from the house.

He watched the factory again the following day, but the mark didn't leave till much later. He decided it would be best do it in the morning when the businessman left for work.

All that was left was to stake out the house.

* * *

He parked by the common near the house for the next two mornings.

Saw the gates open just after eight on both occasions and the businessman's car speed by in the direction of the factory.

A man of regular habits. Good.

* * *

All this had taken longer than expected.

Time was moving on.

The job would have to be done as soon as possible.

Monday morning.

* * *

He found a way in over the weekend.

Walking in the woods near the house he'd located a couple of loose planks in the fence at the back of the property. After making sure no-one was around, he pried them and the ones above out a little, and stood behind a tree to listen. No sound of alarms or dogs barking.

* * *

Monday.

He left his vehicle in the car park next to the common shortly after dawn, and in the guise of an early morning walker, went through the woods to the fence. No disguise this time, just a cap pulled down tightly so as to partially hide his face.

It was cold for the time of year, and his feet crunched on the frozen grass while he located where the loose boards were. He could see surprisingly clearly in the half light. Not another soul about as he worked the planks loose and slipped through the narrow gap, remembering to push them back into place in case another walker noticed them.

There was already a faint glow in the east. Time to make his move before the sun came up. Staying close to the fence and keeping hidden behind the trees and bushes that lined the garden, he carefully made his way to the front of the house, concealing himself behind a clump of rhododendrons next to the garage.

He looked at his watch. Five to seven.

The dawn chorus of birds chirped and sang all around. A squirrel stopped just in front of him on the manicured lawn, then ran to the nearest tree.

A light went on upstairs at seven fifteen, and went off at seven thirty. He checked the gun and silencer. By now he could hear cars on the road outside. No problem. The hedge should give sufficient cover.

Ten to eight.

He was startled by the noise of the front door opening as the businessman came out, smartly dressed, dark overcoat, carrying a slim, tan coloured briefcase, walking the short distance to the garage, fumbling for his keys, shoes crunching on the gravel.

He grasped hold of his gun and emerged from behind the bushes.

Saw the front door still open, and . . . a girl of ten or eleven coming out yelling, "Daddy, wait for me." Dressed in a school uniform. Light blue and yellow. One of those posh schools, he found himself thinking.

Too late for hesitation. He could see the look of surprise on the man's face as he ran towards him. Saw him take something from the pocket of his overcoat. Metal. A gun.

He stopped immediately, aimed, and fired. The man stumbled, dropping his case, the gun slipping from his fingers.

Screaming from the girl.

He fired once more. This time the man went down. He went closer. Saw blood spreading on his chest, the eyes looking up as he shot him a third time.

More screaming. A woman. Youngish. In a pink dressing gown. Standing in the doorway. Beside her a boy. Tall. Tee shirt and jeans. Something slack, almost flabby, about his face.

The woman holding the boy's arms. Restraining him.

* * *

He turned and ran to the back of the house, pushing through branches and leaves, once almost falling, before he smashed his way through the fence, and staggered through the woods towards the car park.

He hadn't realised how out of condition he was. Panting after a minute or two. Chest heaving. Almost sick.

Relax. Take deep breaths. Five minutes before they contact the police. Another five minutes at least to get hold of a patrol car in the area. More time before the car arrived.

Put the gun in your pocket. Take the gloves off. Catch your breath. Slow down. You're a man taking a short stroll before going to work.

He smiled and nodded to a man walking his dog.

* * *

The car. He could see his car parked, but now with another one beside it. Don't rush. Take it easy. It's just the fellow you saw. Put your gloves on. Don't want to leave any prints.

His hands shook as he unlocked the door, though whether from cold or fear he couldn't have said.

He started the engine. Hid the gun under the seat. Drove off in the opposite direction to the house, joining the rush hour traffic.

Nothing. Not even a siren.

* * *

He left the car in a side road a couple of miles from his room. No-one would bother about it for several days, by which time everything would be over.

Home safe. Showered the sweat away. Slept till mid-afternoon. Tried to put the sound of the girl's screaming out of his head.

* * *

The story appeared on the evening news. Shots of the house cordoned off by the police.

"Man gunned down in front of his family."

In the absence of hard facts the piece concentrated on the cowardice and cruelty of whoever did the deed. The policeman in charge of the investigation indignant at this affront to a person's expectation of safety in their own home, particularly when the victim had been shot while his wife, young daughter and autistic son were watching.

Finally, a request for any witnesses to come forward so the perpetrator could be quickly brought to justice.

"Businessman shot on doorstep by lone gunman. Motive for murder unknown." His morning paper said.

No mention of the murdered man's real profession, or the gun he'd dropped at the scene of the crime.

* * *

Only one left now. The loan shark.

The boy who was keeping an eye on the mark told him that he spent the first part of the week in his office, visiting his other interests on Thursday, Friday, and the weekend.

He'd do him Tuesday morning.

He cut up some notepaper to the size of bank notes and put the pieces in an envelope together with some used ten and twenty pound notes picked up as change in shops and pubs. Never use money drawn from the bank, which could often be traced.

* * *

The office, if you could call it that, was a rundown building attached to a car showroom which was also owned by the loan shark. Wandering up and down at different times the previous week he'd noticed a brand new silver BMW convertible, which he assumed belonged to the fellow he was looking for, parked outside.

The main problem was the number of characters that wandered in and out the building during the course of the day. Not too many, but more than enough to disturb him. In the circumstances all he could do was go in early in the morning, at eight, an hour before the showroom opened, when he hoped things would be quieter.

This time he'd wear dark glasses, a baseball cap and a false moustache.

* * *

He went up the steps, gun in his pocket, the envelope with the money in his left hand, and pushed open the door.

A small office, bare, apart from a calendar on the wall. A man, unshaven, squat, tough looking, sitting behind a desk. One of the enforcers, he guessed. Behind him, another door, reinforced steel, by the look of it.

He waved the envelope in front of the bodyguard.

"It's what I owe Frank." He said, opening it to give a glimpse of the notes inside.

"What?"

"What I owe him. Frank Henderson."

"You pay on the street. Not here. . . . What's your name?"

"Gerry McArthur."

An old villain. The first name that came into his head.

"Wait a minute." The bodyguard said, reaching for the phone on the desk beside him.

He took out the gun and shot him. The man looked up in surprise as he slumped across the desk, mouth open, blood dripping on the drab, grey carpet.

He quickly replaced the phone and bent down beside the body. Yes. There it was. A button on the side of the desk. As he pressed it, there was a loud click from the door behind. He got to his feet and pushed it open.

Another room, similar to the first. An older man this time, leathery skin, puzzled expression at first, then getting to his feet, pulling a short bladed knife out of his pocket.

"Drop it." He said, levelling his gun at the man's head. "Or you'll join your chum in the front."

The knife clattered to the floor.

"Right." He said, keeping his voice low. "Easy now. No trouble. I just want to talk to Frank. Let me in."

"And what if I don't?"

He pressed the gun against the man's temple.

"I pull the trigger and I let myself in. Now, be a good chap, and open the door."

"Ok. Ok."

The bodyguard bent towards the desk and pressed a button. There was a loud buzzing noise followed by the sound of raised voices coming from behind the door.

He shot the bodyguard in the stomach. Looked down, and saw two buttons, one white, the other red. He pressed the white one and barged in.

Henderson and another man. Both on their feet. Henderson pulling at a drawer in his desk.

"Stop!" He shouted. "Police."

"What the. . . . " Henderson started to say, as he shot him at close range.

The other man began screaming. He hit him hard over the head with the gun, and after putting another two bullets into Henderson, walked out, slamming the door behind him. Past the bodyguards. One moaning in pain, the other quiet, not moving.

Through the car lot, pausing to glance at a couple of vehicles.

"Just looking around." He said to an approaching salesman, and walked out into the busy street for some distance before taking a bus back to his room, getting off a couple of stops earlier to throw the gun and remaining ammunition into a pond in the local park.

He didn't even bother to watch the evening news.

* * *

The next day he cleared the room, destroying his papers, files, and any other incriminating evidence, and later in the day he went to the agent, paying for another week plus a month's notice in cash, saying he'd been called up north on urgent business.

* * *

He met up with his children and grandchildren as arranged.

Had to turn away to hide his tears as they were saying their goodbyes.

"Did dad seem funny to you?" His daughter said to her husband as they were driving home. "I've never seen him like that before. I think he was almost in tears."

"D'you think so? Probably broke up with his girlfriend. Hey look—they've almost finished that new supermarket."

* * *

Maybe booking the trip to India was a mistake. He needed to go back to his flat to pack clothes for the hot weather the brochure told him to expect. Could the police have found something? Be waiting for him? Ready to grab him the moment he appeared?

"Come on." He thought. "Don't be stupid. There's nothing to link you to any of it."

He had to take the chance. He put on a simple disguise. Hat and glasses. Walked round the area. Checking.

No sign of any surveillance, although they could be in the van parked down the street or watching from one of the properties across the road.

He felt himself starting to panic, went to a cafe nearby and had a coffee to steady his nerves, going through it over and over in his head. No. There was nothing he could think of that led back to him. Except DNA. Those boffins could produce wonders out of nothing.

No. He was sure he hadn't left anything for them.

"Don't be such a damned fool." He told himself. "Better now than later. Do it, for fuck's sake."

One more look around and he was up the front steps and into the flat.

He dragged the suitcase out from under the bed. Threw clothes, shoes, some other gear inside. Sweating despite the chill.

Done. A glance out the window, and he was off to spend his last few days in the rented room.

* * *

Just one more thing left to do.

He phoned his son and daughter the next day to tell them he was going away for a couple of weeks.

"Where're you off to dad?" His daughter asked.

There was no point in lying.

"India."

"India? Why you going there?"

"I don't know really. I just fancied it."

* * *

The flight was long and boring.

He hadn't travelled much recently. When the kids were young it was different. They'd gone away every summer—touring or staying at the seaside. Even abroad a few times. Nothing too far away. Belgium. Northern Spain. France twice.

Once the children left home he hadn't taken all the leave due to him. Too busy, he told his wife. And when he did have time off he usually just pottered about the house or garden doing odd jobs. His wife complained. Took herself off to her sister's in Devon a couple of times a year.

He'd preferred to stay at home or go to work. That's where his life was. On the street with his boys.

* * *

They landed at night.

The heat hit him immediately he got off the plane, the fans in the customs hall barely making an impact. Hundreds of people milling around, talking, yelling, carrying luggage. It was not until he'd got onto the air-conditioned coach with the other people on the tour that he felt a little more comfortable.

* * *

He sat on his own near the back during the hour's ride to the hotel, the other passengers, mainly younger than him, already laughing and talking to each other.

The streets were in darkness, only alleviated by the weak lights of the small shops and restaurants that lined the road, some of the signs in English, others in a script he couldn't understand. The buildings were mostly white with cracked plaster peeling off the walls, some garishly painted in yellows, blues and pinks. Dark hordes of men, women, and, although it was late, children, crowded the sidewalks, wandering this way and that, shouting, gesticulating. Bicycles. Thin white cattle. Battered looking cars, the occasional gleaming four by four, incongruous on the narrow potholed streets.

* * *

The lights of the town soon faded away, the road no longer paved, only lit by their coach's headlights, trees and people emerging without warning from the darkness from time to time, disappearing into the gloom as quickly as they'd materialised.

"Only another few minutes, ladies and gentlemen." Said the courier who'd met them at the airport.

Bright lights in the distance as their coach swung off the road through double gates, a uniformed attendant saluting as they passed up the drive towards a big, well lit building with parapets and towers all around.

Attendants rushing to help them off the coach, while others unloaded the luggage and followed them into the entrance lobby where the travellers were offered cold drinks and warm towels to refresh themselves. A painting of a roaring tiger gazed down on them from behind the reception.

* * *

His room was large and well appointed. A basket of fruit, flasks of tea and water, and a plate of sandwiches awaited him.

He was too exhausted to have any of it.

Despite his tiredness he had trouble sleeping. Feeling disorientated, the low buzz of the air conditioning keeping him awake. Tossing and turning. Wondering about his family and what was happening back home. Eventually dozing off, to be woken by the phone ringing after what seemed like only a few minutes.

A moment of panic before he realised it was his wake-up call, arranged by their guide. Remembering through the haze of tiredness they were to make an early start, before the day hotted up.

* * *

He shaved, dressed, and hurried down to breakfast.

Now he could properly see the magnificence of the hotel, once a maharajah's palace. The rooms lavishly decorated and furnished. High ceilings. Chandeliers. Carved, wooden doors. Marble floors covered by intricately woven carpets.

The rest of the group were already sitting at the table reserved for them, talking amongst themselves and to a short, bearded man, the local guide who would be looking after them for the three days they'd be spending at the reserve.

Breakfast was a buffet spread out on two long tables overlooking a terrace and the hills beyond. He hadn't eaten much on the plane and was starving. He went over and filled up his plate.

"Looks like you're going to enjoy yourself." Said one of the men with a smile as he sat down.

He nodded back, and as he ate, listened without joining in to their conversation about travel, houses, restaurants.

"Right." The guide said eventually. "As I have told those who were here earlier, my name is Naseem. And now could you please tell me your names and a little bit about yourselves."

He told the truth when it was his turn—that he was a retired policeman. What was the point in lying?

At first there was an embarrassed silence, before. . . .

"We'd better behave ourselves then." Said one of the women, giving him a glance, and touching her husband on the arm.

He could think of nothing witty to say in reply.

"We'll be leaving in half an hour." The guide said. "I know some of you have visited Africa where the game is in great numbers. Here it is different, so I must warn you there is no guarantee we will see tiger or leopard. Still, we will try our best, and I hope we'll be lucky this morning. If not, there are many other animals, and we've got several more drives before we leave. One other thing. When we do see the animals please to be as quiet as possible so not to frighten them."

He paused to take a sip of tea before continuing.

"We travel here in open vehicles. They use elephants at the next park you're going to, because the grass is taller. Please bring jackets or pullovers, as it will be cold at first. And remember, ladies and gentlemen. No leaning or putting arms out of the vehicles. And certainly never get out unless I tell you it is safe. If you need a call of nature, please tell me. If we aren't near one of the toilet areas, and it is an emergency, I will find somewhere safe for us to stop."

He looked around the table.

"Are there any questions? Right. Then we'll meet outside at six thirty."

* * *

He still felt hungry, though somewhat embarrassed to fill a second plate in front of everybody.

"To hell with it." He thought. "Who gives a damn what they think."

And took even more the second time.

By the time he got back there was no-one at the table.

* * *

There were three vehicles waiting in the chilly mist.

He was the last out and squeezed his way into the back of one of them.

They drove through the grounds of the hotel, past the outdoor restaurant and the swimming pool and though the gates where a little knot of taxi drivers, pale under the entrance lights, stood around stamping their feet to keep warm, their breath white in the cold air.

He blew on his hands and nervously fingered the binoculars he'd bought for the trip in anticipation of what was to come.

* * *

The morning was interesting; deer, monkeys, crocodiles and a profusion of birds. No sign of any tigers though, just a tantalising sighting of some paw marks by the side of the road, shortly after their mid-morning stop for tea and biscuits.

Their search for game took them along a myriad of the well-worn tracks the vehicles used. Left. Right. Forwards. Back. Only the odd ruin, lake, or unusually shaped hill to help you get your bearings.

Their route was so convoluted that he'd never remember any of it. It would have to be written down.

* * *

They returned to the hotel before it got too warm, for a swim, a rest, whatever they wanted, followed by a sumptuous lunch in the outdoor restaurant, which he finished quickly so he could get away from the others in the group.

He walked round the hotel and grounds, at first sitting in the sun, then moving into the shade when the heat became too intense. He must have dozed off, because when he looked at his watch it was almost time for the evening meal, followed by the night-time drive.

The drive was no good at all. He couldn't see a damned thing, the lights and torches lighting just few yards back. Beyond, impenetrable blackness.

* * *

He made sure he was first on the vehicle the following morning, sitting in the back so no-one could see what he was writing in his notebook. If any of them were surprised to see him scribbling away they didn't show it. No doubt they thought he was keeping a diary of the trip.

They drove into the hills for a view of the valley and the mountains in the distance, then across a narrow wooden bridge to a village on the edge of the park, to be shown the benefits tourism was bringing to the locals. A machine for de-husking rice. A new water pump, women in orange saris laughing as the water splashed into their polished metal pots.

At the end of afternoon drive they made a stop at a viewpoint on the way back for a magnificent sunset.

As for the animals, more of the same.

Still no tigers.

* * *

He went down to dinner late. Another buffet. Food piled high on the tables. Far too much of it. He wondered what the waiters, standing around attentively in their smart red and black uniforms, thought of all this excess.

Saw the others sitting on the terrace outside, chatting and laughing. He had a drink in the bar, then ate on his own.

A night drive was scheduled, but he felt too tired to go on it.

At breakfast early next morning the talk was all about the leopard they'd caught a glimpse of, its eyes glowing in the dark.

* * *

This time the morning drive took a different route which ended up in a place where a stream splashed over a small waterfall into a pool surrounded by trees, thick grass, and rocks.

As they drove along the low ridge on the side of the glade the guide suddenly told the driver to stop, and, putting his finger to his lips, pointed. Everyone craned to look. He focused his binoculars. At first he could see nothing. Then . . . Yes . . . A glimpse of a head. A flank half hidden in the grass beside the pool.

They moved slowly forward allowing the other two vehicles to come up behind them. Now he could see better as the head moved in their direction.

"It's a male." Whispered the guide.

Seconds, maybe minutes, passed until there was a faint cry in the distance. Too far away to tell if it was a monkey or a bird.

The great head swung towards the sound, and the tiger got to its feet. A good view, but from the back, as it drifted silently away through the long grass.

There was a sigh from someone at the front. No-one else made a sound.

"We'll wait a little." The guide said, still whispering. "He may come back."

He felt a knot of anticipation in his stomach. Fifteen minutes passed. Nothing. Another five minutes before the guide whispered it was time to go.

The people relaxed when they drove off, started talking, laughing, as the tension diminished.

He wrote feverishly in his notebook on the way back to the hotel.

* * *

That afternoon they had a sighting of a female with a cub—just over a year old, the guide said—crossing the road in front of them, then waiting by the side for a minute or two.

Silence, only the cameras clicking and whirring.

"Thank you, Naseem." He said, slipping the guide some cash when he got down from the vehicle back at the hotel.

"Don't forget." The guide told them before they went inside. "Breakfast tomorrow will be at seven. Put your luggage outside your room before you go down. We leave at eight. The drive will be long, but there are some interesting places on the way."

He ate alone again that night, and went to bed early.

* * *

He'd set his alarm for four o'clock. Got up and dressed, remembering to take his torch and note book, and his thick leather jacket against the cold.

He neatly packed everything else. Clothes, camera, binoculars. The lot.

Shut the case and put it on the bed.

Placed most of the money he had left in a neat pile on the table by the window.

Let himself out quietly, and made his way down the deserted corridors into the lobby, nodding to the tired looking clerks on the desk, before opening the door to the open.

It was cold, his breath hanging in the air. He zipped up his jacket. The night was clear, a half-moon casting its silvery light over everything. The harsh cry of one of the peacocks that roamed the grounds startled him as he approached the gates of the hotel.

The guard was clearly surprised to see one of the guests up and about at such an early hour.

"Good morning sir. Can I help you?" He said, rubbing his eyes, as he stepped out of the little gate house.

"I couldn't sleep. I need a walk."

"Yes sir. A walk is good."

"I want to go outside."

"No sir. Not allowed. It is too dangerous."

"Just five minutes. I won't go far."

"No sir. Not allowed."

"Just five minutes. I won't go far. I'll pay you." He said, putting his hand into his pocket.

The man hesitated before replying, his brow furrowed in thought.

"You will stay near the gate?"

"Yes . . . Of course."

The man unlocked the double doors.

"Only five minutes. Then I will open for you."

He took the rest of his money, rupees, dollars and sterling, pressed it into the man's hand, and stepped through the gate.

Behind him he heard the man cry out.

"But sir . . . This is too. . . . "

He heard no more as he walked quickly away along the track, eastwards. The direction they'd taken the day before.

* * *

It was still dark with maybe the merest hint of pink in the sky. Once he thought he heard voices behind him. Maybe they'd sent out a search party already.

He would have to hurry.

Although he had a good sense of direction, without his torch—which the brochure had advised travellers to bring in case of power failures—and the notes he'd written in his book he would have found it impossible to find the way. As it was he had to stop from time to time to shine the beam on the path and his notebook so he could be sure of taking the right track.

A ruin loomed up ahead. He peered at the notebook. Yes. There it was—one of the maharajah's hunting lodges. He turned left just before it, down the track he was looking for.

Here the forest grew much thicker, and he experienced a sudden moment of panic as leaves and branches brushed against his face and arms. Thought for a moment he could feel eyes watching him. Claws ready to grab. Was startled by a cry and a flutter of wings, an owl of some sort, large against the sky.

He hurried on, keeping the torch focused on the track.

Not far to go. The low lying morning mist slowly dissipating. The colours and shapes around him much clearer now.

He turned the torch off.

It was gone five thirty and almost light by the time he got to the waterfall and glade where they'd been the previous morning.

* * *

He had to wait several minutes to get his breath back before climbing down to the water's edge.

It was getting warmer by the minute, and he was sweating profusely by the time he'd got down.

He took his jacket off and sat, his back resting against a rock, on a flat piece of ground which gave a good view of the pool. Through the trees he could see the golden ball of the sun rising into the sky.

Apart from the sound of the breeze rustling the leaves the forest around him was quiet. As if it was waiting for something.

A faint noise. Movement nearby. He felt his body tense.

The noise came nearer. Four deer, females, appeared by the water's edge, glancing nervously around, smelling the air, nostrils quivering, until, apparently satisfied, they commenced drinking.

A bird cry in the trees nearby. The deer looking up, ears twitching for one, maybe two seconds, before hurling themselves into the bushes.

More cries. Monkeys this time. Then silence.

His senses felt alive, as though he was floating high above the forest.

The crack of a twig breaking, and there it was. By the side of the stream.

The male tiger, muscles rippling through sun and shade. Crouching to drink. Large pink tongue lapping the water.

He moved a fraction, lifting his right hand, the outstretched palm facing the animal.

The tiger drunk some more, then got to its feet, calm, unhurried, the narrow, golden, yellow, eyes moving round the glade until they lighted upon him, looking straight in his direction. Expressionless, as the great beast moved effortlessly towards him, its paws splashing through the water.

As he sat there he thought he heard the sound of an engine approaching, and possibly the sound of his name being called. But he was no longer listening. All he could hear was the sound of his and the tiger's breath merging into one.

He stood up, and, opening his arms wide, went forward to embrace it.

Ambush

You should never break the rules of a lifetime, however tempting the prospect. Although . . . Some would say rules are created precisely so they can be broken. Whatever the consequences.

* * *

The car was a white Toyota, shot full of bullet holes, lying in a ditch, its engine still smoking. An ambush, typical of the time, in the early evening on the road leading to the mountains just over an hour from the capital.

The victim, though, was not typical. A multitalented writer, poet, and singer, fairly well known outside the country, famous within it, his works concentrating on love, loss, the countryside, day to day life in the cities. Bold and innovative, yes, but not particularly outspoken against the government.

The government. The government, of course blamed the killing on the rebels, and though by this time the rebels didn't pay too much attention to what the government said or did, one of their main groups went to the trouble of making a standard denial on its website, accusing the authorities of "stifling yet another voice of the people."

To tell you the truth, none of us knew for sure who'd done it or what their motive was. In this particular case my betting was on the government or its supporters, though like most of my fellow citizens—in other words those of us not directly involved—I'd learned over the years that appearances could often be deceptive. It wasn't the scruffy, unshaven man, mumbling nonsense under his breath, who was the danger. No. It was the well-dressed young man standing quietly beside you who was more likely to stab or shoot you, or blow you to pieces.

That night the TV showed police and ambulance men doing whatever they usually did in such cases, the whole scene unnaturally lit up by bright spotlights. I switched it off, did a little work, and went to bed.

* * *

The following morning one of the sub-editors of the paper I worked for called me into his office to tell me he wanted a piece on the dead man, to be ready by the weekend. An article, exactly like others I'd written before in similar circumstances, part obituary, part appreciation of the deceased's work, together with a few pictures and some "non-controversial" extracts from his books and poems.

As the sub editor put it. "A review of his life. Nothing political of course."

Adding, not that I needed reminding.

"And nothing about the killing. No details, motives, and so on. Nothing like that. Just the human angle. You know. His early life and background. And his work. That's what I want and that's what will interest our readers. The sort of thing you're really good at."

A little flattery never going amiss in these situations.

And then.

"The funeral's in two days from now. Go up to his village tomorrow, before everyone else arrives. Describe what it's like up there—a quote from that song of his would be good. You know the one. About wanting to return to the peace of the mountains. Talk to his neighbours, his family, people who knew him when he was a kid. Before he was famous."

* * *

Once I'd produced a draft both the sub and main editors would check the article—"in view of the sensitivity of the subject"—and make any changes they deemed necessary.

"Is that OK?" The sub editor had said, staring at me, as if I had a choice in the matter.

I nodded. Over the years all of us—well, not quite all, there were still some idealists and maniacs who were prepared to put their economic or physical well-being on the line—let's say *most* of us had come to accept that we had to walk a narrow line, a very narrow one, constantly looking over our shoulders at the government on the one hand, and the rebels on the other, so as to avoid censure or closure of the paper, or, as two of our competitors had suffered, physical attacks on our premises.

And as for us individuals—journalists, photographers, and the like—arrest, or even assassination or torture by one of the warring factions, was always on the cards for some real or imagined affront.

This was no idle concern. One of my fellow journalists had been shot dead, another badly beaten, and a third had disappeared without trace.

Still, we survived somehow, even blossomed, despite the—what shall I call it—the *unusual* situation we found ourselves in over the past few years, and we'd become pretty adept at reporting most, if not quite all the news, in such a way that controversy was largely avoided and as few feathers ruffled as possible.

Our paper also benefited from the fact that our largest shareholder was one of the country's leading businessmen. Someone with his fingers in many pies, and with excellent connections to the government, the army top brass, and various other movers and shakers here and abroad. As well as, it was rumoured though never proved, the rebel groups, some of which, people said, he funded, thereby making sure he had a foot in both camps.

The other shareholders were the editor, and a number of companies based in overseas tax havens. The view around the office, depending on the political inclinations of who you were talking to, was that the people behind these companies were either the CIA, our own security services, a Russian billionaire, a wealthy oil sheik, or even, farfetched as it seems, one of the rebel groups.

In truth no one knew for sure, and it was more than your job, possibly even your life, was worth to attempt to find out. I was informed by someone whose opinion I respected that the reason why one of our journalists had disappeared was that he that he'd decided to do a little investigating on the side, and was getting uncomfortably close to the truth on the particularly sensitive matter of press and media ownership and control in our country.

Fact or fiction? A warning to the rest of us never to try the same thing? In the state of affairs that currently existed, who could say for sure?

* * *

The sub editor sent me on my way, reminding me once again that he wanted to see the first draft of my article before the end of the week.

And, after I'd stood up to leave, the sting in the tail, just to make absolutely sure I was in no doubt about his concern for my wellbeing.

"Only go up there if the security situation allows it. I don't want you taking any unnecessary risks."

Note the use of the words—"I don't want you taking any *unnecessary* risks". Not—"I don't want you taking *any* risks".

But that would have been ridiculous, given the nature of the job and the times we were living in.

* * *

I spent the rest of the day doing desk research on the dead man's background, arranging to see his publisher, who I vaguely knew, when he'd returned from the funeral, and instructing one of our assistants to find extracts of poems, songs, articles, as well as archive photos we could use, reminding her to make absolutely certain that nothing that could be construed as the slightest bit "political" was among them.

247

* * *

The poet's family lived in a village in the mountains. I consulted a map. Yes, there it was. A couple of hours away. He must have been heading there when he got caught. I checked with a contact at one of the ministries who confirmed that the road was still closed by the security services, but was due to be opened at midnight—as if anyone would be stupid enough to travel at that hour, snaking up the narrow, winding twists and turns, when their headlights could be seen for miles around.

The suggestion for me to go to the village the day before the funeral made a lot of sense. It should be relatively quiet, and hopefully a number of the poet's relatives should already be there, able to give me the benefit of their personal reminiscences about his youth and development. I would, of course, try to be most careful not to make any reference to, or discuss the cause of his death. Well, maybe I'd ask a few questions of my own if the opportunity arose. Not for the article, merely to satisfy my own curiosity.

* * *

So here I was, on a fine, spring morning, travelling on the very same road the dead man had followed.

I'd left before dawn, the city quiet, the air cool and refreshing. Very few vehicles on the streets, mainly pick-up trucks crammed with workers bound for the building sites and farms around the city.

Although the road had been reopened there was still a strong security presence. I was stopped at two roadblocks before I started the climb into the mountains, waved through when they saw my new car and my journalist's pass with the name of my newspaper, and there was a third one just before the spot where the shooting had occurred.

I slowed down a little after being let through by the young soldiers on duty. Apart from the gaping hole in the fence caused by the poet's car crashing through, there was nothing left to see. The car was no longer there, removed, I guessed, with any other evidence that had been found.

Through my mirror I could see the soldiers staring at me. There wasn't any point in giving myself problems by showing an unhealthy interest in the incident. I accelerated round a bend in the road, leaving the roadblock quickly behind.

* * *

I stopped at a restaurant half an hour later and had breakfast on the terrace overlooking the plain. No-one else about, just me watching the sun come up, sipping my coffee and nibbling at the delicious, sweet cakes, which, the owner proudly informed me, had been baked by him and his wife that very morning.

Below me I could see a couple of cars and a lorry making their way slowly up into the hills. Tomorrow would be different, with people, including journalists like myself, arriving in droves, all heading for the funeral. The numbers would make the authorities nervous. Delays would be inevitable. Problems. At best it would be chaos. For the moment though all was peaceful, the hills around covered with thickly growing trees of all kinds, open areas of grass dotted with wild flowers, sheep and cattle grazing, the sun glinting on a river in the distance and the roofs and walls of a village nestling across the valley.

I found myself thinking, as I often did, why a beautiful country blessed with such generous people should find itself in such a terrible mess, but put the thought immediately out of my head. That way lay only madness or, of course, emigration, starting over again, new place, new language, something I doubted I could face.

My musing was interrupted by the proprietor asking where I was bound for.

"I'm going to visit a friend." I replied, pointing vaguely in the direction of the mountains.

"We've had no-one here except you since the shooting." He said. "They closed the road. They don't care what that does to someone like me. I'm sick of it. We've had six incidents so far this year. People don't come up here anymore unless it's essential. We used to get visitors walking in the hills. Staying in the villages or hotels round about. Now, there's no-one."

He stared out over the valley at a flock of birds flying towards the south.

"More coffee?" He asked.

I said no thank you and left, the restaurant owner watching me as I pulled out the car park.

* * *

The sun was already hot as I gathered speed, mapping out the article in my head. I was looking for "the human angle." A horrible phrase, maybe, but one which summed up adequately what I was trying to do-describing the setting where my subject had been born, his childhood history, personal recollections from the people he'd been brought up with, with inserts of his work at appropriate points in the narrative, his death and funeral only mentioned in passing in a brief paragraph.

A couple of photos, one of my subject as a child, another as a young man, if my colleague could find them in the newspaper's archives, would complete the job. I wouldn't be taking any photographs while I was in the village. I didn't even carry a camera. Cameras are threatening in a way a notebook isn't. Something I'd learnt to my cost, having had mine smashed on several occasions, and being beaten up a couple of times for good measure. So cameras were definitely not for me. Words were my building blocks. And no tape recorder. A few scribblings in my untidy scrawl bothered nobody, although I always took the precaution of asking whoever it was I was interviewing whether they minded me taking notes. And when we were finished, enquired politely if they wanted to see what I'd written. They seldom did.

Non-threatening, you see. Making them in a sort of way complicit in my work. No problems.

* * *

The lack of traffic meant I made good time, and I arrived at the village just after eight, passing the small cemetery on the outskirts where the dead man would be buried the following day.

I stopped the car in what seemed to be an unofficial car park, alongside a lorry and a couple of battered trucks, got out, stretched, took a deep breath, and looked around me.

The air was fresh and clear with a hint of pine and newly mown grass about it, the view with its backdrop of mountains, magnificent. The contrast with the village couldn't have been greater. Although a number of people were already up and about, the place had an air of desertion, even desolation about it. Dusty. A collection of houses huddled on either side of the road. A few rundown shops. Not even a place of worship. No inn or hotel to be seen, the look of the area confirming the correctness of my decision to arrive early, not staying overnight for the funeral, leaving at the end of the afternoon or early evening unless some matter of particular importance detained me.

Normally I would have been concerned about travelling back on the roads so late, not reaching the city until after dark, but the continuing security presence gave me some reassurance on that score.

The first thing I needed though, was another coffee.

* * *

There was a cafe down the street, the few men who were sitting and talking inside and on the small terrace in the front staring at me as I sat down and placed my order, identifying me, no doubt, as a city boy, not to be trusted.

Dealing with suspicion was a major part of my job, convincing people who didn't trust me to eventually open up and tell me the things they wanted to, and, if I was lucky, things they didn't intend to, and sometimes—and this was often the most important—things they never even realised they knew. That was my job, and without wishing to brag, I was good at it. That was why they'd sent me up here. I never, or almost never, offered money. Maybe it was my tone of voice, or my appearance, seeming younger than I was, that reminded people of their sons or brothers, or maybe something else I wasn't aware of that persuaded them to open up. I didn't know exactly what it was, and there was no point in over-analysing such a thing. All I can say is in the majority of cases I got more or less what I wanted.

And then, our country being what it is, the editors or, on an increasing number of occasions, the censors, proceeded to cut out the really interesting bits, and occasionally give me a good hassling if they still took a dislike to the article that was eventually printed, however watered down it was. I'd been manhandled, warned, threatened, brought in for questioning several times. I'd learned to be philosophical about it. Just an occupational hazard. At least I wasn't like those poor bastards I'd seen in the city lining up for work, or the fellows in this cafe, stuck miles from anywhere, whiling away their time in the only place available.

So you can understand why the looks of the other customers in the cafe, whether merely interested, or just plain hostile, didn't concern me.

I needed to get started, so after I'd paid my bill, I asked the owner of the café, who'd started splashing a number of dirty plates and cups around in the sink, if he knew the man who'd been shot.

"Of course I did." He said. "Everyone here did. The whole village. We all followed his progress, even though he lives. . . . " He stopped to correct himself. "He lived in the city. But no airs and graces. Whenever he came here, we. . . . "

He stopped washing the plates and dried his hands on a dirty towel.

"Who are you?" He asked, staring at me aggressively. "And why are you asking all these. . . . "

But I already had my press card out. Name. Photograph. The paper I worked for. The good old card, which could so easily be forged, and was done so regularly, by both the security forces and the rebels to gain access to places where nobody would willingly permit them entry.

"Oh." The owner grunted, craning forward to examine it. "So you've come to pick over his bones, eh. Don't you know the funeral's not until tomorrow? And there's nowhere round here for someone like you to stay tonight."

Not a promising start. Still, over the years I'd learned that telling the truth, or a version of it, is preferable to not. At least most of the time. Opening my bag, I took out a book of the dead man's poems I'd had for many years, in fact since I was a student, suitably battered and well thumbed.

"I'm not here for the funeral." I said, holding up the book, wondering if he could read, and mentally patting myself on the back for having the good sense to bring it with me. "I've always been a fan of his poems. I just want to find out some things about him for an article I'm writing. When he was a child, and after. Before he got famous. From the people who really knew him."

"Ah yes." He replied. "His poems. I like his poems."

Maybe he could read after all.

He started washing the plates again before continuing.

"He used to come up here three, four, times a year. To see his family and relax."

He pointed outside to a table under a tree.

"He'd sit there drinking coffee. Talking. Sometimes writing. He told me this was the one place where he could really unwind. And also . . . .."

He lowered his voice. I waited for the revelation to come.

"I never charged him, of course. Everything he wanted. On the house."

"Can I quote you on that?" I asked, hoping my disappointment didn't show too much.

"Of course. Of course." He paused before continuing.

"Don't say I told you, but the last couple of times he didn't write at all, just sat for hours looking at the mountains. I thought he looked old. Tired. Not talking. Not his usual self at all."

"Anything else?"

"No. Nothing else." He suddenly seemed nervous of saying more.

"What about when he was a child? Growing up?"

"Not really. I remember him as a kid. Nothing special. Running around. Playing. Helping his father out. Then he went to university, and suddenly his first songs came out, and he was gone like so many of our youngsters."

He smiled a fraction.

"But at least *he* didn't forget us."

The smile faded.

"And we won't forget him. Everyone here knows it was. . . . "

He stopped in mid-sentence and, picking up another plate, rubbed it so hard that I thought it would break in two.

"I won't forget him either." I said, a suitably mournful expression on my face.

I wasn't being cynical here. I did in fact harbour fond memories of the dead man. The slim volume I'd shown the cafe owner wasn't something I'd produced like a rabbit out of a hat. I'd read it and reread it in my student days, when the poet's writings and songs of yearning and contemplation seemed to echo exactly my frame of mind, but expressed so much more elegantly and passionately than I could ever contemplate. I'd actually met him a couple of times, and was most upset, no, not just upset, more than that, I felt a frustrated anger at his pointless, unnecessary death. His murder.

I decided to change tack.

"Maybe you can help me." I continued, when the fellow's anger seemed to have dissipated. "Is there anyone else around who knew him well? Apart from his family?"

Proprietorship. Complicity. The pride of being able to help, combined with a dose of curiosity, and the desire to seem important. A potent mix, few, I'd learned, could resist.

"Yes. Over there."

He pointed to a man, aged, I guessed, in his late thirties, in tee shirt and jeans, sitting with two others at a table in the corner, and called him over.

Perfect. Ripples in a pond, spreading when the stone hits the water.

"This is. . . . " The owner said, proudly stating my name and profession, and explaining what I was doing in the village, as if he'd been the one who'd brought me up here in the first place.

The man who joined us was, unfortunately, not so easily convinced. Asking me several times exactly why I was there; who I worked for; did I realise what a difficult time it was . . . and so on. . . .

The one thing I was grateful for was at least he hadn't told me there'd been someone up there the day before asking exactly the same things as me.

"So, you're going to do a piece on our village, are you?" He finally remarked, spitting out the words with a scowl on his face. "I'll bet you never gave us a second's thought before all this. Never bothered to come up here, and now here you are, snooping around asking questions as if we owe you something. I know you people. Now you've got your claws into us you won't leave us alone until the story goes cold, and then you'll spit us out like a piece of rotten fruit."

"No. You're wrong. I have been here before. Several times. On holiday."

Sometimes you have to lie, or at least exaggerate the truth. I *had* been to the area a number of times when I was student. Now I preferred more peaceful places, where you were less likely to disappear or get gunned down on the road. The coast. Other cities. And, after a long, horribly convoluted process, abroad on a couple of occasions before the troubles really took off.

That took the wind out of his sails, though he recovered quickly.

"Not here." He said, shaking his head. "You weren't here. I'd remember if you were."

Be prepared. Always be prepared,

"No. It was. . . . " I mentioned the nearest town, the name of which I remembered, luckily, from the map I'd looked at the night before. "And I had a different car, and . . . and a beard."

"I'm told you were a good friend of. . . . " I said, hurrying on before he had the opportunity to say anything further.

Flattery. Not just a friend. A *good* friend, no less, of such a famous man.

That did the trick.

"Yes. I was. Before he left. And he always looked me up when he came back here. Without fail. Every time."

I thought I detected the glint of a tear in his eye.

"You know." He said. "When we were young . . . I knew there was something special about him. I remember. . . . "

Once he'd got going there was no stopping him.

I bought two coffees, and we sat down at an empty table. I started taking notes—with his permission of course, as well as his agreement to use what he was saying in my article.

"You won't use my name will you?" He suddenly said after he'd been going on for a while.

I promised I wouldn't. And wild horses wouldn't drag me from that promise. You may think me cynical, but I do have my standards. I won't lie in my writing, knowingly put anyone in danger, or disclose my sources if they don't want me to. Everything else is fair game. And when I'm on the track of a story the gloves are off. I won't stop at anything. Within reason.

He carried on at full pelt, me struggling to keep up.

All useful stuff. Nothing too exciting, but good, solid background material on the human angle—those words again—that I could build up a bit and pad out to a couple of pages of my article.

I was feeling better already. The tiredness I'd experienced earlier that morning had completely gone.

I ordered two more coffees.

"So?" I asked when he'd stirred several spoons of sugar into his. "Anything else?"

"Yes. There was something."

He looked around as if frightened of being overheard, and lent towards me, speaking softly.

"The last time he was here he told me he was thinking of going away. Emigrating."

"Did he say why?"

"He said he was tired of it all. And. . . . " He looked round again, dropping his voice to little more than a whisper. "He hinted someone was after him."

"Did he say who?" I asked, leaning forward so I could hear.

"No. He didn't. But I thought it was. . . . "

He stopped in mid-sentence.

"You're not writing this down are you? If you are. . . . "

"No. Look. You can see." I hurried to reassure him, showing him my note-book. "I'm not doing anything political. I told the owner of this place the same. Just about your friend's life. Some of his poems and songs. Nothing else."

"Good. I had to check. You understand."

"Yes of course I do. And so, what else did he say?"

As he took another sip of his coffee, avoiding looking at me, I realised the moment had passed. If he had indeed been about to reveal something, the break in the conversation, though short, was enough to make him clam up for good.

"Nothing. Just that he was thinking of leaving . . . Nothing else. . . . Did I tell you about the time when he. . . . "

And he continued with his reminiscing, me scribbling away, barely listening, all the time my head in a turmoil.

My antennae were waving wildly.

A story. A hidden story? Something dangerous? Maybe. Maybe not. After all, it wasn't unusual for people to leave, those who could afford it, or could pursue their art or business in more congenial climates.

The poet fitted the bill exactly. A substantial following not just in this country but also abroad. Why shouldn't he leave, like so many others?

But then the words and music of one of his songs, a recent one, played day and night on the radio came into my head. So much passion and love about the country, the people . . . .

No. He wouldn't have wanted to leave. At least, not willingly. Surely his con-science wouldn't. . . .

The man's voice interrupted my thoughts.

"I'll miss him. We all will." He said sitting back in his chair, then suddenly leaning forward, speaking softly again.

"You won't write anything about what I said before, will you? About him wanting to leave."

I smiled as I put my notebook away

"No. Not a word. I promise."

"Thank you."

He finished his coffee, wiping his mouth with the back of his hand.

"Is there anyone else you'd like to talk to?" He asked.

"His family perhaps? His parents?"

"No. I don't think they'd want to. Not so near the funeral. Although . . . ." He stared out the door. "Maybe his brothers." He said, getting to his feet. "If you want, I'll take you there."

* * *

As we walked along the street, my companion still talking about the dead man, the hot sun beating down, the few people about staring at me as we passed, noticing like they always do in such places the stranger in their midst, I found myself becoming increasingly angry.

Not at the poet's lonely death on the dark road, or the other stupid, wasteful deaths over the years. No. Not at these.

It was myself I was angry at. The compromises I'd agreed to. The cuts to my work I'd accepted with barely a complaint. The so-called serious work I'd written over the years. Who was I kidding? Most of it was trash. Damned, inconsequential, useless trash which I'd produced under the guise of serious work, while all around me the world was falling apart.

* * *

The voice beside me droned on and on. I had to stop myself from grabbing him by the throat and telling him to shut up.

The words of one of the dead man's songs came into my head:

"A man is defined by what he does.

By those he loves.

And who love him back."

A man is defined by what he does.

Thinking about it, I felt the tears come to my eyes for all the opportunities I'd wasted.

Damn it. This time it would be different. Sure, I'd write the piece they wanted. Stupid. Uncontroversial. Useless. But on my own I would try to find out the reason for his death, who it was that killed him, and why he was thinking of getting out the country.

Quietly. Carefully. No deadlines to meet.

A memorial to his death. A proper memorial. Not a load of bland reminiscences.

I had no illusions. It could be dangerous. Very dangerous. But on the other hand I had connections. Some in the most unlikely places. People I trusted and, more importantly, who trusted me. Favours to be called in. Information supplied.

I'd find out what I could without exposing myself too much. . . .

There I was. At it again. Trying to protect myself. Like I'd been doing for so many years. I just couldn't help it. It had been ingrained in me. Like pretty well all of us, compromising ourselves in ways big and small each and every day.

I felt myself getting angry again.

"Here we are. We've arrived." My companion said.

* * *

The house was at the far end of the village, standing on its own small plot of land, larger, and better kept than most of the others. Two stories, the walls painted a yellowy white, doors and window frames, dark blue.

Several cars and pickup trucks were parked outside, no doubt friends and family already gathering for the funeral.

I didn't know what his family did for a living. Whatever it was, clearly there'd been a little money to spare. Just enough to send their clever son to the nearest town, an hour or so away, for the secondary education which would give him the opportunity to escape from the confines of his upbringing. And, of course, to develop that spark of inspiration, genius, whatever you care to call it, coming from goodness knows where, that enabled him to produce such relevant work over the years. The work which, I assumed, had ultimately led to his death.

A brave man? A man unafraid to face the consequences of his beliefs? Or so I always believed. But also apparently a man who was starting to think seriously about leaving the place that was the source of his inspiration.

* * *

"Wait here." My guide said, knocking loudly on the front door, which immediately opened to let him in.

I sat down on the low wall outside the house, and looked around. In the distance the road snaked up into the mountains, dirt tracks running off it towards a couple of isolated buildings a mile or so from the village. More activity on the street now. People walking up and down, going into shops and houses. Some young boys running past, shouting, laughing. No shoes. Tousled, untidy hair. The same, I supposed, as he was at their age.

The glare of the sun was dazzling my eyes. I was about to try to find some shade when the door opened and the man who'd taken me to the house beckoned me in.

* * *

The house was cool after the heat outside. As my eyes grew accustomed to the lack of sunlight, I saw the rooms were of a reasonable size, and comfortably furnished, though rather old fashioned to my city eyes.

Through an open door into what I took to be the lounge I could see a number of people milling around a couple in late middle age, the parents I presumed, seated to one side on two low chairs. The usual babble of conversation you get when friends and family gather together was conspicuous by its absence, just a low, subdued sound of people talking in whispers, occasionally punctuated by the cries of children coming from nearby.

"Wait here a minute." My guide whispered, leaving me in the hall, while he went into the lounge, coming back after a short time.

"Ok. His brother will see you in the garden."

He led me through the kitchen—women crowded into the small space, cooking and baking—to a small but well-kept garden at the back. Neatly cut grass, a tree for shade, with a couple of chairs and a table under it, several large earthenware pots filled with shrubs and flowers.

"He'll be out shortly." He said, then hesitated, nervously rubbing his hands together.

"I told him your article would show his brother in a good light." He continued.

In my current mood I didn't take kindly to someone telling what I should or shouldn't write.

"I don't see why it shouldn't." I replied, biting my tongue, and avoiding the desire to tell him to mind his own business. "Do you?"

"No. No. Of course not. It's just . . . You'll remember not to include that bit about him wanting to. . . . "

"I promised, didn't I?"

"Yes. . . . You did. Thank you."

And he was gone, leaving me alone.

* * *

Beyond the low fence at the back of the garden there was an open area patched with brown grass and a few scrubby bushes. Several piles of rubbish, bottles, newspapers, cans and the like were scattered around while further away, a fire, tyres from the smell of it, was smouldering near the wrecks of two rusting, burnt out cars.

How ironic, I thought, all this at the back door of a man who wrote so passionately about the beauty of nature and the need to preserve it, to be confronted with such an affront to everything he stood for each time he took his ease in his parent's garden.

I heard voices coming from the house. I was wondering if they were discussing my arrival, when the kitchen door opened, and a fellow in his early forties, with a definite resemblance to the murdered man, came towards me. Tall, well built, dressed in a dark suit, white shirt, open at the neck, shoes well-polished. In contrast to his clothes, however, his physical appearance was unprepossessing—unshaven, hair uncombed, bags under his eyes. The older brother, I assumed, wondering where the younger one was.

He stopped some distance away, staring intently, as if trying to sum me up before addressing me

"Congratulations. You're the first." He eventually said in a low, hoarse voice. "I wondered how long it would take for you vultures to arrive."

I saw his fists clench by his sides, and could feel my muscles tense as he took a step towards me.

"Whatever you do, don't hit him." I thought. "Don't let it get out of control."

He was taller and heavier than I was, but I was younger and I'd boxed a little at university. If he threw a punch I'd try to block him but not retaliate.

My fears, however, proved unfounded. He stopped short, his fists unclenched, though, judging by the look in his eyes, killing me where I stood would have given him enormous pleasure.

"Vultures . . . Filthy vultures. Every one of you." He spat out.

I breathed a sigh of relief. So it was going to be verbal not physical abuse. Good. This at least I was well equipped to handle.

"All I wanted. . . . " I started to say.

"You wanted? You wanted? Don't you people ever stop to think what somebody else may want?"

He took a step forward, staring into my eyes.

"Do you know what it's like for a mother to lose her son? My brother's barely cold and. . . . "

He turned away and slumped down on the nearest chair.

"I'm sorry." I said. "I didn't want to impose. I thought it would be better if I came here before the funeral. You'll have enough on your plate tomorrow."

"Oh. So you're doing this for our benefit, are you?"

This gave me the opportunity I was looking for. If you're patient, one usually comes.

"In a way, yes. All I want to do is show our readers some of his work, and. . . . "

"They know his work. Those that want to."

"Yes. And also to explain something about his background."

"Well. You're here. You've seen his background." He waved his hand in the direction of the mountains. "Now you can go. You're lucky it's me you're seeing.

Some of my relatives inside aren't as civilised as I am. Someone like you. They'd like to. . . . "

He got to his feet.

"If I were you I'd keep well away from us. Go back to where you came from."

"I'm sorry you feel like . . . ."

"I do. Now get off our property."

"Ok. Ok. I'm going." I said, making for the path on the side of the house.

"You know." I said, turning towards him just before I was out of sight. "I met your brother twice. He probably didn't remember me, but I really loved his work, and I'm sorry he's dead. I really am. Please give your family my condolences."

But I doubt if he heard me. He was standing by the fence, looking away into the distance.

* * *

I hurried away from the house, not a little scared, I must admit, that some of those relatives he'd spoken about would take it into their heads to come after me. I was completely alone up there. A knife or a bullet was all it would take. My body and car tossed into one of the gullies nearby. No-one admitting to seeing me. The police with more important things to do than spending their time looking for yet another missing journalist.

Sure enough after a few seconds I heard a door slam behind me, and footsteps coming in my direction. Walking quickly. Running. There was no point in trying to get away. I stopped and turned to face them . . . Him.

About my age. A grey suit. Creased. Not worn, I guessed, very often. White shirt. A younger version of the man I'd left in the garden.

"You." His voice was loud, almost shouting, as he approached.

"You." He repeated. "My brother told me."

So, He *was* the third, the youngest brother. Coming to put in his two cents worth of abuse

I decided that saying nothing was the best option for the moment.

"You've upset him, you bastard." He continued, shouting now, looking around as if seeking an audience. "Don't you think things are bad enough without you interfering?"

I put up both my hands in a gesture of resignation.

"Look." I said. "I'm sorry if I upset him. I'm going to my car. I'm leaving."

"Good. Fuck off out of here. And don't come back" He shouted as he turned on his heel and walked away.

I looked back and saw several men standing at the door of the house. Whether the older brother was with them I couldn't tell.

It was time to leave. The sooner the better before things started getting too hot for comfort.

* * *

I walked briskly down the street, but not so fast that it seemed I was running away.

Something was yelled in my direction as I was passing the café. Some insult or other, I supposed. I ignored it, and walked on.

There was barely anyone around, the street almost deserted in the mid-morning heat, that was until I noticed half a dozen men in the distance, waiting by my car.

Well, I thought. So this is it. Maybe I'm destined to die here, shot or stabbed, left to bleed to death on this dusty road.

There was nothing I could do but grasp my shoulder bag, ready to swing it at them in the vain hope of downing a couple before the rest finished me off. But no. This wasn't destined to be the day I was to die. They moved away as I passed, staring at me, daring me to challenge them, one of them pushing me hard with his shoulder as I fumbled for my keys.

And then I was in the car, my hands shaking as I started the engine, my heart beating fast.

While I was turning in the direction I'd come from earlier that morning I felt one, then another, blow to the back of the car, but I didn't give a damn what the damage was. I just wanted to get out of there as quickly as possible.

* * *

I drove slowly at first, testing the brakes hadn't been tampered with, before gaining speed and checking the rear mirror to see if any vehicles were coming after me.

It was not until I was a fair distance away, and behind a hill, that I stopped the car and got out, leaving the engine running.

I looked back. The road was empty. Blue sky. The sun bright overhead. Wooded hills all around. A more tranquil scene you couldn't have wished for.

Next I listened, in case they'd decided to follow me. Not a sound.

I examined the car. Tyres first. No cuts. Solid when I kicked them, but two indentations above the side of the boot.

I looked back once more. Something coming up fast. I shielded my eyes against the glare. Relief. Just a tanker, no doubt hurrying back to town after being delayed by the road blocks.

I drank deeply from my water bottle, washed the sweat from my face, and drove off.

* * *

I was unable to properly concentrate until I reached the relative safety of the plain. Ridiculous, I know, but the feeling that a sniper's bullet could hit me at any moment unavoidable each time I slowed down on a bend or narrow stretch of road, my uneasiness gaining in intensity as I approached the area where my subject had met his end.

I tried to distract myself by thinking about the article. It was clear I didn't have too much to go on. Some memories of the dead man from two villagers who'd known him; a description of the village, the area, and the house he was brought up in; something about his family gathering for the funeral.

Not a lot. Still, if I could find somebody who'd known him at university, or even better, had taught him there, and I'd interviewed his publisher, together with the archive work and the extracts I hoped the research assistant had unearthed, I should have just about enough. Together with photos, three, maybe four, pages.

Yes. It'd be enough. I'd start work immediately I got home.

* * *

Once back in my apartment, I had a quick shower, made a cheese sandwich and a cup of tea, sat down at my kitchen table and started looking at my notes.

I'd gone through the first couple of pages when my phone rang. My sub editor, I thought, checking to see if I'm back in one piece.

But it wasn't the sub editor. It was a voice I didn't know. A woman's voice.

"Is that Monsieur. . . . ?" The voice said, sounding distant and muffled.

"Yes. And who. . . . ?"

"Ring this number in fifteen minutes if you want to learn something more than you did up there today."

"But who. . . . ?"

"Call back in fifteen minutes. Use a phone box or we won't pick up. I'll repeat the number."

"How did. . . . ? I started to say as I was scribbling down the phone number, but the call had already been cut off.

My head was spinning. Whoever was on the phone apparently knew I'd been to the village. Had I been followed? No. I was sure I'd have seen them on the winding deserted road leading into the mountains. Could it be someone who'd seen me up there? But if it was, how did they know my private number? The number that only my family, friends, and a few work colleagues knew . . . What would. . . .

But then my damned, fatal curiosity took over. To hell with it, I thought, let's find out what this "something more" the woman mentioned is all about. The article can wait till tomorrow.

I gulped down a glass of water, grabbed my watch, some cash and loose change, hid my notes of the morning's visit in the small compartment I'd constructed at the bottom of my wardrobe, slipped a couple of pens and some paper into my jacket pocket, and left my apartment, locking the door behind me.

* * *

The one thing I did understand was the insistence on me using a phone box to return the call. Even a slightly sensitive conversation was best made from one or a pay as you go mobile – paid for in cash—as phone taps and traces had become commonplace on journalists, lawyers, in fact anyone the security agencies wanted to keep tabs on.

Luckily there was a phone box – one that actually worked—near my apartment. I looked at my watch. Almost fifteen minutes gone. I counted to ten and dialled.

The number rang several times before it was answered.

"Hello." It was a man's voice this time.

"Is that. . . . ?" I asked, reading the number out.

There was some hesitation before the reply came. Harsh. Defensive. Unfriendly.

"Yes. Who's that?"

"I was given this number fifteen minutes ago."

"Who by?"

"I don't know. A woman phoned my apartment."

"And you are?"

I told him, resisting the temptation to remind him they already knew my name when they first made contact.

In any case I only lied professionally if there was some clear benefit to me, and there was no way the person I'd lied to could check on the veracity of what I was telling them.

"Wait."

I heard voices in the background, and then the man was on the phone again.

"We'll phone you back." He said.

Three or four minutes passed before the phone rang.

"What's your job?" The same voice asked with no preamble, sounding if anything more brusque and threatening than before.

I was on the verge of telling him that it was a bloody stupid question, given they knew my name and private phone number on top of where I'd been that day, but I'd learned it was best to go along with whatever requests were made—at least at the beginning of the process.

"I'm a journalist." I replied.

"What paper?"

I told him.

"Wait."

More talking, muted, as if he'd put his hand over the receiver.

Then. . . .

"Go to another call box. Not in your neighbourhood. Phone this number in half an hour."

And the connection was cut off before I could respond.

Cat and mouse. Cops and robbers. I was used to these games. Necessary for people who needed to avoid the security services or the rebels.

* * *

I knew a nice little restaurant about twenty minutes away. I'd take a leisurely stroll there, make the call, then have a meal.

It was getting dark and the streets were coming to life. The approach of night, which by rights should have been far more threatening than the bright sunny days we were accustomed to, always seemed to have a positive effect on our citizens. You could feel people's confidence increasing as dusk fell, and it was a fact that for the average man or woman the nights were an awful lot less dangerous than the days.

Why on earth should this have been? I suspected it was because the perpetrators of the atrocities committed on both sides preferred their deeds to be seen in the glare of the hours of daylight, revelling in the knowledge that they didn't need to resort to skulking in the darkness like common criminals, should anyone have the audacity to compare them to such scum.

A constant state of crisis creates some strange situations. For example, the shops and cafes would clear as if by magic, minutes after a particularly nasty incident. But not for long. Within a few hours their customers would start drifting back, a trickle at first, then a flood, until in a very short time, things had apparently returned to normal.

Sometimes it wasn't an actual event, merely the circulation of a rumour that cleared the town centre. I had no idea how these rumours, often untrue, arose, and were subsequently circulated so that in the space of a couple of hours everybody seemed to have heard them.

The study of the dissemination of such phenomena would make a fascinating topic for an article in a learned journal—if one had the time and resources to undertake a proper investigation, which I, unfortunately, did not.

But I digress.

I found a call box a few minutes from the restaurant, stood in a doorway to make sure I hadn't been followed, before slipping inside, piling up my change by the side of the phone and dialling the number.

It was a different voice this time. A woman's. The one who'd phoned me at home? I couldn't tell. But just as abrupt as the previous speaker, telling me to wait.

I fed more money in, before a man came on, not, by the sound of him, the same as the one I'd previously spoken to.

"Name?"

"Newspaper?"

"Where are you?"

I told him.

"Do you know the old post office?" He asked after a short pause.

"Yes."

"Take a bus there. Get off at the stop before. The one by the river. Check that no-one's following you. There's a footbridge nearby. Do you know it?"

"Yes."

"Cross the bridge, walk down street opposite, and turn left at the end. There's a coffee bar three or four buildings along. Make sure you're there at exactly twenty five past seven. Check again that you haven't been followed, then wait outside the coffee bar. If anyone asks, tell them you're waiting for a friend. A car will pull up at seven thirty. Open the back door and get inside."

"But . . . How will they. . . . ?"

"Seven thirty. They won't wait."

The phone was cut off.

I looked at my watch. Ten to seven. No time for the steak and glass of wine I'd promised myself.

* * *

I found the bus stop I needed, looking around while I was waiting and when I got on the bus to see if there was anyone who seemed the slightest bit suspicious. There was nobody, or at least nobody who stood out from the crowd. No-one else got off at the stop where I'd been told to, except for a middle aged man and woman, holding hands and laughing.

I hung around, watching them walk across the bridge until they were out of sight, and dived into a nearby cafe, first glancing at the menu, then at my watch as if debating whether or not to stay, before quickly hurrying out and looking around.

The street was completely empty. I looked at my watch again. I had more than enough time. I knew the area, and decided to take a slight detour before returning to the route I'd been given, in case anyone had watchers keeping tabs on me, feeling, as I always did on these occasions, a mixture of fear and elation at all this cloak and dagger stuff. This time, though, the fear factor was to the fore. Definitely to the fore.

* * *

In fact I was more worried about being picked up by the authorities than whoever it was I was going to meet. I'd been stopped several times after dark by the security boys and taken in for questioning on three occasions. Knocked about a bit—complaints not advisable—luckily the good old press card and one or two phone calls getting me back on the street, accompanied by a smile and a handshake from the very same people who were apparently prepared to blow my head off or pull out my fingernails just a couple of hours earlier.

On top of that practically every block had one or two snoops paid a small sum each month to inform on any unusual goings on in their area. These bastards, who in normal circumstances would have merely been harmless gossips and busybodies—put their nosey inclinations to a more sinister use, watching the streets whenever they had a moment, or peeking out from behind their curtains in the hope of spotting something, however small, that could be of interest to the authorities.

When these activities first emerged, friends used to complain about such "disgusting, despicable behaviour". It was only advisable to use such disparaging words about government policy in the company of those close to you who you could trust—not necessarily the one and the same thing. I, on the other hand, would say—"You're wrong. This is a fantastic development. The authorities will be so overwhelmed with a mass of information, about Mr X's comings and goings, the furniture delivery at flat number 8, and so on, that the whole stupid system will collapse under its own weight."

And then the smile would be wiped off my face by the standard response.—"Great. Leaving us to the tender mercy of the rebels."

The system did not in fact collapse. After a couple of months the authorities issued what they referred to as "guidelines" for the sightings they were interested in. Anyone who consistently reported nonsense would lose their stipend, and could also find themselves on a charge of wasting police time. So, Mr X could continue his amorous adventures, and Miss Y could once again take her afternoon stroll by the river without the fear of being subject to a report.

As for the rest of us, the arrests, killings, and acts of terrorism went on as before, neither side able to land the killer blow that would finish it off once and for all, for good or bad.

Between a rock and a hard place is the expression that best summed up our circumstances.

This impossible situation was why such a high proportion of those who were able to leave, did, and, difficult though it was to believe, maybe even the murdered man, who many of us considered to be the soul of our country, was planning to do the same. Could that be why he was killed? Because he wanted to leave? Or . . . Maybe someone was worried he'd speak out of turn when he was safely abroad?

All these thoughts were buzzing round in my head as I walked around the block to the rendezvous point outside the coffee bar.

Don't let you mind drift, I had to keep reminding myself. Concentrate on the job in hand. Your life could depend on it.

* * *

I looked at my watch for what seemed like the twentieth time that evening. It was almost half past seven.

Although I'd suffered it a couple of times before, the thought of being taken away by strangers was starting to terrify me. The dark inside of the car. The hood or blindfold half choking you. Being forced to lie on the back seat or on the floor, your face pressed up against the vile smelling fabric. The silence during the ride, to goodness knows where. The dangers of a shoot up with the security services, or a change of heart in the group who were taking you. Bullets tearing into your flesh. Passers-by too frightened to lend a hand. The slow response of. . . .

My God I thought, was I being a complete idiot in setting myself up for this this without any prior knowledge or preparation? Of course I was. Panic, uncontrollable, set in. I broke out in a cold sweat. My hands began to shake.

Keep calm, for God's sake. Don't lose it. Try to console yourself by thinking this is *not* a kidnapping or an abduction. It's just an arranged meeting, like at your office or your bank.

Office? Bank? Who was I kidding?

* * *

Seven thirty five . . . Seven forty. . . .

I was on the verge of turning heel and walking away when I saw headlights moving slowly towards me.

The car, a Fiat. Not new, but in good condition. Slowing down. Stopping. Figures inside. Two in the front, one in the back, leaning over to open the door. No light.

Me, coming forward gingerly, half expecting to see the barrel of a gun pointing towards me.

No gun, just a whispered voice.

"Get in. Quick."

I got in the back seat, slamming the door as the car moved off, hearing the sound of the central locking shutting off any hope of escape, the man beside me slipping a hood over my head, and making me slide down, half on the seat, half on the floor.

The car accelerated. Slowed down. Accelerated again. No-one talking. The radio on, not loud, but loud enough to block out any of the outside sounds the noisy air conditioning permitted to slip through.

Nothing to be seen through the canvas hood, just the occasional impression of a bright flash of light, once accompanied by a loud hoot as something big—A bus? A lorry?—overtook us.

I felt hot and uncomfortable, crouched down between the floor and seat, unable to move. All I could do was stay still, ignore the crick in my neck, and hope the ride would be over sooner rather than later

It had, I reckoned, been about half an hour. The road suddenly seemed a little quieter, slightly less bumpy. The car stopped once, reversed, then continued slower, climbing now. I guessed we were still in the city, most probably in the suburbs, my captors not wanting to risk encountering the roadblocks on the edge of town.

One of the men in the front started speaking on a phone, but much too softly for me to hear. The car slowed, then stopped. There was the noise of gates opening. Metal, by the sound of it. The car moved forward again. Stopped. Voices outside. The doors of the car were opened and an arm took mine, and led me across what, by the echoing sound of our footsteps, seemed to be some sort of enclosed courtyard.

Not a sound. The stink of petrol fumes that pervaded the busy streets no longer perceptible. Almost certainly one of the suburbs. Probably in the hills in the northern part of the city.

Up some steps. Walking on a wooden floor. Then into the open again.

Another door. An outhouse of some sort?

Something softer underfoot, a rug or a carpet. The hood taken off leaving me blinking several times before getting used to the semi-darkness.

A large room lit by a single lamp. The walls whitewashed, with nothing on them except for large mirror at one end of the room.

"Sit down."

A hand pushed me onto a chair, a glass of water was placed on the small table beside me.

"You must be thirsty. Drink."

The voice deep, melodious, educated, came from a high-backed armchair facing away from me, placed at an angle so the occupant could watch my reactions and body language in the mirror. Impossible though for me to see much more than the top of the speaker's head. Thick hair, dark brown or black, I couldn't tell for sure in the half light.

Bizarre. Still it was better than remaining blindfolded or hooded, or having a bright light shone into your face until your eyes watered.

As I lifted the glass of water I turned my head slightly to see if anyone else was in the room.

"Don't. Just look straight ahead." Came a voice from behind me.

"So. How did you get on up there today?" Asked the man in the armchair, once I'd finished drinking.

"Up where?"

"Where? The mountains. His village. A few hours ago."

"I'm sorry. I can't tell you that."

I could see the hand wave dismissively above the chair.

"A man of principle, eh. That's rare in your profession these days."

I couldn't tell, but I imagined from his tone that he was smiling.

It was most disconcerting to be talking to a voice emanating from the faceless, disembodied, head in front of me. Still, if that's how they wanted their fun, so be it. I'd learnt from similar interviews in the past that there was no point in complaining about or criticising your interrogators' methods. Each group would play the game as it suited their particular plan. All you could do was try to follow your own agenda as closely as you were able. This though, was different. I didn't really know what I was doing there. In this case I had no plan, no agenda.

They held all the cards.

"That's how I work. And besides." I added. "I don't know who you are."

"Who do you think?"

"No idea. You could be government. . . . "

He laughed.

"A joker as well as a man of principle? No. Not the government."

"One of the anti-government groups?"

"That doesn't leave much else, does it? Exactly who we are doesn't matter for the moment. Maybe I'll tell you later. When we've decided what we're going to do with you."

What they were going to do with me? If these words were intended to scare me, they didn't have the desired effect. This approach was fairly common at the beginning of the process. All they wanted to do was rub it in at the outset that you were in their hands, at their mercy to deal with in whatever way they cared to.

Besides, if they'd intended to harm me, why go to all this trouble to find out how much, or, in this case, how little, I knew?

No, this was just the sparring before the contest began in earnest. For my part all I could do was bow my head gracefully and submit myself to their tender mercies, knowing it was the ones who couldn't be bothered to make their point who were more likely to put a gun to your head and leave your body in a ditch or a rubbish dump.

In fact I could feel my confidence returning with very second the process continued. I reckoned I was safe. For the moment. And although still completely in the dark as to their intentions, I had my own little game to play. Which was to tell the truth, or at least most of it, whilst at the same time trying my best to see what information I could gather from my interrogator.

I'd learned that sometimes the odd throw away remark could be worth more than an entire paragraph. So, having made my point about not revealing my sources, I told him about the reason for my visit to the village, leaving out only the details of who'd given me the phone number, realising of course that they most probably knew very well the identity of the individual concerned.

"So." The voice said, when I'd finished. "What exactly is your interest in our dead poet?"

I told him the truth again, at least as far as my "official" work was concerned.

"Just a reminiscence, with poems?" He said when I'd finished.

"Just that. And some photographs."

"Nothing controversial?"

"No. Nothing controversial."

There was a pause. By moving my head slightly I could see the man's hands, or at least the tips of his fingers pressed together, then opening and closing again.

"You know Monsieur. . . . " He said. "I'm surprised you haven't asked me why we wanted to see you."

"Firstly, you're young and ambitious." He continued, without waiting for my reply. "Secondly, we've been following your work for some time, and we like what we see. And most important, we've been told you're an honest fellow who speaks his mind, and we hope you'll do the same for us."

So the bastards had been checking me out. In other words spying on me.

Keep calm. It's quite normal in our country. Nothing to get concerned about

"Thanks for the compliments monsieur" I said, trying not to sound too angry. "But with all due respect, I'm waiting for you to tell you what this is all about, and you want from me."

"You see what I mean?" The voice said to whoever else was in the room.

"He's not frightened to say what he thinks."

A pause. More of those damned fingers opening and closing.

"Would you be interested in finding out why your friend the poet died?" The voice asked after a while.

Wait a little before replying. Don't seem too eager. Play it cool, even though your heart is beating fit to burst.

"Well. Would you?" He repeated.

"Not for this article, and I doubt if my paper . . . But personally. . . . " I paused as if I was thinking about it. "Yes . . . I would."

"Personally, eh? Well, who do you think killed him? Personally."

"I assume it was the most probably the government . . . or perhaps one of you people."

"*You people?* I haven't told you who we are yet. And why do you think *us* people would want to kill him?"

"I don't know why . . . So everyone would think the government had done it?"

"And I was told you were a clever fellow. Is that the best you can do?"

That damned chair. Have you ever tried talking to the back of someone's head, knowing your life could depend on your answers? I paused, racking my brains, trying to think of some other reason, one that would impress him with my erudition.

"Maybe . . . Maybe . . . It was someone he'd upset. Written the wrong thing. . . . "

I paused again, my mind a blank. Unable to think of anything that would have disturbed the government or the rebels enough to justify their killing him.

Then . . . remembering how I'd been told he was thinking about going abroad.

"Or . . . Something. . . . " I said, scrambling for a reason, but not wanting to say too much, for fear they'd think I knew more than I actually did. "Something he hadn't written yet. Maybe . . . Maybe it was something he was going to write. And someone didn't want him to."

There was a sound of slow clapping from the chair.

"Not bad. I knew you were smart. And, Monsieur . . . do you think the people who killed him, whoever they are, would appreciate you delving around to find out who committed the murder, and more importantly, why they did it?"

It was only then I realised what a hole I'd dug for myself through my efforts to impress him. A deep, dangerous hole.

Time to backtrack.

"Look. I'm only guessing" I said quickly, trying my best to disguise the rising panic in my voice. "Even if I'm on the right track, I wouldn't be able to publish anything."

"Too dangerous?"

"Yes. There's no way my paper would take the risk."

A snort—was it disgust? Disappointment?—came from the chair.

"What about if you published it abroad?"

I was starting to wish I'd never phoned the bloody number in the first place.

I took another sip of water, suddenly feeling tired of all this fencing around hypothetical situations. I drunk again, more deeply this time, emptying the glass.

"You're tired? Hungry?" The voice asked, no doubt seeing it etched on my face.

In fact I was exhausted both physically and mentally, and despite my best efforts I could feel my eyes getting heavier and heavier with each moment that passed.

"Yes. I've had a long day, and. . . . "

"We'll give you something to eat and drink. Then we'll continue."

I saw his fingers waving above the chair.

A hand from behind me picked up the glass.

A few minutes passed in silence. I heard the sound of a plane high overhead, then the door opened and a hand placed a cup of hot tea, and a plate with some bread, cheese, and meat on the table beside me.

* * *

I ate self-consciously, aware I was being watched in the mirror and by whoever was on guard behind me.

"Feeling better?" The voice from the chair said, as the plate and cup were cleared away.

"Yes, thanks."

"Good."

The hands and fingers were placed together again. Apart. Together. Apart. Together.

I felt a desire to rush over, look him in the eye, and tell him to stop playing his stupid cat and mouse games, but that would probably mean. . . .

The fingers separated once more, and the head bent forward.

"Right." The voice from the chair said. "As I said, we think you're the right person to some research for us. See for yourself what's caused all this trouble. But not here. It's too dangerous, and not secure enough. You'll have to go abroad. Switzerland to be precise. There's some documents there for you to examine.

There's a lot of them, but two weeks should be enough. You'll have to work hard, but your expenses will be paid, and we'll reimburse you for your time. A lot more than you're used to—and in hard currency. No strings attached. Think of it as a well-paid working holiday. All we need is. . . . "

This was happening much too quickly.

"Hold on." I said "I haven't said I'm going yet."

The fingers pushed themselves together again.

"Of course you haven't. You need some time to think about it. That's ok. There's a lot to take in. One of my colleagues will give you a number to phone before they take you back. But be sure to contact us no later than Wednesday morning, or we'll have to come looking for you to find out your answer."

There was a pause, no doubt to let me take in his threat, and surprise, surprise, his showing me they knew where I lived, before the voice continued.

"Do you have any questions?"

I had a lot, but felt much too tired to ask them.

A piece of paper was thrust into my hand.

"Phone this number as soon as you've decided." The voice said. "And remember—not later than Wednesday. If you want to go, I'll see you again soon and give you some more details. And don't forget to bring your passport. You do have a passport do you?"

No sooner had I mumbled "yes" when the hood was placed over my head and I was taken out and pushed into the back of a vehicle, different to the one I'd been brought in, by the sound and smell of it.

The car stopped after what I guessed was about three quarters of an hour, the hood was whipped off, and I was unceremoniously shoved out as they accelerated away, leaving me standing at the entrance to a park no more than five minutes from where I lived, and wondering what sort of mess I was getting myself into.

* * *

My apartment had been searched. My hidden compartment seemed undisturbed, and there wasn't much of a mess, just sufficient so I'd know someone had been there. Who the someone was, I had no idea, but it was this intrusion more than anything else that persuaded me to go, that is as well as my darned curiosity, my desire to get away for a while, plus the hard currency I'd been promised. In any case were they really giving me any choice?

I phoned the number I'd been given when I got home from work the following day, and then had to go through the whole absurd cloak and dagger process again—a different pick up point this time; the hooding, the drive, back to the same room where I somewhat reluctantly handed over my passport.

"You'll get it back with an exit and re-entry visa." Mr. Fingers, as I thought of him, said. "And also an air ticket to Geneva."

"A return?"

"Of course a return. Some cash for expenses—Swiss francs—a good, hard currency, as well as a fee deposited in an account in your name at a Swiss bank."

He quoted me a sum which I reckoned was three or four times what I was earning.

"Shall I continue?"

"Why not?" I replied, trying to hide my growing excitement.

"As I mentioned the first time we met, there's some documents we want you to have a look at. It's as simple as that."

"As simple as that?"

"Yes. As simple as that. What I can tell you is there's a lot of them, and they were all produced by your friend the poet. I don't want to give you any more details. We'd rather you read them for yourself and make up your own mind. Give us your opinion on which parts you think are important and worth publishing, and which aren't."

"But how did you get them, and will I . . . ."

"No more questions. You'll find out everything when you get there. All I need now is for you to confirm that you'll do it."

"Yes. I'll do it."

I saw his hand taking a glass to his mouth.

"Good." He said, after he'd had a sip of whatever it was he was drinking, "When you arrive in Geneva you'll find a train station inside the airport. Buy a ticket to a place called Aigle. The trains leave every thirty minutes. It's only about an hour round the lake. Nice views if you sit on the right side of the carriage. When you arrive, wait outside the station. Someone will come up to you after a while. Do exactly as he says even if it seems strange. He won't harm you. We have to take precautions—for your sake as well as ours."

One or two other bits and pieces, and I was back in the car.

On the way I wondered for the umpteenth time if I was doing the right thing. To hell with it, I thought. The money's good and I need a break. This, and that damned, stupid curiosity of mine were more than enough to persuade me.

* * *

An envelope was dropped through my letter box a few days later. It contained my passport, with exit and re-entry visas stamped inside—unusually quick, the convoluted process of getting permission to travel abroad normally took a couple of months, often more—together with a return air ticket to Geneva and fifteen hundred Swiss francs.

Luckily I had a month of unused holiday available. I asked my sub editor for two and a half weeks off, saying I wanted a break from the city. No problem. My article had gone down well and things were relatively quiet, partly due to the intense summer heat, which was usually the precursor to a kind of unofficial truce between the various warring parties.

To those of my colleagues who asked, I told them I was going to visit the coast and the mountains—no planned itinerary, staying wherever I fancied.

* * *

It was raining when I arrived in Geneva. Not a good start.

Still, the coffee in the station wasn't bad and at least the train left on time.

Clouds obscured the lake for the first part of the journey, but after a few minutes the rain stopped, the sun came out, and I could see mountains in the distance and the water gleaming through the trees and buildings lining the lake.

I got off at Aigle and waited as instructed in the little square outside the station. Five, ten minutes passed. The few passengers who'd got off with me had long disappeared. The sun was hot now, and I took my suitcase into the shade of one of the trees nearby.

I didn't see him approach until a voice next to me murmured in French.

"You're Monsieur . . . .?"

One of my countrymen, judging by his appearance and the accent—in his thirties, broad and muscular, well dressed in sports shirt and slacks, military bearing, some sort of enforcer or bodyguard, I guessed.

I nodded.

"Go round the building into the toilet." He said, speaking in little more than a whisper. "I'll follow you in a couple of minutes."

I went to the toilet at the side of the station. There was no-one else inside. The door opened after a minute or so and the man came in, turning towards me after checking the two cubicles were empty.

"Right." He said. "Hands over your head." And carefully patted me down, relieving me of my mobile phone, and presumably also looking for a wire or a weapon, as if I'd be stupid enough to carry either.

I didn't object to any of this, if these were the rules of the game, I'd go along with them—for the time being.

"Now your suitcase." He said when he'd finished, and bending down, checked it thoroughly.

"Ok." He said, straightening up. "I'm going out. Follow me in a few seconds. Walk up the road in front of the station. You'll see signs leading to the chateau. It'll take you about twenty minutes to get there. There's a restaurant called Des Alpes next to it. One of the tables is reserved in the name of Monsieur Argient. Someone will join you."

By the time I'd come out he was nowhere to be seen. Pulling my suitcase, I followed the road to the north of the town. The sun grew even warmer, the sky a deep, clear blue, the houses more scarce. Neat rows of vineyards loaded with green and red grapes stretched away on either side of the cobbled lanes.

* * *

The restaurant was where I'd been told it would be, nestling by the chateau walls.

I was directed to a courtyard at the back where a table laid for two stood in the shade of an umbrella, somewhat apart from the half a dozen others. As I sat down I noticed the bodyguard type who'd met me at the station studying the menu at a table nearby.

"Ah, Monsieur . . . I'm so pleased you could make it".

I looked up. A man in his fifties wearing dark glasses, stood over me. Impeccably dressed in a conservative grey suit, light blue shirt, a few inches of cuff showing, grey silk tie, hair also grey, trimmed short, neat moustache. Every inch the typical Swiss businessman or banker, but the accent, slight though it was, definitely from my own country.

The thought ran through my head that he could be the person who'd interviewed, interrogated me—whatever you care to call it—back home. It was something about the voice. But that person had thick, wavy, black hair. So what? Hair can be dyed. Cut. And the moustache? A disguise? For a second I had a crazy desire to try to pull it off. As for his. . . .

" . . . nice place, isn't it?" He was asking.

"Yes. Very." I replied absentmindedly.

"Let's order, then we'll talk." He said as he sat down opposite, looking directly at me, his own eyes though, hidden behind those damned dark lenses.

After the waiter had gone, the man who called himself Argient, though I very much doubted if that was his real name, made some small talk, about the weather, the area, and the like, before speaking softly, leaning forward so I could hear.

"We've got somewhere for you to work." He said. "Not far from here. Nice and quiet. All mod cons, computer, printer. Everything you'll need. No internet or phone, I'm afraid." He smiled, "We can't have you distracted. Pierre . . . " He indicated the bodyguard sitting at the nearby table. "Who you've met before, will be staying with you. He'll drive you, cook, do the shopping, and generally look after you."

"How long will I be here?"

"Two weeks. That's what you were told wasn't it? You'll be busy though, there's a lot of material to get through. We want you to have a good look at it before we decide what the next step is. Ah, the food. Let's eat."

* * *

Argient filled me in with more details during the meal.

There were three suitcases of papers written by the dead man to be examined. Notes, reminiscences, diaries he'd composed over the years; some personal, some political, some of it boring, repetitious, but also, Argient said, "some very interesting stuff". What they wanted me to do was to run through the lot and, as Argient put it, "sort the wheat from the chaff", and then put the wheat in some sort of order, and break it down into its different components.

"I won't say any more." He told me. "We don't want to prejudice you until you've seen the papers for yourself. We want you to look at the material with fresh eyes. Imagine you found it in a bus or on the back seat of a taxi." He said giving no hint of whether he found the concept amusing. "When you've finished tell us what you reckon are the most significant parts, and then we'll decide what, if anything, could be released in the form of articles in the press, or made available on the internet. Whatever we think is the best way the best to deal with it." He concluded.

"Best for who?" I asked.

"Let's not run ahead of ourselves. Look at the material first." He said, and refused to be drawn any further.

* * *

After we'd finished our meal we went outside to the car park where Pierre was waiting.

"Ok." Said Argient. "Pierre will take you to the house where you'll be working. If you need anything, or have any problems or questions just tell Pierre and he'll contact me. I'll be popping round in a day or so, once you've had an initial look at the documents, to see how you're doing."

He paused, and smiled before continuing.

"We've invested a lot of time and money in you, Monsieur . . . and we need everything to go smoothly. All I ask is that you do your best, and we'll get on fine."

He put out his hand. I took it.

He motioned to the bodyguard, who opened the doors to a Toyota—a newer version of the very same model the poet had been driving when he was murdered—that was parked next to a black Mercedes.

"Pierre's got the documents." Argient said "They're copies by the way. The originals are somewhere safe. We've numbered the pages for your convenience, and you can mark or tag them as much as you want. If for any reason you need another set or sections, I can get them for you, but it will take several days." He said, before getting into the Mercedes and driving away with a wave.

I should have realised there and then that something was wrong. If I was only going to be there for two weeks and I did need extra copies, there'd barely be enough time to get them to me.

But of course this only hit me later when. . . .

I'm running ahead of myself. We'll come to that part in due course.

* * *

"Put your case on the back seat." Pierre said, before moving off in the opposite direction to Argient, across the valley, and up a steep twisting road past neat houses with red and white flowers hanging from their balconies.

There were wooded hills all around us and behind them mountains with patches of snow on their peaks.

"We're going down there." Pierre said after a while, pointing to the left as he swung the car off the road down a narrow track running between pine trees, the occasional glimpses of a fast flowing river below us.

"Here we are," He said, pulling up in front of a house near the bottom.

Swiss chalet style. Pitched roof. Shuttered windows, and a balcony at the front with a view across the valley to a small village opposite, not much more than a church with a few houses clustered around it.

We got out the car. The air smelled fresh and clean, like in the mountains back home. Pierre took my suitcase from the back seat, then opened the boot of the car, grunting as he lifted out three large aluminium suitcases, each of them padlocked.

"Give me a hand." He told me brusquely, and we carried them to the front door.

* * *

The house was modern inside. White walls. Wooden floors with rugs. Vaulted ceiling to the lounge. A large, well equipped kitchen. Four bedrooms upstairs, two with en-suite facilities, one of the others made into an office. Computer and printer as promised. Pens, notepads, but no photocopier, in case, I presumed, I was tempted to make some copies on the sly.

We put the aluminium cases in Pierre's bedroom.

"You need two keys to open the padlocks." He told me. "One for you, the other for me. Whenever you're not looking at the documents tell me and we'll lock them back in the cases. And only look at one case at a time else the papers will get in a muddle."

I nodded, realising that although Argient had affirmed if I did my best everything would go along swimmingly, their faith in me wasn't even sufficient to allow me the sight of more than one suitcase at a time, or open one without Pierre's assistance.

Well, I thought, if that's the way you want to play it, so be it. If you want to join the club play by the rules. All *I* wanted was to be let loose on the papers as soon as possible.

* * *

I started work that afternoon with a quick thumb through the documents.

So far as I could see, the writings had started about six years before, gaining in quantity and intensity after about four years, and reaching a crescendo of anger and desperation in the last few months before the poet's end.

Sometime later, when I'd sorted the papers into some semblance of order, I found the last piece was dated just over a week before his murder, but for all I knew he'd continued writing up to the day of his fateful journey into the mountains.

* * *

My bedroom and office had windows that gave panoramic vistas across the valley to the mountains beyond, but I barely gave the view a glance so caught up was I in what I was reading.

I wanted to say to someone.

"It's like Leonardo. His work is fantastic, but if you really want to see into his soul, look at his notebooks."

What I was poring over was exactly that. The dead man's soul. His loves and hates—private and public, mixed up with rumours, facts, names and dates, politics, business dealings, and economics, rumours and gossip mixed up with what appeared to be hard facts. A lot of what I was looking seemed, at first glance to be explosive inside information. God alone knew how he'd got hold of it all. All written in his small, neat hand, crossings out, changes, the lot, his bare, raw, unadorned passionate soul shining through more than any of his more polished works for public consumption.

Sometimes, I confess, I felt like an intruder looking at something that had been written for the author's eyes alone.

Or was it just for himself?

I wondered if what he'd told his friend up at the village that he was thinking of leaving the country was true. If it was, was he also intending to put his past behind him in a great outpouring of invective once he was safely abroad as Shelley had done when he left England?

Could that be why he was killed? To stop it happening?

* * *

The main mistake I made was insisting on phoning Argient after just two days.

Correction. Not my main mistake. My main mistake was agreeing to go up to the dead man's village in the first place.

Let me rephrase that.

One of my mistakes, my many, many mistakes, was insisting on phoning Argient after only two days.

"This is sensational stuff." I burst out in my enthusiasm, without thinking what I was saying. "I reckon it could bring down the government."

Stupid I know, but I had to tell somebody.

And when there was no response from the voice at the end of the line, I continued blabbing all that nonsense about Leonardo's diaries and so forth in a similar vein, full of myself like a stupid, excited child who'd just been given a present of his favourite video game.

"There's a lot of stuff here." I continued. "I've already run through half the first case. I should be able to start looking at the second one tomorrow."

And then . . . Like a fool.

"I reckon it'll take a longer than a couple of weeks to go through everything in detail. I could e-mail my boss for a bit more time off."

There was a pause before Argient responded.

"I'm going away for a few days, but I'll be down next Tuesday." He said. "We'll talk about it then."

Another pause. Then.

"Keep up the good work, Michel." He said, using my Christian name for the first time before ringing off.

Of course Michel isn't my real name, just the first one that comes into my head. For my protection—you understand.

* * *

I kept up the good work, as Argient called it, with a vengeance. Through the days and a good part of the nights. Only managing to snatch a few hours sleep. Trying my best to avoid our shopping trips, which of course Pierre wouldn't allow, clearly under strict instructions never to let me out of his sight. Three times a week to the local town to stock up with supplies. Me trailing behind, feeling like a child taken somewhere against his will.

Pierre, though, was a surprisingly good cook. A mixture of European dishes, and those from back home. Most evenings a bottle of wine from the cellar in the basement.

The doors and windows were locked at night, and alarms set by Pierre.

I was never left alone. Not quite true. I *was* left to my own devices when I was in my bedroom and the office, but even then Pierre was always around.

He even insisted on accompanying me when I went for my short walks in the area, which I needed to clear my head, usually mid-morning and early evening. Not enthusiastically though. Saying nothing. Walking a few feet behind me, kicking at stones. Nervous when we encountered the occasional walker, his body language leaving me in no doubt that he wanted to get back to the house as quickly as possible.

I wondered what was bothering him apart from his instructions to keep me out of mischief. In those early days I had no desire to get away, and even I had, what was I going to do, attack him with a stick? The man was built like a tank, and I was sure he was armed—if not with a gun, then a knife or some other weapon, easily able to deal with any trouble I could give him.

His response to any criticisms I made about my lack of freedom was always the same, "Monsieur Argient's instructions", until eventually I stopped bothering to ask.

Not that I intended to make any trouble. The money, as I'd been promised, was good, very good, but far more important in holding my attention were the contents of the papers; some on lined notepads; others on scraps of paper; some dated, some not; some in ink, some in pencil. All of them punched, put on lever arch files and numbered in red ink in the top right hand corner.

As for the content, I'd finished my run through the first two cases, and what I'd found confirmed my initial impressions. It was indeed sensational, particularly the parts that dealt with the shenanigans of both our recent and current governments.

Yes. Sensational. There was no other word for it. I sometimes found my hands shaking with excitement unable to believe my eyes as I read and re-read the documents and made my notes.

How he'd managed to compile such a catalogue of errors, corruption, crimes and double dealings I had no idea.

I moved on to the final case.

* * *

By the time I turned in on the night before Argient was due to arrive, I'd looked at every one of the documents.

The next job, once I'd seen Argient and given him a summary of the mass of information, was to start sorting them into some sort of logical order under different headings—politics; economics; personalities, the arts, and so on.

Finally, I'd have to go through the documents with Argient or one of his cohorts, and try to decide which bits it was best to release.

And still the obvious question went unasked. How on earth would I ever manage to do all this in the few days that were left?

* * *

You should never break the rules of a lifetime, however tempting the prospect. However tempting. . . .

But there it was, all my caution thrown to the wind. Everything I'd learned so painfully over the years.

Authenticity for a start. Sure the documents seemed genuine, but we all knew how with the application of sufficient time and money forgeries could be made of almost anything.

Then there was the questions of how the documents had come into the possession of the people Argient was representing. And who was paying for all of this and why?

And finally, once everything was in the public domain—because I assumed from what Argient had told me that this was going to be the end result of all this—what effect would it have?

I could go on and on about the myriad of questions I either ignored or didn't ask.

It was as if I was in a kind of trance, all the time I'd spent perfecting my craft thrown completely away without a second thought.

* * *

Argient turned up as arranged, listened to my explanations and looked at what I showed him, not saying much, merely nodding from time to time, and stroking his moustache.

"Good, Michel." He said when I'd finished. "You've done very well. Is everything else ok? Is Pierre looking after you?"

Then continued before I had a chance to reply.

"Look. I've got to go to a meeting. I'm running late. I'll phone you tonight."

"Alright. But I wanted to. . . . "

"I'll phone you tonight Michel."

* * *

The phone rang as Pierre and I were finishing dinner.

"Hello Michel." Argient's voice sounded faint as though he was a long distance away, and I had to strain to hear what he was saying.

"Look." He said. "I've spoken to our people, and we're all agreed that you're doing a fantastic job. The problem is. . . . "

Here it comes, I thought, feeling a chill in my stomach.

"Problem?" I asked nervously.

"There's a lot of material, and judging by what you showed me, most of it is extremely important. The problem is. . . . "

"Why do you keep using that word?"

"What word?"

"Problem. I don't know why anything should be. . . . "

"Let me finish. Ok?"

I could feel my heart thumping in my chest, and my throat going dry as I waited for him to continue.

"I'll be frank with you. The point is that if the material's to be dealt with properly—which I'm sure you agree it should be—you're going to have to stay here longer than two weeks."

"Just a minute." I said. "It was me that told you it would take longer. I've been thinking about it. I've got some leave left. I can spend another eight or ten days here."

"Oh no, that won't be any good. It's going to take much more than that."

"What do you mean much more?" I could hear my voice rising shrilly.

"You've seen what's involved. It's going to need months, not days."

"I don't think you understand. I can only do an extra couple of weeks, and that's it."

"Look Michel. We're paying you very well, and we're giving you the chance to do something really worthwhile. Sensational stuff. Those were your words, not mine."

"To hell with what I said. I have to go back in two weeks."

"You're behaving like a spoilt child."

"I don't care how I'm behaving. Look, Monsieur Argient, it's been great, and I appreciate the money, but I can only do two more weeks, and then I'm going home."

"You're sure?"

"I'm sure."

"Ok Michel. If you're sure you really want to go home, that's not a problem. Pierre will take you to the airport tomorrow."

"I didn't mean right now."

"No. I insist. You'll leave tomorrow. There's a flight at midday. You can change your ticket for a few francs."

"But I. . . . "

"Don't worry, Michel. You won't lose out. We'll transfer all the money we agreed to pay you to your account."

And the phone went dead before I could say another word.

* * *

I couldn't work anymore and spent the rest of the evening watching TV with Pierre, neither of us saying a word.

Later, trying to sleep, I couldn't help wondering how easily Argient had allowed me to leave.

It shouldn't be too difficult for them, I thought. With what they're paying they should be able to get someone else to finish the job rather than spending their time fighting with me.

And as for me keeping quiet, they knew where I lived and worked, and if I spoke out of turn there was no doubt in my mind what the consequences would be.

I eventually slept, buoyed up by the thought of all the money I'd earned.

* * *

The following morning, having first checked my suitcase, Pierre drove me to Geneva airport, insisting on accompanying me into the terminal in order, as he put it, "to make sure you get off safely".

It was only afterwards that I understood what the real reason was.

After wishing him a cursory goodbye I joined the queue for our national airline. Very few people. After all the country was hardly on the list of most popular destinations.

When my turn came I told the young man on the desk that I'd been unexpectedly called back home and wanted to change my ticket.

"No problem. There's a charge of fifty francs though."

I paid him out of the cash I'd been given.

"Thank you." He said, giving me a receipt. "Your passport?"

He thumbed through it once, then again, a puzzled expression on his face.

Suddenly I had a dreadful premonition that something awful was about to happen.

"Could you wait a minute, please?" He said, disappearing through a door at the back of the booth, emerging a couple of minutes later with an older man.

"Could you come over here, sir?" The older man told me, indicating an empty booth nearby.

"I'm afraid there's an irregularity in this visa." He said without any preliminaries. "You can't travel on it."

I leaned across and grabbed hold of the passport.

"What d'you mean, I can't travel? What irregularity? This runs until the twenty second." I said desperately, showing the visa stamp to him, stabbing my finger at the page.

He glanced at it cursorily before handing it back.

"I'm sorry, sir. But it's no longer valid."

"Look at it, for God's sake. There's the date. The twenty second. It *is* valid." I was shouting now. "Look. There's my Swiss entry stamp from a couple of weeks ago"

"I've looked sir. My colleague's looked. And it's not valid."

"But it is. For God's sake. It's there in front of you. It's obvious."

"I'm telling you for the last time. It's not valid and there's no way you can travel on it."

"I've got my entry stamp. The Swiss will let me out."

"You won't be allowed on the flight without a valid visa."

"This is bullshit. For hell's sake why can't. . . . "

"Look sir. I've been very patient with you, but if you persist in arguing and making a scene I'll get the police to escort you out of here. The Swiss don't take kindly to disturbances in their public places."

I could feel my aggression dissipate like a punctured balloon.

Calm down. Think. *Think*.

"Ok. Ok." I said trying to keep my voice under control. "There's obviously been a mistake. Can you tell me what the problem is?"

"The visa's not valid." He repeated, like an actor reading from a script.

It was clear I'd get nothing further out of him.

"Alright." I responded, as calmly as I was able. "If it's not valid what can I do about it?"

"All I can suggest." He said. "Is that you try our consulate in Bern. Just a minute."

He opened a drawer and handed me a sheet of typed paper.

"There you are. There's the details."

"Thank you." I said, quickly looking at it. Open for enquiries weekdays from ten thirty to one. Too late to go now.

"I'll go there tomorrow." I said half to myself, and half to the official. "They'll sort it out."

He gave a sort of half smile, whether of sympathy or contempt it was impossible to tell, and went back to the other desk.

* * *

I saw Pierre standing nearby as I turned to leave.

"You knew, didn't you?" I said to him.

"Knew what? I was told to wait till you'd got on the plane."

"Well. Guess what. My visa's no fucking good. I'm not going anywhere. I want to speak to Argient. Now."

"He's away for a few days."

"How bloody convenient. Right." I continued. "You're taking me to Bern. To the consulate, tomorrow morning. And I want to be there before they open."

Pierre shrugged

"If that's what you want." He said, apparently quite relaxed about my demand.

"It's what I want. Come on, let's get out of here."

It wasn't until we were halfway back to the chalet that I realised I hadn't asked for my fifty francs back.

* * *

In normal circumstances I would have lingered in Bern, joining the tourists and locals taking their ease in the cobbled streets and open air cafes, but I had far more important business to attend to.

After having to ask for directions a couple of times we eventually found our way to the consulate, a large villa surrounded by high walls, situated in a residential area to the north of the town.

Although it was only just after ten—I'd insisted on arriving early—several people were already waiting outside the large metal gates.

I joined them somewhat reluctantly. I would have preferred to wait in the car, but didn't want to risk anyone else coming in front of me. In the event only two people, a middle aged man, accompanied by a younger woman, joined the queue after me.

Thankfully, there was no conversation. Clearly the people there had as little desire as I did to discuss their business with strangers, particularly strangers who were their fellow countryman. Over the years we'd all learned to keep our mouths shut. Far better to keep quiet than take any risks.

* * *

The gates clanged open just after ten thirty. Pierre waited in front of the building as we filed past two security guards dressed in what I can best describe as a kind of brown tracksuit.

After being allocated a numbered ticket we were directed into a waiting room off the entrance hall, where we were handed forms to fill out stating what our business was.

I have to say I felt most peculiar sitting there as people's names and numbers were called out. Although the building was a typical Swiss suburban villa built, I guessed, in the early 1900's, once inside I felt as though I was waiting for an appointment back home.

The surroundings—the furniture; the pictures on the walls; the newspapers strewn on a table—the paper I worked for, I noticed, not among them; the lighting, yellow shades and weak bulbs—were so typical of my country that I could have been in any of a hundred government offices or institutions in the capital or one of our other cities, rather than in the heart of Europe

Even the smell, though barely noticeable, was evocative, what I can best describe as a mixture of perfume, strong pungent cigarettes, and what I thought was the slight, but unmistakable whiff of rice, lamb and spices simmering in a pot.

I sat back, closed my eyes, and for a moment imagined I was driving to one of my favourite restaurants along the coast back home, in the late afternoon when the sun had lost its strength and a cool, welcoming breeze wafted in from the sea.

* * *

Like all our citizens I'd learned the hard way that one had to be patient with our bureaucracy, and I wasn't surprised that it wasn't until well after twelve that my name and number were announced.

I was shown into a small office upstairs where I sat twiddling my fingers until two men, both dressed in identical blue suits, came in.

"Ah, Monsieur. . . . " The older one said in a friendly fashion. "I understand you have problem with your passport. May I have a look at it please?"

"Mm. . . . " He said after glancing at it. "Could you wait a few minutes" And left with his colleague.

My hopes increased. Clearly some technicality, easily remedied. A new stamp, maybe an additional charge, and everything would be back to normal.

Several minutes passed before they returned, accompanied this time by a third man, wearing the same kind of tracksuit as the guards on the gate.

My heart sank as he placed himself by the door, arms folded, while the other two sat down opposite me, the younger one pushing my passport across the desk.

There was a horrible inevitability about what happened next, as I heard a jumble of words and phrases emerging through a kind of haze.

"Serious error; incorrect entry contrary to Article 16 of the Act; annual quotas now exceeded; and finally,—"You may re-apply. . . . "—and here my hopes rose for a second before being dashed again—". . . .in six months, but there is no guarantee that. . . . "

I knew our bureaucrats. It was a waste of time arguing with them. I couldn't bear to hear any more. Picking up my passport, I clambered to my feet, pushed my way past the guard, hearing the words—"let him go"—behind me as I rushed down the stairs, slammed the front door, emerging, breathless, into the bright sunlight where Pierre was waiting, kicking his feet on the gravel.

"Well?" He asked.

"Take me home." I said. "And tell Argient, I don't give a fuck where he is. I want to see him. Tonight."

* * *

What a bloody fool I was, caught like a rat in a trap. And even worse was my increasing suspicion that as this process unfolded it appeared to have all been orchestrated by Argient or whoever it was he worked for.

Every step I took seemed to have been foreseen from the very beginning.

It was what I imagine playing a grand master at chess is like. Each of your moves anticipated before you've even thought of it yourself. * * *

"You won't starve, Michel." Argient told me when my screaming and shouting—which he'd listened to without saying a word—had petered out. "We'll look after you. You have my word on it."

"Besides, there's a lot of work for you to do here." He continued, ignoring my snort of derision. "Important work. For the life of me I can't understand why you don't appreciate how lucky you are. Your colleagues would give their eye teeth to be in your shoes."

"Yes. I'm sure they would." I said, gritting my teeth "I've only got one question. Why are you doing this?"

"Doing what?"

"This. *This.*" I answered, indicating the piles of documents on my desk and on the floor. "All these papers. Keeping me here."

"You could say I'm a patriot." Argient replied. "Someone who wants a better life for his country. Someone who recognises how important these papers are in showing what's going wrong back home. Also, you know as well as I do how interesting they'll be to the wider world. For God's sake, Michel, they're significant historical and literary documents. It would be a crime not to bring them to a wider audience."

"A crime? And how did *you* get them?" I asked. "Steal them? Persuade the dead poet by putting money in a Swiss bank account?"

Nothing I said or did seemed to disturb Argient. The man had skin like a rhinoceros. He just smiled, glanced at Pierre who'd been there throughout the proceedings standing by the door, and said.

"Now Michel, you wouldn't expect me to disclose my sources, would you?"

He looked at his watch.

"I'm sorry. I have to leave. I'll tell you what, though. I'll come back tomorrow. Take it easy, Michel. We want you to stay until you've finished everything. Sleep on it, and think about the wonderful chance you've been given. I'll see you about ten, and we'll discuss what to do next."

* * *

I tried to get into Pierre's room that night, thinking to catch him asleep, knock him out, tie him up, and take the keys to the car.

Whether he heard me or not I couldn't say.

It didn't matter. The door was locked.

In any case, say I'd been lucky and got away from there. Where could I go?

Without a valid visa there wasn't a chance in hell of getting home. And as for Switzerland, Argient's people would probably find a way to withdraw the money in my account, and the cash I'd got left would last a month the most. I wouldn't even be able sell the car. I didn't have the papers, and the Swiss are sticklers for doing things by the book.

Oh yes. Whichever you looked at it I was well and truly in the shit.

All I could do was wait for Argient to show up in the morning.

* * *

After returning from my abortive expedition to Pierre's room, I spent the rest of the night tossing and turning, struggling to consider my increasingly limited options.

However, I tend to be an optimist—you had to be in my job and the state my country was in. I couldn't leave, and that was that, but thinking about the god-awful mess I'd allowed myself to be drawn into it seemed to me there were, at least, a couple of rays of hope. The money, paid into the bank account that had been set up for me in Zurich was good, very good, and, as Argient had said, they wanted me to finish the work on the documents.

After all, I thought, trying my best to cheer myself up, I could at least agree with him on two things. I *was* being given a great opportunity, and the papers were important, very important. As much as I hated to admit it, I was feeling something I could best describe as proprietorial towards them. Except for eventually getting home in one piece, there was nothing I wanted more than to see them in print.

* * *

I got up early to find Pierre in the kitchen, drinking coffee, barely acknowledging me, and not a word about any disturbance he may have heard during the night.

The phone rang shortly after nine. Pierre handed it to me. It was Argient, saying he couldn't make it in the morning, but would treat me to lunch in the restaurant in Aigle where we'd first met.

"Is that alright, Michel?" He asked.

"Have I got a choice?"

He didn't reply, but asked to be put on to Pierre.

A lengthy conversation followed, most of the talking done by Argient. Pierre's part just being the occasional yes, no, and, of course. I had no doubt that Argient was telling Pierre to make sure I came, and didn't try anything foolish.

There was nothing for him to worry about on that score. I needed to get out of that damned prison if only for a few hours, and confront Argient face to face.

* * *

"You know the old proverb." Argient said, the ever present Pierre keeping an eye on me from a nearby table. "When things go wrong, all you can do is make the best of them."

I was tempted to quote another one back at him.

"Better leave one of your legs in the hunter's snare, than succumb to his knife."

In fact, though, in this case, there was a much more appropriate saying that applied.

"Never bite the hand that feeds you."

Particularly if the hand has just poured you a glass of expensive wine, and is offering you a lifeline in the form of an apartment, regular money, and, as Argient put it—"The chance to make a difference."

What choice did I have?

And so, dear readers, I did what most of you would have done.

After half an hour of ranting and raving, I succumbed.

I succumbed.

* * *

I looked at several apartments recommended by Argient, eventually choosing one on the outskirts of Montreux, not right on the lake, but only a leisurely stroll away. Pierre picked me up from there each day at eight, and drove me to the chalet where I continued work on the documents.

The rent, as Argient had promised, was 'taken care of' and on top of this my Zurich bank account was credited each month with fifty percent more than they'd been paying me before, more than enough to cover living, entertainment, and other expenses, and set a tidy sum aside.

"Until we decide what you should do next." Argient replied in answer to my question, and I didn't have the energy or interest to ask him any more. Besides, I had no option except to take what was offered until it was decided whatever the 'next' job would be.

Who paid my rent? I had no idea. I didn't even know who owned the apartment. I never saw the landlord, and I was told to pass the bills and correspondence I received to a p.o. box in Geneva. As for the source of the monthly transfers of money, my bank wouldn't give me any details other than they originated from a company registered in the Caribbean.

I told the few Swiss friends I made that I was a journalist who also did consulting work for Swiss and other overseas enterprises who were considering doing business with or investing in my country, though who in their right mind would consider such a course of action the situation back home being what it was?

The violence and unrest were to be expected, but recently a more than usual volatility on the political front seemed to have been added to the brew. Hardly conducive to the sort of activities I claimed to be engaged in.

The Swiss, though, bless them, have a quality—namely discretion—which I've come to increasingly admire, and did not probe beyond what I chose to tell them or ask any awkward questions.

As for my own countrymen, of whom increasing numbers were starting to appear throughout Europe, some in the part of the world I was living in, I didn't seek them out, and positively tried to avoid them.

* * *

I think it was the sale of my apartment back home—I still thought of it as home then—that upset me more than anything else.

You may think me naïve, but I still believed that once my work on the documents was finished my visa would be sorted out and I'd be able to return to take up the life I'd left behind. My friends and my apartment would be waiting for me as if nothing had changed. My job as well.

I'd managed to clear an extended unpaid leave of absence with my editor, e-mailing him that while on holiday I'd heard from a long lost cousin in the States, and had been given a once in a lifetime opportunity to visit him there. Whether he believed this story or not, the cynical old bastard had agreed without asking me a single question, no doubt with an eye out for anyone who may have been snooping on his correspondence.

"Fine, Michel. Have a great time. We'll see you when you get back." He e-mailed me a couple of days later.

As for my apartment overlooking a pretty square in the old part of town, that I'd so lovingly decorated and refurbished, Argient had assured me on several occasions that all the maintenance, mortgage payments, and other expenses would be taken care of.

I'd no intention whatsoever of selling it, but sold it was, without my authority, and with no papers signed by me to transfer the ownership and pay off the mortgage.

* * *

It happened shortly after the task was complete, the most important extracts of the papers published in the press in Europe and the States, and great chunks posted on the internet a few weeks later.

The first inkling I had was notification from the bank in Zurich of a large amount deposited into my account. I requested the details, and had to call them several times for additional information before ascertaining with growing incredulity and horror that the deposit represented the amount realised from the disposal of my flat after deducting the outstanding mortgage.

So far as I could make out the sale proceeds in local currency were well over the market price, and even more surprisingly, once translated into Swiss francs, I received not the derisory sum one would have expected, but something which approximated to the official exchange rate. The exchange rate, which, as everyone knew, could never actually be realised in a genuine transaction.

These unexpected benefits though, did nothing to stem my fury. I drove to Zurich, and stormed into the bank demanding to know where the money had come from, only to be told that this information was strictly private, protected by Swiss banking laws, and to be reminded politely but firmly, that I'd previously been advised this when enquiring about the source of the regular deposits to my account.

Afterwards, I sat on a bench by the lake. Around me people were laughing and talking with friends, colleagues, lovers. Their voices though, sounded jumbled and distant, my eyes filling with impotent tears as I stared into the distance.

No home to go back to. No visa. Stuck like a rat in a cage. A well fed, well looked after rat, but a rat all the same.

* * *

When I got back to my apartment I immediately telephoned the number I'd been given in case of emergencies and demanded to speak to Argient.

"He's not here." The remote, disembodied voice told me.

I knew from past experience there was no point in enquiring where he was or when he'd be back.

"It's Michel . . . Tell him to phone me. Urgently." I said, before slamming the phone down.

Argient phoned me back in less than half an hour.

"I hear it's urgent. What. . . . " He started to say.

"You know damned well what, Monsieur Argient. If that's your real name—which I doubt. It's probably phony like everything else about you. You know bloody well why I'm phoning. My flat's been sold without me knowing a thing about it. That's what."

There was a pause before he replied.

"Ah, yes. You've got the money. Maybe I should have said something, but I wanted to give you a surprise."

"You surprised me alright, you fucking bastard. You sold it without telling me."

Another pause.

"How much did you get?" He asked.

I didn't answer.

"Come on. I can easily find out."

"Fuck off."

"I reckon in hard currency you got three, maybe four times what it was worth. Think. When you go home, with that sort of money you could buy a villa or a penthouse in the best part of. . . . "

"Go home? You know I can't. I've got no home. No visa. I'm stuck here, you bastard."

"Look. Don't let's shout at each other over the phone. If it upset you, I'm sorry. Come on, let me take you out for lunch, by way of an apology."

"I don't. . . . "

"Come on. What've you got to lose?"

I felt like saying to him, nothing, I've lost everything worthwhile, but I was so darn sick and tired of this constant manoeuvring and playing around that I reluctantly agreed.

"Good I'll see you at the Chateau d'Ouchy. Twelve thirty on Thursday. And Michel, dress smartly, they expect a jacket and tie."

* * *

The Chateau d'Ouchy is one of the best restaurants in Lausanne, situated in well-kept grounds overlooking the lake

Argient was already sitting at a table on the terrace when I arrived. No Pierre that I could make out. In fact since the work was finished and I'd stopped going to the chalet I'd not seen him at all.

Argient waved when he saw me, got up, smiling broadly. Sometime after, I wondered if his good mood meant he had prior knowledge of the events that were shortly about to unfold at home.

He put his hand out for me to shake. I pointedly ignored it. I still felt bitter about what had happened, and his false bonhomie riled me even more. It was all I could do to resist the temptation to punch him in the mouth, turn heel and walk away.

This no doubt showed in my demeanour because no sooner had we sat down then he said.

"No hard feelings?"

"What do you think? No hard feelings? Tell me, Mr Argient. How would you feel if you were trapped like I am?"

"But what a trap, Michel. It may sound unpatriotic to say it, but you could do a lot worse than spend your time here."

He gesticulated at the lake.

"Beautiful place. Nice climate. Laws you can rely on. Trains that run on time. Women. Attractive. Available. And people who aren't busy blowing each other to pieces. What else could you ask for?"

"Don't you get it? Whatever you say, I'm still trapped."

"Don't be a fool, Michel. Most people would murder to be in your position. Relax. Enjoy yourself. Get out more. Buy yourself a decent car. You can afford it."

"Don't patronise me."

Argient's voice hardened.

"You know, Michel, you should realise that now you've finished the work you were brought here to do you're not as useful as you once were. There are other ways in which you could have been dealt with, and I can assure you they wouldn't have been anything like as pleasant as what you've ended up with."

"Is that a threat?"

"A threat? Why would I. . . . "

He broke off as a waiter hovered near our table.

"Ah the menu. We'll order in a few minutes." He said, before turning back to me, a smile on his face once again.

"I particularly recommend the veal. It's really exceptional. Or if you prefer fish, the sole bonne femme is. . . .

* * *

In fact Argient had far more important matters to concern himself about than my situation.

Developments at home.

Following months of government resignations, reshuffles, suicides, you name it, news started filtering through of trouble brewing in the capital, followed by full blown riots and demonstrations which rapidly spread throughout the country.

The government fell in a matter of days, the army taking over, promising a transformation of the country thorough economic reforms, and a much harder line against the rebels and terrorists.

There was no doubt in my mind that my efforts—the series of newspaper articles published all over the world, and the detailed extracts from the poet's papers posted on the internet, showing the extent of double dealing, corruption and criminality at the highest levels of government, as well as his complete disillusion with the forces that had been running the country for the past few years—had been one of the main contributing factors to the air of hopelessness and frustration that allowed the military to make their move.

When the articles and extracts were first published I kidded myself they would act as a memorial, a sort of last will and testament, the dead man's final legacy addressed to his country and the world at large. Now, with the military takeover it was clear that what I'd been instrumental in producing had, like so many legacies, the completely opposite effect to what was originally intended.

The new masters of the country and their friends didn't give a damn about the poet's legacy. All they were interested in was the releasing of the details of the wrongdoings that were rife in our country to an incredulous public back home. I'd done exactly what they wanted. I'd stirred the pot to such an extent that it overflowed.

The very generous lump sum Argient offered me during our lunch in Lausanne was clearly a reward or bonus for my efforts—a very small reward given the spoils now available—through which the people who'd come to power were expressing if not exactly their gratitude, then at least their debt to me.

As for my future, well, Argient told me, toasting my health for the umpteenth time, that was under 'active consideration at the highest levels', adding he was sure I'd be be, as he put it "over the moon" at the arrangements he'd shortly be offering me.

* * *

The war against the rebels was pursued with a ferocity and tenacity previously lacking. Glued to Swiss television night after night I saw shots of tanks on the streets, dead bodies in the gutters, and listened to reports of massacres and atrocities.

Most people back home, had become so inured to violence that the actions taken were, so the military controlled press (including my paper) and TV reported, welcomed by the vast majority of the people as long as they resolved the 'unacceptable situation' once and for all.

Where Argient fitted into all this the lord only knew. What I did come to realise, though, was that everything, including my role, had been planned in advance.

If I was right about this, and the more I mulled over the events of the past few months, the more I was convinced I was, the poet's documents had been an integral part of the manoeuvring by the plotters to undermine the government.

And I . . . I was nothing but a pawn in a very big game manipulated and duped by Argient and whoever it was that was pulling his strings. A game played out by the very people who the poet hated to the depths of his soul. The same people who, I was now certain, were behind his assassination.

* * *

So fuck Argient and his friends, with their 'active consideration' of my 'future at the highest levels', and my presumed feeling 'over the moon' at all their bullshit.

I drove up to the consulate in Bern shortly after the coup. Not a word to any of my friends, and certainly not to Argient.

I was surprised to find the place completely transformed. Modern décor. No more smells of rice or lamb. No smoking allowed. No faces that I recognised. The security guards no longer in creased, ill-fitting tracksuits, but in smart blue blazers and well pressed grey trousers.

Despite these improvements though, my own position had distinctly worsened.

"Certain passports, including yours, Monsieur . . . have been rescinded. You're going to have to re-apply for a new one. At this stage, that can't be before three years from the date of the change in government." (Note the use of the words "change in government". No mention of a coup—that might give the wrong impression, frighten people off.)

My heart sank.

"And you should also understand there's no guarantee that approval will be given for a replacement."

"But they told me six months." Was all I could plaintively reply.

"The law's been amended." The official brusquely informed me.

"You're not the only one who's been affected." He added, with what he no doubt thought was a reassuring smile, as if it made a blind bit of difference to my situation.

"Thank you very much." I said as bitingly as I could. "My passport, please."

He held it up, still with that supercilious grin plastered over his face.

I grabbed it from him and stormed out, slamming the door behind me.

* * *

I stopped off at a bar in the old part of town, and stayed till closing time.

How I managed to get home in one piece I'll never know.

* * *

To tell you the truth I didn't know what my status was.

Refugee? Hardly. Stateless person—albeit one in a gilded cage?

But a couple of weeks after I'd been to the consulate an extremely strange document was pushed under my door one evening.

It was a permanent Swiss visitor's visa—a document bestowed on individuals, only, I gathered, in the most exceptional circumstances. But not a passport though. Who'd ever arranged it clearly had no intention of letting me out the country—at least not for the time being.

Why on earth should I have been given such a privilege—albeit a somewhat limited one? I had absolutely no idea—I assumed somewhere along the line strings had been pulled for my benefit—and I had no intention of sticking my neck out trying to find out why and by whom.

I guessed Argient had a hand in it. Argient, my handler, as I now thought of him, who told me that now I had the Swiss visa in five to ten years I could become a fully-fledged Swiss citizen with all the considerable advantages this brought. If—he added—*if* I behave myself and can show sufficient income and a reasonable lifestyle. All of which, as he's well aware, are in my case completely dependent on the largesse of the people he represents, and as we all know, what's been given can just as easily be taken away.

However, as Argient has informed me on several occasions, if I keep my nose clean and don't rock the boat, there's no reason why the pleasant state of affairs that I find myself in—no hint of irony on his part—shouldn't continue indefinitely.

* * *

Back home—yes, in spite of all that had happened I still thought of it as home—the internet which had played a key role in the protests against the government, and the circulation of the poet's documents, was heavily curtailed.

Censorship was tightened; the newspaper I'd worked for closed down along with several others, leaving just two who strictly towed the junta's line.

'Peace at last' trumpeted the government controlled media. And I had to admit that from where I was sitting it appeared to be true. Things had quietened down after a couple of months, the junta claiming the rebellion was completely crushed, never to soil our great country's reputation again, the way now clear for economic reform.

Within a year every one of the state enterprises and plants, including the oil and gas fields and mineral concessions were, what was euphemistically called, 'privatisated'. In practice the shares were sold at a hefty discount to those rich or well-connected individuals who'd somehow managed to lay their hands on the hard currency required, thereby becoming even more wealthy, in several cases fabulously so.

In addition to its privatisation programme, the military government also pushed ahead in a big way with the opening up of the country to outside investors, enticing them with a raft of generous concessions and incentives, access to cheap labour, and an un-unionised workforce.

Those who did invest concentrated on supplying high-priced goods to those who could afford them, and developing tourist projects, luxury hotels, villas, golf courses for our own rich as well the affluent foreigners who'd started to holiday in our country and also buy expensive holiday homes, attracted by our climate and beaches, the relatively low cost of living, and of course the improved security.

* * *

The previous government, despite its many faults, had followed the long established custom of giving benefits and subsidies to the less well off in our country—in other words, the majority.

These were abolished at a stroke increasing poverty and accelerating the desire of those who dared to risk the journey to the honey-pots of Europe and beyond.

So there it is. Each day hundreds of well-heeled foreigners arrive at our capital's recently modernised airport to be whisked away to spanking new hotels or holiday homes, complete with swimming pools, golf courses, spas, and whatever else money can buy, while at the same time an ever increasing flood of my countrymen are moving in the opposite direction in unseaworthy rusting hulks or small fishing boats, hidden in the back of lorries, freight cars or containers in a desperate attempt to gain a foothold, however tentative, in the prosperous countries of the West.

Do you blame them?

Take a look at the world. Increasingly little work in the countryside, growing populations, the one billion people in slums expected to double over the next twenty years.

This, my friends, *this* is the world we're living in.

* * *

And what about me?

What about *my* world?

Argient's "over the moon" offer materialised a few months after the coup, and I'm doing very nicely, thank you.

I'm drawing an excellent salary, and have recently moved to a new apartment—rent still paid by a company in the Caribbean.

It's larger and more modern than the previous one, and, most importantly, that little bit nearer the lake. I spent a fair amount furnishing it, and, on top of that, have recently ordered a new car. A Mercedes convertible. Metallic blue. Very smart.

Correction. It wasn't me, but my company that ordered the car. Yes, you heard right, I've got a company.

Actually it's not exactly *my* company. Although I own 49% of the shares, allocated to me for a nominal sum, they're non dividend bearing, and the controlling 51%, fully subscribed for in cash, and entitled to whatever dividends are declared, is owned by a Foundation in Zurich.

My co-director who represents the Foundation, and who I've only seen once at our inaugural Board meeting, is a lawyer, also from Zurich.

Precisely who controls the Foundation, or what its objectives are, I've no idea.

Although I own 49% of the company, certain controls have been established to keep me on a very tight leash. My shares can be bought back at their nominal value by the Foundation at any time without prior notice, and all payments over one thousand francs have to be countersigned by Argient or our co-director in Zurich despite the administrative delays that sometimes result from this arrangement.

The message these conditions send me is crystal clear. If you dare to step out of line we will break you.

* * *

Ironically the company specialises in what I used to tell people who asked what my source of income was, namely advising and facilitating individuals and corporations who are investing in or doing business with my home country.

There I go again, still using the words "my home country" even though currently it's definitely neither.

The idea for the company, needless to say, came from Argient, who I'm sure has had a hand in putting business our way, aided by his contacts here and at home, and he helps to grease the wheels for those clients who require it, or at least the ones who're in his good books—as I seem to be at the moment.

* * *

The business was off the blocks extremely quickly, and due to the opportunities which arose after the military coup, expanded far more rapidly than I'd expected.

The work soon became too much for me to handle from home and we moved to an office in the business district of Montreux, just a short drive from my apartment. I say *we*, because there's three of us now. Myself, a secretary, and a bookkeeper come accountant. Both Swiss. The bookkeeper in his fifties and the secretary in her thirties both coming "highly recommended" by Argient.

As you'd expect, they're extremely efficient, although business is so brisk Argient has suggested we think about taking someone on to manage the office, as well as a qualified individual to help me handle our promoting of investment and property opportunities in my country

"I'll find some people for you to interview." Argient, who pops in to chat things over at least once a week, told me. "I don't trust agencies or adverts. You never know who you'll end up with. Much better to rely on personal recommendations. And it's cheaper."

And then, with one of his knowing smiles.

"You know Michel, if things go well you should think about moving to a larger office next year, take on some more staff, maybe get involved in a bit of commodity trading for some people I know."

* * *

The following year we opened a larger office as well as a representative office in the capital back home, manned by a go-ahead young economics graduate appointed by Argient.

I, of course, can't travel anywhere without a visa or valid passport, but I keep in regular contact with the manager by phone, skype and e-mail. He seems efficient and personable, and those clients who've dealt with him speak very highly of his efforts. I never let on to them that I've never actually met him face to face, and am unlikely to do so for the foreseeable future.

* * *

And then there are the 'special' customers, the ones Argient personally introduces to me. Russian, South American, English, Chinese—you name it, the one thing they have in common are the large amounts of money they have to invest.

The bit of the journalist that's still left in me would love to delve into their circumstances, even ask a few probing questions as to the source of their cash, but it would be unwise if not downright dangerous to do so, and definitely not good for business.

Besides, I tell myself, surely any questions regarding the legitimacy of their funds would have been taken care of by the bankers, accountants and lawyers whose job is to deal with these sort of things, and are clearly more aware than I could ever be of all the applicable rules and regulations.

All I can do is try to convince myself that I don't need to worry about such matters. So I keep my trap shut and tell these individuals what they've come to hear—how stable the situation in my country now is, what wonderful opportunities and tax breaks are available, and how delighted my company and I would be to commence a mutually beneficial relationship.

Argient's interest in the business, isn't, I'm sure, purely altruistic. I'm convinced he benefits somewhere along the line from those 'special' clients grateful for the favours he provides them, as well as from the regular dividends and management charges we pay to the Foundation—not to Zurich as one might expect it being the Foundation's place of business, but to a bank account on an obscure South Pacific island.

"Do me a favour, Michel."—the lawyer, my rarely seen co-director, oh so softly whispers on the phone—"It would be very useful if you could e-mail me as soon as possible what you estimate is the maximum amount we could pay the Foundation this year given your profit and cash flow predictions."

Only a polite request, but one I know I cannot refuse.

* * *

After a number of short-lived affairs—apparently my exotic looks combined with the air of mystery I exude make me very appealing—I took up with a young Swiss woman of whom I grew extremely fond.

It wasn't until I'd been with her for several months that I told Argient about the relationship, not in any way to seek his approval, but merely to see what his reaction would be—that is if he didn't know already.

If he did know I had to admit he gave a damned good impression of being pleasantly surprised.

"Excellent. Excellent. I'll order champagne" He said, beaming and rubbing his hands together, looking for all the world like a benign father who'd been given good news by his favourite son.

Despite all that had gone before, he'd become, in a strange sort of way, if not exactly a father figure, a kind of confidante, and his reaction gave me a feeling of pleasure I hadn't anticipated, at least until, driving back home, I found myself wondering maybe uncharitably if he was only acting this way because this liaison was one more cord, albeit a silken one, that further bound me to my life here.

Thinking about the way things had worked out, a notion resurfaced I'd had several times before, that this latest women, as well as the previous ones, and for that matter anyone else I had dealings with were all part of Argient's web, planted to keep an eye on me and report any deviation from "normal" behaviour.

No. Impossible. Ridiculous. Only in the movies.

* * *

Later that night lying in bed, unable to sleep, my girlfriend beside me moving gently in her deep, innocent slumber; me thinking about the rotten state of affairs I'd had a hand in creating; wide awake despite the drink and the pills.

Getting up to pour myself another drink, and after, standing in the dark in the sitting room, looking out at the lake and the deserted streets below, it seemed to me I was not in the heaven that Monsieur Argient had described, but in a sort of hell.

A few lights were twinkling on the hills across the lake. A couple walked down the road holding hands.

I went to the drinks cabinet and had two more whiskeys—a drink I found myself increasingly resorting to.

Hearing a sigh I glanced behind me at the profusion of blonde hair on the pillow.

Tomorrow was Saturday. We'd drive up to a village in the mountains. Walk around. Take in the sights. Have lunch at a little restaurant I knew.

No. Hell was far too strong a word for this.

Purgatory would be better.

* * *

So, my friends, there we are. This is the wonderful world I've ended up living in.

It may be rude of me, but I have to ask.

What sort of a world do *you* live in?

Escape

Meeting—Number 1

The attached Report and Appendices as well as the Agenda for this Meeting have been produced by Members (2) and (3) of the Committee at the request of the Chairman—Member (1).

The authors apologise for the length and complexity of the documents. However, in view of the severity of the situation, full details are considered essential for Committee Members to gain a proper understanding of the issues confronting us, particularly as the information regarding the Project will not have been previously known to the majority of Members, and may therefore come as both a surprise and a shock to them.

While it is admitted that errors of omission and commission have been made in the past, the Chairman, who will not able to attend for the first hour of the Meeting, has expressed the hope that the Committee concentrates its efforts on deciding what action should be taken to alleviate the crisis we face. He believes that spending time looking backwards and trying to question the whys and wherefores of what occurred is not a constructive use of the Committee's resources given the extreme severity of the situation the Committee is charged with confronting

It is hoped these comments will be taken into account, and will lead to a full, frank, and open discussion during which Members should feel free to raise any matters which, in their opinion, have either not been included, or fully covered in the Report and Appendices without, however, attempting to attach responsibility for any errors that may or may not have occurred in the past.

* * *

1. Ground Rules.

- In view of their extremely sensitive nature, copies of the Report, Appendices, the hand-written attachments, and the Agenda have only been circulated to Committee Members.

  Under no circumstances should they or any part thereof, or any of the information contained therein, be handed to, shown to, copied, or discussed with any parties other than the recipients, unless by the express written permission of the Chairman or his Deputy.

- The Report, Appendices, Agenda, and any other subsequent Reports, documents or other written material must be kept in a safe place known only to the recipient. If any Committee Member does not have access to such a place, arrangements can be made by Members (2) or (3) for safe keeping. The list of Members' names, chosen codenames, code-numbers, and their mobile phone numbers referred to below, should also be kept in a safe place, but separate from the other papers.

- Attached to the Report and Appendices will be found a hand written sheet of paper which lists the Committee Members' names as well as a code number which will be used to identify them in this and all subsequent documentation. Numbers for the pay as you go mobile phones which will be handed out at the end of the Meeting are noted next to each Committee Member's name. (See below for details regarding the use of these phones.)

- Each Committee Member should choose a code name for his or her self with a minimum of five letters and give this to Member (2) at the commencement of the first Meeting for copying and distribution to the other recipients. This code name will be used in all subsequent documentation, and may only be changed by prior agreement.

- Telephone conversations with other Members should be kept to a minimum, and should be only by means of the aforementioned mobile phones which will be distributed at the first Meeting.

- After the first Meeting, the Committee will convene on an ad hoc basis, the frequency of such Meetings depending on future developments. It is not possible at this stage to state how often Meetings will take place, but initially they will be two or three times a week, and more if deemed appropriate.

- All Meetings will be held at this location, unless circumstances render a change necessary. In order to make attendance easier for all Members and it less likely for questions to be raised as to their whereabouts, Meetings, wherever possible, will be convened on early evenings. These Meetings should, to as great a degree as possible, take priority over other matters, both official and personal. In the event that attendance is not possible, the Member will be subsequently advised of the content and decisions of the Meeting by way of the Minutes which will be circulated before the following Meeting. All Minutes should be kept safe with the other papers.

- If any Member feels that an unscheduled Meeting is required—for example, on the basis of information obtained formally or informally—they should immediately contact Committee Members (2) or (3), who, if they feel the requested Meeting is justified, will make the necessary arrangements.

- The above should cover all the arrangements for contact, Meetings, and security. If, however, any of the recipients have any queries, criticisms, comments, or additional suggestions, it is essential that these be raised at the initial meeting so they can be addressed, and changes made if required.

2. Background.

The First Item on the Agenda will deal with any questions or points of clarification Members may require regarding the Project—see below.

- Committee Members will have no doubt read about yesterday's explosion at a Research Facility near the Welsh border. Among other things, this Facility, housed a top secret Project. Unfortunately, paperwork hidden at the home of one of the Project workers who died in the explosion indicates that it had taken a completely unauthorised direction for, we think, about eighteen months. Apart from the potential problems emanating from the Project itself, the nature of this unauthorised work could possibly cause additional complications to the problems we are confronting. (Appendix 1 sets out full background information and details regarding both the Project and its unauthorised elements.)

- A selection of press cuttings regarding the explosion can be found in Appendix 2. So far media coverage here and abroad does not contain anything that should cause this Committee any concern.

- The area of greatest, in fact of almost total destruction, was at the part of the Facility where the Project was being undertaken. A glance at the photographs in Appendix 2 will give an idea of the devastation that occurred. It is difficult to imagine anything surviving it unscathed. The benefit of this is that we believe, but, we stress, are not completely certain, that all, or, if not all, by far the greater part, of the information on site regarding the Project, as well as its potentially dangerous physical results have probably been completely destroyed.

- There is as yet no information as to the cause of the explosion. Although sabotage or terrorism cannot be ruled out, the facts so far all point to nothing more than a pure accident.

- Investigations into the explosion by the police and fire services are currently being conducted on what we understand is a 'normal' basis. It is therefore not considered necessary at this stage to try to influence the process in any way. This situation may, of course change, and rapidly. We are therefore keeping in close touch with the progress of the investigations, and in the event of a change or of something 'abnormal' emerging the Committee will be immediately informed in order to decide whether or not we wish to alter our stance towards these investigations.

Item 2 on the Agenda will cover further discussion of this whole area.

- It cannot be stressed strongly enough that we urgently need to adopt whatever measures are required to ensure that no details of the Project, and in particular its unauthorised elements leak out into the public arena. If though, either by accident or design any information, or even more seriously, the actual physical results of the Project, have been smuggled out, or have managed to escape from the Facility (see Section 3 "Personnel" below) or have survived the blast, then we will have a far more serious problem to contend with.

- On the positive side it has to be stressed that as yet there are no indications of any leaks of information regarding the Project or its physical results. However, in order to plan for contingencies, and thoroughly review and discuss the most effective ways to deal with the possibility of any leaks, as well as various other issues, the following need to be considered in detail:

Personnel. Item 3 of the Agenda;

Monitoring / Management of the Situation. Item 4 of the Agenda,

Other Matters. ('5' below) will be taken as Item 5 of the Agenda.

3. Personnel.

- We are fortunate in that the number of individuals who survived the accident, and have detailed knowledge of the Project is extremely small—in total six people. These are the three personnel directly involved on the Project, and the three senior site executives—the Site Director, his Deputy and the Finance Director. These last three individuals were aware of the nature of the Project, but at this stage we do not know precisely how much, if anything, they knew about the unauthorised direction it had taken in recent months.

- Of the six people working directly on the Project, three were killed outright in the blast. Of the three surviving individuals, two were severely injured, and are now in a local hospital in critical conditions—one is not expected to survive; the other's chances are described as "50:50". The final surviving member of the Project team was in another part of the Facility at the time of the accident and was only slightly injured. He is presently at home, as are all the other individuals employed at the Facility, except those who are in hospital or are needed to help the police and fire services with their enquiries.

- The personnel working on unconnected matters at the Facility do not concern us here. Secretaries and other administration and support staff should not, unless there has been a serious breach of protocol, possess any information that could cause a problem. However, for the record, in addition to the individuals mentioned above another four are listed dead or missing; seven are severely injured; and just under twenty slightly injured.

- All the staff at the Facility have, of course, signed the Official Secrets Act. In addition, given the extremely sensitive nature of the Project, the six individuals directly involved in it, as well as the three executives referred to above, were required to sign an Additional Protocol at its outset—Copy attached at Appendix 3. As will be seen, the Protocol, amongst other things, permits members of the Special Agency with which Committee Members (2) and (3) are involved, to issue orders without prior warning, for the production of a search warrant, interview signatories under caution, search their offices and homes, impounding whatever documents or possessions are deemed necessary, and hold the signatories themselves for up to fourteen days with no access to a solicitor.

- On the face of it, it would have been extremely difficult for the six members of the Project team or the three aforementioned executives to have signed the Protocol if at the time they were aware of the unauthorised direction the Project was about to take. What we do not know is whether, when signing the Protocol, any of these individuals was already undertaking or planning any aspects of the unauthorised development, and if any other individuals in addition to the nine referred to were involved in or informed about it.

- The Project offices having been completely destroyed, members of the Special Agency searched the homes of all nine signatories to the Protocol within a short time of the accident. Where partners, children etc. were present, documents were produced which gave suspicion of terrorist involvement in the accident as the reason for the search. In all cases this ensured full compliance and, hopefully, a lack of any leakage. It was also possible to examine the three executives' offices, which were not damaged to any great extent.

- Appendix 4 contains a summary of the Agency's findings. It will be seen that nothing untoward was unearthed either at the offices and homes that were searched apart from certain documents and other information discovered at AJ's house—see below for more details.

- AJ was one of the three people working on the Project who were killed in the accident. He was employed at the Facility after completing a PhD at one of our major universities, and had been working there for eight years, the last three being devoted exclusively to the Project. The checks undertaken at both the time of his joining the Facility, and later, the Project, disclosed nothing of concern. In the light of what follows, AJ's work, personal background, contacts, political affiliations and so on, are being subjected to intensive re-investigation by the Agency.

- AJ lived on his own in a flat—owned by him, and appropriate to his status and salary—a short drive from the site. During a search of his flat and car by Agency staff a number of documents, and a private diary belonging to AJ were discovered hidden under some sheets at the bottom of a wardrobe in one of the bedrooms. The documents and diary are currently being subjected to forensic tests, the results of which will be disclosed at the Meeting. Surprisingly, no personal computer belonging to AJ has been located, a fact which is of some concern.

- In the main the documents consist of copies of highly sensitive material relating to the Project going back some fifteen months, as well as detailed papers regarding the unauthorised work, with notes in AJ's handwriting of both a technical and a personal nature in the margins, and on the back of some of them.

- Clearly the copying and retention by AJ of this material was contrary to both the Official Secrets Act and the Additional Protocol. In normal circumstances the culprit would be charged, but given AJ's death, the extreme sensitivity of the material, and the paramount need to keep all information regarding the Project out of the public domain, the Agency will not be informing the police of this development. They will also pursue further enquiries if forensic or other evidence discloses the involvement of any third parties.

- The diary does not disclose any close relationships with either sex—AJ seems to have been a 'loner'. What the diary and the notes on the documents do however, indicate is a rambling and growing concern about the Project, and particularly the unauthorised direction it was taking, as well as considerable soul searching about AJ's role in it. The diary continues with the complaints growing in confusion and intensity, until two days before the accident.

Despite a number of references to "the need to make the whole mess public before it's too late", or words to that effect, there is no indication in AJ's writings or evidence from other sources that he did in fact leak or try to leak information regarding the Project to the media, post details on the internet, or sell it to other powers or criminal or terrorist organisations. Of considerable concern though are AJ's assertions in some of the later diary entries that other participants in the Project were also having grave misgivings about it. No names are mentioned—and it is possible that these allegations were figments of a disturbed imagination. Any hint of similar concerns raised by others connected to the Project—living or dead—will needless to say, be most vigorously followed up.

- It should be noted that an initial evaluation of AJ's writings by a senior psychologist working for the Agency concludes that he may have somehow caused the accident in order to destroy the Project—the "abomination" as he referred to it on several occasions—thereby working out his acute moral dilemma. We do not at this stage know whether or not there is any truth in this assertion and it has to be said there is no indication in either the notes or the diary that AJ was contemplating or had the means to undertake any acts of sabotage or destruction against the Project.

- Again, given the risks involved, there is at present no intention to disclose any of the above matters to any authorities outside the Agency and the Members of this Committee. This stance may have to be reviewed if any evidence emerges from other sources linking AJ to the accident.

- The above brings us on to the crucial question of how to ensure that no details of the Project and its unauthorised development leak out to the wider world and also how best to handle the personnel involved. The essence is speed of response, whilst not attempting any actions that could of themselves cause media or other attention to focus on the situation, the very thing we are trying to avoid. All possible solutions or a combination of them must be considered, including, in order of preference; payments of 'hush money', temporary or longer internment, and, as a last resort, executive action.

- Having read the documentation, recipients will be aware that it is the unauthorised expansion of the Project which could present an extremely grave danger to the general public. It is not clear at this stage how and why this work was undertaken, and how it was apparently successfully hidden for well over a year from the executives with day-to-day responsibility for the management of the Facility—the Site Director, his Deputy and the Finance Director. Should the facts ever emerge into the public domain it will definitely be to our advantage that the original brief for the development of the Project was changed and extended without the knowledge or authorisation of the Facility management. This could clearly be used to defend our own position. For if the people in charge of the Project on a day-to-day basis did not know, how could the higher echelons of Government and the Civil Service be expected to?

- The fact that unauthorised work on the Project was undertaken without the three Executives' knowledge can be used to persuade them to remain silent in exchange for us not throwing the book at them for negligence, gross dereliction of duty, and whatever else can be dredged up. That is the stick. It is also suggested that a carrot in the form of a substantial lump sum payable from secret funds be made to cement their compliance. As a guide, an initial offer of a tax free amount of between two and three times their current gross salary is considered adequate. In the event of all or any of them holding out for more, this will have to be discussed at the next Committee Meeting, but in any case it is recommended they be held for an initial period of up to fourteen days without access to lawyers as permitted under the Protocol, until a satisfactory agreement is reached.

Enquiries from family, colleagues and friends, can we believe, be dealt with under the guise of national security, which should keep them satisfied for the moment.

- As for the surviving Project staff, experienced Agency people are present at all times at the bedsides of the two who are injured with documentation available to ensure they are immediately left alone with them should they ever regain consciousness. If either of the two do survive, it is intended they should be immediately be held under the provisions of the Protocol, giving them and their families the same explanation as that used for the three executives. Once again, a carrot and stick approach will be utilised to ensure the two surviving individuals' continuing compliance. The slightly injured individual presents more difficulties. Taps are being kept on his phone and computer, and any controversial incoming or outgoing traffic will be immediately terminated. All incoming and outgoing mail is being monitored, his house is subject to twenty four hour surveillance, and teams are available to follow both he and his wife should they leave home. Despite these precautions it is strongly recommended that he and his wife also be taken into custody under the same terms as the other two groups.

- It should be made clear to Committee Members that the proposed holding of these six individuals is not solely for the purpose of keeping them isolated from the outside world. Each of them will also be subjected to intense questioning in order to discover precisely how much they know about various aspects of the Project, in particular the unauthorised work, the possible cause of the accident, and so on. This requirement for information can, if required, also be used as the reason for detaining them further under the terms of the Official Secrets Act and Protocol, which they have all signed.

4. Monitoring / Management of the Situation.

It is essential to quickly find acceptable methods of monitoring and managing the situation in the immediate vicinity of the Facility and beyond, but in such a way as to avoid unnecessary attention being drawn to the Project.

- The main elements to be monitored in and around the Facility are firstly animal life, both wild and domesticated, through local vets, road-kills, and police reports of any unusual activity, and secondly, human activity—through reports from doctors, schools, hospitals, and the police.

- We have considered setting up an exclusion zone and evacuating an area of say five to ten miles around the Facility, blaming the necessity for this on an outbreak of avian flu, but have discarded this because of the panic such a course of action would cause; the link that will inevitably be made to the accident at the Facility, and the fact that it is clearly impossible to contain all the animals in the area. Even if an intensive cull were undertaken, it would be highly unlikely to eliminate 100% of mammals, let alone birds and insects. In addition, such actions will have the effect of concentrating media activity on the Facility.

Given the above situation, there are, we believe, three main courses of action to be discussed:

1. Expand the numbers of individuals undertaking various motoring activities beyond the Special Agency staff currently involved by secondments from other areas, the funding coming from special funds available at the Prime Minister's discretion.

If such a staff expansion is agreed it will have to be implemented extremely rapidly to have an effect, with the requisite risks of appointing inappropriate personnel and so on. These risks, we believe, can be overcome by strict vetting procedures, the use of the Act and Protocol to ensure compliance, as well as giving the persons concerned minimal information as to the reasons for their involvement.

It is important though, to be aware that even if these extra people were seconded on a purely need to know basis, such an expansion would present a greater potential for leaks, and consequently, outbreaks of panic in the general population.

The other risk to this strategy is that if word does get out the resultant storm of criticism from Parliament, the media and the public will be difficult if not impossible to deflect or control.

2. Release a modified version of the truth, for example blaming the whole incident and any resultant problems on AJ possibly suggesting he was some sort of deranged eco-terrorist acting on his own.

The whole, unvarnished truth is not considered a viable alternative, but even a modified version such as the one suggested above is extremely high risk. It could make the situation virtually impossible to control. Once any information started to emerge the press would start to take an increased interest. It could cause panic and chaos, and would almost certainly cause the fall of the Government as well as untold effects on every sector of the country's institutions and economy, and would considerably slow down our response with the possible adverse consequences that have been set out in Appendix 1 to this Report.

3. Do nothing. Let events take their course, responding only when absolutely necessary, and for the meantime continue giving the media, public, and Parliament as little information as possible.

One benefit of this strategy is that by taking no action, the resulting lack of panic and interference in our work and the monitoring process will make it easier to spot any untoward developments on the ground. When and if these become visible we can then take action under the guise of some other emergency to evacuate, quarantine or destroy in a more focused way, and also deny any prior knowledge of the problem.

This course of action may, however, take the initiative out of our hands in a number of areas, and we would have to rely on the good sense of the general public to act responsibly, something which these days seems distinctly lacking.

Each of these alternatives is high risk, but whichever of them, or whatever combination we decide to utilise—it must be clearly understood that time is not on our side.

At least the state of readiness of the country in the face of potential terrorist threats and avian flu, should make any response as positive as can be expected, given the circumstances we find ourselves in.

To this end whether the heads of the armed forces, health and police should be appraised of the situation—either wholly or partially—is for discussion at this Meeting.

Whichever of the above alternatives—or for that matter any others—are adopted, it is, we believe, essential to promptly put out a convincing cover story as to the reason for the accident at the Facility. Clearly no reference will be made to regarding the Project in any shape or form, and the story given out should, as far as possible, aim to limit any further probing. A number of suggestions based on how best to utilise options such as potential terrorist and avian flu threats are attached at Appendix 5 for Committee Members' comments.

In any event we will be obliged to try to keep tabs on the public mood by monitoring the local, national, and international press and media coverage of the accident and its aftermath as well as, most difficult of all, internet comments, both here and abroad.

4. Other Matters.

• It is strongly recommended that the Additional Protocol is expanded to include anyone, including the Members of this Committee, who is directly involved in this matter, in whatever capacity.

• We need to consider whether all or some of our allies as well as other countries, should be advised of the situation and the potential problems that may emerge. It is strongly recommended that this does not occur, but if the Committee considers this should be done we will have to decide to whom, when, and to what extent, the information should be given, bearing in mind the severe level of criticism we will undoubtedly face should any of the adverse possibilities outlined in Appendix 1 be wholly or even partially realised.

• It is therefore proposed that because of the international repercussions and ramifications involved in this decision a special sub-committee be formed to develop urgent recommendations regarding this aspect of the problem.

• In the event that matters do start getting out of hand, the plans for the protection of Government as well as other important elements of the country's power structure, should be available for prompt instigation. (See Appendix 6 for an up to date appraisal of the current state of readiness.)

Finally, although we well understand that the contents of this Report will be highly disturbing to Committee Members, we feel it is important to stress once again that—*there is every likelihood that: (a) All the physical results of the Project, whether authorised and unauthorised, were destroyed in the explosion, and (b) The various measures set out in this Report will be successful in reducing, if not eliminating, any adverse information fallout regarding the explosion at the Facility.*

We have gathered here a group of the most appropriately qualified individuals to deal with this problem. If we all work together, and keep our heads this crisis can, we are certain, be contained.

* * *

STRICTLY PRIVATE & CONFIDENTIAL.
FOR THE EYES OF RECIPIENTS ONLY.
Meeting—Number 11

It's strange how, in spite of all that has happened, *is* happening I still can't stop sticking to the formalities.

For instance, although this will almost certainly be our very final Meeting, I've numbered it in sequence, and have prepared a Formal Agenda.

As for keeping Minutes of the proceedings, that is if anyone else turns up, what would be the point?

Noting. Recording. All of it quite ridiculous, as nothing we say or do will make the slightest bit of difference to our situation.

* * *

Except for myself, our numbers have been reduced to Gerald and Veronica.

I'm sure the two of them won't object to my using their real names—in the light of developments the code names we so solemnly gave ourselves seem to be completely unnecessary.

Thinking about it, perhaps Gerald, always one for the niceties, won't approve. Still, if he doesn't turn up to this Meeting it's highly unlikely that he'll have the opportunity to voice any complaints as I'd be surprised if any more of these gatherings, pleasant as they are, will take place.

Having not heard anything from Gerald since the last meeting I was surprised that he arrived on the dot of 2.30 pm, dead on time, neatly dressed and shaved.

Quite a feat given the circumstances.

But not a query from him as to why there were just the two of us present.

3 pm passed, and as the Meeting—the third at a location in the outer suburbs, where the Committee moved when the centre of town became too dangerous—was scheduled to commence at 2.30, I assumed Veronica wouldn't be attending, although neither Gerald nor myself had received any notification of the reasons for her absence.

Somewhat surprisingly, the other three people present at our previous Meeting—just under a week ago, although it seems like a year—did at least have the good grace to phone me to say they wouldn't be coming to any more of our little get-togethers.

However, the similar phrases used by each of them—"a complete waste of time", "a bloody farce", and worse, led me to believe they'd discussed this among themselves before reaching their decision.

I didn't think it appropriate to ask, but I dare say they had far more important things to worry about like trying to get to somewhere safe, spending time with their families, and so on, than wasting precious time on our feeble attempts to control the uncontrollable.

I found myself wondering why the last half a dozen of us had stuck with the Committee for so long, particularly as it was obvious, at least to me, after the fifth or sixth Meeting, that every initiative we'd come up with was doomed to fail.

I suppose you could say the people who'd stayed on were all bloody idiots, and it was the smart ones who'd had the good sense to make a run for it early on.

* * *

As for the rest of the Committee, I don't know what happened to them, and to be honest, I don't particularly care.

I guess some may have succeeded in escaping the quarantine. Even in the current situation if you have access to enough of the right currency or possessions—art, jewellery, and the like—or even better, your own boat or private plane it's still possible to get out.

The clever ones did it early on, immediately the news broke, before the border controls were fully implemented. As for those trying now, I don't reckon their chances very highly. In the unlikely event of them making it away from here their boats will most probably be sunk, their planes shot down well before they reach their final destination.

And if, by some miracle, they're lucky enough to escape, what then? The moment they open their mouths, how long do they think they'll be allowed to survive?

I daresay a few will somehow make it despite all the obstacles, sitting it out in some godforsaken place, hoping to return once the crisis has died down and pick up the pieces—maybe even making a killing.

So many properties, factories, restaurants and showrooms empty, abandoned. All there for the taking, unless of course the looters or arsonists have beaten them to it.

Good luck to them.

If they seriously think they can resurrect anything worthwhile from this damned rotten mess. Good, bloody luck to them.

* * *

The really lucky individuals are the people who form part of the innermost circles of power.

There are some things I'm not privy to even with my top security clearance, but I'd lay money that Tony, Patricia, together with some other ministers—the ones who are currently in favour, the top military men, business people and bureaucrats, including a few of those solid citizens who've disappeared from our Committee over the past few weeks without, I would add, any explanation or warning, are now safely ensconced in some deserted coal mine or iron workings deep underground, with enough supplies to last for years in a valiant attempt, as a spokesman put it on one of the last TV and radio broadcasts to be transmitted—"to do our best to keep the wheels of government and commerce turning in these troubled times".

Bullshit. It's obvious all they're planning to do is sit tight until they think the coast is clear before emerging like rats out of their hole, having in the meantime left the rest of us to our own devices, facing the music, well stuck in the shit, so to speak.

Yes, I admit I feel bitter, or maybe it's that I'm just upset that I wasn't considered important enough to be one of the chosen ones.

* * *

To get back to the Meeting.

It's strange how you can work with someone for years, without really knowing what motivates them at the deepest level.

Actually I'd written Gerald off, put him down as a runner, but here he was insisting on me reading out the Minutes of the previous Meeting, even going so far as to request some minor changes, which I agreed to, even though the two of us didn't represent a quorum.

As I mentioned before, I'd already gone through the farce of producing an Agenda, but informed Gerald there was no way I was going to the bother taking Minutes for just the two of us, given the utter futility of pretending we could influence the situation in any way.

Gerald though, objected to this vehemently, so vehemently at one stage I seriously thought he was going to hit me, saying that despite the difficulties we found ourselves in we had a duty, a *moral* duty, he called it, to do our best to retain the norms of government and civilisation for future generations. Like the monasteries and seats of learning had done during the Dark Ages and the Black Death despite the chaos and destruction all around them.

I hadn't the heart to disillusion him regarding this historical inaccuracy, or the pointlessness of his insistence on my taking Minutes; on our discussing if further controls should be placed on the media—a media which barely existed anymore; considering what steps should be taken to reduce the level of violence spreading rapidly from the cities to the countryside; and on me producing a paper regarding the feasibility of reopening the Facility; all for consideration at our next Meeting—which I didn't have the heart to tell him didn't have a snowball's chance in hell of happening, either in the short term or the foreseeable future.

Following this Gerald and I discussed I don't know what for well over an hour before I called the proceedings to an end—I was keen to get away well before nightfall—although before I managed to escape into the gathering gloom he was adamant on setting the time and date of our next Meeting, as well as handing me his notes of our deliberations which, to avoid wasting any more time, I promised to type out with my comments, and send him along with the Minutes, despite knowing full well that, like the feasibility study, I wouldn't be bothering to do any such thing.

Not a smile or a grimace crossed his face as we went through this charade, not even when I locked the office, and he said—"See you next week, or sooner if it's necessary," before we both walked away in our separate directions.

No final handshake or goodbye.

I really think he's gone quite mad.

No. Not quite mad. *Completely* mad.

* * *

I supposed I've survived so far because of the inoculations myself and the other Committee Members were given at the end of our third Meeting. The one after which Tony and the others made their escape.

A middle-aged man, who I'd never seen before, was called in shortly before we were finished, and proceeded to give each of us a series of four jabs.

Telling us we'd experience flu like symptoms for two or three days afterwards, and recommending we should take it easy until we felt better.

* * *

Lord knows what the jabs contained, but I barely made it home, collapsing on the bed, vomiting and sweating for a day and a half before the symptoms cleared up as quickly as they'd arrived.

Good old me, obeying our instructions to the letter, lying to my wife, saying I had a touch of the flu.

Writing about this stupid, pointless deception, all I can say. . . .

All I can say . . . No. Don't make it worse. There's nothing I *can* say.

No excuses.

* * *

Though still a trifle weak, I was able to return to work after two days.

Two vital days lost in order to save a handful of people.

Ladies and gentlemen of the jury, all I can say in my defence is at that point I don't think I fully realised the seriousness of the situation.

And ... Yes ... Yes ... Yes. Ladies and gentlemen of the jury.

I *was* one of the Committee Members who asked the obvious question once the doctor had left. How come that an effective antidote—if it was indeed effective—was available so soon if no-one knew about the direction the Project had taken other than some of the half dozen people working on it directly.

Anyone looking at the Minutes will see there was no answer to this until, after an embarrassed silence, one of the more senior Committee members eventually promised to look into it in time for the next Meeting, adding he understood there was limited availability of the antidote for about a thousand or so "key individuals".

At this Veronica lost her temper, saying she couldn't understand why the *expletive deleted* antidote was only available for us and a few hundred others and not the *expletive deleted* general public, and she wanted an answer at this *expletive deleted* Meeting, and not next week or next month.

Some of us supported her, including, I would add, myself, ladies and gentlemen. The Minutes do not of course give a feel of how heated and lengthy the discussion was, only terminated by the onset of the ill effects of the inoculation and a solemn promise of a clear answer at a specially convened Meeting at the end of the week.

Which Meeting, needless to say, never took place due to the fact that those who were due to present the facts to us so conveniently chose to disappear.

"We'd better have a proper fucking answer." Vanessa mumbled, loud enough for everyone to hear as we got up to leave, most of us already feeling sick and starting to sweat profusely.

* * *

Once our news channels, BBC, ITV and the rest of them, ceased transmitting, I changed to CNN, though they too soon curtailed their coverage from here—I assumed they'd withdrawn their personnel when the utilities started to fail or when it got too dangerous.

Without anyone on the ground they were obliged to confine themselves to describing other countries' efforts to protect themselves, and showing maps, graphs and harrowing shots of our nationals, holiday makers, business people and the like, stranded abroad trying unsuccessfully to get home or contact their loved ones through mobile phones or e-mail until everything ceased, slowly dying away like the sound of a fading echo.

* * *

I managed to pull a few strings to send my own family abroad shortly before things really got out of hand, and transport in and out of the country was suspended.

My wife has relatives overseas, and I persuaded her and our two children to go to them for a three week break, stooping to the ruse of buying a ticket for myself for the final week of the holiday, pretending I'd be joining them in order to persuade her that the crisis—the full gravity of which I did not, of course, disclose, nor my role in the Committee—would be over by then.

Even though at that stage it was clear that something was very wrong I poo-pooed it, blaming the rumours and growing panic on media scare-mongering.

* * *

I knew from information I'd received as a Member of the Committee that there'd be delays on the motorways crowded with people without tickets fighting to get to the airport in the hope of picking up empty seats—to anywhere, as long as it was as far away as possible—so we left shortly before dawn several hours before the flight, driving by the back streets, even so taking almost four hours for a journey that would normally be less than one. Having to leave the car and walk the last mile to the terminal, before forcing our way through the crowds towards the cordon of armed police and soldiers who were only allowing ticket holders through the doors.

Saying my farewells there, outside in the cold, hordes of desperate, screaming people milling all around us.

Hiding my fears for the future, trying to act casual, concealing my tears. Joking about seeing them in a couple of weeks, when they'd be nice and brown, and I'd show them up with my paleness. Knowing all the time it would never happen.

* * *

I managed to speak to my wife and daughters a number of times on the phone before communication became impossible. The later conversations, once all was revealed, tearful, them blaming me for deceiving them. Me saying it was all for the best, trying to make light of it, promising to join them at a later date once the crisis had blown over.

My wife cursing me through her tears for being not only a liar, but also a fool for not getting out when I could.

* * *

So why didn't I go as well?

The trouble is I'm somewhat old fashioned. I don't believe in deserting the ship even if it's sinking.

I remember being terribly impressed by a painting in one of my father's books as a child.

'Faithful Unto Death' it was called.

A solitary centurion remains on guard in Pompeii, molten lava falling all around him, buildings collapsing, facing certain death, refusing to leave his post while the citizens he's supposed to be protecting are fleeing from the eruption.

Most, no doubt, would think him stupid to stay, ridiculous even, the whole event full of Victorian claptrap, but not to my way of thinking.

Soldiering on, I call it.

* * *

At least my wife and kids are safe—for the moment, although all it needs is one incident—a failure of control, someone unauthorised slipping across a border, and their origins could mean quarantine or worse.

As anyone who's studied history can tell you the capacity in human beings for sudden violent changes against all the norms of society is. . . .

Stop. I don't want to think about it. . . .

May God—if indeed there is still a God—may God have mercy on us all.

* * *

The soldiers and police disappeared from the airports a few days after my family had left.

The news showing mobs rampaging, smashing and burning, looting what little was left to take, as they realised no more flights would be leaving.

The planes that were left dumped any old how in the bays and blocking the runways.

The few reporters who were still doing their jobs describing the stink of rotting food and un-cleared waste inside the cabins, until the power finally failed and nothing else was heard.

My portable radio/cd player kept working thanks to the batteries I'd had the foresight to stock up with, giving me the dubious pleasure of listening to the news and other radio stations, dying away one by one.

At least I'm left with my collection of CDs. Mozart, Verdi, Beethoven and the rest.

As for modern music I'm mainly stuck with Bob Dylan, Leonard Cohen, and Townes van Zandt. Fantastic—but not exactly the most cheerful offerings around.

Why on earth didn't I replace my old Elvis, Little Richard and Neal Sedaka records?

* * *

After that final Meeting with Gerald I considered making a run for it to the holiday cottage which we own in the West Country, a four hour drive away. But the petrol I'd got left would have only got me about halfway.

And if I had eventually managed to get there. What then?

No. I preferred to stay on the outskirts of the city, leaving the car hidden in the back garden, covering it up with leaves and branches, hoping no-one would notice it or me swimming on the edge of a shoal of millions.

Safety in numbers.

I decided to use the car only in an emergency, or when, hope against hope, things got back to normal. Dreamt of the day when I'd drive to the airport, park early, have a coffee and maybe a cake or croissant while I was checking the arrivals screen, before standing at the barrier to watch my family coming through the doors, smiling, waving, running towards me.

In the end though, I suspect when I get ill or the food runs out I'll take the car for one last run on the motorway at double the speed limit, Beethoven's Ninth blaring out, until I crash into a convenient bridge or even better skid off the road, flying out of control down a steep bank coming to a smoking rest, slumped over the wheel, in a quiet dell where water bubbles over moss covered rocks.

Or maybe I'll forget the car altogether, and in a few weeks when the heat has dissipated fill a back pack with provisions and walk north or south, whatever direction I fancy at the time, avoiding the city, along the lanes through fields and woods, bedding down for the night in empty houses and pubs.

Try to make it to the coast in one piece.

Or maybe . . . Just sit it out here . . . Waiting. . . .

* * *

I ate like a king for the first week or two after the power had failed trying to finish as much as I could of our perishable and frozen food before it was uneatable.

Now it's all gone, eaten or ruined, everything I didn't scoff buried in the garden to hide the smell. No point in advertising one's presence.

I'm left with all the stuff I hoarded when I realised—a crucial couple of weeks before the general public—that things were seriously getting out of control. Tinned meat, fish, vegetables and fruit, packets of cereals, long life milk, bottled water, soft drinks, beer and wine. More than enough for the moment, though I've already started to ration myself.

I've lost weight, looking fitter than I've done for years.

* * *

What's the definition of heaven?

You come across a massive store of tinned food of every possible variety, untouched, ready for the taking.

And what's the definition of hell?

Once you've lugged them all home you can't find your tin opener.

* * *

My short, nervous, and largely abortive excursions for food and provisions are becoming increasingly dangerous as well as useless

Nothing of value left in the shops. Desperate people on the streets.

* * *

The sirens of the emergency services died out after a few days, followed in fairly short order by night after night when the air was full of the sound of breaking glass, bangs and crashes, cries and explosions, and I had to force myself to keep awake for fear of some sort of attack or incursion.

Now there's virtually nothing. No traffic. No shoppers or noisy youngsters coming home from the pub, leaving me to ponder why I, of all people, was spared the tender mercies of the ravening, desperate crowds wandering the streets.

* * *

Despite the silence I find myself unable to sleep—a phenomenon that's been occurring with increasingly regularity.

I've become what I imagine a wild beast is like, constantly on the alert, never able to relax, one ear always cocked for trouble.

* * *

Talking about wild beasts, there used to be plenty of rabbits and other creatures on the common and the fields round here, but I wonder how long these will last when faced with the influx of family pets let loose on the outside world.

My own cat, or more correctly my daughters', went missing one night.

In the old days I would have asked the neighbours; checked with the police; put notices on trees; maybe even an ad in the local paper. Now all I could do was make a quick, cursory drift around the area as it was growing dark, whispering the animal's name so as not to draw attention to myself, stopping even this limited activity after I thought I heard something or somebody moving in the under-growth on the third night.

After all, I reasoned, once I'd calmed myself down with a stiff drink, what was the point?

If she was nearby she would have heard me well enough. If not she'd come back when she was hungry—I still had plenty of tins of cat food available.

Nothing. Two weeks passed, without a whisper. A couple of times some sounds in the bushes, but no sign of her.

I found myself missing the damned creature, thinking I saw her in the shadows or slinking round a corner.

One night I thought I heard a faint cry and a scratching coming from the back door. Grabbing my revolver—one of the ones handed out to each of the Committee Members by one of the military men during our second Meeting—I crept downstairs, hoping she was back—any company is welcome these days—but there was nothing there.

* * *

The howling and cries of dogs and cats that disturbed my nights for the first month or so have died down recently.

I suspect, like most of them, our cat's dead by now.

As for me, I feel more confident of venturing out now that the domestic animals seem to have gone for good. There are very few people about, and apart from encountering my fellow citizens, the thought of being cornered and torn to pieces by a pack of starving dogs frightened me, I think, more than anything else.

* * *

With the demise of the domestic animals I'd imagined I'd be seeing many more birds and wildlife, but this was not the case.

The sound of bird song is a rarity, and as for the foxes and squirrels I used to come across regularly, they seem to have completely disappeared.

It's like that old folk song we used to sing at my parents' house at the end of the Passover service—"The cat ate the kid; the dog bit the cat."

And so on. And so on. Until the Angel of Death slaughters them all.

Finally though, everything is neatly tied up in a happy ending of sorts as God rides to the rescue and consumes the Angel of Death.

I doubt very much if we, the ones who are left on this earth, will encounter anything even approximating a happy ending.

* * *

It's remained quiet for the past few weeks.

Only rarely the sight or sound of a car or lorry. Usually filled with men armed to the teeth. Keep well out of sight when they're around.

No vehicles. Virtually nobody on the streets. The army, previously in evidence from time to time on foot patrol, or in armoured trucks, seems to have completely disappeared.

No commercial airplanes overhead, but occasionally the faint noise of something in the sky, too high to see even with my binoculars—military aircraft I suppose.

Each time I hear them I wince, half expecting to see a bright, blinding flash, the familiar mushroom-shaped cloud rising over the city, feeling the unstoppable force of the blast knocking me off my feet a few seconds later.

Better make the main danger areas safe by completely destroying them rather than risk the results of the Project spreading even further.

Fanciful? This possibility was already being seriously mentioned at our third Meeting when it was clear that our attempts at containment were failing, but the view of the majority of military men on the Committee was that such a course of action would be counterproductive. Firstly, because it wasn't physically possibly to obliterate the whole country, thereby risking the continuation of the problem, and secondly, the fallout would most probably spread to our neighbours, risking retaliation.

Notice I used the word *"the majority of military men"*. How heart- warming that not all of them were willing to reduce our population to a crisp—at least not yet.

These, of course, were the very same military men who disappeared with Tony and the others, probably safe and snug at this moment several hundred yards underground, drinking fine wine after a good well-cooked dinner, watching a video or listening to their favourite opera, maybe flirting with the female secretaries and administration staff. All of them, no doubt, specially selected, young, attractive, and, most importantly, still alive.

I know what I'd do. I'd drop the bomb, several in fact, after waiting till the wind was blowing in the right direction, as a concession to our friends and allies.

Vapourise the whole damned country.

* * *

One thing the long, undisturbed nights have done is give me the opportunity to catch up on my reading.

I creep into the local library from time to time, not during the day, but in the evening, before it gets too dark to see.

Among the mess of papers and rubbish and half empty shelves I occasionally find books that interest me, slip them into my bag, and take them home.

Why not? No-one else is likely to have any use for them.

One day after a bit of searching around I turned up not one but two books I hoped would be of particular relevance to our situation. 'Journal of the Plague Year' by Daniel Defoe, and 'The Plague' by Albert Camus.

One, fact, the other, fiction. Both very apt in the circumstances. I couldn't wait to see what insights they could offer into our own predicament

Bad idea. I don't know what on earth possessed me to take the damned, depressing things.

If I thought they'd give me useful information or some guidance I was sadly wrong. The only thing I did learn was the pretty obvious one that each disaster is unique and that the ones in the books were different from ours in the worst possible way—namely that, terrible as they were, these plagues eventually burnt themselves out and life, albeit bruised and damaged slowly returned to normal. A phoenix rising from the ashes.

But what we have is not like that at all. No hope whatsoever of a return to anything even approaching normality.

I couldn't summon up the interest to finish either of them. I threw them out the back door in a rage and left them to rot in the garden.

To hell with plagues and disasters. Only escapist stuff for me in future. As little connected to our world, the better

* * *

Better. Things Can Only Get Better.

That awful, bland little ditty that did its bit to help elect one of our more rotten, recent Prime Ministers.

Well. Ladies and gentleman of the jury. I worked for the swines, and I swear I didn't know if things were getting better or not.

They even had me believing this latest debacle could be contained.

That is, until I realised far too late. . . .

Here's Johnny!

Axe smashing through the door.

Weighed in the balance and found wanting.

* * *

I wonder what Gerald would say?

Not to worry. Keep calm. This present little problem is just another blip on the screen of progress.

Like his delightful Black Death. When, as he informed me on a number of occasions when this whole business started, in a generation or two mankind bounced back even stronger than before.

I hope he's right.

I hope so. With all my soul. I do hope so.

And yet . . . Try as I may, I can't bring myself to believe it.

I miss the crowds. The stupid, rowdy, pushing crowds. The noise. The rubbish on TV.

Most of all I miss them . . . My wife, and my. . . .

Don't cry. Stiff upper lip and all that.

Gerald wouldn't cry, would he?

* * *

There's an RSPCA centre fairly close to where I live, not more than two, three miles by road, double that across country.

I decided to go there on foot, a sort of mini expedition to see if any of the animals were still alive. Useless of course, I knew what I'd find, but at least it represented an attempt to relieve the increasing boredom I was feeling from being cooped up at home, particularly as of late the weather had been unseasonably cold and wet.

Besides, the streets round about had been eerily, silent of late.

No people, no danger, I reckoned, and decided to go on the next decent day.

* * *

The road leading to the centre, not much more than a track between high hedgerows, looked the same as it had always done, except for the two burnt out RSPCA vans obstructing the entrance to the car park.

I squeezed past them thinking that at least the blockage would give me time to make a dash for it across the fields if anyone turned up by car or lorry while I was inside.

Apart from the burnt out vans, the place seemed untouched. Car park empty. Doors and windows intact. Inside a little grubby, but computers still on desks, posters on the walls.

No-one in reception of course. No volunteers. No excited children waiting to take their new pets home.

My eyes started to water as I remembered visits in the past with my family when we'd picked up a couple of. . . .

Maybe it wasn't a good idea to come here. Memories, or at least the good ones, were better left dormant.

I thought I heard a sound coming from the back where the animals were kept. I wiped my eyes and made sure to cock my pistol before carefully opening the door and going outside.

* * *

You'd usually be greeted by a cacophony of barking and growling from the kennels the moment you emerged, but today there wasn't a murmur.

I expected the worse. Cages with their occupants dead from exhaustion or starvation, injuries caused by their vain attempts to escape by unremittingly hurling themselves against the bars of their prison.

But there was none of this.

Every cage door had been carefully jammed open. Not one animal left. Not a dog or a cat.

Even the tortoises had disappeared from their enclosure, the ponies from their paddock.

Set free to take their chances? Eaten?

I had no idea.

* * *

I scoured the place for supplies before leaving. Found some dog biscuits and a couple of tins of cat food which I put in my rucksack.

You never knew when they'd come in handy.

A handful of broken pencils, and a penknife in reception on the way out, and that was it.

* * *

Before I'd visited the centre I hadn't realised how much confidence having a loaded gun would give me, though whether I'd have the guts to use it was another matter.

In fact the question of controlling unauthorised weapons which were appearing in increasing numbers, not only in the hands of criminals but also of law-abiding citizens—if indeed any such creatures still existed—was one of the items discussed at the second, no, I think it was our third Committee Meeting.

The one after which Tony and some of the other big shots disappeared.

It couldn't have been a coincidence. By this time things were getting really out of hand. Of course I now realise they must have been planning it all along, a group within our group, all the time kidding us poor saps who they were about to leave in the lurch that everything was under control, and the work we were doing day and night was paying off.

Needless to say our attempts at controlling the flow of weapons, once the floodgates were open, were a complete waste of time, as was pretty well everything else.

* * *

A couple of weeks had passed since my visit to the centre, and I was feeling bored again. Sick of the same four walls and my patch of overgrown garden.

It got so bad that one day, in a fit of impatience, stupidity, whatever you want to call it, I decided to throw caution to the winds and take a trip in the car.

Only a short one, but almost my last.

* * *

I had what I thought at the time was a brainwave and decided to drive to a health club situated in the grounds of the local orthopaedic hospital, where there was a cafe and several food and drink machines. An idiotic notion that a profusion of supplies would be waiting for me untouched and all I needed to do was take my pick.

In retrospect, I probably knew deep down this would never be, but hope springs eternal, or maybe I just needed to get out, albeit a distance of only twenty five minutes by road from where I lived.

Sorry. Make that fifteen minutes.

No traffic any more. No speed cameras. No police.

* * *

The moment I drove into the deserted car park it was obvious that my journey was a complete waste of time.

Somebody had been before me.

The doors to the building were smashed, as were the vending machines in the lobby.

No point in going any farther.

* * *

Before I left I glanced through the plate glass windows of the swimming pool.

The pool was almost empty. Just a foot or so of dirty, brown water.

On the side, lined up neatly, as if waiting for their occupants, half a dozen wheelchairs, and incongruously, propped up against one wall a prosthetic limb, unnaturally pink and shiny, and at the bottom of the pool. . . .

I pressed my face close to the glass.

Three bodies, curled up, the arm of one of them flung out in a gesture of. . . .

I should have heard them before.

Voices from nearby, coming in my direction. Talking loudly.

Luckily for me I hadn't explored any further or they would have caught me in the building, or, having seen my vehicle, waited for me outside.

Either way would have been the end of me.

* * *

I jumped in the car and got the hell out of there, in my haste grazing the wing as I swung out the car park.

As it was I encountered them on the road just outside the main entrance.

A group. No. More like a small crowd. Fifteen, maybe twenty, I couldn't tell for sure.

The glint of sunlight on metal. Knives. Swords. A spear?

I accelerated hard, seeing faces and bodies falling away.

Thirty, forty, yards. A loud bang. Then another. The sound of what I assumed were bullets hitting the boot.

I took a bend almost skidding out of control as another shot glanced off the side of the car, catching a glimpse of them in the back mirror, waving and gesticulating, thank goodness much too far away to catch me on foot.

Down the hill. Fast. Stopping a few hundred yards on, leaving the engine running, to check if the damage was serious. It wasn't.

The fields and woods all around, quiet, peaceful.

Then a raw, invasive sound. The growl of a motor bike engine. Not one, but two of them. Rapidly approaching.

I drove off, looking in my mirror. Seeing them faintly in the distance.

Gaining on me. A couple of minutes, probably less, before they'd catch up.

No point in trying to outrun them.

Fortunately I knew these roads well. After the next bend I turned off down a side lane, then drove in low gear along a tree lined track that led to what had been a local riding club.

I parked behind one of the barns, switched off the engine, and listened.

I heard them go past a few seconds later, then waited several minutes before they came back, no doubt not keen to expend more fuel than they had to.

Quiet again.

I drove slowly back up the lane, stopping a hundred yards or so from the end to check all was clear, engine ticking over.

The small cottage on my right was in surprisingly good condition. White picket fence. A good sized front garden, albeit untidy. Flowers and weeds run riot in their fight for survival.

I was about to move off when I noticed the front door opening.

Foot on the accelerator. Ready to make a run for it.

Then saw it was a young girl. Sixteen, seventeen, at most. Long black hair. Jeans. A tight, green blouse. Low cut. Top buttons undone.

Smiling, as she came towards the car.

Healthy, white, clean, teeth. Smiling.

I turned the engine off, and put the window down a fraction to hear what she was saying.

A soft, quiet voice.

"I thought you wouldn't stop. My parents went for food, and they didn't. . . . "

I thought I saw a tear in her eye as she bent down towards the window, revealing the tops of full breasts, brown from the sun.

"Please . . . I'm so frightened. I'm all alone. I need help."

Something I hadn't felt for some time stirred.

I was about to open the door when she turned her head slightly in the direction of the cottage.

A curtain moving slightly. A vague outline in the window, as she looked back at me.

"I need help . . . I'd. . . . "

But I'd already started the engine, seeing the blade in her hand out the corner of my eye, and the three men running out the door as she smashed her hand against my window, her smile turning to a snarl.

I drove off to the sound of her curses and the shouts of the men, not stopping until I reached the safety of my home, almost forgetting to hide the car under its cover of leaves and branches.

I drunk some whisky to stop the shaking and spent the next day in bed or stretched out on the couch, wondering if I'd ever have the guts to venture out again.

* * *

But venture out I did.

My tinned food supplies, though still plentiful, were becoming increasingly unsatisfying, so I decided to take a walk to the common, just after it got dark, to gather the blackberries which I reckoned would be ripe by now.

That is, if somebody hadn't been there before me and picked the lot.

* * *

A warm, clear night with a smell of autumn in the air, a slither of the moon casting its silvery light.

No-one around as I made my way to my destination, gun fully loaded, knife in my belt.

Frequent stops in the shadows of buildings or behind trees listening.

Listening.

Once I thought I heard something in the distance.

An engine of some sort? I couldn't tell.

I waited until it had died away before carrying on.

Normally a short stroll, now it took me over half an hour.

Past the empty car show rooms and smashed up shops. The estate agents, their windows full of fading pictures of properties no-one would buy.

* * *

The houses round the common were quiet and in darkness, apparently deserted.

It was not, of course, advisable to advertise your presence, especially at night. And yet . . . You could never assume that houses in darkness, even those with broken doors and windows were unoccupied.

The original occupants could still be there, leaving the damage untouched, or in some cases inflicting it themselves in an attempt to fool any looters or refugees from the city that this particular desirable abode was no longer worth their attention.

On the other hand, they may have been driven out or got stuck somewhere unable to return, and the house may have been taken over, by God knows who—a salubrious five or six bedroomed residence, bathrooms ensuite, still desirable despite the manicured lawns now overgrown, the swimming pool empty—no water, just a green, evil smelling slime.

As for the light in the window, previously a welcome sight to the guest or traveller, this was now definitely to be avoided, for who, except someone crazy, or so armed and dangerous that they weren't scared of intruders, would be so foolish as to advertise their presence.

Or . . . Maybe the lights were only on as a bluff to try to convince people that a dangerous beast lived there, while all the time a helpless family or a woman alone with her children cowered inside fearing the knock on the door or the footstep on the gravel path.

For my part I avoided other houses—whatever state they were in, and when I lit my own candles, one at a time in order to extend my dwindling stock, made sure to firmly draw my curtains so not a crack showed through, and for additional protection, stuck down the newspapers I'd secured at the top of the windows.

* * *

I checked again.

Everything quiet. Dark.

Wait.

Flickering lights across the common. One of the big mansions backing onto the woods.

I took out the binoculars I'd stuffed in my pocket.

Lights blazing. Clearly a plentiful supply of candles.

Cars and motorbikes in the drive. Shadows flitting across windows.

Flaunting themselves. Unafraid.

* * *

I moved a little closer, making sure to remain hidden behind the bushes.

Was that music, women's laughter, I could hear on the breeze?

There it was again. Definitely laughter.

Warmth. Conversation. Company.

Tempting. Like the sirens reeling you in.

Best though to keep well away. Whatever it was you saw or heard, or hoped for.

* * *

The blackberries were just about ripe, and working by the light of the moon—too dangerous, I thought, to use my torch—I picked as many as I could, piling them up in the plastic boxes I'd bought with me.

Needless to say someone *had* been there before me, taking the easily reachable berries at the edge of the grass, while I had to search and push my way into the brambles to get a good haul.

I hadn't eaten fresh fruit for several months, and couldn't wait to get home, relishing the thought of stuffing myself, the purple juice running down my beard and staining my fingers. I'd polish them off over the next week or so, before they went bad, maybe pouring a good slug of sherry or liqueur over them, getting drunk as I seemed to do more and more these days, and to hell with the consequences.

* * *

I filled three boxes to the brim, tasting the welcome sweetness of a few before making my way to the top of a hill which gave a good view of the city, some eight or ten miles away.

* * *

Scanning the scene in front of me through my binoculars, the city, or at least the parts of it I could see, looked peaceful.

Empty streets. One or two plumes of smoke hanging motionless in the sky. Most of the buildings gutted, lights surprisingly on in several others, mainly on the higher floors, though how on earth the people inside—if there were any—had managed to hold out, and how the emergency generators—if that's what was supplying the power—were still working I had no idea.

Nothing like that terrible night when, alarmed by the appearance of a strange, orange glow in the distance, myself and several others had gathered in the same place I was now standing from where we could see a pall of black and white smoke spreading out over the city, bright flashes of fires engulfing the horizon in all directions, and a mass of headlights moving aimlessly to and fro on the maze of roads, caught like rats in a trap, going God alone knew where.

I knew it was impossible, but as I watched, I could have sworn I could hear the buzzing and crackling of the flames; the revving of the motors of cars and buses frantically manoeuvring to escape; the sounds of gunfire; and above them all the yells and screaming of men, women and children.

How long ago was that? Four, five months? More?

I couldn't remember.

And now . . . Quiet as the grave.

I put the binoculars away, and headed for home.

* * *

On my way back I ducked into some bushes to relieve myself, and almost fell over a dead baby lying on the ground, its large head twisted round at a strange angle.

You didn't see many bodies. Most people preferred to die indoors unless they had no choice in the matter.

I bent down to touch it. . . .

And . . . laughed out loud.

It was a doll. A child's doll.

Left there. Forgotten. Probably after a picnic.

I picked it up and carried it home with me.

It sits on the dressing table in my bedroom regarding me with its vacant, slightly sinister, stare.

Always alert. Never sleeping.

* * *

I've got into the habit of reading through a good part of the night, buried under my blanket, candle giving barely enough light, like a mischievous child hidden away from prying eyes, dreaming of the journeys he'll make one day to exotic places. In my case, places I'll never get to see.

* * *

I've always liked history, but I can't be bothered with it any more.

Depending on my mood, I now find so much of it either far too depressing or abominably smug with its insistence on man's inexorable rise to greatness and self-improvement.

Look at us.

Look how clever, how innovative, how democratic we are . . . . .*Were.*

* * *

Talking of this sort of thing, I found a book called "The End of History" in the library the other day under a pile of magazines and newspapers.

This story of our greatness, perfection, triumphs . . . . .whatever you choose to call them, particularly inappropriate given the situation we currently find ourselves in.

After flicking through the first few smug, self-congratulatory pages I couldn't take any more, hurling it with all my strength against the wall, watching the pages flutter to the filthy floor.

The End of History.

Maybe the author got it right, but not, I think, in the way he intended.

* * *

So . . . No more history. It's only fiction for me now. The more escapist, the better.

I've been rereading some of my favourite books, including two paperbacks I hadn't looked at for years. 'Hiero's Journey' and 'Against a Dark Background'.

Several pages missing, but I make them up as I go along.

Both science fiction, about risky, dangerous, quests in perilous times.

Heroes and monsters.

Reading them I feel the urge to get away whatever the consequences. I need a break, a holiday of sorts.

* * *

As if to emphasise my desire to escape, I had a particularly vivid dream a couple of nights ago.

A wooded valley lit by a pale moon.

Streams and rocks.

Ruined buildings.

Vague, ghostly forms drifting though empty doorways and between broken pillars.

A feeling not of terror as I would have expected, but more one of peace and a mysterious, intense, tranquility.

* * *

It wasn't until I'd finished my breakfast the following morning that I remembered what the place in my dream reminded me of.

Fountains Abbey in Yorkshire.

I'd visited it with my wife when we were first married, almost twenty years before.

A cold misty day. Virtually no-one else around as we wandered round the site, talking softly, almost in whispers, as if frightened to disturb the magic of the place. Full of plans for the future.

* * *

I grabbed my road map. Just over two hundred miles, give or take, door to door.

I should be able to make it there and back with the fuel I had in the tank and the spare couple of jerry cans I'd so laboriously siphoned from jettisoned vehicles over the past few months.

As much water and food as I could squeeze into the boot of the car. Clothes and other supplies on the back seat. My weapons, such as they were, next to me.

I felt a wave of excitement flow over me.

The route? My hands were shaking as I checked the map again.

Motorways or side-roads?

The latter. Motorways were too easy to block. That is if anyone was still out there.

* * *

I grabbed a pen and pad and started to plot my way northwards.

I would leave as soon as possible. Probably early the following day.

With luck I could be there by nightfall.

And after . . . Why not go further?

York. Edinburgh.

The Highlands.

Quiet. Empty.

Back in a couple of months, before the winter sets in

* * *

I drafted a note explaining what I was going to do.

Tore it up.

Tried again. Not happy until the fourth attempt.

Wrote out three copies in capital letters. Stuck one on the kitchen door. The others in the upstairs and downstairs halls in case my wife and the girls returned.

Who was I kidding? The chances of us ever meeting up again were minimal.

Still. You never know.

Imagine they came back and thought I was dead or gone for good.

* * *

And what about the piles of Government papers, the files and the Project Committee Reports and Minutes I'd so carefully hidden away?

The Top Secret and Circulation Restricted stuff that seemed so important at the time, all so irrelevant now.

Should I destroy them, or take them with me?

No. Damn it.

I got the lot out from their various hiding places, and piled them up neatly on the dining room table, welcome to anyone who found them.

* * *

Later that afternoon I went along the high street to the local church.

The door was off its hinges, the inside stripped of anything that wasn't nailed down.

I climbed the stairs to the top of the tower

It was a clear day, and I could see for several miles in all directions.

The roads empty of traffic, just the occasional wreck blocking the way, lying on the pavement or in a ditch.

The pub near the green. A burnt out shell.

The large house by the common where I'd seen lights blazing a few weeks before, apparently deserted, its windows broken, the cars and bikes all gone.

Here and there gaps in the tree-line. Ragged stumps disfiguring the landscape.

* * *

At first glance the fields round about appeared well kept, the corn and rapeseed, sown before the catastrophe, ripe and ready to harvest.

But of course there was no-one to do the work. In time the crops would wither and die. Weeds would choke the fields. After one, maybe two, years all of it would return to the wild.

God knows what entity would eventually emerge to hold sway over the world.

In the meantime, though, everything so calm. Peaceful.

Wait. Something moving in the distance.

Sheep? Cattle? People?

I couldn't tell. Too far away to see clearly.

Time to go.

I shivered despite the warmth of the sun, and hurried down the stairs and back to my house to finish getting together my supplies for the trip.

The Oldest Man in the World

"Christ, Tom. It's almost five. I was getting worried."

"Long meeting. They bought in lunch."

"What was it? The budget?"

"No. Not the budget. Come in, and shut the door."

They go into Tom's office. A city landscape of skyscrapers can be seen through the large window behind Tom's desk.

"You'd better sit down, Jake. I've got something important to tell you." Tom says.

"It's not the old heave-ho is it? For fuck's sake, Tom, I know I haven't . . . "

Tom laughs.

"Relax. It's the opposite. Something big's come up, and I want you to give me a hand on it. We'll be working alongside the finance and legal boys, and the top management lot. Claude, Marie and the rest."

"Big, eh. What is it?" Jake says, sitting down.

Tom points to several sheets of paper on his desk.

"I can't say till you've signed this."

Jake stretches out his hand towards the papers.

"Hold your horses." Tom says, interrupting him. "I'll tell you a bit about it first. It's a special job. A one off. They say it'll take three months, but I reckon it'll be more like six. If you decide to join, this is what's going to happen. The team will be taking over the whole of the eighth floor. Everyone will be given special entry passes. No-one except for the team in or out, and not a word about what we're doing to anyone except the other people involved in it. We'll be working 24/7 until the damned thing's sorted one way or another. No lunch or supper breaks. Meals bought in. And if that isn't enough, we'll all be staying at a hotel nearby. No time off. No private phones or computers. Limited phone or text contact with wives, families, girlfriends, and someone will be checking everything we say."

"Isn't that a bit. . . . "

"That's how it is. Take it or leave it. The good news is, as I said before, you'll be working alongside all the big shots, which can't be bad. And the package is bloody generous. All expenses paid, and a bonus equivalent to four times salary at the end of the project, whether it goes ahead or not. So, it if takes six months, you'll pick up two years extra. Not bad, eh?"

Jake nods, and Tom continues.

"There's a briefing meeting tomorrow morning for everyone who's in, and we'll be giving out some bullshit cover story to stop too many awkward questions from inside the company and out."

Tom leans forward.

"I can tell you, Jake, I promise you've never seen anything like this before, and you probably won't again."

"So what's the big mystery?"

Tom holds up the papers.

"Can't say till you've signed this. It commits all of us to complete secrecy on anything and everything about the project. Everyone's had to sign, even Claude, and once you've signed, you're in for the duration. No backing out. And one other thing, Jake. If anyone leaks or gives out any information about this unless it's properly authorised, they're out of here quicker than their feet can touch the ground, and we'll make damned sure they won't work anywhere else in this town. And, for good measure, we'll sue the arse off them."

Tom pauses, and leans back in his chair before handing the agreement to Jake.

"On top of that the darned agreement stays in force even if we leave here. In fact, so far as I can see, it lasts until they put you six feet under. So you'd better read it carefully, before you tell me what you think."

Jake reads through the document, occasionally checking back on pages he's already looked at. He eventually puts the papers down.

"Fuck Tom, they've really got us by the balls."

"I warned you. Well, are you in or out?"

"In, I guess, but I hope I won't regret it. Can't you tell me anything else before I sign?"

"Sorry. No can do. But I promise you won't regret it."

"Alright then. Let's do it."

"You're a hundred percent sure?"

"Hundred percent sure."

Tom takes out a pen.

"There you go. Sign and date it."

Jake signs with a flourish.

"Great." Says Tom, shaking Jake's hand. "Welcome to the club. I think this calls for a drink."

They sit down on a low couch.

"What's yours?" Tom asks.

"Whiskey, please. With a dash of water."

Tom pours them both a whiskey.

"Cheers. Here we go, then. Have you ever heard of Liu Zhang?"

"Can't say I have." Jake replies, sipping his drink.

"Neither had I till this morning. He's a Chinese billionaire. Forbes top hundred. Houses and estates all over the world. Made his money in computers, but also big in residential development, raw materials, agriculture, tourism, and God knows what else. Mainly in the Far East, but moving into Africa and South America. All those millions of people wanting to eat better, go on holiday, have somewhere decent to live. They reckon if he carries on the way he's going, he'll be in the top ten in a few years. No-one seems to know his exact age, but the best guess is mid-forties. He's well educated. Big collector of art, mainly oriental. He's sponsored seats in several universities, and he's very interested in history, particularly Chinese. Same again?"

"Yes please."

Tom pours two more whiskeys.

"What's this fellow Zhang got to do with us?" Jake asks him. "Is he taking us over?"

"No way. Actually, Jake that's not a bad idea, but it's definitely not on the agenda."

Tom stands up and stretches.

"Right. Where was I?"

"Chinese history."

"Yeah. History. Have you heard of the First Emperor?" Tom asks Jake as he sits down. "You know, the one who built the terracotta warriors?"

"Yeah. Of course I have. I'm not stupid, Tom."

Tom smiles.

"Sorry. Of course you're not. That's why I wanted you in on this. Well, our friend Mr Zhang is obsessed with him. Apparently this Emperor spent a fortune on trying to find the elixir of eternal life."

"And did he?"

"What do you think? The fucker died young, but Mr Zhang, bless him, has got another idea. He doesn't want eternal life, that's impossible, but he wants multiple resurrections for a long, long time. Guess how long."

"I dunno. Two hundred years?"

"Higher."

"Five hundred? But that's . . ."

"One million years."

"One million? That's bullshit."

"It maybe bullshit, but it's fifty million worth of bullshit, with more to come."

"What d'you mean?"

"This all kicked off last week. Half a dozen of Zhang's representatives came to see Claude, and asked us to do a feasibility study on this. At first Claude thought the same as you. Complete nonsense. And then they handed him a banker's draft for fifty million. Non-refundable, once we've signed heads of agreement, even if the project doesn't go ahead."

"But it's crazy. The whole thing's fucking crazy."

"It's dead serious. Why d'you think we're going through all this cloak and dagger stuff? Actually, the final resurrection's after one million and nine years, with another eight planned before that. The first one's twenty nine years after Zhang's first put under. The next one fifty nine years later. Then, after five hundred and nine years, and so on."

"I don't believe you."

"That's what he wants. I swear."

"Jesus. I don't know what . . . What's this with all the nines?"

"Nine's some sort of lucky number for the Chinese. So it's all nines except one of the comebacks, the fourth or the fifth, is after exactly ten thousand years. No nines, because they told Claude that ten thousand's a particularly auspicious number."

"Unbelievable."

"You haven't heard the half of it. It's not just for Zhang. He wants to take twenty or so people with him. Family, friends, assistants. God knows who else."

"Twenty?"

"Something like that."

"I can't . . . Why's he chosen us?"

"Haven't you read our website? We're the biggest, the best, the longest established, and whatever other bullshit the PR people have thought of."

"But we haven't bought anyone back yet. The first ones aren't due for a couple of years."

"Zhang's willing to take the chance. They won't need us for some time, and Zhang's people told Claude he has, and I quote, "the utmost confidence in our ability to solve any problems that may emerge.""

"But what if we can't?"

"If the results are, I quote again 'considerably worse than expected', whatever the hell that means, they'll have the right to cancel everything. I wouldn't like to be in Bill Jackson's shoes. He's between a rock and a hard place. All the definitions and agreements are down to him, but Claude's already warned him that he doesn't want any legal piddling around to screw this up, unless it's a complete deal-breaker."

"And the fifty million?"

"That's ours whatever happens."

Tom gets to his feet.

"I don't know about you, but I'm starving. What d'you fancy? Chinese? Pizza?"

"I'll have a pizza. Chicken and pineapple."

"I'll have ham and olives. We'll share. Fifty, fifty. And to drink?"

"Coffee please."

Tom phones down their order, and sits down again.

"Any questions?"

"D'you reckon it'll work? You know, with so many comebacks?"

"No idea. That's down to the lab. They'll be working flat out on mice, rats, monkeys, and whatever else they use there to make damned sure it does."

"But if it doesn't . . . We could fiddle the results."

Tom shakes his head.

"No chance. Zhang's a smart fellow. He's already thought of that. He wants his people on site to make sure the results are kosher. Claude and the others aren't keen, but the other side's playing hard ball on this. If we don't agree to have his people in our labs, there's no deal. Frankly, I don't give a shit. Let's get our hands on the fifty million, and then they're welcome to check up on us as much as they want."

"But even if it does work. A million years? Fucking hell. Anything could happen. There could be a disaster, like they all die before they can be brought back."

"Maybe. Maybe not. It's our job to try to make sure that sort of thing doesn't happen."

Tom leans forward.

"Between you and me, Jake, I couldn't give a fuck if something does go wrong, only that it doesn't happen until we've got our dirty little paws on the money. There's a bloody great fortune to be made for everyone on this, particularly the lucky buggers like you and me who are in on the ground floor."

"What, more than the fifty million?"

"For Christ's sake, Jake. Haven't you been . . ."

There's a knock on the door.

Tom opens it, takes the food and drink, pays, and brings it over to the table.

"Where was I? Oh yeah. I know I've given you a hell of a lot to take in, but I told you before, the fifty million is just for starters. We're going to charge the bastard a hell of a lot more than that. The only question with a contract that lasts for so long, is how we calculate it, and how he pays. And most importantly, what it does for our bonuses and share options. Thank God, that's not up to us. Fred and the finance boys can worry about that. All I know is Claude's already said we're going for as much as possible up front. I mean what's the use of a shed load of money a couple of hundred years from now, let alone a million?"

"Yeh, Tom." Jake says. "But even a hundred years. What about climate change? Asteroids. Social breakdown. Not to mention that bloody great volcano under Yellowstone."

"You forgot to mention alien invasion. Don't you think we haven't thought about all that? Look. You don't know what's going to happen. I don't know. Nobody knows, not even Mr Zhang. But if we do get a deal, and he's willing to cough up straight away whatever figure accounts eventually come up with, I couldn't give a damn."

Tom takes a slice of pizza, eats it, sits back, and stretches.

"That's better. Actually, those sort of problems are good for us two. D'you fancy a trip to Switzerland, all expenses paid?"

"Yeh. Of course. But why?"

"As I said before, our Mr Zhang's very smart. He's been thinking about the sort of problems you mentioned. He's got a bloody great estate near Geneva, and he reckons that Switzerland's a good bet for his crazy idea. It's stable, at least at the moment. Reasonable climate. No hurricanes or droughts. It's in the middle of Europe—well away from things like tsunamis and seawaters rising, and on top of that it's protected by high mountains."

"So's Tibet."

Tom laughs.

"Are you serious? Would you like to spend a million years stuck up there? You'd go fucking mad. And there's something else."

Tom drops his voice.

"It's not exactly secret, but we've got facility just outside Berne."

"I've never heard . . ."

"Why would you? We don't publicise it. It's for ultra-rich clients who reckon they'll get tax advantages from being kept there until we bring them back. The service is very expensive. Each case is bespoke depending on where the clients live, where they keep their assets, and so on. Well, somehow Zhang found out about this, and Claude needs the two of us to go see whether it's best to expand our Berne facility to deal with Zhang and his people, or build a completely new one for him on the Geneva estate—which Zhang prefers for security reasons. Whichever way, it's going to cost Zhang a hell of a lot, but according to Claude, he doesn't care. He just wants the best. Coffee?"

Tom pours them both coffee.

"So, my friend, we're due to fly out there next week. The downside is no luxury hotels, and no chance of sightseeing or clubbing. We'll be stuck in the Berne facility, and they'll be the same restrictions on outside contacts as here. The upside is we'll also be going to Zhang's estate. Same restrictions, but who knows, we may even meet the great man himself. What d' you think?"

"Sounds good to me."

"Good? It's fucking great. At least we'll be away from this madhouse for two or three weeks."

Tom leans forward.

"And Jake. I want to hit the ground running on this. If it goes ahead, we're set to make a hell of a lot of money. Remember that when we're stuck in lockdown here or in Switzerland twenty four hours a day. Another whisky?"

* * *

The experiments on multiple resurrections of rats, mice and monkeys being deemed successful by the company's scientists and Zhang's observers, the deal was completed seven months later.

Zhang's companies went from strength to strength resulting in him becoming, according to the Forbes List, the fifth richest man in the world.

After various medical interventions, blood infusions, and enhancements, he was frozen for the first time at the age of fifty nine, still in good health and at the height of his powers, together with the group of people and the two cats he'd chosen to accompany him on what was formally referred to as 'The Project' but was described by Zhang as 'The Great Adventure'.

The age of fifty nine was considered by Zhang to be highly propitious for the commencement of The Adventure because five is regarded as a lucky number connected to the elements and the senses, and nine also boded well as its symbol signifies 'long-lasting', and in addition, it had been traditionally associated with the Chinese Emperors.

All the participants, animal and human, were considered, in the jargon of the agreement, to be 'disposable units' to be discarded or replaced at any time during the multiple resurrections should Zhang consider their future participation 'undesirable to the wellbeing of The Project.

* * *

After much debate, in the interests of security, and to avoid what was described as possible 'contamination from other clients', the freezings were undertaken, not at the company's Berne facility, but at one specially constructed in the grounds of Zhang's Geneva mansion, with direct links to the facility in Berne, the company's Chicago head office, and its Seattle research laboratories.

The Geneva facility was manned by a combination of company technicians, and Zhang's own staff specially trained for the purpose.

* * *

The composition of the entourage accompanying Zhang was considerably different to when the agreement was first drawn up.

Always one to cover all foreseeable eventualities, Zhang had inserted a clause in The Project agreement specifying that his written authorisation was required for the advanced freezing of any individuals in the entourage who'd had the misfortune to die before The Great Adventure commenced.

In the event his consent was given for the advanced freezing of two individuals who'd passed away, but withheld for three others—an executive who'd committed suicide after falling out of favour; his wife who'd died in a company plane crash several years earlier; and his youngest son, killed in a motor accident.

The absence of his wife gave Zhang the opportunity to marry his longstanding mistress, and add her to the list.

Unfortunately, or maybe fortuitously for the wellbeing of The Great Adventure, Zhang's current mistress who he'd also intended to join him, was killed in a domestic accident. The two young sons she'd borne him, though, were scheduled for inclusion.

As for the son who'd died, he was considered unworthy of resurrection, being of a highly unstable and disrespectful nature.

* * *

Apart from Zhang's immediate family and the cats, the names of the other members of the entourage were only announced at the very last moment.

Despite the secrecy surrounding their identities, several individuals were found to be missing when they were summoned to the Geneva facility for preparatory work a month before the first freezings.

Their whereabouts remained unknown despite strenuous attempts to track them down. It was never discovered why they'd disappeared, how they'd found out in advance they were to be included, and, particularly galling for Zhang, what possible reason anyone could have for turning down the opportunity to participate in The Great Adventure.

However life—or in this case the extending of life—goes on, and Zhang set about finding last minute replacements with his usual energy.

* * *

The resurrection company's share price soared on the back of the enormous fees generated by The Project, which were classed in the Annual Report as 'other income'.

Under intense pressure from regulators, auditors, and institutional shareholders, the company eventually agreed to release some limited information about the source of these funds.

This only served to stoke the rumour mill even further, pushing the share price to record highs.

In due course the inevitable happened.

The facts about the deal, and the long term financial arrangements with Zhang and his companies emerged. The source of the leak was never discovered in spite of an intense and wide-ranging investigations by the company and Zhang's people to unearth the guilty party or parties.

By this time, though, things were far too advanced for Zhang to make good his threat to withdraw from The Project should any details become public knowledge.

The company's share price rose to stratospheric levels.

* * *

Zhang and his parties' first resurrection occurred as planned after twenty nine years with only one human and one cat fatality.

Zhang, apparently still in a good mental and physical condition, took up the reins of his empire, stepping down after just three months in preparation for the next freezing, and secluding himself with the other participants on his closely guarded Geneva estate, having refused to attend any more meetings or have any dealings with the media.

Apart from family members of the participants, who were allowed to visit them on a strictly controlled basis, Zhang's insisted on complete isolation from the outside world.

However, one participant, aged eighty three by normal standards, but in practice only fifty four, decided to ignore this restriction, and broke out of the estate despite all the security, the dogs, and the sensors.

He surfaced two days later, in a night club in the south of France accompanied by a number of beautiful women, and surrounded by bodyguards and admiring crowds.

The paparazzi who subsequently dogged his every step spotted him over the next few days partying into the early hours of the morning in various fleshpots along the Riviera.

This state of affairs, though, only lasted three weeks, after which, apparently suffering from severe depression, he retreated to a secret location, rumoured to be an isolated sanatorium in the French countryside.

Needless to say, the gentleman in question wasn't invited to join the second freezing, along with three others, including Zhang's wife, formerly his mistress, who'd incurred his displeasure for various unspecified reasons. These four individuals as well the one who hadn't survived the resurrection were replaced with new participants, and a Pekinese dog was substituted for the deceased cat.

The reasons for the human exclusions were never disclosed to the outside world as each of those involved received an extremely large monthly stipend which would cease immediately, and be followed by legal proceedings, should any of them leak any information about 'The Great Adventure'.

These constraints, though, were of little avail. A few weeks after Zhang's party had moved on to the second freezing, one of the security guards, and the head chef on the Geneva estate sold their stories to rival newspapers, whose online readers revelled in hearing the lurid details of the relationships and disagreements between the villa's inhabitants during their short stay, as well as details of the various delicacies, movie choices, and exotic entertainments enjoyed by them.

What, however, particularly fascinated the public most were the accounts of the growing resentment the established members of the entourage felt towards the five new participants, particularly Zhang's new girlfriend, a young manicurist he'd met when she came to the estate to cut and manicure the nails of the resurrected individuals.

* * *

Jake was promoted soon after the agreement with Zhang was signed, and, like the other senior executives involved on The Project, became the recipient of very large annual bonuses, and, more importantly, substantial share options, boosted in value by the company's ever increasing share price.

He cashed in his chips, and retired at the age of thirty three, keeping his apartment in Chicago, but spending most of his time at the beach front house he bought in Florida, or exploring the Caribbean and the Yucatan peninsula on the fifty foot yacht he purchased.

After four years he sold the Florida and Chicago properties and relocated to San Francisco, where he went to work at a nominal salary for a charity that supported and funded birth control in poorer countries. Back home the charity campaigned for tax incentives for smaller families, and for urgent legislation to halt or drastically reduce the freezing and resurrection arrangements which were becoming increasingly popular for those that could afford them.

The industry, of which Jake's former employer was by far the largest player, lobbied intensively at the very highest levels against any form of curtailment of their activities on the grounds that—a) everybody had the intrinsic right to determine their personal fate; and b) they were on the verge of reducing the costs to a point where, as they put it—"for the first time in history the man or woman in the street can experience the joy of seeing their great, great, great grandchildren, and be granted the additional time to pursue their deepest personal interests."

* * *

Two years after the agreement with Zhang was signed, Tom, now a wealthy man, retired to spend more time with his family.

He moved to the country, and was last heard of trying to complete the two books he'd been working on since leaving university.

One was an fictional account of the early settlers in the far west and the trials and tribulations they had to endure. The second, non-fiction, was a history of the effects of taxation on political and social developments throughout history.

None of the books have been published yet, and it is not known if either of them have been finished.

* * *

To date neither Tom nor Jake has expressed any desire to be frozen and resurrected.

* * *

As for Zhang.

I see. . . .

I see him dancing happily with his girlfriend and entourage in a futuristic disco.

I see his dismembered, headless body lying in a pool of blood.

I see him inspecting the wonders of the First Emperor's tomb, first opened to the public in 2048.

I see him looking out over a desolate, apocalyptic landscape—fires, explosions, the sky dark and threatening.

I see him celebrating his ascent of Olympus Mons, the giant Martian volcano.

I see him in a ruined city, desperate and at bay, surrounded by a horde of starving children wielding knives and clubs.

I see him sailing on an azure sea bounded on an unknown planet. His boat is followed by several silvery blue dolphin-like creatures. Flocks of large, yellow and green sea birds fly overhead.

I see technicians and robots trying desperately to revive him.

I see him watching the floodwaters seep over the deserted, cobbled streets of Geneva's old town.

I see him being readied for freezing on a space ship, about to start its exploration of the outer reaches of the solar system.

I see him in a red sanded desert swaying in time to the pulsating beat of music played by a group of impossibly tall, white robed nomads.

I see him sitting alone by the side of a lake, weeping.

I see him. . . .

I see. . . .

* * *

As with any life, particularly with one lasting, perhaps, over a million years, the possibilities are endless and unknowable.

And so, dear reader, I find myself in a similar position, to what I believe, may have happened to Tom. Namely, a writer with a story he's unable to complete.

In the circumstances all I can suggest is that you choose which, if any, of the above scenarios you prefer or feel is most likely, or, even better, decide for yourself what kind of future you envisage for Mr Zhang.

There is nothing more to say.

THE CHOICE IS YOURS